The Gristmill Playhouse

The Gristmill Playhouse

• • •

A Nightmare in Three Acts

Don Winston

This is a work of fiction. Names, characters, businesses, places, events, and incidents are either the products of the author's imagination or used in a fictitious manner. Any resemblance to actual persons, living or dead, or actual events is purely coincidental.

ISBN: 0692370099
ISBN 13: 9780692370094
Library of Congress Control Number: 2015900844
Tigerfish, Los Angeles, CA

THE GRISTMILL PLAYHOUSE

a nightmare in three acts

DON WINSTON

TIGERFISH

For Benny and Mae

Author's Note

For more than seventy-five years, generations of aspiring and established actors have flocked to the fabled Bucks County Playhouse in New Hope, Pennsylvania, for a summer season of hijinks, camaraderie, and most of all, to feed their all-consuming passion: performing before a live audience.

Countless legends got their start here. Broadway hits launched their runs here. The golden age history of American theatre is very much linked to this magical enclave nestled on the Delaware River.

The playhouse and town in this story are riffs on the real places. Some of it is authentic, some a composite, and some completely fabricated. The world in the pages ahead is more a state of mind than a physical place. "Summer stock" itself doesn't really exist anymore, but for the purposes of our story, it is alive and well in our New Hope.

And so are the dreams of the myriad actors—young and old, journeymen and stars—who make the annual pilgrimage with a burning zeal to prove themselves, night after night, for a few cherished, fevered months in a quintessentially American summer town.

♫ *"Why do we work our asses off?*
What is it for?
Cares disappear, soon as you hear
That happy audience roar!
'Cause you've had a taste of
The sound that says 'Love!'
Applause! Applause! Applause!" ♫

Applause
Full Company

Cast of Characters

Betty Rose Milenski—*a young actress*
Julian—*her boyfriend*

<u>The Gristmill Playhouse</u>
Rex Terrell—*artistic director*
Dottie—*actress and director's assistant*
Alistair—*actor*
Phyllis—*actress and apprentice*
Gwen—*actress and apprentice*
Sutton Fraser—*actress*
Rachelle—*actress*
Caleb—*actor*
Baayork—*choreographer*
Becky—*stage manager*
Myron—*music director*
Baub—*costume designer*
Mimi—*dance captain*
Roger—*set designer*
Geraldine Roberts—*legend*
Clyde—*a goat*

Town of New Hope
Mr. Arbor—*barkeeper*
Calvin—*sheriff*
Erma—*librarian*
The Mansion Inn Innkeeper
The Panama Man and Strudel—*a local and his pet monkey*
Florist
Mailman
Phillip—*young boy*

New York
Wes Ward—*talent agent*
Erin—*waitress*
Danny—*bartender*
Claudine—*pianist/singer*

Marian Maples, Broadway

Legend, Dies at 88.

By PAUL YARDLEY
Published: June 11

Marian Maples, the irascible, brassy four-time Tony Award winner and stage, film, and television actress for more than six decades, died Tuesday night in Manhattan. She was 88.

She died onstage at the Booth Theatre during a performance of the revival of *A Little Night Music*, according to her long-time agent, Wes Ward.

A prolific performer in regional theatre, on tour, and in summer stock, Ms. Maples appeared in more than three dozen

Broadway shows throughout her career, including her final stage role, for which she was nominated for Best Supporting Actress in a Musical at last week's Tony Awards.

Equally accomplished in comedies and dramas, she began her career as standby for Ethel Merman in the 1950 musical *Call Me Madam* before moving on to starring roles in *Bus Stop*, *Sail Away*, *Company*, and many more.

Ms. Maples went to Hollywood sporadically in the 1950s and '60s and appeared in a handful of B movies, including *The Violent People* with Charlton Heston and *Who Killed Teddy Bear?* with Sal Mineo. She also did a two-year stint on the daytime drama *The Edge of Night* in the mid-1980s as well as numerous guest spots on primetime programs, for which she garnered four Emmy nominations and two awards.

But it was in the Broadway theatre that Maples made her mark, with star turns in musicals by Rodgers and Hammerstein, Cole Porter, and most indelibly, Stephen Sondheim, who famously called her his "salty muse."

A workhorse till the end, Maples encapsulated her career eleven years ago in a one-woman show entitled *Look Who's Here*, for which she won her final Tony for Best Special Theatrical Event. The *Boston Herald* called the retrospective "Not just a witty catalog, but a deeply moving fast-forward through a life filled equally with love, loss, joy, and regret."

In addition to her talent, Maple was known for her tart take on the vicissitudes of a mercurial industry, about which she could be equally sanguine. "It's like the old prostitute once said," she quipped in an NPR interview last November, "'it's not the work. It's the stairs.'"

An invitation-only memorial is scheduled for Friday at the Shubert Theatre. On Thursday night, Broadway theaters will dim their marquee lights for one minute in honor of the late actress.

Act One

Scene One

"He just called, stuck in traffic," the girl said, poking in with her cordless headset. Roughly her age, stringy hair yanked back in a band. "He's on his way."

"Thank you." Betty Rose smiled back from her straight-back chair, hands in her lap.

"Can I get you coffee or tea or something else?"

"Water's fine, thank you."

"Sparkling or flat?" the assistant asked. She was too young to have such dark circles.

"Flat, please."

"Chilled or room temperature?"

"Oh." Betty Rose thought and said, "Either. I'm easy."

The girl seemed relieved and pulled out again, tapping her earpiece, answering another call with a "Siren Talent" sighed into her mike.

Poor girl, thought Betty Rose. *Run ragged here.*

Her chair felt awkward, which she blamed on nerves, but after a few repositions and shuffles, she realized it was almost imperceptibly diminutive, shorter to the ground. The modern slab desk loomed taller in front of her, as did its chair with a monogrammed "WW" back pillow. Betty Rose smiled; she'd read about this old trick. And then a fresh pang of nerves at the realization these people knew what they were doing.

It was common, she knew, for agents—the crafty ones—to stage dominance over anyone across the desk, especially actors. Each did it in their own way. The lower-rent ones, she'd learned over the past few months, were the most heavy-handed and obnoxious: hours-long waits in cramped rooms choked with other desperate actors, snippy receptionists, dismissive, hostile responses to the responses from their grilling. Agents who ran their offices out of musty apartment buildings were the worst. Mostly failed actors themselves, exacting revenge on new dreamers.

And Betty Rose endured it all, even from the lowest rent, because without an agent, any agent, she wasn't going anywhere. She couldn't even start.

But Siren Talent Agency was high-rent and bicoastal—both here in prime midtown and new offices out in Beverly Hills in the same building, she'd learned, as Ron Howard's production company and Gersh. Siren was on the rise, gaining on the Big Three. She could never have gotten a meeting here on her own.

So when a Siren agent summoned her, even with a half day's notice, Betty Rose scrambled to cover her waitress shift—easy enough, as Friday's tourist arrivals were a tip cash cow—dropped fifty for a blowout at the Tribeca Drybar, and arrived twenty minutes early, cooling her heels in the lobby, so the June humidity wouldn't cause her hair to frizz. The assistant had sounded urgent on the phone—"Wes needs to see you this week, tomorrow"—so maybe, just maybe, Siren needed an actress just like her for an audition soon, this week, today.

Here the lobby was spacious and calm, almost soothing. The office energy was frantic but orderly, as agents closed deals on Broadway star turns, national tours, the occasional guest spot, both in New York and L.A. Everyone on the floor was pitching clients, fielding offers, booking jobs.

Here they offered visitors—even nonclient, out-of-work actors—four choices of water.

Betty Rose sat up straighter. Katharine Hepburn, she'd read in the Garson Kanin book, had four-inch platform shoes custom built for her meetings with Louis B. Mayer and insisted on standing so she would tower over her MGM boss. Betty Rose needed Hepburn's moxie.

She lifted up to pull and smooth her floral charmeuse skirt taut. She'd chosen her outfit with care: artistic, but classy. Betty Rose knew her "type" from the three-week casting workshop she'd found in a *Backstage* ad. "Great look, great read," the former casting director of *All My Children* had said after Betty Rose's cold read. "All-American girl next door. I wish I'd found you when I worked on the show." And a delighted Betty Rose had said, "Thank you!" and thought her $295 decently spent.

She studied Meisner Technique twice weekly at City Center, with its repetitions, activities, intentions, and breakthroughs. She climbed the creaking, uneven stairs to the Ripley-Grier Studios for jazz dance on Monday/Wednesday/Friday (in Studio C, eyeing, with hope and envy, the spirited Broadway replacement dancers rehearsing in B), and was saving up to train with the voice guru/legend who taught Rachel York and Cheyenne Jackson and, until a rumored falling-out, Patina Miller from his fabled apartment at the Apthorp. Maybe Betty

Rose could take her spot, if she passed her audition and made the waiting list. The guru's name on her résumé would, she knew, open magic doors. For the time being, she did her vocal warm-ups every morning in her kitchenette, with the windows shut and the exhaust fan on, so as not to bother the neighbors who loudly stayed up late and likely slept late.

She read *Backstage* daily with its tips on dressing for auditions and finding the spiritual core of her characters and the moment before "zero"—useful and silly in equal measure, she thought, knowing the difference between obscurity and superstardom was a quantum leap of intangibles and sheer guts.

She knew you submitted headshots to agents only midweek, never on Monday, when they were ornery, and certainly not on Friday, when they were rushing to get out of the office.

She'd learned the difference between "theater" and "theatre." "*Theatre*," her college acting teacher had lectured on their first day, "is an art which is practiced inside a *theater*."

She'd spent dearly for her new headshots—trendy photographer/makeup/retouching/reprinting—and opted for clean line framing over full-bleed for a more classic look. She stapled them to bright white, heavy-stock paper on which she'd laser printed her acting résumé at the FedEx office, crisp and clean. She leaned over to straighten it perfectly on the glass desk, so he couldn't miss it.

On the long, stainless table under the mounted television sat a proud row of photographs in silver, brass, and leather frames: the same flamboyant, pudgy man beaming with the archly buff and plucked Nick Adams on the *Matilda* red carpet; an openmouthed guffaw with Stephanie Block at Sardi's; at Joe Allen's with Idina Menzel, mock wrestling away her fresh Tony; genuflecting before a seated and bemused Rosemary

Harris at the Russian Tea Room. At the table's edge sat a little sock monkey wearing a *Urinetown* sweater, next to a company-autographed *Playbill* cover of *Forever Plaid*.

Gay, she thought, with some relief. She could dial back the sex appeal, her shakier hand, and focus on her fabulousness. The gays loved fabulous, and it loved them back. So did she.

Betty Rose inspected her reflection in the window over-looking the Avenue of the Americas—it was just gloomy enough outside to double as a mirror. She swiveled and posed and grimaced; nobody looked fabulous, let alone movie star, with a fluorescent key light.

The New York actor's learning curve was steep, but she'd scaled it quickly, handily since arriving in January. At the bottom of the agent scale was the Bruce Leonard type, who charged actors up front, and whom Betty Rose had enough sense to flee. Up several notches was the Dulcina Eisner ilk, a reputable veteran with clients on Broadway and off. She ran her boutique agency from a West Village brownstone basement and held open singing calls the first Tuesday night of each month. Betty Rose had waited her turn with a dozen other incarnations of herself, listening awkwardly to those ahead of her, and when called, had unleashed the final sixteen bars of "Johnny One Note" to showcase both her belt and high notes in front of Ms. Eisner's desk. The agent, elegant but weary, thanked her for not singing anything from *Wicked* and regretted she already had three of her "type" in her stable. "But you're a strong high C," she encouraged. "I wish you all the best."

Siren was top tier: They worked in teams, coddling each treasured client for stage, television, and film, both coasts. Even a hip pocket arrangement, just their logo on her résumé, would catapult her to the next level. She knew, of course, whose back they were scratching, which ironically burdened her with more pressure, not less.

The voice arrived first.

It materialized abruptly, she gathered, from the elevator and grew louder, sonarlike, as it moved from the lobby and through the hall, toward her. It barked, harried and playful, as it traded good-natured barbs with an unheard opponent over its Bluetooth. It multitasked orders at its assistant as it exploded into its office. Betty Rose smoothed her lips and her skirt once more.

"...relax, Dot. This isn't my first rodeo. If he doesn't trust me by now, why'd he ask in the first place? Look, I'll call him after tonight's show. Of course I know the number....He changed it again? *Lauren, do you have the new number?*" the agent spat, rounding the desk as he pocketed his phone, and then murmured, "Sorry I'm lateish...." He wore a solid navy suit with a candy-stripe shirt and a pink-and-white polka-dot bow tie and a heavy watch. Fortyish, he had round tortoiseshell glasses and wild, flaming hair that almost matched the orange silk spritzing from his breast pocket. He was a jolly, classy confection. He stood over his desk, Joker-like, surveying the battlefield.

"The memorial at the Booth went long," he said without looking up, and before Betty Rose could answer, he added, "And then I had to say 'hi' and 'hello' and 'thank you' to that whole cabal clusterfuck. And then traffic and all. Tourists. From Iowa, I'm sure."

"That's quite all right," Betty Rose said, "I was just..."

"Marian would have liked it, I think," he pondered. "The Battle-Ax Brigade turned out—Lansbury, Stritch, *Chee-tah*—although, really, what else do they have to do? Marian swore she'd outlive them, but *c'est la guerre*. Sondheim. Woody and his daughter-wife. Bernadette sang 'Send in the Clowns.' God, what a vision." He studied his computer screen. Scrolled up and down.

"Marian Maples?" Betty Rose asked. "Her memorial?"

"I mean, dying onstage," he *tsk*ed with a laugh. "*Quelle drama!* She would howl at the cliché of it all, but it was rather inevitable. She was rarely anywhere else. At least she'd finished 'Liaisons.' *Lauren, where's the Big Guy's new number?*"

"On your call sheet, Wes!" Lauren shouted back from her assistant's perch.

"Do you mean Marian Maples?" Betty Rose repeated, inserting herself.

"My client, yes. Know her?"

"I know *of* her. She's a legend. I saw the lights dimmed on Broadway last night. For her."

"Oh, I missed that," Wes said, still scanning his computer. "How was it? *Where on my call sheet, Lauren?*"

"It was very moving. The whole district was dark and silent for a full minute, right at eight." *District.* Like a pro. An insider.

"At the very top!" Lauren called back, and Wes, squinting, said, "Bingo. *Thank you!*" He plopped down in his chair, looked over at Betty Rose, and said, "What?" even though she hadn't said anything. And then he added, solemn, "You know, we'll never see another like Marian again."

"I know," Betty Rose said, hushed, sympathizing.

"This new crop, I mean, *bleh…*," he spat, shrugging in boredom. "They want it easy. As Uta Hagen said, 'They have no disciplines.' No offense."

"Not at all," said Betty Rose. "I agree."

"Lauren, who is this skinny wisp of a thing in my office?" the agent asked abruptly and then picked her headshot off his desk.

"Julian's girlfriend! Yes!" he eureka'd, clasping his hands. "His college sweetheart!"

"That's me," Betty Rose said with a laugh and then made a point: "But he's older."

"Oh, he talks about you constantly. My *actress* girlfriend. Oh, he's a big fan."

"He'd better be," she said, winking and wondering if she were being too chummy.

"We love him here. People still talk about his set for *Salome* at the Houseman last fall. He worked magic in that sardine can."

"Yes, I've seen photos…."

"His career, in the past year"—he clap-zoomed his hand straight up—"like a rocket! Is he still doing the *Cloud Nine* revival at Minetta Lane?"

"Oh yes," Betty Rose said with pride. "He's finishing the model at our apartment. It looks—"

"And I hear he's up for *Streetcar* at the Acorn, for Daniel Sullivan! How you make that set look fresh and new, on that stage, I'll never know…."

Betty Rose nodded blankly, unaware. Julian didn't count his unhatched chickens. "The doors are flying open for him…," she said.

"You got that Kate Middleton thing going," the agent interrupted, comparing her live to her headshot. "You get that before?"

"Yes, I have," she said, happy to pull focus.

"Waity Katie they call her."

"Ha. Yes."

"There's always a demand for that fresh kind of look."

"I hope so. Yes. That's good," she stammered. *Turn up the fabulous*, she scolded herself. *Chill, he likes you.*

"Betty Rose. Excellent name. So memorable."

"Thank you," she said. "Technically, it's Elizabeth, but my father shortened it to Betty as a child, and it stuck."

"Smart fella. Got some Laura Bell Bundy going on there. Know her?"

"I know *of* her. I think she's—"

"The original Sister Christian in the workshop of *Rock of Ages*. Did you know that?"

"I didn't."

"Why'd you add 'Rose'? To the 'Betty'?"

"It's what Dad always called me," she said, shrugging. "Both together."

"'Betty' alone is a bit old-fashioned. A little *Mad Men*."

"Yes," Betty Rose said. "It does sound lonesome by itself."

"Rose is very *Golden Girls*," he added. "Love it. You're a sight for sore eyes."

She laughed. He laughed. She leaned closer, folded her hands on his glass desk.

"*Ack!* What is this?" he squealed, squinting at her headshot. "Betty Rose *Milenski*?" He scrunched his nose.

"Yes," said Betty Rose.

"Nails on chalkboard. Have you picked a stage name?"

"I would never change my last name," she said simply.

The agent laughed and looked upward. "Well, you *will*. And I'd suggest sooner. Today. That Polish thing won't work."

Betty Rose sat still.

Wes the agent clasped and Simon Legree'd his hands. "Bernie Telsey would love you," he said. "He's a grizzled ol' bore, but he casts almost everything. He'd put you in regional first. Maybe bus-and-truck. Probably *Mamma Mia!*"

"That's excellent," Betty Rose said, relieved to pivot off her last name. "I'd love to meet him." She leaned in, coconspirators.

"Look at these roles!" he said, excited, studying her résumé. "Laurie, yes, yes, of course. And Julie and Nellie. And both Marias—German and West Side. Good, good." He looked up. "No Marian?"

"I did Marian," Betty Rose corrected, straining forward, pointing.

"Yes, I see it. All the standards. And Sandy, of course. And what's this? Ophelia? *Hamlet*? Shakespeare?" He peered at her. "Is that where you go bat-shit crazy and off yourself?"

"Yes." Betty Rose nodded. "Well, sorta..."

"Ye Gods," he said, and then jumped. "Wow, wow, wow. Emily?" He lowered the résumé, impressed. "*Our Town*? How very versatile."

"Yes, that was the most rewarding because it was a straight drama and a good reach," said Betty Rose, thrilling at his appreciation.

"'Does anyone ever realize life while they live it...every, every minute?'" he quoted, swiftly moved to emotion. "We don't, do we? We don't."

"'Saints and poets maybe...,'" she finished for him, commiserating. "That's such a beautiful line."

"And then she croaked, right?" he said, bursting into shrill laughter. "Such a long fucking play."

They discussed Douglas Carter Beane's new musical and the upcoming season at McCarter Theatre and dished on the latest catfight between Kristen and Idina—manufactured and mined for publicity, they agreed. Wes primed her about the new projects that would start casting in the fall, including a hot Broadway revival of *Applause*—"The first since Bacall! They're looking for the next Penny Fuller"—and dangled an invitation for her and Julian to visit his country home in Woodstock over the summer.

They swapped anecdotes about the stage legends—Duse, Laurette Taylor, and, of course, Hepburn—and dissected the teaching techniques of the long-gone titans Meisner, Strasberg, and Stella Adler, who once taught Wes and whom he called "the sexiest bitch I've ever met, and my dear, that's a watershed statement coming from me." Betty Rose knew them all, emboldened by passing Wes's theatre history test.

The agent fawned. Betty Rose blushed. And basked.

They bonded. Betty Rose felt fabulous.

"Now I'm going to give you some advice, Betty Rose. Maybe the most important you've ever gotten. Are you listening, Waity Katie?"

"Yes, Wes," she said, coquettish.

"Do something else with your life."

"Oh."

"Give this up. Right now."

She sat back in her chair, holding a tight smile. Wes got serious, leaned closer.

"I've been an agent for fourteen years," he said, centered. "And it's just not going to happen for you, my dear."

"I see," Betty Rose heard herself say.

Her throat tight, she looked around for the water—sparkling or flat—that the turncoat assistant had failed to bring.

"You're unusually lovely and apparently talented and clearly intelligent," the agent went on, "and it's a waste to go down this dead-end path. Marry Julian and have babies and develop a skill set, and then come back and thank me in twenty years for this moment."

"Yes," Betty Rose said, and then said, "No. No, thank you."

"Northwestern is a good school," Wes said. "You'll get a real job."

"I'm a theatre major. With honors," she managed to say.

"But this résumé is bullshit," he accused, waving it.

Betty Rose reddened. "No, sir," she corrected. "It's all true."

"It's college. And Beech Grove, whatever the fuck that is..."

"It's a...school...."

"A *high* school. Goody. It's amateur. It's worthless."

"Oh," she said. She felt sweat in her scalp. It would frizz her hair.

"You haven't a single professional credit to your name. At your age!"

"I'm only twenty-four," she said, instantly wishing she'd shaved off three.

"At twenty-four, Julie Andrews had three Broadway hits and a Tony nomination. Bebe Neuwirth was wowing in *A Chorus Line*. Betty Buckley was already starring in—"

"I...had to take a little time off," Betty Rose interrupted.

"Nobody nobody nobody cares," Wes said, tapping his watch. "Tick tock!"

They sat. Wes sighed and fidgeted.

He bolted from his chair, paced by the window.

"Jay Binder takes chances," he said. "And he still owes me for Kelli O'Hara. He's holding Equity calls this week for Roundabout."

Betty Rose shrank.

"What?" Wes challenged. "You're too good for an open casting call?"

"I...can't go to an Equity audition," she said.

"Behind in dues?" Wes frowned and reached for his wallet. "Good grief, I'll spot you. Just go straight to their office on Forty-Sixth and settle up...."

"I don't have my Equity card," she said quietly. "I'm not in the union. Yet." She felt a trickle down her lower back. It would stain her blouse.

Wes sat. Glanced back at her résumé, tossed it to the floor, buried his ginger mop in his hands.

"Worse than amateur," he said. "A dilettante."

"No," Betty Rose protested, but the agent cut her off.

"Betty Rose, I've seen thousands of wannabes flit into town, all with the same dream of landing on Broadway...," he explained.

"It's my only dream," said Betty Rose. "Ever."

"...and one thing is constant," he went on. "Those who have what it takes, that motor, prove it immediately. We're talking the point-zero-zero-one percent. They live, sleep, breathe the business, obsessed. They don't just want it. They will not, cannot, live without it. The other pros sense that obsession, give 'em a shot, feed 'em to the wolves. And ignore the rest. Like they're ignoring you."

"But they haven't seen me," Betty Rose insisted. "Or heard me."

"Only five percent of Equity members make a living wage from acting, and of that five percent, almost all are poor," Wes continued, his frustration rising. "And here you sit, not even in the union. Do you realize how Herculean, how practically impossible the task before you is? Wake up, Betty Rose! I am begging you—*begging you*—don't start down this road!"

"But it's too late, you see," she said, trying not to hear him. "I've already started."

Now he was angry. "Do you know why Hepburn never had children? She said if her child were sick, and she had a show, she'd smother her child rather than miss a performance! Could you do that? That's why I got out of that game. I'd sell my mother but not kill a child!"

Betty Rose recoiled. "I doubt she meant that literally...."

"And that's why you'll never win this game!" the agent erupted. "You're not 'fresh,' you're not 'undiscovered,' you're not 'misunderstood.' You're just not cut out for it!"

Betty Rose stood up, refusing tears.

"I'm very sorry about your client," she said politely. "And I'm sorry to have bothered you. Good afternoon."

"Betty Rose, wait!" He stopped her just in time. "Close the door." She did. He sat back down. She stood still.

"I apologize," he said. "It's been a tough week, losing Marian. I shouldn't take it out on you. Julian is very important to us here, and I'll do anything I can to help you. But without your union card, my hands are tied."

She knew he was right.

"What can I do?" she asked, an open plea to a new, fabulous friend.

Wes sighed, spun his chair toward the window, thought. It had started to rain. He sucked his cheek and moments passed and he spun back to the wall, past signed posters of *Aida* and *Grey Gardens* and a vintage *Oh! Calcutta!*

He focused on a framed and faded photograph of a red and white barn with a large water wheel behind an ancient elm. It stood apart.

He winced.

"No, I can't," he muttered. "I really can't."

Wes pivoted a glance at Betty Rose, unflagging by the door. Back to the barn. Tapped his tooth, exhaled.

"Well, maybe...," he continued to himself. "God help me. Dear God help me. Maybe there is something...."

Scene Two

SURPRISINGLY, JULIAN DIDN'T LIKE THE AGENT'S IDEA.

"Summer stock?" he asked. "Does that still exist?"

Betty Rose had raced downtown on the R to their apartment on Mulberry, stopping into Duane Reade for a cheap umbrella to protect her blowout. It frizzed anyway.

"It's not just any summer stock," she said, palming argan oil down the lengths of her hair. "The Gristmill Playhouse is the most famous in the country. It's a renowned training ground."

"Oh, is that what he told you?" Julian asked. He was in his typical work uniform: white wife-beater, gray sweats, barefoot. He darted around his maquette in the dining alcove, obsessively tweaking the dollhouse model set against bright green grass and cloud-spotted blue sky. Betty Rose thought it looked dreamy.

Julian didn't like her account of their meeting. He thought the agent sounded "abusive." He was irresistibly protective.

Betty Rose defended him—he was just trying to help her get her Equity card, the crucial first milestone. Union membership rules were impossibly catch-22: You couldn't work without one, and you couldn't get one until you worked. *Backstage* devoted whole issues to this nightmarish obstacle that vexed most new actors. But the union also had a Byzantine point system and ephemeral loopholes and shortcuts desperate actors were always looking to exploit. The agent potentially had one.

"Yeah, I've heard of the Gristmill," Julian said, squatting for a head-on angle of his model. "It's in that Pennsylvania artist's colony-tourist-trap hippie village. Between the candle makers and glassblowers and fudge shops."

"Do you know how many theatre legends got their start there?" Betty Rose instructed, clearing cups and plates and coffee press from the tile kitchen counter. "Not just actors, but musicians, directors, even set designers."

"Wow, he did the hard sell," Julian said with a chuckle. "Did he mention its reputation as a weird, all-controlling commune? The word 'cult' pops up a lot...."

Betty Rose clicked the countertop ironing board open. "That's 'cause actors are freaks!" she said. "Especially in a group. But they're my peeps, babe. With the Gristmill on my résumé, earning points, people will take me seriously. No one has yet."

"An apprenticeship? AKA 'free work.' Formerly known as 'slave labor,'" Julian pressed. "Why do they need someone now? Hasn't their season started already?"

Betty Rose tested the iron, put it to work on a black skirt. "Wes knows the director. He's going to ask a favor. He got his start there, too."

"A lot of good it did him," said Julian.

"I'm behind, Julian—two years!" Betty Rose said, her voice pitching up. "Even Monica has an agent and a manager and a touring gig with *Bring It On*"—Monica, her eager, half-talent classmate who'd stolen the show at Northwestern's New York showcase only because Betty Rose had missed it.

"Hey, I know directors," Julian said. "And I meet new ones all the time. I can ask a favor, too."

"It's not the same," said Betty Rose, ironing harder. "You're my boyfriend. There has to be a sense of discovery, word of mouth. That's how you made it."

Julian looked around at the cramped apartment. "I made it? When?" he said, laughing. "Is this all there is?"

"You paid your dues," she went on. "And it paid off. Now it's my turn."

Julian turned to her. "It's just…you're green, B.R. Naive. I don't want them to take advantage of you, that's all."

"Well, I gotta find my way, like everyone else." She stopped ironing. "What's wrong? You really don't want me to go?"

"Not there. Not the Gristmill Playhouse. It has a weird rap, B.R."

She rolled her eyes. "It's two hours away. You'll come visit. I'll be back right after Labor Day.…" She grabbed the iron as it scorched her skirt, burning her hand.

"Dammit, what am I talking about?" she said. "They haven't even said yes. I set myself up every time. Even the smallest thing, free work, such a minefield! What am I doing?"

Julian held her hand under the cold water. Gently patted it dry. Held her, still trembling.

"Hey, what is this?" he chided. "Where's the tigress I know?"

"I don't know," she said. "I'm just frightened. All the time."

He kissed her forehead.

"You've had a hell year, B.R. It would have crushed anybody else. I'm not just in love with you. I'm pretty much in awe."

"At least I have one fan." She laughed, wiping an eye.

He kissed her mouth. Her neck.

"Are you seducing a young, needy actress?" she asked with a smile. "God, you're all the same."

His hand moved down.

"I can't be late to work," she protested. "They'll write me up."

On the counter, her cell phone buzzed. She jumped, grabbed it.

"That terror's kinda hot," said Julian, unrelenting.

She checked the screen. Her acting class scene partner. Ignore.

"We have time," Julian told her, lower. "Take the express."

"Nice try, jackass," she said as she succumbed. "They're all local."

● ● ●

Rain and near-lateness notwithstanding, Betty Rose kept to her afternoon ritual of getting off at Forty-Second Street—her favorite street—and walking five blocks through Times Square in the pre-Broadway crush.

She maneuvered the rubberneck throngs along Broadway Beach, darted west on Forty-Fourth to the less-congested and inspirational Shubert Alley, heralding *Jersey Boys* and *The Book of Mormon* and *Chicago*-now-with-Billy Ray Cyrus. She weaved back and passed the pigeon-hatted George M. Cohan sentry over Duffy Square, targeted the bloodred TKTS staircase and pealed off again on Forty-Seventh toward the Hotel Edison bar.

The Rum House was typically sparse until pre-theatre, then hectic for an hour, and quiet again after curtain. During the first-act lull before the intermission mini rush, Betty Rose served Brooklyn Lagers to a polite, ticketless couple from the hotel and kept checking her apron pocket for cell phone vibration.

"Excuse me, miss," said the tourist woman with Midwest apology. "We ordered the Dark 'n' Stormy."

"Yes, you did," said Betty Rose, checking her pad. "Be right back." She dabbed sweat off her forehead with a cocktail napkin.

"Who stole my beers?" howled the other waitress from the bar. "God, you're a hot mess tonight. You poach my table and now this?"

"I'm sorry, Erin," said Betty Rose. "Hot mess is right."

Like Danny the bartender and Claudine at the piano, Erin had worked at the bar so long, she could anticipate its every move. Good-natured and jaded—and defiantly sour—Erin was, for a not-yet-made-it-actress, the impossible age of thirty-three. She was still striking and poised and instinctively stood in third position, waiting for stage directions that would never come. The Rum House now suited her; she'd never leave, thought Betty Rose, who'd been there an unexpected four months.

"How was your meeting?" Erin asked, and Betty Rose said, "It was nice, thanks."

"They gonna hip pocket you?" Erin pressed, and Betty Rose said, "I hope so."

She'd learned not to share much with crepehanger Erin, lest she abandon all hope herself.

Danny, midfifties, smiled and separated fresh egg whites for a pisco sour. "They'd be lucky to have you," he said. He'd been handsome once, thought Betty Rose. A young leading man. A potential star.

Claudine had worked there the longest. Over-dyed, overly made-up, and wearing gauzy black blouse and slacks whose slimming effects had long-diminished returns, she finished her set with a torch-songy "I Feel Pretty" and fished the singles and pocket change from her tip jar and lumbered grandly out the back. She'd sit out her break, Betty Rose knew, in the hotel lobby, playing sudoku on her phone and telling eighties Broadway tales to any visitor who cared.

"How long will the singer be gone?" asked the timid Midwestern wife when Betty Rose brought the corrected cocktail. "She's a bit loud, don't you think?"

Betty Rose winked in commiseration. "She does bang a bit," she said to the tourist. *Probably from Iowa*, Wes the agent would say.

Wes, who'd promised to call the Gristmill and then call Betty Rose and had clearly forgotten to do both. Typical agent. Unless they'd rejected her outright and he was protecting her from a double dose of bad news on the same day.

She busied herself at the bar in case the lobby manager poked in. Erin asked her to cover her Saturday shift so she could go to Southampton with her new "boyfriend." There was always a new one. "I'll be back before the Sunday-night rush," Erin promised.

"Do you know anything about the Gristmill Playhouse?" Betty Rose asked.

Erin yanked the chewed-up stirrer from her mouth. "My God, the New Hope Freak Show?" she said. An acting classmate of hers had gone a few summers back and had fled soon after. "And I mean *fled*," she added. "The stuff that goes on there..."

"Like what?" asked Betty Rose.

"My friend wouldn't tell me everything, I think she was scared or something, but it's like a concentration camp. They work them to death, especially the newbies. I'm surprised Equity doesn't crack down."

Erin's friend sounded lazy, which was common. She "had no disciplines," as Uta Hagen would say.

"Plus they're so secretive, so underground," Erin added. "They must, like, recruit their own members, like Hogwarts. Have you ever seen them post a casting in *Backstage?*"

Betty Rose hadn't. The Paper Mill Playhouse, the Long Wharf, the Goodspeed Opera House, yes, all the time. Not the Gristmill. Then again, the vocal guru she longed for didn't advertise either. He didn't need to.

"Tons of stars come out of there," Danny piped in, muddling mint. "Every so often, another pops. Sutton Fraser's just the latest."

Broadway's long-standing "it" girl, on the cusp of queendom. Last year's Tony winner for *Anything Goes*, after three consecutive nominations.

"Overrated," sniffed Erin. With her tray and apron.

"If they ever offer you a gig," Danny encouraged, "I'd grab it. I'd grab everything."

Older, wiser Danny was at the acceptance stage of his non-career, where he wished the best for those just starting out. Erin would get there, thought Betty Rose, once she worked through her own bitterness. It crept up fast, she feared, catching herself in the bar mirror.

Betty Rose covered Erin's tables while she went to smoke outside under a scaffolding. The rain lingered.

There'd be no call, no offer. There never was. Which was just as well, since Julian was so against her going. He'd stayed loyal to her after graduating a year ahead and moving to New York to start his career while she finished out her degree. And then her unexpected return to Indiana, much longer than either had expected, had caused a barely perceptible but bound-to-happen strain, in spite of his caring and understanding and insistence otherwise. She shouldn't risk another separation so soon on a whim dangled by an agent who'd turned his nose up at her Polish name.

Christine Baranski, anyone? she thought. *Jane Krakowski?*

She'd find other opportunities in town, with a flurry of castings for fall and winter shows and tours, roles she'd win on her own, or with Julian's help, which she'd be a fool not to accept. After all, he had a head start and was her biggest fan.

But Wes the agent had no reason to feign his professional and personal interest. He seemed genuinely invested in her career, her newfound champion. That's how careers took off. He said he believed in her and promised to help. She'd win him 'round on her name.

There was no call that night. Nor Saturday, Saturday night, nor Sunday.

The Rum House was always bedlam after Sunday matinee, starting with *The Boy Friend* revival at the Friedman across the street. The young cast had pegged it as their go-to spot from the beginning, celebrating nightly since previews, through opening night, and now in their second month, still giddy with their fresh hit. Their weekend started Sunday at five thirty, and they tipped big and knew her name, and she'd take pictures for them, as a group or with visiting friends and family, proud parents who'd come to their kids' Broadway debut and couldn't stop beaming. The gang was always loud and Betty Rose's age, or younger.

She was at the bar, loading her tray with daiquiris and skinny margaritas when her apron pocket vibrated a steady purr.

"Where you going?" Erin demanded, sun-kissed from her Hampton weekend. "Now?"

"Hello?" Betty Rose said into her phone, huddled under the outside scaffolding, avoiding drips from the late-afternoon shower. "Hello?"

She nodded and nodded. "Yes. Absolutely."

She scribbled instructions on her pad, her phone tucked against her shoulder.

She said "thank you" many times. She dabbed her eye.

Betty Rose stood in the rain, watching the twilight river of taxis and the crush of summer tourists, trying to catch her breath.

Scene Three

BETTY ROSE STAYED UP MOST OF THE NIGHT doing laundry, ironing, and packing smartly, as she was allowed only one bag.

She checked the bus schedule and picked a too-early departure to guarantee an on-time arrival. She was due to report at three p.m., but there were only two buses that stopped in New Hope per weekday. The first one would get her there at noon. She would not miss it.

Night owl Julian stayed up late with her, tweaking and fretting over his *Streetcar* sketches for his upcoming meeting and made one last stab at keeping her in New York for the summer. They made love while her clothes dried downstairs in the basement, and she slipped quietly from bed at daybreak while he slept. Outside, the rain thrummed louder, having picked up.

Wes had been true to his word, a refreshing surprise. He'd called the Gristmill after their show that Friday night and finally heard back Sunday. He'd "pitched her" to the "top dog." He painted an epic struggle, and Betty Rose thanked him repeatedly, and he rattled off specific directions, which she scribbled on her waitress pad and read back to him, although he'd moved on to his next topic.

"It's not a role, or a gig, or a guarantee of anything," he insisted. "It's an apprenticeship. It's probation."

She said nothing to Erin, not only to shelter her parade from rain, but also to heed Wes's advice against "counting her chickens."

"You might fall flat on your face," he'd warned. "They might kick you out. Do yourself a professional favor and keep it to yourself for now."

The bar manager wished her luck on her ambiguous gig and promised to find a spot for her upon her return. "You're a good worker," he said. Betty Rose thanked him, confident she'd have real, better opportunities come fall. Four months with tray and apron were enough.

Betty Rose showered and blew out her hair, unconcerned about waking Julian, who slept like the dead. She desperately needed a haircut, a trim of her split ends, a professional touch for her big debut, but there was no time. Hopefully, she'd find someone good in New Hope; in the meantime, her miracle-cure argan oil would have to suffice. She polished her teeth with Crest and baking soda and applied light makeup and slipped on her silk knit top embroidered with daisies over a pastel charmeuse bias skirt—not the shrewdest travel attire, she realized, but a smart, young look for a first impression.

She ran down her mental checklist and pondered her packed suitcase. She paused and removed a few pairs of socks and pushed her character shoes and curling iron to the edge. From the top drawer of the chest she and Julian shared, she lifted a small, brown, leather-trimmed lockbox, fitted it into the suitcase corner, and then sat on the suitcase to zip it closed.

She brushed back Julian's bangs from his closed eyes and gently kissed his forehead. He stirred, murmured, reached out. She deflected his grab and tucked his arm back under the sheet.

"It's no farther than the Hamptons," she'd insisted earlier, while giving him veto power. "I won't go if you really don't want me to." And, because he loved and supported her, Julian gave his reluctant blessing, as she'd known he would.

"But no summer fling!" he'd ordered, and Betty Rose begged, "Pretty please? With all those chorus boys?"

Julian opened one eye and mumbled as she stood to leave, and Betty Rose said, "Shh. I love you."

Port Authority was busy, cavernous, labyrinthian. She shook the warm rain from her umbrella and navigated briskly through the crowds, rolling bag in tow, scattering pigeons who'd taken up residence inside. She passed Au Bon Pain with its early-morning coffee line, the frenetic Hudson News, billboard posters for *Matilda* and *Pippin* and the new revival of *Sweeney Todd*, and easily found the main ticketing center, which she'd charted out online.

"The Gristmill is allowed one apprentice union card per summer," Wes had told her. "Or none. It's up to them. Your best shot is to work harder than anyone else, wow them with your talent, and pray for a little luck."

The emerald Trans-Bridge bus pulled into the downstairs gate at 9:20 and idled in its own exhaust while the spirited driver loaded the belly with luggage and collected tickets. Betty Rose, third in line, settled into a window seat near the front, pulling her skirt to prevent wrinkles. She successfully radiated unwelcome vibes to ward off a mouthy young punk who trolled farther down the aisle.

"This ain't Mickey and Judy putting on a show in the barn," Wes had warned, coachlike. "This is basic training for the theatre—how the sausage is made. Summer stock is the most intense, grueling regiment an actor can face."

The bus descended from the steady rain and purred through the Lincoln Tunnel, seizing the reverse commute at rush hour. Betty Rose hugged the wall to give her elderly woman seatmate elbow room for her *Newsday*. She rested her head on the cooling window and watched the tunnel lights traffic by. She regretted staying up all night.

"Just remember there's only one person at the Gristmill you gotta please. And it's not yourself." Wes chuckled and said, "I'll leave it at that."

The bus rolled and hummed along in the darkened tunnel. Betty Rose covered her yawn. The temperature was perfect.

"But one tip of his head is the difference between a wasted summer and the gateway to a career." Wes teased out a finale. "A nod means a solo. And then everything changes...."

Betty Rose yawned again, covering it.

● ● ●

Her mother always said *42nd Street* was to blame. More likely, it was the kettledrum that had unleashed the magic in the dark that had hooked her instantly.

Her father had taken her to the matinee at the Tarkington in Indianapolis, when she was seven. The massive red curtain was exciting enough, but when it rose during the overture, revealing those dancing feet from the knees down, she knew her future. By the end of the second act, she *was* Peggy Sawyer, ready for her debut, going out a youngster but coming back a star. Her father indulged her with a souvenir program, poster for her bedroom, and an original cast recording CD that would eventually wear out from overuse. She didn't even remember the ride back to Beech Grove that night, having unsuccessfully begged her father to stay for the evening show.

Her mother never forgave her father for this first taste or for the season tickets that followed through the years and led to acting, voice, and dance classes and charted her on a course that would take her far away from them.

Betty Rose shifted in her seat, awakened by the old woman next to her rustling the pages. She cracked open her eyes to the rain outside the window, leaned against it, closed them again. She yawned anew.

Wes looked funny in the plastic grammar school chair on the second row. All the grown-ups did, smiling up at the gym stage. Miss Marcia didn't have to prod or push Betty Rose like the others. She marched on, led her class, took center. Her father was the proudest, and most handsome, holding her mother's hand, right up front. Betty Rose watched old Mrs. Ross at the piano and, on cue and pitch, sang about your land and her land, and the others mumbled, safe in the background.

She hit the Mouse King with her slipper, saving her fifth grade prince, recruited seven brides for the seven brothers, and flapped and sassed her way through Atlantic City as Nanette. Her father laughed and cheered and applauded, still so handsome and smartly dressed for the evening, but older, grayer, thinner, and she begged them to hold the curtain for him, he was just a little late and had never seen her play Kate before, much less a Cole Porter. But the show was on a grand stage, with a full chorus and orchestra and elaborate sets, and it had to go on, and the old woman with her *Newsday* and the mouthy punk left in the middle of her "So in Love" and went to the ticket taker for a refund. Betty Rose's throat closed up in the middle of her solo and she went silent, so frantic and desperate and terrified she was, searching for her father who had never, ever missed her opening night before.

A gentle hand shook her shoulder.

"New Hope, ma'am," said the mustached Trans-Bridge bus driver, smiling down from the aisle. "I believe this is your stop."

"Oh!" Betty Rose said with a start. "Yes." She squinted out into the sun and checked her watch. Right on time.

She grabbed her bag handle once he'd pulled it from underneath and thanked him again for waking her. "I conked right out!" she said with a laugh as she slipped him a five, and the driver smiled and tipped his hat.

The bus rolled out of town, disappearing around a curve. Betty Rose turned around. And around.

The town, the village, the hamlet, hugged her instantly.

It was weathered wood and aged brick, still bright in its faded sugary shades of pink and blue and yellow. It was Victorian and layer-shingled and candy-stripe-shuttered, haphazard and pristine in the post-rain gleam.

The air was warm and wet and drowsy. It smelled of just-cut grass and fresh water and jasmine.

A steam whistle jolted her. She spun to a vintage locomotive idling at its station, its chimney erupting clouds and beckoning guests who climbed in its cars, children first. She crossed its tracks, following the life deeper into town.

She turned at an intersection onto the mainest of main streets, which the corner sign, resisting cliché, called "Carla Avenue." One end led to woodsy outskirts; the other, which she chose, into the action. She rounded the corner at the Mansion Inn, its vacancy sign welcoming her to town. A Donna Reed–looking woman in a rosy dress with apron swept the wide, wooden porch dotted with wicker rockers and smiled warmly as she sized her up.

There were shops and houses and garages and doors, lacework and clapboard, all nestling the cracked sidewalks and cobblestone alleys. They were painted in sherbet colors of orange, lime, and lemon, trimmed in café au lait.

Flags flew: American, internationals, and prideful rainbows. Balloons bunched outside storefronts, under circus awnings, next to giant gum ball machines with spiraling chutes.

Betty Rose pulled her bag, half expecting to hear a barbershop quartet sing "Lida Rose" or see the Wells Fargo wagon coming down the street. Instead, a hippie-era VW Bug puttered past blasting Bob Marley, a worthy consolation. She passed a wooden Indian guarding Stuber's Smoke Shop and heard big band music crackling from an AM radio through its open door. From a child's rocking chair next to Penny Whistle Toys, a bespectacled mechanical stuffed bear blew bubbles. Next door, a vintage clothing store stationed a mannequin with fiery red pig tails and Dorothy-gingham dress by the front holding a warning sign: "Unattended Children Will Be Sold as Slaves."

From a narrow alcove called Nifty's Knife Sharpening came a whining sawlike noise, as a middle-aged man with goggles—presumably Nifty—honed a cleaver's blade edge right inside the open door. Two spots down, in the Gypsy Heaven Witch Shop, a neon pentagram hung in the shrouded window.

General store. Public library (housed inside a beautiful, repurposed white church building). Christmas shop. A whimsical antiques alley whose entrance cautioned "No Eating, Drinking, or Screwing on Premises." A quaint, feisty, psychedelic Mayberry.

She nodded and said hello to a slim Asian mailman with blue hat and messenger bag on his delivery rounds. He ignored her, seemingly in a hurry as he ducked into one shop and then the next, working his way down the block.

She passed a Starbucks, its sign and scent curiously comforting.

It was easy to peg the tourists—herself included, she knew. A bohemian cluster of young locals, in straw hats and camo shorts and espadrilles, smoked and nodded as she passed Café Carla's sidewalk patio, and when Betty Rose turned for another look, she found them doing the same.

On a mosaic-tiled bench near the New Hope clock, in front of a pair of rusty iron gates the plaque read came from the town's first jail, sat a bearded man in a bright Hawaiian shirt and wide-brimmed straw hat. On his shoulder perched a brown and white spider monkey wearing a tiny Shriner's fez. The monkey alternately grinned and chirped at passersby, and when Betty Rose stopped to smile, it tipped its hat and then groomed its owner's beard until he fed it a peanut. "Gentle, Strudel," the man said, thumbing through the *New Hope Gazette*. "Gentle."

Gerenser's Exotic Ice Cream also sold fudge—and boat tours on the Delaware—and she smiled at the New Hope Candle Shop, which reminded her of Julian's taunts. She reached for her phone to let him know she'd arrived safely. There was no cell reception.

At the town center, she weaved back and forth by the historical society and a painted horse statue, luring bars on her service.

"Excuse me!" she said, whirling to the foot she'd carelessly stepped on. "I'm so sorry, sir. I'm trying to get a signal."

The round, great-uncle-looking man didn't flinch. "Try outside the tattoo parlor on Mechanic," he said. "If you're lucky."

"Tattoo on Mechanic…," Betty Rose echoed the balding, mustached man in short-sleeve oxford and khakis, clutching a striped Rx bag from the New Hope Pharmacy. He had a sheep dog aura and openness. "Thank you."

"The town's been debating a cell tower for years, but they always vote against it," he added, peering down the sidewalk, as if waiting for a friend. "People come here to escape all that stuff. That's the argument, at least."

And then he said, "Are you looking for the Gristmill?"

Betty Rose laughed and said, "Is it that obvious?"

"The eyes give it away," he said with a twinkle. "Bright and seeking. Keep 'em open."

"I will, thank you!"

She shot out her hand and introduced herself to Mr. Arbor.

"Are you the new star of the season?" he asked, and Betty Rose said, "Well, why not?" Then she added, "No, actually. I'm just an apprentice. A nobody."

"That can change in an instant," Mr. Arbor said, and Betty Rose smiled, and he didn't.

He was a lifelong resident and owned a tavern on one of the canals. He had season tickets to the Gristmill Playhouse. He led her toward it.

"You have a lovely town," she told him. "Magic, really."

Mr. Arbor nodded as they crossed Carla Avenue. "A unique brand. Keeps 'em coming, year after year after year." He hesitated and almost spoke, but instead pointed and said, "There you go."

Betty Rose looked at the empty gravel lot.

"Just follow the music," Mr. Arbor said, inspecting her. "Can't miss it. Like a big jack-in-the-box."

He offered the landline phone at his bar whenever she needed it.

"That's very generous," said Betty Rose, "but I'm sure the theater has a phone." Lest she sound ungrateful, she added another "Thank you."

Mr. Arbor repeated his offer and waved her on.

"I'll look for you in the audience!" she called back as he walked off with a slight gimp.

"Good luck, Betty Rose," he replied, turning for one last look and then shuffling on. She felt the urge to pat him on the head.

No-nonsense Yankee, thought Betty Rose, who'd grown to appreciate them. *Good stock.*

At the parking lot's far edge was a rustic "Now Playing" sign hawking the Gristmill's summer season, with *The Mystery of Edwin Drood* just closed and *Oklahoma!* on deck. Bordering the sign under glass were full-color cast head-shots—perfect hair, skin, big teeth, mostly her age or younger, all a step ahead. There were a few people of color, but the Gristmill certainly wouldn't be mounting *The Wiz* anytime this season.

Along the bottom was the sun-faded title "Artistic Director" and an even more faded name that started with "R" and was in desperate need of repainting. Betty Rose stepped back and absorbed it all; the sign alone promised excitement.

In the near distance she heard faint carousel music and the white roar of water. She followed the foliage-canopied path from the gravel lot through to a broad clearing across the tributary that rushed into the Delaware. A footbridge, lined with lush flower beds, spanned the divide. A tarnished copper plaque marked the gated entrance:

THE JOURNEYMAN BRIDGE
In Memory of the Gristmill Players the World Never Knew.
Their Stars Shine Forever in Our Hearts.

Betty Rose pulled her luggage through the open gate and across the bridge, past explosive rosebushes in a bright spectrum of colors and sizes. Some looked ancient, others barely established. All were robust and magazine-worthy. Fuzzy bees shopped from bloom to bloom. The rich, peat-smelling beds were tilled and tended and composted.

Down below, a waterfall churned up rapids around the rock outcrops that begged to be sunned on, dived from. The waters calmed into an eddy, clear and sparkling and protected. A perfect swimming hole.

A roving hummingbird dipped in one flower and then another. It darted up to Betty Rose, hovered in front of her nose. It floated level with her eye, curious, and leaned in to drink.

"No!" said Betty Rose, gently swatting it away with a laugh. "No nectar here!"

She felt a disturbance in the air and looked across to a flock of large black birds taking flight, disappearing into a thick tree. The disrupting culprit—a brown, baby goat with mini-bell collar—scampered toward her, puppylike. It sniffed her ankles and calves and fingers and, satisfied or bored, started digging in the flowerbed. She reached down to pet its young, fresh fur.

Betty Rose looked up and caught her breath.

The Gristmill Playhouse loomed ahead. On the promontory, alone, waiting for her.

Grander, prouder than its faded office photo, it was a white brick barn with wood-shingled roof and red trim. A large waterwheel churned at its front; a tall silo sat attached to its side. Behind and apart, little log cabins clustered around thick lawns. On the river beyond, a houseboat with fringed awnings bobbed at its dock. Towering elms and oaks sheltered and shaded it all.

The Wurlitzer organ music pulled her closer.

On the red front porch, white wicker rockers sat idle under pink geranium hanging baskets and a chasing-light marquee that heralded "*Oklahoma!* Opens Tuesday!" Corner speakers played the crackly carousel music. Betty Rose climbed the stairs, past the large brass farm bell, opened the western split door, and walked inside.

The still, silent lobby looked lovingly restored with fresh paint and new-smelling green carpet. There were upholstered benches and wheelchair-accessible restrooms and a hands-free drinking fountain. Pioneer-looking lanterns dangled from the ceiling, illuminating the Certificate of Appreciation from the New Hope Chamber of Commerce, among other honors. Framed, vintage posters lined the flagstone walls— *Irene, Ten Nights in a Barroom, Pal Joey*—productions stretching back through the decades. The room was refreshingly chilled, bordering on icy.

Between the shuttered box office windows for "Will Call" and "Advance Sales" hung a tall sign with hooks and removable cards that announced the fifteen shows of the summer, in order, like a racing board. The current season had kicked off with *Kiss Me, Kate* on Memorial Day and would wrap up with *Godspell* on Labor Day. In between was a dizzying list of classics and a few unexpected choices whose jubilant fonts alone quickened Betty Rose's breath. One card teased *The Rocky Horror Show* on select midnights, with a special prompting to buy tickets early.

On a shelf to the side sat a wooden suggestions box, next to a stack of comment cards and a Gristmill coffee mug stuffed with pencils, the sharp ends sticking up. Across two sets of double doors was a festively painted sign that read "Theater." Beyond, Betty Rose knew, lay the magic. Centered high above the doors, near the ceiling, was a small, discreet window looking down. Its sliding panel was cracked slightly open, and inside were shadows and flashes of activity. The control booth, she realized, where the stage manager could call the show and keep an eye on the lobby at the same time.

A portable sandwich board in the center of the lobby begged "Quiet Please! Rehearsal in Progress." A battery of can lights and spotlights were lined up in neat rows along the floor to the side of the front door, their power cords carefully coiled and tucked around their clamps. Taped to the top was a hand-scribbled note that read, *For pickup—Nelson Electric.* The lighting rig from the last show, she figured, dismantled and to be switched out for the new one when the delivery truck came.

She inhaled. The room smelled of cedar, a bracing scent in the air-conditioned cool.

Betty Rose gravitated to "The Gristmill Wall of Fame": glamour black-and-white portraits of the titans who'd performed there through the ages. Bette Davis, Katharine Hepburn, Dolores del Río, Barbara Stanwyck, Margaret Sullavan, a murderer's row of legends, loyal members all. Marian Maples, a can't-quite-place-her former starlet named Geraldine Roberts, and new-honoree/current Broadway darling Sutton Fraser peered down at Betty Rose from their well-earned star perch. She absorbed them and turned to the theater doors.

Centered between, the largest and most elaborately framed, hung a cracked oil portrait of a precocious, wide-eyed adolescent— Lillian Gish? Clara Bow?—dressed Big Girl in a sparkling red sequined dress over a petticoat and a flash of knickers. The dress matched her hair, which hung in shimmery ringlets about her shoulders. She towered between the doors, staring down her admirers with an impish smile of near–*Mona Lisa* mystery and her hands tucked behind her back. Both coy and seductive, she seemed to withhold a surprise.

Betty Rose drew closer. The worn plaque at the bottom was engraved "Carla," a recurring theme. The town's mascot, she thought, or perhaps its original prima donna from turn-of-the-last-century. She held the lobby's place of honor, eclipsing the other legends with their mass-produced photos, her shrine hand-painted by a real artist.

A gleam caught Betty Rose's eye, and she squinted up at the gold medallion around the child idol's neck. She rose higher and strained to decipher the engraved insignia.

"I'm sorry, we're dark Mondays," a pixie voice said with a tinge of scold. Betty Rose spun.

"Oh! My bad!" the girl said, flustered, covering her mouth in apology. "Betty Rose!"

She was younger, eager, with a rosy, open face. She wore a paint-spattered halter dress in dusty pink denim over a prairie floral blouse. She wore white tights on thick legs and beige character shoes. Her sandy hair was pulled back in a pink-and-white headband, and her freckled face was makeup free. She smiled broadly and stuck out her hand.

"Did you find us okay?" she asked. "I'm Phyllis." Then she sighed and shook her head, sweetly beleaguered, and said, "I was supposed to meet you at the bus, but we're in tech. It's always a zoo. You got here just in time; boy, do we need you!"

"Well, I'm here!" said Betty Rose, rising to the excitement. "Put me to work!" She tipped her luggage on its wheels and added, "If I could just put this somewhere..."

From inside the theater came a rushed piano vamp, followed quickly by a full orchestra.

"Oh hell!" said Phyllis, covering her mouth in gleeful panic. She grabbed Betty Rose's hand and said, "Onstage!"

"Right now?"

"Yes, silly! You know 'Oklahoma!' right?"

"Yes, of course," said Betty Rose.

"Phew! Thank God!" Phyllis said with a filly laugh, pulling her away. "'Cause you're on!"

Scene Four

PHYLLIS DRAGGED HER DOWN A PITCH-BLACK CORRIDOR by the box office, toward energy and noise as the orchestra grew louder and more expectant.

Betty Rose resisted; Phyllis pulled harder.

"Just do what I do," she shouted over the swelling music.

She rounded a corner under blue running lights, threaded through dark wing curtains, and yanked Betty Rose into the hot glare of the open stage.

There was a crinkly scrim backdrop of brilliant sky and sun over brown fields and green plains, windmills, and barns. There was a plywood cottage and front porch, half-built and unpainted and puddled with sawdust. Strategically propped around the stage were a well water pump, a butter churner, and four bales of hay.

There were two dozen cowboys and cowgirls, farmers and daughters, grouped in a finale panorama, singing to one another and the black abyss of the audience with Broadway precision. Phyllis snuck her upstage to the rear, and shoulder-to-shoulder they faced the backs of young heads and blinding trees of spotlights. Phyllis opened her face and sang to the sky; Betty Rose caught on quickly and found her words and notes with ingrained ease.

She responded with the chorus to the solo verses. She took the high soprano line when the unison branched into harmony. She bent and bounced, hands on knees, for the repeating bridge building toward the finish. She breathed deep from her diaphragm and modulated up with the key change.

The cast abruptly broke into a swirling square dance, swinging partner to partner with alternating elbows. Betty Rose, flummoxed, followed Phyllis's lead and folded in, spinning from one to another. Familiar fresh faces sprang to life from their headshots on the board. She twirled from a spot-on Will Parker to a potential Ali Hakim, and do-si-do'd with a token older couple who tipped their heads, good-neighbor-like. Aunt Eller, she reckoned, and either an ill-cast Andrew Carnes or maybe Ike Skidmore. Betty Rose laughed and turned to face a striking and sinewy young buck who was just a cowhand now but would someday make the perfect Curly. He winked and grinned at her through his "yip-ee-ay" and linked elbows for a series of spins. She didn't miss a step, hiding the blush from his attention, as she felt his biceps against her upper arm. She released on cue to reach for her next partner.

The group immediately parted into two rows, leaving Betty Rose abandoned in the middle. Panicked, she fled toward one side, but they'd already sashayed together and back again. She followed, clodding, out of sync and now lost in her words. She reached out to no one reaching back and mimicked, in desperation, one step up and one step back.

"Stop this," said a strong, calm voice from the black abyss.

The chorus sang on, spelling out the song's letters toward the crescendo.

"Cut!" the voice called louder, irritated.

The cast reached the "A" and took a breath for the big finish.

"STOP! CUT!" the voice raged. "STOPFUCKINGCUT!"

The stage fell silent. Then a shuffling retreat to the wing flats, leaving Betty Rose alone, stage center. She turned to follow.

"Don't fucking move!" the blackness warned. Betty Rose froze.

There was a deep sigh from the dark house. A deliberate wipe of the face.

"In a few hours, just a few hours, mind you," the man said in a normal voice, having regained his calm, "strangers will join us here, in the dark, a communal gathering, a tribal ritual, really…craving an intimate and sensual experience.…"

Betty Rose, afraid to squint, looked out evenly, the hot lights scorching her eyes. In her lower periphery, orchestra members in the pit put down their instruments and assumed crash positions. The man's voice traveled down the row and into the aisle.

"After a slow, arousing buildup—comforted and seduced by songs they don't even remember learning,"—he sounded weary, almost bored—"stimulated by precision dance, thrusting them deeper and closer to the climax…"

He emerged into the light—stout and robust, white-bearded and ruddy—dressed in a black Pittsburgh Steelers T-shirt and rumpled khakis, a Caterpillar baseball cap, and clutching a metal clipboard and yellow legal pad loaded with scrawl. Making his way around the orchestra pit, he looked slightly down and at no one, as if working through this heavy dilemma for himself.

"And with the sap rising," he went on, ascending the side stairs to the apron, "methodically stroked to the edge as they tense to pop their collective cork…" He scanned the stage without focusing and gravitated, by chance it seemed, toward Betty Rose in the center.

He got close and stood still. "Suddenly, a mutant freak clown bursts onto the stage! Leaving them limp, shriveled. And demanding a refund." He peered at the company lining the deck and held his stance in the silence.

Betty Rose, still at attention and blinded by lights, giggled against her will. Her hand shot to her mouth to stifle.

The man turned, as if alerted to her presence, and stepped closer, and closer still. He inspected her face. He seemed to sniff her.

"Do you…" he asked her in a low voice, close enough to feel his breath on her cheek. "Do you find this—this monumental catastrophe I'm describing—I'm just curious; do you find this…*funny?*" He was, underneath his eerie calm, boiling.

"No, sir, no!" Betty Rose insisted, afraid to look. "I…can't help it!"

Surely he wouldn't smack her in front of the cast. Once he'd finished humiliating her, she predicted, he'd just dismiss her and send her to back where she came from. In the moment, that seemed a relief.

He grabbed her face gently and turned her head to him. He steered her eyes up to his. He held her terrified stare while her eyes adjusted. Then he rounded his face into a warm smile and toggled her chin playfully. He became Santa Claus.

"Please control yourself," he said *entre nou*s, nodding toward the floor. "We just mopped the stage."

Mortified, Betty Rose looked down at the floor, found it dry, and looked back up at the jolly man seizing with laughter.

"Oh you!" she *tsk*ed, mock punching his arm. He erupted, his body shaking with glee.

The horseshoe surrounding them joined with raucous laughter of its own.

"Welcome, Miss *Milenski*!" He shrugged and said, "Well, what's in a name? When I first landed from the Old Country, I was Takas Patikas. Or so I'm told..." The cast laughed anew. Betty Rose, not getting it, laughed along.

The man stepped back and indicated Betty Rose as exhibit A.

"Our giggling schoolgirl has already mastered the crucial art of 'winging it,'" he lectured as he paced. "An especially critical skill with the pressure we work under here every day." He sized her up, tapping his cheek, and decreed, "You'll be on running crew this show. Maybe chorus in the next."

"Thank you, sir," Betty Rose said, exhaling. "Thank you, Mr. Takas!"

There was a gasp upstage and then fresh silence.

"Or...what's your name now?" she asked, on edge again. Another gasp from behind her.

Santa carried on, ignoring the question and the room's shock.

"Dottie." He beckoned to the maybe-Aunt Eller who, with her salt-and-pepper pageboy cut and bookworm glasses, now seemed impossibly cast. It must have been by default, as the only age-appropriate woman in the company. She sprang to her boss's side.

"Yes, *Rex*?" she emphasized for Betty Rose, shooting a quick glance.

Rex whispered in her ear an unheard list of instructions, and Dottie nodded in hushed obedience. "Yes, Rex," she said,

and repeated "Yes, Rex" with each new order. He released
Dottie's shoulder and turned back to his subjects with a smile.

"Keep trusting your instincts," he told Betty Rose for the
benefit of the others. "All you need is training, discipline…and
to lose eight pounds. Right, Dot?"

Dottie frowned. "Oh, Rex," she pleaded. "Maybe five?"

"Eight," Rex repeated, and Dottie nodded. Neither looked
at Betty Rose.

"Get our preemie settled in, gypsies," he commanded the
cast. "I'll see you in the morning."

He made a final stop in Betty Rose's ear.

"Make it happen, Betty Rose," he urged her privately.
"That's all you need to know here. Make it happen, and let it
happen."

He disappeared back into the dark house and out the front.

The company descended upon Betty Rose, congratulating,
welcoming her. She spun in a circle, trying to greet them all.

Dottie took her face in both hands and Eskimo'd noses.

"Daddy likes you," she said, scrunching.

● ● ●

Betty Rose struggled to keep up with Dottie's pace and rules.

"You'll bunk with Phyllis and Gwen, the other interns," she
said, abruptly professional, strutting up the aisle into the lobby. She
was bony and tomboyish in her oxford shirt and paint-spattered
khakis. She'd changed from character shoes into dingy white Keds.
"Rex Rule Number One: no drugs."

"Booze is fine," added Alistair, the older ill-cast man who
seemed Dottie's sidekick. "Just don't overshoot the runway."
He was mannered and foppish with clipped, vaguely British

speech—better suited for Cole Porter or Noël Coward than farmer or cowman. Dottie tolerated him like an old married couple, which was unlikely. "He means don't get drunk," she clarified. "In his own queer way."

Betty Rose looked around the lobby and then paced it, abruptly panicked.

"Excuse me…," she started, searching.

Dottie grabbed a sales report from the box office manager, ran her finger down the last column, and flared her nose, unimpressed. "But no dope!" she stressed. "Rex has zero tolerance for that nonsense. One strike and you're out."

"I'm sorry," Betty Rose said, more urgent. "My luggage is gone."

Dottie put down the report. "Gone where?" she asked.

"I left it here, right here, with my purse, when I went onstage."

Dottie sighed. "Did the stupid techies load it out?" she asked, scanning for the guilty party. "No matter. We've got everything you need here."

"Yes," Betty Rose said, "But my ID. My money…"

Dottie turned, indignant.

"No one's going to steal from you, Betty Rose," she said.

"Oh, I know that!" Betty Rose insisted. "I just…need to get a haircut at some point. I didn't have time before…"

Dottie reached out to finger her lengths and shook her head. "Keep it long," she said. "It reads better onstage."

She led Betty Rose across the manicured, parklike grounds, past weathered Adirondack chairs and lawn umbrellas, with chatty Alistair in tow. He peppered her with personal questions.

"Beech Grove," he repeated with breathy flair when she revealed her hometown. "Why, it sounds like dancing."

"You just broke the seal," Dottie said to Betty Rose, shaking her head. "You've got him quoting Philip Barry. It only gets worse." They bantered like a vaudeville comedy act. Comden and Green, she thought. Nichols and May.

Inside the "Artists Entrance" to backstage, Dottie tapped the clipboard with its dangling pen. "Sign in and out on the call board every time you leave the theater, whenever you cross the bridge," she said. "We must know where you are at all times. Union regulation." Betty Rose nodded, scanning the list of names and boxes and checks.

They passed a line waiting for the wall-mounted telephone, next to the oversized chalkboard. "Two minutes a day limit, domestic only," Dottie instructed and then squinted at the chalkboard. "Your boyfriend has already called," she added with slight reproach.

Betty Rose found her name scribbled, with *Call Julian* circled after. "How did you know he's my boyfriend...?" she started, and Dottie said, "Who else would call so soon?" The line was long, and Betty Rose made a mental note to call later, when it had thinned out. She thrilled to see her name on the board with the others.

"A boyfriend?" Alistair teased, feigning naughtiness. "You'll have to tell me all about him, B.R...." She laughed at the old man's gossipy talk and said, "B.R.—that's just what *he* calls me."

"Let's get you changed before dinner," Dottie interrupted, spiriting ahead.

The mess hall extended out from the theater, toward the river. It had a vaulted and beamed ceiling with rows of banquet tables covered in red gingham cloth and dotted with pizza parlor candles. Betty Rose wore the red and white "Gristmill Playhouse" T-shirt and surplus painters pants they'd loaned her, as she had no other clothes. Dottie tried unsuccessfully to reach the techie who'd loaded her luggage and purse into the truck along with the lights and fog machine they'd rented for the last show. He'd realize his mistake, she hoped, when he unloaded at the rental shop.

"We'll get it back," Dottie assured her. "That worthless techie's on thin ice. I swear he's a stoner, but I can't prove it. Yet."

Betty Rose sandwiched between Phyllis and a punchy jester boy who cracked loud, corny jokes and appeared high on something himself. Rex's zero-tolerance policy seemed more honored in the breach than the observance. The bill of fare, dished out cafeteria-style, included grilled T-bone steaks, macaroni and cheese casserole, and steamed broccoli mixed with red peppers and water chestnuts. It smelled delicious.

Dottie, however, served a special plate for Betty Rose.

"What...is this?" she asked politely when the aproned Dottie slid the scoop of gray pureed mush across the steam table.

"It's low carb, high protein, that's what," Dottie said. "Doctor's orders. Until you lose some of that baby fat. You'll feel better."

Betty Rose nodded, although she felt fine and hadn't been aware, until today, of her baby fat problem. It looked like oatmeal mixed with spinach and raisins and ribboned with ketchup, which Dottie confirmed was, more or less, correct. "That's Sriracha on top," she corrected. "Sweet and savory."

"It's a twist on an old theatre recipe," she added. "It worked for Judy Holliday. It'll work for you. We'll whittle you down in no time." Sweet and *fiery*, Betty Rose thought, her mouth burning from the first tentative spoonful. She pledged to acquire a taste, and it was more palatable than it looked, like a vegan Thai experiment. Still, she mostly stirred it.

The room was loud and gossipy with outbursts of laughter from here and there. Betty Rose scanned the packed tables and thought of church summer camp back home. She looked at the sea of paint-stained denim overalls and jumpsuits and halter dresses in light blues and dusty pinks, the striped shirts and floral blouses, individual and yet all of a piece, like the not-quite-matching singers in the Lawrence Welk reruns she'd discovered as a child and had imprinted on her ever since. If Lawrence Welk hosted *Hee Haw*. They'd all ditched their character shoes for moccasins and sneakers.

Phyllis sawed at her steak and drew Betty Rose into the table's conversation about the day's rehearsal gaffes and final fittings for Laurey's dream ballet and Mrs. Ellsworth, the blue-haired subscriber whose hearing aid always whined from the third row and would inevitably do so again tomorrow night, no matter how often the house manager alerted her.

"I just wanna see my main man Strudel again," said Phyllis, hammering the table. "He's my groupie." The table seconded the notion, and Phyllis explained the spider monkey whose straw-hatted owner—the "Panama Man," they called him—was a local and season subscriber. Apparently, he brought his little pet to every show. "I saw them in town!" said Betty Rose, eager to add to the conversation. "In his tiny hat."

"Does anyone…," Alistair mused from a nearby table, "… still wear…a hat?"

"Batten down the hatches!" Dottie called out from the kitchen. "Alistair is quoting Sondheim!"

At the next table, an animated gang swapped quotes from their worst theatre reviews, which they remembered to the letter. "The *Times* said the cast of my one-woman show was 'too large,'" laughed a breasty and clean-scrubbed redhead, as if it were a badge of honor. *"Time Out* wrote: 'It was hard for me to enjoy his *Amadeus* because of adverse conditions out of his control,'" said a prematurely balding youngish fellow. "'By that I mean: The curtain was up.'" The table roared, and Betty Rose felt a pang of envy for a reviewer's mention, however scathing, from a professional, non-student newspaper.

It was a sunny group. Upbeat and pure without the petty backstabbing bitchiness she'd witnessed with nonworking actors like Erin back at the Rum House. This team glowed with a joyful focus on the game they'd been hired to play. No one spoke of the Kardashians or *The Bachelor* or Instagram. And no one, after their initial burst of welcome, paid her special attention, which suited her fine. She was happy to meld in.

Betty Rose the Outsider mostly listened and laughed in the right places, having little to add besides "Really?" and "That's terrible!" and "That's wonderful!" Better inane, she reasoned, than standoffish. That didn't bother Gwen, the third intern, who sat across from Phyllis but acted like she was at her own private table.

Gwen was a stunner, with bright jewel eyes and rich lips and sun-kissed hair. She was hard to look at and impossible not to. She nibbled at broccoli and sat silently. Too gorgeous to be self-conscious or shy, thought Betty Rose. Just superior. Gwen had never had a baby fat problem, or likely any others. The little princess caught her staring and returned a half smile and dismissive glance at her mush before looking back down at her own plate. Betty Rose didn't go out of her way: A drop-dead young actress with attitude was a perennial cliché and not to be indulged.

She spread the mound around her plate and speared raisins and said "soprano" when the jester asked her vocal range.

"But I can belt, too," she added, which was a fact and not a brag. Dottie paraded from the kitchen with a silver-domed plate on propped fingers and said, "Who's feeding Daddy tonight?"

All forks hit the tables, but the lanky young buck who'd ignored Betty Rose once offstage was first to spring up. "Got it!" he announced, and Dottie said, "Good boy, Caleb," passing it off.

"My, my," Alistair called from his table. "*Someone* wants to be Daddy's favorite...." There were titters and whistles, but eager-beaver Caleb had already pushed through the swinging door out. He moved like a gymnast.

Betty Rose heard a familiar bell tinkling and turned toward the spontaneous commotion to see the brown baby goat had snuck in the swinging door and was making the rounds. "Clyde!" one table cried out, and then another, vying for his spastic attention with scraps.

Dottie wasn't amused. "Whose idea was it to trade season tickets for this beast?" she demanded.

Sutton Fraser popped up from her table across the room; Betty Rose hadn't seen her yet, although she'd been looking. Less striking in person and out of costume and makeup, she was camouflaged like the others until she reared up and turned on the Tony wattage.

"I thought it was a fair trade," she said, shoulder-clapping Dottie. "Organic goat's milk has so many uses: soap, lotion, cheese." And Dottie said, "But who's going to milk the damn thing?"

"The only thing milked around here," came Alistair's clipped diction, "are the curtain calls." His corny jokes seemed more calculated for groans than laughter.

Clyde paid a quick visit to Betty Rose's table. He wolfed down Phyllis's steak scraps but, dispelling goat myths, had no use for the oatmeal-Sriracha mashup.

After dinner, she stood behind Phyllis in the plate-cleaning line. Phyllis was practicing, with spotty results, the alto line in "Out of My Dreams," and Betty Rose gently guided her into the right pitch. "It's a tough harmony," she conceded, not wanting to upstage her new friend.

The line curved to a brick room off the kitchen, where sat a giant, vintage iron contraption with a wide open mouth facing up. It was bolted to a massive, round concrete slab and was powered by thick rubber belts snaking through a constellation of large rusty gears. It made a tremendous racket.

"What...is that?" asked Betty Rose.

"THE gristmill," Phyllis shouted above the noise. "They really did a solid by preserving it from the day. Aren't agrarian artifacts so old-school groovy?" Betty Rose nodded, acclimating to Phyllis's mix of urban and King's English.

One by one the line dumped leftovers into the yawning hopper and used a long, sharp metal pick to stuff them down. The mill rattled and clunked and churned and pulverized. Betty Rose backed off from its violent outburst as it shattered steak bones and spat the pulpy, partially digested waste into a large red fire bucket on the side. Its spout dripped and belched in between feedings.

"What do they do with it?" asked Betty Rose, nodding at the slop bucket. It made her slightly queasy.

"Compost for the roses on the bridge," Phyllis said. "Reduce, reuse, recycle. They're very green around here. 'Stewards of the Earth,' Dottie calls us." Betty Rose nodded. The roses did look well fed.

Someone right ahead fed the mill more than it could chew, as it made a terrible *thunk* and choked and shuddered and overshot jagged chunks past the bucket onto the floor.

"Shut it off!" yelled Dottie, storming from the kitchen in a panic. A boy flipped a switch on the wall, and the belts slowed, calming the monster garbage disposal. "I think it's clogged," he said.

"You don't say?" said Dottie, patting the machine, listening. Then she reached down into the hopper, shoulder-deep. "NO!" Betty Rose cried out, and Dottie shot her a perplexed look. "The...blades!" Betty Rose softened, self-conscious that no one else shared her alarm. Dottie waved her off like a pest. "Jeezus Christ," she mumbled, shaking her head. "It doesn't have blades."

She dug around and fished out a twisted scrap of metal. "What brainiac dropped their fork in? Anyone? Bueller?" No one fessed up, and Dottie bellowed to the sky, "For the love of God, do NOT put silverware in the mill! It dulls the goddamned stones!" She fished out more shards and wiped her befouled hand down her apron, streaking it. She groused and told them to use the garbage can until she "got this disaster cleared up." She circled the metal brute, distressed and motherly.

"Does anyone know a mill Maytag Man?" asked Alistair, and Dottie said, "That joke does not improve with age, you old fop."

They stacked and slid their scraped plates toward the "pearl divers" on dishwashing duty. Phyllis linked arms and guided Betty Rose out. She glanced back one last time at Alistair offering useless tips as Dottie, increasingly agitated, probed the injured beast with the long pick, like a surgeon.

"This can*not* happen," she muttered. "Rex will kill me."

Scene Five

As undistinguished as she appeared in person, Sutton proved her star worth when she opened her mouth to sing.

She lit up with her roller brush, leading the gypsies in an impromptu "Do-Re-Mi" sing-along as they finished painting the set onstage after dinner. Mary Martin, Betty Rose had read, underwent a similar metamorphosis from relatable Plain Jane to megastar under the lights. Sutton had the combination to that safe.

"God, I'm too old for 'Maria,'" she groaned with a laugh, interrupting the final round. "Someone tell Rex we need a new ingenue. Stat!"

The pianist in the pit kept playing, and Sutton scanned the stage and pointed at the reticent Gwen to pick up where she'd left off. Gwen dropped her attitude and blossomed into a clear, sweet, and powerful soprano, eclipsing the star. Betty Rose caught herself gawking at the ringing vibrato and tried to recover; the talent gods had, almost cruelly, stacked the deck with this one.

Gwen led the company to the song's jubilant end and tipped her bashful head at the applause before returning to Aunt Eller's half-painted door.

"Gwen sings just like Barbara Cook," Alistair gushed, holding a dry brush just for show. "Oh, I took such a shine to her, back when I thought I was straight."

"You're a natural," Sutton chimed in, clearly impressed. "You've gotten even better the past few weeks." Gwen smiled down and said, "Thank you," and pivoted to the door she was painting. Betty Rose painted her own window and kept to herself. Above, techies on ladders hung Parcans.

"Hey, what's my type?" Phyllis demanded with puppylike urgency. "Your *line*," Alistair corrected. "That's what we call it in stock."

"What's my line?" she pestered. "Am I an ingenue, too?" Alistair inspected her with a diplomatic pause and said, "Not in the traditional sense of the word." Phyllis nodded.

"But that doesn't mean you can't be a big star," he added quickly. "You're a Kaye Ballard type. Second banana." Phyllis said, "No clue who that is, but I'll take it!" "Or even a hybrid like Marilyn Miller," Alistair went on. "They called her 'Mademoiselle Sugarlump.'" Phyllis feigned offense and said, "I'll stew on that one."

"Proud second banana here!" announced Rachelle—leggy and feisty, with wild hair and perfect body and challenging, angular face. "I call it 'low maintenance, high visibility.' We waltz out and steal the scene while the star does the heavy lifting and takes all the slings and arrows. We have longer careers." She stuck out her tongue at the more angelic Sutton and cackled. "They'll put this one out to pasture soon." And Sutton laughed back and said, "*Mangez moi*, beeatch."

Betty Rose studied Rachelle's sharp features and thought that had they been just a few degrees softer, she'd have been a leading lady, too. From the back-and-forth conversations, Betty

Rose gleaned that Rachelle had been at the Gristmill a few years longer than Sutton, although she'd fallen short of that level of stardom. Even so, she seemed every bit the Broadway workhorse. She was the perfect Gertie Cummings for the new show.

And then Phyllis said, "What about Betty Rose? What's her line?" Betty Rose smiled faintly, uneasy in this spotlight. Alistair looked her over and said, "Well, that's up to Rex, of course. But so far she's mighty handy with a brush." She nodded an awkward thanks and finished the sill.

"A character actor holds all the cards," Dottie agreed, backing Alistair up, and Sutton explained the "star's journey" to a young, pudgy techie slicing thick hemp into long pieces with a stage knife. "Ingenue, leading lady, character actress," she schooled. "And then you die, basically."

"Thanks, Sutton!" Dottie called out.

"Or in my case," said Alistair, migrating toward Betty Rose's window, "young butler, aging butler, butler needing diapers... Oh, it's been a looong journey." He stood over her shoulder, and she felt his expectant stare. "How...long have you been here?" she asked, sensing her cue.

"I joined the Gristmill forty-one years ago this summer!" he announced and acknowledged the room's congratulations. "I've done Broadway, regional, national tours, but nothing thrills like a summer at the Gristmill. Forgetting one show, playing another, learning the next, all at the same time. Wondrous!"

"You've certainly mastered the 'forgetting' part," Dottie grumbled. "Get some paint on your brush, you big pansy."

Betty Rose pointed toward the lobby. "All the portraits out there—the big stars, I mean—are women," she said. "Is there a separate wall for the men?" She was curious who else had started out here, for bragging rights to Julian. If, by chance, a young Steve McQueen or Paul Newman or even Brian Stokes Mitchell had spent a summer at the Gristmill, her stock in Julian's eyes would rise to that of pedestaled goddess.

"That, my dear, is an excellent question," said Alistair, who explained how the Gristmill's legacy of celebrating its female stars stretched back to its earliest days.

"And Rex supports that fully even now," Alistair added. "After all, theatre is really the medium of women. Think Duse, Bernhardt, Laurette Taylor. Men might rule the movies, but the dames command the stage."

"Damn straight!" said Rachelle, wielding a Makita. "Back off!"

"I do miss the dramas we used to do here," added Alistair, inspecting paint cans but not finding the color he was looking for. "We switched to an all-musical repertoire in the seventies, for economic reasons. Summer crowds just can't sit still for a straight play these days. But, oh, how we used to light up the sky!"

"Damn the torpedoes!" Dottie taunted from across the stage. "Alistair is quoting Moss Hart!"

"I like your necklace," Sutton said, surprising Betty Rose with her abrupt attention. "What's it say?" She reached out her hand.

"Oh," said Betty Rose, taken aback by the star's focus. "It's...from my father." She dangled the tiny silver pendant into Sutton's gentle fingers.

"'Go boldly...,'" Sutton read, squinting.

"'...in the direction of your dreams.'" Betty Rose finished the quotation. "'Live the life you have imagined,' although that wouldn't fit. It was a favorite of his." Sutton nodded and said, "Thoreau. Or a variation. Your dad has good taste." And Betty Rose said, "Thank you. I never take it off."

"It's lovely. And so discreet," said Sutton, reaching down her own neck. "Unlike *this* Frisbee!" She pulled out a gold medallion with a rustic-looking insignia and swung it, hooker-like. It was slightly larger than a silver dollar and seemed to match the child star's lobby portrait. But it triggered an earlier memory.

"You wore that at the Tonys!" Betty Rose blurted, instantly feeling fan-stupid and borderline stalkerish for having remembered. Then again, it was hard to miss, especially with a plunging neckline, at the podium, on national television.

"I never take it off either," said Sutton. "My good luck charm. Although it didn't help much with *Little Women* or *Leap of Faith*. Thank God the Gristmill takes me back, no matter what."

"When the wolf's at the door, run for the barn!" Alistair bellowed, dripping red onto the stage. "The drop cloth, ding-bat!" Dottie yelled.

Betty Rose inspected the medallion's engraving: the comedy/tragedy masks, which she knew were called sock and buskin, from Greek theatre days. They were a variation on the traditional masks: decidedly feminine, with long eyelashes and flowing hair. They looked human, childlike. One gleeful, the other wailing.

Separating the girly faces was a long stick with a pointed end.

"It's beautiful," she said. "What's that between them?"

"Part of the old mill logo," Sutton answered, monitoring her. "Maybe you'll wear one someday."

"Curfew!" Dottie called out, yanking Alistair's useless brush away. "Believe it or not, we do sleep around here!"

"We need you fresh-faced for opening night," she insisted, herding the reluctant troops offstage. "La-di-da-di-everybody!"

● ● ●

Now the playhouse dress code made sense.

The spattered paint and tech work scuffs would have ruined her clothes and everyone else's. It was smart and thoughtful for the Gristmill to provide a knockabout wardrobe. And her frilly Laura Ingalls nightgown, while not particularly sexy, was country-chic and the perfect summer weight. Even after the rogue techie had returned her luggage, which would be—they assured her—*tomorrow,* she'd leave it packed and wear the Gristmill's denims and khakis and chambrays. Offstage, there was no need to dress up. It was liberating.

Betty Rose scrubbed her face in the freestanding camp bath house just beyond the log cabin barracks. She'd waited for the end-of-day rush to subside, not yet comfortable with the unisex setup, in spite of the harmless, familylike vibe. She'd slipped off her nightgown in the solo shower stall and hung it under her playhouse-provided towel on the outside hook. Soaped, rinsed, dried off, and perked up at the sound of curtain rings from another late arrival two stalls down. She donned her nightgown and crept quietly from her stall, in flip-flops, past the billowing steam and late arrival's towel, toward the trough-style sink and mirror.

She exfoliated and moisturized with Burt's Bees from her Gristmill-issued beach pail of toiletries. She quelled a burp, and then another, and made a note to hold the Sriracha sauce, which had needled her since dinner. Surely Dottie wouldn't object.

She twisted her damp hair into a bun and marveled how doomed and despondent she'd felt just twenty-four hours before, trapped with Erin and Danny and Claudine at the Rum House, perhaps forever. What an odd miracle the day had brought. She was exhilarated, and exhausted. It seemed like days since she'd kissed goodbye the sleeping eyes of...*Julian!* she thought with a start.

She scolded herself for not calling him right after dinner. Phyllis had been prattling on so eagerly, trying to be helpful and to show her everything and explain it all, that it had simply slipped her mind.

She'd call first thing in the morning—predawn, if necessary, and leave a message if he was asleep, which he would be—to explain the sketchy phone situation, so he wouldn't worry or think she'd forgotten. It was too late tonight; she couldn't risk sneaking back into the theater after Dottie had shooed them out.

She brushed her teeth with Tom's of Maine, which seemed a very Gristmill brand, although she missed her Crest and baking soda. She rewiped a clean patch on the steamed mirror.

The shower stall ringed open. Caleb stepped out naked.

Betty Rose caught her breath.

She looked down and away. Doglike, Caleb shook out his hair and stretched, centered too perfectly in the mirror's clear patch. Tom's of Maine, which typically just sat in the mouth, felt frothy now.

The mirror must have had a slight, fun house warp; no one had shoulders so broad, a waist so small.

Not a gymnast, she reconsidered. *A swimmer.* Michael Phelps, with a face.

And gall.

He sauntered, still dripping, toward the sink, mercifully into the fuzzy, steamed-over mirror side. Betty Rose brushed and brushed, ignoring him.

"Hey, you," he said with happy surprise. She nodded halfway, her mouth full.

"Sorry I missed the painting party," he said, now beside her. "I was running lines with Rex." With one swipe of his towel, he cleared off the mirror, stood naked in the reflection, still glistening.

Betty Rose brushed and nodded and made brief mirror eye contact before looking away.

"I always get supertense before an opening," he added, tousling his hair. He leaned forward to check his teeth. Betty Rose sawed one set of molars and then another.

"Sorry for all the steam," he said with a laugh, sizing himself up. "I find a hot shower does the trick. Among other things…"

She held foam in her mouth, trying not to swallow or gag. She kept her eyes locked on the mirror they shared. Laura Ingalls and naked Michael Phelps with a *Glee* face.

He reached over and caught a drip of pasty drool from her bottom lip. Rinsed his hand under her faucet. "You should try it sometime," he said, with an unlawful grin.

Betty Rose leaned down, cupped water into her mouth, tried to avoid her periphery.

Caleb wrapped the towel low on his hips, tucked it. Ran fingers through his locks, which responded perfectly.

"Sleep well, Betty Rose," he said, flashing whites. She nodded downward, held up an "OK."

She held until he was gone.

Jackass, she thought, swishing. She spat.

Scene Six

BETTY ROSE HAD MISJUDGED GWEN; she wasn't so bad after all.

The three apprentices shared a cramped dorm room off the mess hall, facing the river. They were on a shorter leash than the official company, spread out in cabins around the compound. There was scarcely room for the college-grade bunk beds and set of drawers they split. Betty Rose, last in, took the top bunk, although Phyllis offered to switch; Gwen had a single by the window. Closet space, at a premium, was less an issue with their spare and interchangeable playhouse wardrobe.

Phyllis called it "cozy." It did have a certain charm. And they graciously divvied up their territory with Betty Rose, considering they had a month on her.

"Are you nuts? My parents have no idea. They would never let me spend my summer at a theater" said soon-to-be-college-senior Phyllis to Betty Rose's question. "As far as they know, I'm 'studying art in Málaga.'" Her eyes widened in mock concern. "Hell, I wonder if Wellesley even has a program there. Guess I should have checked."

"I didn't bother to tell my sister," said non-college Gwen, filing her nails as she sat Indian-style on daisy-patterned sheets. "And my parents don't give a fuck." She looked up at Betty Rose. "Why? Did you tell yours?"

Betty Rose shook her head. "I'm an only child." And then she said with a laugh, "It's sorta funny, if you think about it: None of our family knows we're here."

"Well, why should they?" Phyllis asked. "None of this makes sense to anyone in the real world. I'm so glad to be away from it for a few months."

"It makes less sense to me every day," said Gwen, and Phyllis said, "Oh, Gwen, don't start bitching again. You're such a Debbie at night. It's so low-budge." Phyllis, Betty Rose quickly realized, classified most everything into categories of low budget and high budget, based on their current worth to her. Broadway, Tory Burch, and Pharrell Williams were "high-budge." Equity waiver, Justin Bieber, and Gwen's general attitude were the opposite.

"Prisoners of the Gristmill freak show," Gwen went on, jest-free. "Slaves, really. Selling our souls for a stupid Equity card." She'd clearly soured on the place.

"Everyone knows you're going to get it," said Phyllis, steering the conversation to the bright side. "You're the star here, and I'm just the second banana having a ball."

Gwen popped open her laptop, plugged into the wall. "I'm this close to letting you two duke it out," she said. "I don't know if we're interns or inmates."

"It is bad business to talk bad business about show business," Phyllis scolded.

"Daddy trained you well!" mocked Gwen and then turned to Betty Rose. "And you get props for not knowing Rex's name. That was my favorite disaster all summer. I thought Dottie's head would spin off."

Phyllis gasped and said, "I thought mine would, too!" and Betty Rose said, "How would I know his name?"

"Rex Terrell is a famous Broadway director," Phyllis said.

"*Was*," Gwen clarified. "And 'famous' is a relative term. So is 'Broadway.' And 'director.'" Phyllis pointed at her and said, "Debbie Downer. Every night. Like the moon."

"Rex directed one show on Broadway, long before we were born," Gwen elaborated. "And it closed in six days. Mega-flop. Sage of the stage, my ass."

"Faith Hill was in it," Phyllis boasted. "Faith *Prince*," corrected Gwen. "Pre-Tony. Big fucking deal."

"Gwen is always throwing shade on this place," explained Phyllis.

"And you're always messing up your street terms," Gwen shot back. "This isn't shade. It's a full-on trashing. And totally legit."

Phyllis settled back on the bed, out of ammo and trumped. Gwen, surprisingly, knew her stuff. She also knew Rex was twice married and divorced, with children and grandchildren scattered in the Northwest.

"He ran for the Gristmill right after that bomb," she added. "Made it his own personal kingdom. Or more likely his own personal—" and Phyllis cut her off with, "Don't say it. Don't say it, Gwen!" She grew abruptly serious with a blue blood arch. "If you say that one more time, I'll…tell someone," she warned.

Gwen took her seriously, censored herself. "Chill out, sugarlump," she said in retreat. Phyllis simmered down. Betty Rose kept to herself in the strange silence, already guessing the forbidden c-word that had been bandied about by Julian and Erin.

Defiant, Gwen shrugged it off and went back to her laptop. Inserted a pink flamingo-shaped flash drive, swirled her finger on her touchpad, started typing. Phyllis propped on her bunk, reading *The Fervent Years.*

"Is there e-mail here?" asked Betty Rose in the dead air. Gwen looked up. "Are you out of your fucking mind?" she said. And Phyllis added, "You can use it at the public library."

"So what are you working on?" Betty Rose asked. Gwen stopped typing and eyed her, sizing her up fully for the first time.

"My summer journal," she said after a moment. "Everything."

"I wanna read the Caleb chapter, Miss Mattress-back," Phyllis taunted and added, "Slutty McSlutster," for Betty Rose's benefit. Gwen said, "Shut it. I was *stupid* a month ago!" Phyllis pounced onto her bed and said, "I'll be retarded if that's what he likes. I hope everybody gets a turn." "They probably will," Gwen said, shoving her while she bounced.

Not me, thought Betty Rose, curling on Phyllis's bunk. She smiled at her friends-again roommates in their frilly night-gowns, talking boys of summer. All they needed were cold cream and hair curlers.

Gwen reached down the side of her mattress, pulled out a crumpled joint and a mini lighter.

"Gwen, no!" Phyllis pleaded. Gwen rolled her eyes and pushed the window open further. She lit it, held it outside and away. "Gwen! He'll see you!" Phyllis said, increasingly agitated. She backed out of window view.

Gwen streamed the smoke out. On the river, in the near distance, the vintage yacht rocked up against its dock in darkness.

"Beware the *Panic,*" Gwen said with melodrama. "Where Dear Leader hatches his plots!"

"You shouldn't go snooping and spying around there," said Phyllis, and Gwen said, "I don't snoop. It's not my fault the river echoes everything from inside. And he wants me to hear. I swear every move at this place is rehearsed...."

"Hear...what?" asked Betty Rose.

Gwen offered her a hit; she declined.

"I've got stronger stuff if you need it," said Gwen. "And you will."

"Put the grass away! You're going to get us all kicked out!" Phyllis hissed, now furious. Gwen took one last, deep drag and put out the joint with her fingers. "Relax," she said, holding it in. "He never dirties his hands. Just watch out for Dottie and Alistair. His flying monkeys." She poked her head out the window, exhaled, pulled it down to a few inches.

Betty Rose laughed and said, "They do kinda remind me of flying monkeys!"

"Lights out, girls," Dottie said from the now-open bedroom door. She stared them down with a touch of reprimand.

Phyllis sprang to her bed. Betty Rose scurried up the ladder to the top bunk. Gwen reclined and stifled a snicker.

"Good night, girls," Dottie said, turning off the light. "Good night, Betty Rose." Unsmiling, she closed the door to blackness.

Betty Rose slid into the tight sheets. Gwen popped out the tiny pink flamingo from her laptop and tucked it into her mattress joint-hiding place. Then she donned earbuds and a night mask. Betty Rose peered down at the bottom bunk: Phyllis, on command, was already asleep. With her own earbuds and mask.

Betty Rose stared at the ceiling and smiled. Her Isle of Misfits for the summer.

Her stomach rumbled again. *Calm down*, she thought. No need for nerves; she was where she belonged. She patted her belly, fingered her silver pendant. Gwen shifted in her bed, the creaky coils boinged.

Ringing the ceiling, she noticed, was a repeating pattern of words. She sat up, squinted in the dim light.

Make Things Happen, it read. *Let Things Happen.*

Rex's pearls of wisdom, lovingly painted in cursive, surrounding them day and night. Like a nursery rhyme.

She settled back. The red exit sign above the door flickered and strobed an erratic pattern. A short, she realized. It was intrusive in the darkness. And hypnotic.

From a distance, through the breeze of the cracked window, came the carousel organ music that had lured her across the bridge. Faint but persistent, in a key hard to ignore, like a car alarm. An odd hour to play, she thought, wrapping the pillow around her head.

She tossed, repositioned, gave up. Too much excitement in one day. Earbuds and night mask, she added to her list. Hold the Sriracha, she reminded herself, burping quietly. She lay, she felt, for hours. The words along the ceiling, the strobing sign, the cycling organ music.

The excitement and anticipation peaked on her big day. Agnes de Mille had choreographed her wedding ceremony masterfully, and the bridesmaids pirouetted in perfect sync against the waving wheat that smelled sweet. An all-smiles Phyllis fluttered up to position the delicate veil onto Betty Rose's head and tucked a June bouquet of pink roses and lilac and baby's breath into her grip.

Betty Rose looked down at her white nightgown and scowled. It was only half sufficient; old and borrowed, but she needed new and blue, in a jiffy. The audience was waiting, the white runner laid, a little girl from town strewing petals. The orchestra swelled. The show must go on. Betty Rose, beaming, stood tall, took a step.

From the wings appeared Gwen, tall and resplendent, in Cinderella white and floor-length veil, holding a larger, lusher bouquet. She floated smoothly down the aisle, absorbing the worship. The stage came alive.

Phyllis pulled Betty Rose to the side with the other bridesmaids.

"But it's my day!" she cried out, although no one listened to her. "It's mine!"

She reached to her neck, panicked. Her father's pendant was gone.

Fighting tears, she backed from the crowd, from the celebration. Gwen turned to her with full wattage.

Betty Rose spun to flee into the house and screamed. Face-to-face she came with a giant.

Its silhouette towered over her. With dress and ringlets.

She stumbled backward, caught herself from falling, looked around. The stage empty and dim, a lone work light cast from backstage. Her hand shot to her pendant, back where it belonged and had always been. The theater was silent and still, save a slight buzz humming from the power box by the stage deck.

Betty Rose took a breath, regained her bearings.

Nightmares were an unwelcome by-product of the upheaval and stress she'd endured over the past year. They were usually freaky dramatizations of insecurity, grossly distorted and relatively easy to dismiss. They'd grown darker and more vivid since her move to New York, with memorable sensations of feeling betrayed, threatened, even preyed upon. On more than a few nights, Julian had woken her to soothe and calm her back to sleep, but his caresses often sparked an even more har-rowing sequel. Her subconscious was clearly uneasy. But the nightmares had never triggered sleepwalking before, as far as she knew. It spooked her.

She looked up at the looming curtain she'd backed into, poked it. Stiff and heavy. The fire curtain, she realized. From the far side, the carousel music played on, slow and soothing. She followed the curtain to the edge, squeezed around to the stage apron. The ghost light stood sentry at the center rim, its cord snaking into the wings. Betty Rose looked up.

Carla the Giant stared down from the curtain. A painted replica from her lobby portrait.

She lorded over her beloved, miniature village—the main street, train station, Journeyman Bridge, the playhouse barn itself. A cartooned mural, spring bright and colorful, peopled with faceless Lilliputian locals in overalls and florals and hats, their arms raised either in worship or in a final dance bump.

Carla ignored them, her impish smile trained on Betty Rose. Her hair looked more fiery, her medallion more radiant. She looked a bit silly, a young girl blown up to Godzilla size, her arms tucked coyly behind, surrounded by her toys. It was weird art. A shrine.

Off to the stage side, in its own alcove, a large, multitiered Wurlitzer played alone. Betty Rose pulled closer, watching the keys move. The melody was lovely and hypnotic.

"Are you one of those creepy somnambulists, Betty Rose?" echoed a voice from the audience.

Caught, she twisted and peered into the blackness. Rex, she pegged instantly.

"I'm sorry, sir. I...don't know how I got here."

There was a click of a remote control, and the player organ stopped, its final notes lingering in the pipes.

"Do you sleepwalk often?" Rex-voice asked, calmly curious.

Not since childhood, she thought. "No, sir," she said.

She felt exposed in her flimsy nightgown. She looked down, barefoot.

"I must have been wandering," she said with apology. "I really don't remember, sir."

"Please...*Rex*," he said. "This place takes some getting used to. I know that. Your mind's likely all a-scatter. And that slop Dot feeds you doesn't help, I'm sure."

She worried her shapeless nightgown made her look fatter than he thought she was. She tucked her hands behind her back, Carla-style, gathering fabric to make something of a waist. She stood in closed fourth position.

"It's not so bad," she said, fighting back a fresh burp. "It's a little spicy."

Rex emerged from the dark. His eyes were red, his face tear-streaked.

"What's wrong?" she blurted. "Are you okay?"

Rex tamped down her concern before placing the organ remote control on a seat arm. "Just reflective," he said. "Losing Marian and all. She was queen of the Gristmill when I started out here. I was just a kid, smitten, watching her every move. Right up there, where you're standing." He nodded toward the apron. "So many memories on that stage." She stood still and respectful of his moment. He seemed fragile, smaller.

"Who's next to go? I wonder," he mused. "Mona? Geraldine?" He considered his own question and answered, "Alas, probably Geraldine." He called upward, as if she were floating there.

"Keep treading the boards, old girl. It's not your time just yet."
He looked back at Betty Rose.

"One by one, time leads us all offstage, doesn't it?" he added and then smiled at her polite empathy. "You'll see...."

"I'm very sorry about your loss," Betty Rose said, with tenderness.

He indicated the Carla curtain. "On nights like this, I lean on the wisdom of our first lady," he said, reciting,

"My song plays on, my song plays on.
Long after the music is gone, my song plays on."

He gazed up at Carla, as if listening. "But who will take her place?" he asked the room. "Youth is the lifeblood of our playhouse. But only a tiny few ever really hear that song." A new thought crossed his face, but he tabled it. "we shall see," he said, turning back up the aisle. "We shall see."

"Sir...Rex," she said, stopping him. "Thank you for having me. For letting me come."

Rex put finger to lip and shook his head. "Not yet," he said.

He grew taller, ascending the raked house. He reached halfway and turned back to consider her, still standing by the ghost light. He seemed to recharge.

"If I were you, Betty Rose, I'd get my rest while you can," he said with the barest smile. "You've got a week ahead."

Scene Seven

THE COWBELL JOLTED HER.

"Up and at 'em!" Dottie bellowed, banging on their door. "Kitchen patrol!"

"We're up!" Phyllis called back, groggy. "Motherfucker," Gwen grumbled to her pillow.

Betty Rose checked the time: 5:48. She'd found sleep only in the past hour. She felt blurry, needing more.

"It's sticking! More flour!" Dottie ordered minutes later in the kitchen, throwing a fistful onto the biscuit dough that coated Betty Rose's rolling pin. "Didn't your mother teach you that?"

She fared no better on the biscuit cutting—"Don't twist!"—or the baking, forgetting to set the timer while she scrambled an enormous bowl of forty eggs. "What's that smell?" Dottie shouted, racing to the industrial oven and then "B.R. burned the biscuits!" when the truth bore out. "Good grief, pick out the shells," she complained into the bowl. "Don't you know how to crack an egg?"

Gwen traded with her the simpler bacon duty. "Just don't start a grease fire," she murmured in her ear, and Betty Rose smiled and thanked her, turning pieces.

"No biscuits today!" Dottie announced to the hungry breakfast lineup. "Betty Rose immolated them all." "I'm so sorry!" Betty Rose called from the stove to the chorus of protests. Even her bacon curled into twists and cooked unevenly, and she served it in shame.

Her stomach was too knotty for her own morning mush. "Suit yourself," said Dottie, sliding the little yellow bowl into the fridge. "It'll save."

She was more adept at scrubbing the lobby toilets, at dusting and vacuuming the lobby itself. She left it spotless and restocked with toilet paper and paper towels and Whoppers, Wise chips, Shastas, and Poland Springs behind the concessions stand. She folded a carton of programs still warm from the printer and inserted flyers of upcoming shows and winced and bled from a gasp-triggering paper cut. The sting was potent, the blood hard to stanch.

The "wardrobe mistress" was a man she thought named Bob until he corrected her. "*Baub,*" he insisted, drilling her until she got it right. He was a fat, sour one at that, especially when the steamer hose clogged after he assigned her to spruce up the costumes. "Did you fill the steamer with tap water?" he said, exasperated with her stupidity. "Distilled water only!" With grand melodrama, he emptied the reservoir and shook it dry. "It's ruined," he kept saying. "We can't steam the costumes. We'll have to cancel opening night." Betty Rose, flummoxed by his insistence on wrinkle-free farmers and ranchers, toweled out the lime scale residue and got it steaming again. "It's not working the same," the fussy drama queen said, lording over her as she worked her way down the costume rack. "It will never work the same again."

The cast did a final speed-through, and Betty Rose, hoping to be helpful, studied the script right offstage for cues, entrances, and scene changes. She kept blocking traffic, and the stage manager, Becky—a boyish, efficient lesbian—banished her to the upstairs dressing rooms to follow on the television monitor feed. Retreating to the corner, she made herself small amid the room's chaos. Everyone was on edge and punchy.

Her sliced finger throbbed, and she switched out Band-Aids from the first-aid kit. She felt a dull pang in her stomach and realized she hadn't eaten anything real since Sunday, before the phone call, before leaving New York. She'd sneak something later.

Julian had left another message on the chalkboard, next to his first, and she swore to herself she'd call back after the show. He'd be worried by now but would understand, especially once she explained her new, hectic routine and phone privilege limitations.

Her leftover mush had grown a skin by lunchtime. A peach fuzz by dinner. Even Dottie told her to dump it. "You'll have to wait till tomorrow," she said, hurrying from the kitchen to get ready for the show. "I don't have time to whip up a new batch."

"Dottie?" Betty Rose called after her. Dottie turned. "What?" she challenged.

"My...luggage," Betty Rose said, with apology for bothering her. "And my purse...did it turn up...?"

"Oh God, yes," Dottie cut her off. "The stupid rental place in Yonkers sent it with the lighting suite to the Paper Mill Playhouse. In Millburn. In Jersey."

"Oh," said Betty Rose.

"They're doing *Assassins* for six weeks, although don't ask me why," said Dottie, and Betty Rose said, "I see. In Jersey." Dottie said, "I spoke to Sheila there, and she's keeping it locked up until they close the show; then we'll get it back." Betty Rose said, "I see. Six weeks?" Dottie nodded and said, "They're regional. They do longer runs." Betty Rose said, "Oh," and Dottie added, "Unless you want to rent a car and drive to Millburn on your day off, but it's far." Betty Rose asked, "How far, do you think?" and Dottie said, "Too far, and how are you going to rent a car without your driver's license?" "Yes," said Betty Rose. "You're right."

"We'll get it back," Dottie said, exasperated. "You can borrow twenty from the box office to tide you over, as long as you pay it back. Don't you have work to do? Don't we open tonight?"

"Yes," said Betty Rose, backing off. "Sorry."

The barn crackled with the arriving audience for opening night. Many brought baskets for a pre-theatre picnic on the benches under the elms. Betty Rose peeked through the front windows at the festive, neighborly crowd that swarmed larger. Off to the side, Mr. Arbor stared up into an elm, biding time before they opened the doors. She smiled at his loyalty.

"*Half hour!*" called Becky over the intercom. "*House open!*"

Betty Rose rang the front porch bell to beckon the guests inside. She took tickets and ushered an elderly couple to the wrong side of the house. "We always sit over there!" complained the old husband, and the wife shushed him. "The girl's new," she said. The house manager sent her backstage to help with costume quick changes as the theater filled.

"*Five minutes!*" said the Becky-intercom in the frenzy. Sutton led the cast in a calming circle while Betty Rose brushed them down for lint, surprised the girls all wore their Gristmill medallions, even in costume. *"Places!"* announced Becky. "Good luck!" Betty Rose called out, and everyone froze in horror and turned to spit over their shoulders. "You *never* say that in the theater," Gwen whispered. "It's terrible luck." Which she knew, of course—everyone knew that—but had somehow forgotten because she was smack in the error zone today and couldn't escape it. "Break a leg!" she said in replacement, but everyone had already fled her.

"Hurry." Alistair prodded the others in their exodus. "Before she mentions the Scottish play!"

"Move it!" the running crew ordered during the first scene change when she stood in the path of Aunt Eller's rolling house. "I'm sorry," she said, jumping aside, and the assistant stage manager hissed, "Quiet!" slicing her finger across her throat. They sent her to the props table, where she confused Laurey's and Ado's auction hampers for the social and, in a horrifying moment, handed Judd "The Little Wonder" instead of his plastic stage knife. "Wake the fuck up!" the props master growled, grabbing them both away. "Go! I'll do it myself."

At intermission, she sold T-shirts, baseball caps, tote bags, and coffee mugs from the concessions stand, all with the Gristmill medallion masks logo, but not the medallions themselves, unavailable at any price. The Lance cracker sandwiches in the basket, along with the boiled peanuts and cheese curls, called her name, but she resisted.

Becky called down from the control booth window overlooking the lobby and ordered Betty Rose to bring her a bottle of Poland Spring and a Snapple for the lighting designer immediately. Betty Rose dashed through the dark catacombs to the backstage, up the stairs, and across the catwalk to the booth, which was airless and sweltering, even with the cracked window into the lobby. The lighting designer complained about the peach flavor, and Betty Rose peered through the little window down to the lobby, where a long, impatient line had amassed at the concessions stand. She promised to bring the designer the lemon flavor and raced back to the lobby, where the house manager had filled in for her and upbraided her for leaving her post. Betty Rose tried to explain that Becky had summoned her, but the house manager didn't care for excuses, and the hungry line grew more impatient, since the lights were flashing and intermission was almost over.

She lent a hand with Ado Annie's quick change just offstage and heard a seam rip when she pulled her dress down over her hips. Dottie heard it, too. "Good God, Betty Rose," she said. "Are you *trying* to ruin our show?" Gwen stepped up and said, "My bad, Dottie. I pulled too hard."

From the wings, she cheered the cast at curtain call, giving the thumbs-up to her fellow interns on the ends of the row. The cast ignored her congratulations as they swept offstage toward the stairs. The lighting designer stormed up and demanded his lemon Snapple, which she'd forgotten about and which he didn't want anymore, although he made a point that he'd suffered through the second act without it.

The dressing rooms were stacked in the old silo tower attached to the back of the stage—cramped, windowless rooms paneled in rustic barn wood, just off the steep, switchback staircase. They were assigned by seniority, with the stars on the stage level and the newbies at the top, each outfitted with a video stage monitor on the wall. Betty Rose started on the seventh floor, hauling baskets of soiled and sweaty underwear, ripped and stained costumes, and dull character shoes in need of polishing. The cast pushed past her as she carefully descended, arms full, foot-feeling her way down the narrow steps. "Today?" Baub yelled from below. "I'm waiting!"

Late that night, with everyone else asleep, she mopped the stage and scrubbed the lobby toilets anew. The industrial washing machine buzzed, and she emptied whites for the second time, the first round rejected by Baub because she forgot bleach. "Dingy," he'd complained. "And sloppy." She'd have to wait another hour for the dryer, to fold and hang, lest the farmers' shirts and knickers wrinkle.

She tried the kitchen door, hoping to find leftovers, or even a saltine, but it was locked for the night. She was too exhausted to take advantage of the now-available phone, and she didn't want to wake Julian. Tomorrow.

Her portions got smaller and spicier by the day, she thought. The mush burned her mouth and throat, and she savored the lone raisins she speared and relished the scent of buttermilk pancakes and maple syrup and link sausage from the rest of the company. She inhaled deeply and steadied herself on the stove at the spin of vertigo, scorching her hand. Dottie called her "clumsy" and brought an ice pack and butter.

"Dare to admit you have real genius inside of you," urged Rex at his daily prelunch lecture under the elms, which Betty Rose was allowed to observe, off to the side. "Dare to accept you're worthy of the world's adoration. Dare to learn, embrace, embody the joy of this journey. You all getting me?" The company said, "Yes, Rex," in unison and sprang to their feet, linked hands, and sang together before filing into the theater to rehearse next week's *Brigadoon*. Outsider Betty Rose, invisible to Rex, took her chore list from Dottie and returned to the kitchen to serve lunch and prep for dinner.

And the shows kept coming.

She struggled to focus her eyes in the dark scene changes and confused the orange with yellow glow tape, setting Judd's stool wildly off mark. She dashed back out to correct it just as the stage lights came up, leaving her marooned and deer-eyed to the roar of audience laughter. Blinded and disoriented, she weaved toward one side, then the other, as the laughter swelled to catcalls. Gwen darted out to usher her back to the safety of the wings.

"Relic? Dinosaur? Guilty as charged," declared Rex at his daily drill. "In a craven world of disposable celebrity and false idols chosen by telephone vote, we proudly endure, shouting into the hurricane, 'Stop!'" Betty Rose sat outside the circle, riveted by his passion, propping herself up in the grass to keep from swooning from hunger and exhaustion.

Julian left messages that morning and afternoon and evening, the most recent two circled and double-starred on the chalkboard for extra urgency. *Soon*, she thought, racing with plunger toward the overflowing lobby toilet that flooded and soaked the new green carpet. She stayed up most of the night, on her knees, blow-dryer in hand.

"You're the front line, wherever you go," Rex urged them another morning, pacing the circle perimeter. "In the world, but not of the world. Devotion, teamwork, sacrifice—our bewildering superstitions and rituals, traditions that are never written down—preserve the Gristmill to this day. You—every single one of you—are the salvation and the future of the theatre." He paused to stare down his chosen ones, letting the pressure build. "Guard it with your life, won't you?" he concluded, releasing them with an uncleish wink.

At breakfast midweek, Gwen slipped half a toasted bagel to Betty Rose, who grabbed it with a lust that shocked her. Alistair reached from behind to snatch it back, wagging his finger.

"Please," Betty Rose said, drained and dizzy. "Just a half..." Dottie came up fast. "What's your problem?" she demanded. "I'm...famished," Betty Rose admitted.

"Oh, everybody's got a bag of rocks!" Dottie fired back, waving it off before launching into a lecture: "Streisand. *Funny Girl*," she recounted, hammering her fist into her palm for emphasis. "A raging fever, no sleep, completely dehydrated, a bucket offstage to vomit in. Never missed a performance or a cue. And never complained. That's a pro. *That's* a warrior!"

She knew what they were doing, of course; Wes had warned her. "Basic training for the theatre," he'd said. "How the sausage is made." They were trying to break her, to teach the newbie—a preemie, Rex called her—a lesson. His accomplices were his flying monkeys, Dottie and Alistair. The company his coconspirators. Her only allies her fellow interns, with Gwen surprisingly empathetic, a preemie herself not so long ago.

The starvation was one of their tools to wear her down, she realized, after Rex's preposterous insinuation that she was fat, the Achilles' heel of every woman, especially an actress. They expected her to crumble, to shrink, self-doubting. They were testing her ego, the most important and fragile part of the actor's psyche. She'd soldier on and pass their silly test.

And she'd teach them all who was a warrior, she vowed, waking with a start early the next morning on the bare stage, her clothes and hands stained black, surrounded by character shoes she'd been polishing all night. Her bedroom, steps away, seemed too far; she curled on the boards and slept until the cowbell.

"Betty Rose, are you resisting?" asked Rex's voice, jolting her awake during one of his morning lectures. She shook her haze to find the company staring back at her, snuggled against the elm trunk. "I'm awake!" she blurted, springing to attention. "I'm listening!"

"See, this is what I was talking about," Rex said to the company before turning focus back to her. "The more you try to understand what I am saying, the less you will never be able to understand it," he said. "Do you understand?"

"…Yes…," Betty Rose said, nodding, although she didn't. "Yes!" She sat higher.

Rex was skeptical. "Self-sabotage," he said to the circle, pointing at her. "So used to getting kicked down, you think that's your place. A *hamal*. The loser in you." Back to her. "But the winner in you wants to soar. Let it happen. You don't have to do anything. Make it happen."

The company stood and said, "Let it happen," in unison.

"Make it happen," Rex reminded them, and they responded in a repeating chant.

Betty Rose, unsure, scrambled to her feet and stood apart, watching. She steadied herself on the elm, slightly dizzy from the thick heat.

A soprano led off a melody that seemed newly familiar: "My Song Plays On." The circle grabbed hands and joined in five-part harmony. Rachelle and Alistair released to make a spot, inviting her in. Betty Rose stepped up, clasped hands, followed along. Her palms were wet, but neither grip flinched. Phyllis sang with gusto; Gwen mouthed the words, lackluster. She glanced up at Betty Rose and then away.

Betty Rose hummed and joined the second chorus, learning. It was a gorgeously complex, vaguely Sondheim-esque harmony, and she took the soprano melody line to be safe. Rex stepped from the circle and watched. The symphony, simple and haunting, richly rendered with professional voices, lifted and carried with the warm breeze.

And the shows kept coming.

The weekend brought "two-a-days" with matinee and evening performances. The frenzy doubled. And Betty Rose found herself outside the circle once more.

"Watch it, B.R.!" she kept hearing, from the sides and back. "Slow down!" and "Hurry up!" They trashed her behind her back, she knew, as they should. She was always in the way, or never in the right place when they needed her, or both simultaneously. She was constantly bumping, turning, recalibrating. And light-headed.

"Are you shivering, Betty Rose?" Dottie asked as she mopped the stage between performances. "Are you ill? Do we need to bench you?"

Betty Rose felt feverish, but she said, "I'm fine. It's just a little chilly in here."

"Rex says musical theatre is best served at sixty-eight degrees," Dottie replied. "Shall I register your complaint with him?" "No, please!" Betty Rose insisted, taming her shakes. "I'm not complaining!"

She rushed back to her room before curtain to throw a peasant blouse over her shoulders and trembled through the first act.

"This is root beer," whined a blue hair at intermission. "I ordered cream soda. I can't drink root beer." Betty Rose nodded and apologized and squinted at Shasta cans, her temples throbbing, flicking her hand to ward off a cramp. She craved a Twix bar from the basket, but others were watching, she knew, from the box office, the lobby, the front porch window. She only had herself to blame for being so fat, she chastised herself. When did she let herself go? And why hadn't she noticed?

Arms loaded with dirty costumes, she hurried toward the laundry room, past the chalkboard of nagging Julians. Why hadn't he warned her she'd packed on pounds? He knew thin was her professional responsibility; he should have said something, tactfully, for her own good.

Her stomach bubbled and flexed, searching for anything. She burped nothingness, tasted faint bile in her throat. "Watch it!" came the angry voice she collided with in the hallway, blinded she was by her mountain of dirty overalls and petticoats. "Sorry," she wheezed, stumbling forward. "Sorry."

Get it together, she ordered herself, dumping the darks into the machine, her trembling hand scattering detergent on the floor as she targeted the washing drum. She checked her forehead, as hot and flush as her cheeks. So why the chill? Hearing her name yelled from a distance, she piled the whites on the floor and dashed to the kitchen.

"I don't trust you with that knife," Dottie said, interrupting her mid-onion-chop as she prepped hash browns for the next morning's breakfast. "You're slipping all over the board." She took away the big blade and said, "Go disinfect the tables. With scalding water."

Her size-four charmeuse skirt, her favorite, still hanging in the closet, hadn't felt tight on the bus ride to New Hope, which now seemed weeks ago even though she knew it had been only days, although she couldn't pinpoint exactly how many, which disturbed her briefly, her inability to focus on simple math. It had fit the same as always. All her clothes had.

She squeezed the thick sponge, slopped hot suds across the picnic table.

Her alarm rose: What if her idea of thin wasn't thin enough? Or her talent, which everyone had praised in high school and college, was only mediocre, or worse, in the big league? No one would tell her that; they'd just humor and ignore her and cast her betters. Which, she realized with a sudden sink, the pros had been, ever since she'd arrived in New York.

The bar was higher here. She'd meet and surmount it. And shrink to size 2, like Thin-Gwen. Maybe less. Rex couldn't expect better than that.

She clutched her stomach to fend off a sharp spasm that reverberated through her groin and lower still. She doubled over, held her breath until it passed.

"Oh. My. God!" Baub bellowed from the laundry room. "*Betty Rose!*" he shrieked. She dropped the sponge and, still holding her gut, hustled toward the drama queen by the open washing machine. She stopped and froze, her hand already shot to her mouth.

The costumes—the denims, the prints, the floral, the stripes—were bleached out into splotchy ruin. "No…," she said. Baub, trembling, hurled the twisted mess to the floor and stormed out in silence. Betty Rose rushed to salvage them, a futile attempt. She scrolled back in her mind, with alarm, at how she could have poured bleach into a load of colors. She couldn't remember the moment at all.

The final two Sunday performances were packed and bizarre-looking, the valiant cast rising above their disastrous tie-dyed costumes but grumbling hotly backstage. "We might as well do *Hair*," said Alistair with ill humor among the other hippie-cowboys. "This is fucking ridiculous," spat Sutton in a rare diva moment in the offstage prep mirror. "Amateur hour," said Dottie during the matinee's intermission, adding, "The blue hairs will be demanding refunds." "These are rentals. We'll have to buy them," announced Baub, loud enough for everyone to hear. "It'll cost a fortune."

Betty Rose, feeling Public Enemy One, was banished from the wings and sent to the balcony catwalk to man the follow spot for the closing show. She swooned on the narrow stairs, having stayed up all night trying to fix the unfixable costumes. Her stomach twisted tighter, less from starvation than the agony of the catastrophe she'd wrought. She was on dwindling fumes.

She'd done hundreds, maybe thousands, of loads of laundry in her lifetime. It was her earliest childhood chore and ongoing college routine that, as an adult, became as effortless, ingrained, and automatic to her as brushing her teeth or washing her hair. She'd never, not once, poured bleach into a color load. How cloudy and compromised was her brain to have made such a disastrous error with the stakes so high?

It hit her: Someone else had bleached the costumes, to pin it on her. As sabotage.

Baub hated her, certainly, and would love to get rid of her, but that didn't make sense. The ruined costumes only made him look like a sloppy supervisor. And the rental cost would be taken out of his budget, which, she gathered from his grumblings, was tight already.

The spot lamp was heavy, unwieldy on its caster base stand. She struggled to turn it, telescopelike, to follow a ludicrous-looking

Sutton singing "Out of My Dreams" before the big, druggy ballet that would put the first act out of its misery. The lamp creaked, its knobs too tight, its gears needing oil. It made her arms ache, into the bone.

Unless one of the other interns, one of her trusted room-mates, wanted her gone, eliminated to increase her chances of winning her Equity card. Actresses certainly had pulled more sinister stunts in the history of show business. But Phyllis, open-faced and guileless, was an unlikely Eve Harrington. Betty Rose doubted she was that good of an actress anyway.

Sutton drifted downstage, singing closer to the audience. Betty Rose unscrewed the lamp's pivot knob to follow more smoothly. The spot lunged too far, hitting the orchestra pit, prompting a puzzled turn from the conductor. She strained to right it, the locked casters wobbling against her efforts. The clamps holding the spot onto its rickety stand squeaked and complained. She held tightly, determined to tame it.

That left Gwen, who claimed not to want her card, feigning indifference, in spite of her front-runner status. Who'd hovered more closely, almost protectively, around Betty Rose all week, even slipping her food when she got too weak. Which had earned Betty Rose a rebuke from both of Rex's flying monkeys and had certainly gotten back to Rex himself. Painting her, no doubt, as just another undisciplined, uncommitted actress, a wishful amateur incapable of following specific orders. And fat, to boot.

The audience tittered below. She didn't remember the dream ballet being a comedy. They must be laughing at the costumes, the streaked and spotted dresses spiraling around the stage. That someone else had sabotaged, to torpedo Betty Rose's shot at her card.

Her initial instincts had been dead-on: Gwen was not to be trusted, or liked, so Machiavellian and octopus-armed were her deceptions.

The audience roared. Betty Rose couldn't bear to look again. The gnawing strain had exhausted her.

"*Psst!*" she heard, with whispered urgency. "*Betty Rose!*"

She jerked up with a start, her face resting on the bannister. Turned to Gwen, in splotchy costume, at the top of the balcony stairs, gesturing, pointing desperately. Betty Rose lifted her head, a string of drool trickling behind. She followed Gwen's frantic finger.

The spot was hitting a blue hair in the fifth row. The old woman turned and looked around, dazed by the attention and swelling laughter. Newly in-the-dark Sutton, marking steps stage center, was befuddled and enraged, in equal parts, glowering up at the balcony, seeking relief.

Betty Rose grabbed the spot, stuck in its downward position, and pulled hard to level it. The casters unlocked, rocketing the stand back toward her. She pushed back, skating the spot up against the balcony's edge. Her feet tangled in the long power cord, and she kicked to free herself.

Gwen came up from behind. "Let me help," she said, and Betty Rose, swatting her off, said, "No, I can do it." She kicked the cord again and threw her weight into spot as leverage.

The spot abruptly unstuck, lurching upward to target the ceiling, where it stuck again. The audience howled louder. The orchestra played on, as the dancers lost their beats and steps. It was a circus.

"The knob's too tight," Gwen urged from behind, scrambling closer. "Unscrew it."

Betty Rose, her eyes hazy in the darkness, fumbled with the base. She strained with both hands. The knob resisted, and her shoulders ached, her elbows too, and she gritted her teeth and turned harder, afraid her wrists might crack. The audience hooted and clapped.

"Not that one!" Gwen cried, rushing forward. "That's the clamp!"

"I've got it!" Betty Rose hissed through clenched, grinding jaw.

The knob gave way, with a sudden spin. Triumphant, Betty Rose spun it faster and faster.

"No!" Gwen screamed. "Get away!" Betty Rose said.

The spotlight groaned and tipped downward with a heavy rush, released from its base.

It fell from the balcony, onto the audience below.

Scene Eight

THE SILENCE UNNERVED HER MOST.

Not the suspended moment between the fall of the spot and its impact below, its power cord tangled around Betty Rose's calves, yanking free as it fell, her reflexive reach out to grab it unsuccessful yet enough to knock it off its trajectory so it crashed into the aisle, headfirst, bouncing and catapulting end-over-end. The crush of bending metal, shatter of lenses, and jolted squeals from the audience—especially the blue hair on the row it ricocheted off—were loud and jarring, but harmless.

Not the feverish chatter in the lobby—"It landed right next to me! I was *terrified*!" "I've never heard of canceling midperformance. Have you?" "I certainly got my money's worth, and then some. Come along, Frances"—where Betty Rose was sent to offer refunds, mostly refused, although she got a steady earful of gripes, imagined injuries, and even a toothless lawsuit threat. "I'm so sorry," she kept repeating, on behalf of the playhouse, as no one in the audience knew she was to blame. "I'm so sorry!" She'd said little else, she realized, for the past six days.

The unnerving silence came from the company itself. They clammed up when, after her lobby duties, she joined them onstage to help strike the set, although she caught the gist of their verdict when she crept through the soundless doors into the theater.

"Who let her run the spot?" and "What the fuck is wrong with her?" "I hope there weren't any producers in the audience," spat Rachelle. "We can't let her ruin the season," whined the Laurey double from the dream ballet. "We're not a day care center."

"Don't put your daughter on the stage, Mrs. Worthington," Alistair sang with droll, British delivery as he took down Aunt Eller's curtains. *"Don't put your daughter on the stage."* The cast tittered in a rolling wave.

Betty Rose felt more an outsider than she had the day she'd arrived.

"It's your fault," Gwen piped up loudly, coiling cables by the large rolling box. "It's fucking insane what you put her through this week." The cast and crew turned. "I mean it," she added, challenging their stares. "The union should shut this place down. And they would in a heartbeat. And you all know it."

Phyllis was the first to spot Betty Rose at the stage edge. "Hello, B.R.," she said brightly. "Are you okay?" The hushed company looked at her, then down and away, back to their work.

Dottie interrupted before Betty Rose could muster her umpteenth apology to an unwilling audience. "The strike crew can take it from here," she said, waving the cast offstage. "Interns, please tidy up the dressing rooms before you go. Everyone else, join the party, if you can."

Betty Rose hung the ruined costumes that had been wadded on the floor in the deluxe, star's dressing room on the stage level, even though Baub said they "should be burned," while Phyllis restocked tissue and makeup puffs and emptied the trash cans into a large black bag. "Chin up, B.R.," she said. "It didn't hit anyone. If you think about it, it's the excitement of live theatre. Anything can happen!" And Betty Rose, her stomach twisting ever tighter, forced a half smile and said, "Thanks, Phyllis."

Gwen, sweeping in circles, waited until Phyllis carried the trash bag upstairs to the second floor dressing room before moving closer. "You'd better listen up," she said in a quiet, tense voice, grabbing her arm. "Breaking you down is their first act. Molding you is their second. I don't even want to know what their third is...."

"What...do you mean?" Betty Rose asked. "Molding how?"

"And you don't want to know either," Gwen went on, locking eyes. "This place is seriously fucked up."

"What's the drama?" Phyllis asked, back with a fuller bag. "What did I miss?"

"Nothing," said Gwen, releasing Betty Rose's arm, back to her sweeping. "Just trying to cheer her up."

Phyllis struck a pose, hand on hip. "Oh, Betty Rose, please drop it," she said with a smile, mock punching her shoulder. "It'll all blow over by the next show. Really. That's how things work around here." She turned to Gwen. "Dottie wants us to set up for the party. I need your help with the tables." Phyllis pivoted and marched out with her trash bag.

Gwen closed in again. "Find me outside," she whispered with urgency in Betty Rose's ear. "*Please.*" "Gwen?" Phyllis called from the hallway. "You coming?"

Betty Rose straightened and pinned the Aunt Eller wig onto its form and bunched her brow, straining to defog her brain and decipher Gwen's message and true agenda. If Gwen were trying to get rid of her, why would she defend Betty Rose in front of the company, especially after her string of disasters that ruined the week? Why not join the mob?

She lined up the wigs on the shelf above the bulb-ringed makeup mirror. Maybe she'd misjudged Gwen and created a villain where none existed, a by-product of her confused and cluttered mind, as underfed and overworked as she'd been all week. Which Gwen had acknowledged to the others, practically threatening them with whistle-blowing union action, a supremely ballsy move for an intern seeking her own Equity card. Maybe she didn't really care about it after all, as she'd insisted that first night.

She hung Ado Annie's social dress, both blotched and stitched from the rip Betty Rose had made in the quick change.

Gwen *had* tried to help her all week, she realized. Sticking up for her, covering her rear, even taking blame for the dress rip, which had clearly been Betty Rose's fault. Why had she been so quick to judge and condemn her? Had she become that suspicious and jaded so quickly?

Betty Rose wiped down the counter, cleaning mascara and pancake makeup smudges, and recapped a powder jar. Overheard ridicule from the all-male tech crew through the stage television monitor suspended from the dressing room ceiling. She looked up to see them mocking her, hurling wise-cracks behind her back—not knowing or caring if she saw—as they dismantled flats and unclamped lights and sliced through thick hemp cables with their stage knives. One cursed and complained about the dull blades, which were slipping across the rope; the overweight, lowly grunt got blamed and was ordered to take them to Nifty's the next morning for sharpening. They ribbed and hazed the hapless fellow for a moment before promptly returning to their ridicule of her.

That's what techies did, she knew. They trashed the actors, mostly out of envy and resentment. Under their macho swagger lurked the mean girls of the theatre. Unfortunately, she'd given them plenty of fuel.

She lined up brushes and mascaras under the mirrors. What did Gwen mean by her "first act/second act" riddle? Or her cryptic warning about this "seriously fucked up" place? It was the first time she'd seen the laid back Gwen so charged, with an urgency and fear. Either the pot had made her paranoid, or it was a doubly Machiavellian—and frankly silly—tactic to scare off Betty Rose. It would fail.

Betty Rose would rise to the occasion, as she had repeatedly through life. She wasn't going anywhere.

"She's not working out," said Rex from the stage monitor. "She's just not one of us."

Betty Rose turned to it. He was just out of camera reach, talking with a hush to a confidante.

"Everyone agrees," replied Dottie in a similar low tone, also off camera. "She doesn't belong here."

Betty Rose stiffened, her senses sharpening.

"I hate this part," said Rex. "I really do."

"We gave her plenty of chances. We just don't have time for more."

"Yes," said Rex. "Very regrettably."

"I'll handle it," Dottie said. "Don't trouble yourself with this one."

Betty Rose gripped the costume rack for support.

"No, the company should do it together," Rex said. "That's the respectable way. Tonight, I think. So we can start fresh tomorrow."

"Whatever you say, Daddy," said Dottie. "I'll spread the word."

"Don't make it a federal case," Rex added. "I'm sure she'll understand. It's not the right fit. It wasn't meant to be." He seemed to convince himself and sounded disappointed, almost sad. He sighed.

Dottie piped up to full voice. "Guys, let's finish later," she called out to the stage crew, still striking the set. "Let's join the party, shall we?"

They laid down their tools and left the theater. The stage was empty and silent.

Betty Rose sat down, for the first time, she felt, all week. And exhaled. She folded her hands in her lap. She'd been cast out after all.

She was going home.

● ● ●

They were looking at her but not talking to her. They were talking *about* her. Whispering behind her back. Like they'd done all week. The cowards.

She didn't care anymore. She was released and carefree, defiant. Almost gleeful.

From the dressing room, after overhearing the news, she'd marched back to her dorm, showered, primped, and dressed in a clean jumpsuit. She'd snuck out stage makeup, since her own was still missing, and dolled herself up tastefully, but with punch. She blew out her hair.

Katharine Hepburn had been fired from her first stage acting job, too. Rather than shrink off in shame, she'd risen to full height and confronted the company, saying goodbye to each separately, so they'd never forget the future legend they'd ousted. And then waltzed out, doubly motivated to leave them in her shadow. Betty Rose made the same resolve.

She gave them just enough time at the closing-night party to spread the word of her expulsion before making her entrance. She strutted straight to the pot-luck bar set up on a picnic table, next to the bowls of cheese curls and mini pretzels and a tray of fish sticks and bendy lemon bars left over from dinner and still mostly untouched. She scanned the liquor offerings and plucked out the liter bottle of Cuervo Silver.

Navigating through the moonlit knoll behind the theater, with Bruno Mars whining from portable speakers, Betty Rose saw conspirators—bullies, really—behind every elm. A coven encircled the keg, passing the spout. Mean girls, all. She lurched forward, having tripped on a root, recovering just short of a face-plant, but upending her cup, mostly drained anyway. After a moment's deliberation as they smirked at her pratfall, she straightened and marched back to the booze table and without looking grabbed the Tanqueray.

"Cheers!" she said to the snarky Laurey double who'd never rise to leading lady, and "Cheers!" to the fat bitch Baub, pitifully huddling with young boys he longed to bed. Off duty, he held court and laughed like a diva with such phrases as "Miss Thang" and "Ain't no thang," channeling his best RuPaul. Apparently, in his mind he was a buxom black woman. He was one-third correct.

"Careful there, missy," said the Cheshire cat Caleb, grinning down at her with perfect teeth and pillowed lips. "That's a heavy pour."

He was undeniably pretty in a shallow, disposable way, with his Olympics body and Disney Channel face. A short shelf life, she predicted. Perfect for chorus boy—and certainly Broadway Bares—or potentially a young leading man until he hit the wall. He lacked the heft that fueled careers through adulthood. He'd never sing "Being Alive," at least not convincingly.

But he was pretty.

"You have your clothes on," she accused with a stabbing point to his chest. "Why?"

"You should eat something," he said, and she wagged her finger and said, "No, no, no. Haven't you heard? I'm on a diet!"

She held her icy cup against her forehead to calm her fever. It was a hot, wet night. She gulped and grimaced, unaccustomed to gin and not afraid of it. It hit fast. She focused her eyes and stumbled toward the clearing where partiers danced to Daft Punk. She marched to the middle, bumping against the others.

They'd never taken her seriously, not as a professional, at any rate. She was a charity case, a favor for the agent Wes, who himself was doing a favor for his hotshot up-and-coming scenic designer client, who also happened to be her longtime boyfriend. They'd humored her for a week, their debt paid, and now dispatched her before the start of the next show.

She'd been a dupe from the start.

She danced, spinning.

It was back to the Rum House, where she belonged. Double shifts covering for Erin, still clinging to her dream, with increasing tenuousness and contagious bitterness. Slinging drinks with almost-made-it Danny, now permanently ensconced behind his bar. Listening to Claudine, well past her prime, overweight and overly made-up, with her depressing torch songs and sudoku app, marking time until she went home to her family of cats. "Look who's back!" She could hear Erin now, having expected her failure and quick return all along.

Sutton danced near. A real star, from day one. With agents and managers, lawyers, Broadway marquees, a *Tony*, for God's sake. *Not one of us*, her pitying smile told Betty Rose, who smiled back and danced harder, sloshing her gin and not apologizing for it. She was done sucking up to these people, so dewy and flush they were with the excitement of her imminent purge.

What are they waiting for? she thought, downing her drink, standing still while the night spun around her. Emboldened and fiery, Betty Rose staggered from the dance pit, pinballing through the mob. Targeted the iPod in its speaker dock, hit the button, silenced Florence and her Machine.

"Hey!" a girl complained from the dance pit. "Boo!" others chimed in, looking for the cause of the abrupt quiet.

Betty Rose carefully pushed aside the fish sticks and lemon bars, the bottles of vodka and tequila and gin and mixers, clearing a spot in the middle of the picnic table. Tested the bench seat with one foot, rocked back once and launched to the top, wobbling. Slide-stepped around to face the hushed, puzzled crowd. She smiled down.

Her Hepburn moment.

"'Scuse me," she said, timid at first, clearing her throat. "May I have your attention, please!" she said louder, quieting those on the periphery, waving them closer. "Step up! Step up!" she barked out. They drew near, curious.

Phyllis gazed up with her toothy smile, but her eyes betrayed a baffled amusement. Gwen, unreadable, stood rigid and stared.

Betty Rose, stage center, curtsied. "Before you all…you know"—she giggled and slashed her finger across her throat—"I just want to apologize. For ruining your show, your whole week, really, and almost killing your audience." She laughed at her own joke, and then laughed harder to compensate for their silence. Frogs croaked a rhythmic chorus in the river distance.

She took a breath, surprised when it morphed into a shallow sob, which she struggled to contain. "But I also want to thank you. For the best week of my life." She looked up into the elm canopied above, centered herself, and returned to her audience. "I was one of you, for the first time," she said, deflating. "And the last."

She scanned the company spread out before her—all industry pros and veterans, she conceded, and many younger than she. With overflowing résumés, countless stage hours, offers lined up for the fall, with backups. And, of course, their Equity cards. She felt, abruptly, un-Hepburn.

"Better I wake up to this now," she said, unloading with ease, "than twenty years too late. And figure out what to do with my life."

She waited for someone, anyone to respond. When they didn't, she choked out a smile and a shallow bow. "And so *adieu*," she heard herself say. "*Adieu*. To *yeu* and *yeu* and…" She tilted, her knees buckled, and she collapsed off the edge of the picnic table. Caleb and the grunt techie rushed to catch her and cushion her fall.

"Whoa!" said Caleb. "Careful now!" said the techie.

Betty Rose found her feet and, catlike, wriggled from their grip, lest they see her tears and grief-twisted face. Careening, she pushed through the crowd head down, staggered toward the river, dark and fuzzy in her view.

"Betty Rose, wait!" Gwen called out from behind. Betty Rose didn't.

Gwen grabbed her arm at the riverbank and spun her around. She seized her by the shoulders.

"Listen!" she ordered in a hushed panic. "You don't want to be one of them. Trust me. We've got to get out of here."

Betty Rose tried to focus on her face. Her exquisite, expressive, heart-shaped face, both photogenic in close-up and easily readable from the back row. She smiled in admiration. "Gwen, you're such a star," she slurred, caressing her cheek. "Every girl's dream. *My* dream…"

Gwen shook her with a single, violent snap. "Shut it!" she said. "They brought us here for a reason. They're grooming us for something fucking awful. I know it!"

Betty Rose recoiled from the unexpected assault and squinted. "Wha—what do you mean?" In Gwen's voice, she heard crisis and fear—but also traces of the steady vibrato, the powerful belt, the lyrical high C. The triple threat of talent that every Broadway casting director and producer would lust over. A megastar on the verge.

"Gwen, Dottie wants you," said Phyllis from behind, interrupting. Betty Rose turned to her by the river's edge and then back to Gwen. The quick movement made her swoon.

"Everybody wants Gwen," she said, smiling, gazing. "The new ingenue."

"Tell Dottie to cool her fucking jets," Gwen ordered, still trained on Betty Rose with her sapphire eyes.

"She says the whole company wants to see you," Phyllis said, persisting. "I'm just telling you what she said." And then she added, "Right now, Gwyneth."

"In a minute!" hissed Gwen, even more glorious when provoked. "Can't you see I'm—"

Betty Rose broke free and ran off, unable to face Gwen's perfection anymore. She weaved and stumbled across the knoll, targeting the playhouse stage door on the far side. Gwen called after, but Betty Rose barreled ahead.

The stage was empty and dark, save the ghost light stage center. Betty Rose staggered through the partially dismantled set, catching her foot on a coil of rope, tripping but recovering to target the apron. She stood on the lip, gazing out on the dim, vacant house. The closest she'd get, she knew, to commanding this stage. Or any stage.

The theater began to swim, and she felt seasick, weaving to stay vertical. The room listed more sharply, and she reeled back from the edge, collapsing on what was left of Aunt Eller's front porch, strewn with hammers, knives, and Makitas the techies had left behind. She banged her tailbone in the fall and cried out, triggering a deeper coil of sorrow and despair, and she heaved and sobbed, shutting her eyes to stop the spinning stage, which now threatened her stomach. She lay down, curled, and poured out her woes, longing for Aunt Eller's soothing caress.

The Wurlitzer woke her first. A melody she'd heard but couldn't place. It comforted her. She yawned and stretched.

Betty Rose opened one eye, then both. She propped herself up on one elbow. The organ, now spotlighted, played itself. She looked around the stage, still empty and dimly lit.

A glint from the back of the theater jolted her. Betty Rose peered into the blackness. She jerked her head up from the porch, squinting harder.

Sparkles caught the ghost light first. A small figure at the back of the house, strolling, in no hurry, down the aisle. Betty Rose struggled to sitting position, still bleary and unclear. She focused.

Into the light emerged Carla, straight from her portrait, sequins and ringlets matching red. She dawdled, meandering toward the stage, her smile vague, her arms folded behind. Betty Rose sat up straighter.

Carla jumped on the first step, childlike, but ascended with a diva's stature. Betty Rose, in her mind, bolted to her feet, but her legs wouldn't work, and she sat frozen, hypnotized. She was unafraid.

The young starlet kneeled in front of her, taunted her hands behind her back in a moment of theatrical suspense, before whisking them to the front, magician-style. Betty Rose jumped in place. Carla opened her fists, palms up, empty, and shrugged. Then she giggled. Betty Rose caught her breath and giggled back. Her new playmate.

Carla gazed at her. She gently took her face in don't-be-afraid hands. She brought her nose close and smiled with love. Betty Rose, warm and centered, secure, smiled back. Carla stroked her cheek.

The Wurlitzer sang louder, and Betty Rose realized it was Carla's anthem, which made sense for her cue. Carla's caring face blurred and changed, her eyes shrinking, her cheekbones jutting, her forehead growing longer up into a lighter wave of hair. Betty Rose faced the steely stare of young Katharine Hepburn, blush with new fame, challenging her with a lecture drowned out by the escalating organ. It was urgent, she could tell, and she hated to miss acting tips from the great.

Betty Rose strained to hear, wishing someone would silence the machine, reaching behind her on the porch, groping for the remote control that Rex had used to stop the organ but finding only a coil of rope, a light gel, a worker's knife carelessly left behind. She nodded at Hepburn, pretending to hear, so as not to seem rude, or obtuse.

Hepburn's eyes widened, her cheeks rounded, her lips curled downward to a surly pout that belied the snarl behind it. Betty Rose flinched a bit at Bette Davis, a real bitch, who locked eyes and prattled on with bullet-quick orders. She snarled her silent wisdom, and Betty Rose tried to read her lips, nodding with gusto. The Wurlitzer was deafening, its repeating chorus both grating and hypnotic.

Davis begat Barbara Stanwyck, of clenched jaw and piercing manner, who passed the baton to Marian Maples, lustrous and young again, like her lobby portrait. Betty Rose fought a swoon, starstruck by the parade of giants and still hazy. Maples morphed into Sutton, the reigning diva, whose eyes and energy betrayed a fresh urgency that startled her.

Gwen took over for Sutton. The next great star, right on the verge. But in her face was panic, like before, but now terror and desperation, which were new. The organ grew louder, and Gwen shook her by the shoulders, as if trying to rouse her. But she was awake, and Gwen's explosive force knocked her off balance. She braced herself on the porch, groping anew for the Wurlitzer remote. This was an emergency.

Gwen's pleadings grew more manic, and she abruptly turned back to the house. Betty Rose blinked twice to clear her eyes and saw the blurred and dimly lit outlines of the audience ushering into the theater. No wonder Gwen was hysterical when she turned back; it was showtime, and they were stranded onstage, the curtain already risen.

Betty Rose tried to calm her, reaching out as the audience neared, and it worked for a split moment, as Gwen stopped talking and took a deep breath. Her sapphire eyes froze, locked on Betty Rose, and her mouth hung open, and the panic mixed with fresh shock, which puzzled Betty Rose, who smiled and tried to speak, but the words wouldn't come.

They wouldn't come for Gwen either, who sat speechless until she gasped, and her eyes stayed locked but her color went off, a sudden pale, and Betty Rose reached out to wipe the tear that threatened one eye. A drop of dark blood leaked from the edge of Gwen's mouth.

Gwen lurched upward, as if struggling to stand, but she held in suspension, trained on Betty Rose, less afraid than confused. Blood dripped from both sides, then streamed. Gwen coughed roughly, and blood spat out onto Betty Rose, who felt and tasted sick rising in her own throat. Gwen hyperventilated, spewing clouds of blood, hot and stinging, with each unsuccessful breath. Betty Rose held her tighter, as the approaching audience, now aware of the crisis, rushed forward to help.

Wake up! she commanded herself, knowing it a nightmare but unable to escape it.

The Wurlitzer shook the theater with Carla's song, and Gwen vomited a dark river, and even through the deafening chorus and outcries from the swarming audience, Betty Rose became aware of her own gasps, and screams, which pitched higher and more shrill and rang down the curtain on top of them all.

Act Two

Scene One

SHE SPRANG UP QUICKLY, TOO QUICKLY, triggering a swarm of nausea. She lay back again, closed her eyes to calm the swooning. The room was still and crisis free.

Another night passed out on the stage, she realized. Dottie would start her rounds soon, barking everyone awake. Betty Rose needed to crawl back to her room. But the stage, this morning, was comfortable. It held her. She turned and curled on it, pulling the sheet to her chin.

She turned back. Opened her eyes, focused on the ceiling. It was white and smooth. She lifted her head off her pillow, then settled back again into the mattress, too exhausted and relieved she'd made it back to her bed last night after all. She could sleep a while longer, until Dottie's obnoxious cowbell.

It never came. Her eyes popped open anew, refocused on the ceiling, too far away to be the view from her top bunk. And clearly not in Phyllis's bottom bunk either. Gwen's? She inhaled her pillow, a different scent. Non-girly. Muskier. She shook her right arm—which she'd slept on and was slow to wake up—propped up on one elbow, blinked, looked around.

The room was small, but a single. On the dresser was a hairbrush, an orange Nerf football, a red bottle of Lacoste cologne. In the open closet hung a few printed T-shirts and polo shirts and two button-downs. Man-sized Nikes, kicked off, lay in angles.

Socks, underwear, jeans, shorts, strewn about the floor. A man-boy's mess, the kind Julian used to make before she trained him. She still hadn't called him, she remembered with a pang.

Betty Rose felt the sheet against her skin. She looked under. Naked.

She scanned the floor for her clothes and found none. She leaned down to look under the bed and felt a sudden swoon again. She righted herself, but stayed alert.

Caleb bounded in the door, glistening, a towel wrapped around his waist. He kicked off his green flip-flops and beamed.

"'Morning, sunshine!" he said, smile widening, tousling his damp hair. Betty Rose pulled the sheet up tighter. She stared at him.

He laughed. "It lives!" he shouted, stretching his back. "And owes me a massage for sleeping on the floor last night. I'm all knots. Least you can do..."

Betty Rose found her voice, dry and crackly. "Did I...go to the wrong room?" she asked, hopefully, steeling herself for the answer.

Caleb laughed again. "You couldn't go anywhere!" he said. "I thought we should just leave you on the stage, but the techies had to finish strike and stuff. So we carried you to bed."

"Yours?" she asked.

"You don't remember anything?" Caleb asked. She shook her head. "Hmm," Caleb teased. "Well, then, maybe I shouldn't tell you."

"Tell me," she urged, stiffening under the sheet, and then pulled her legs up into a ball.

Caleb relented. "After you yakked all over your own bed," he said with care, and Betty Rose said, "Oh no!" and he went on, "Phyllis and Sutton cleaned you up and dumped you in here. They didn't know where else to put you."

"Oh God," she said, and glanced up at his wolflike grin. "We... I mean...," she stammered. "We didn't...I mean you didn't..."

He dropped the act, shook his head. "I'm not a necro, B.R.," he said. "You were dead to the world. And likely to hurl again."

Betty Rose grimaced but was relieved. And not surprised. Of course she hadn't cheated. She never had before, no matter how drunk, and as her fog cleared, her body told her she'd stayed pure. Her memory, still muddled, creeped back, too. She vaguely remembered the shower—being undressed first, which she'd briefly resisted, until she realized her jumpsuit was wet and soiled down the front. Now she knew why and with what.

She remembered Sutton's soothing voice as she unzipped and disrobed her in the bathhouse—initially embarrassing, even as it dawned on her she was being taken care of, in her foulest, most vulnerable state, by a Tony Award winner. Phyllis pitched in, too, running the shower and checking the temperature, before they dragged her in. "Keep her head down," Sutton said. "And her mouth closed. Don't drown her." And Phyllis, propping her up from behind, said, "Hand me the soap. A fresh bar, please."

"It won't come off," Phyllis complained, scrubbing her face and neck with a scratchy washcloth, and Sutton said, "It will. Keep at it," and Betty Rose felt freshly self-conscious about what she'd thrown up, although it couldn't have been solid since she'd hardly eaten the past week. Unless Dottie's nasty mush, which burned her mouth and stomach was made even more toxic and staining when vomited back up. She sat helpless on the shower floor, feeling the water pelt and tasting suds as Sutton scrubbed harder and shielded her eyes to protect from stinging. They bantered back and forth like a team on a mission, but the shower blurred out the conversation, and Betty Rose feared she'd stay there forever when the water abruptly stopped.

They dried her off still seated, using two towels and occasionally giggling at what was—Betty Rose would have acknowledged had she been able to speak without slurring—an absurd situation. And entirely preventable and completely her fault. A messy and fitting end to her very brief Gristmill career. She said "thank you" over and over to them both, unable to think of anything else. At least they didn't dump her on the road to find her way back to New York.

Instead, they wrapped her wet hair and swaddled her in a seersucker robe with terry lining and held her up on either side, leading her across the deserted grassy knoll, where empty bottles, strewn paper plates, and the still-playing iPod hinted at the party now disbanded. From the theater came the destructive noises of set strike and the violent clunking of the gristmill off the kitchen, which sounded especially petulant at this late hour. It ground with an erratic, angry force that seemed to shake the building, and Betty Rose just wanted to hide in her bed, to sneak away in the morning.

Dottie, wearing yellow dishwashing gloves and a sour face, stepped from the back of the playhouse and blocked their path. Alarmed, she waved them away. "Where the hell do you think you're going? Get out of here!" she ordered. "We're taking her back to her room," said Sutton, and Dottie said, "No, you're not. Dump her in yours." Sutton protested, saying, "Absolutely not, Dottie. She cannot sleep in my room. I refuse."

And ever-so-vaguely Betty Rose recalled Caleb, scrubbing sponge in hand, popping up behind Dottie and volunteering his own bed. "Really?" said Phyllis, and Sutton asked, "Are you sure?" and Dottie, problem solved, said, "Good. Go. Now," before pivoting back into the theater.

And so now here she was. Naked. And bleary.

"You okay?" asked Caleb, breaking her trance. He was still in his towel, staring down at her.

"I...think so," said Betty Rose, feeling an urgency to get back to her room, to her friends and fellow interns. She looked around the room. "Where's my...robe?"

Caleb shrugged. "They must have took it."

"*Taken* it," she corrected automatically, before considering her options. The sheet wouldn't do. She squinted at Caleb's closet.

"Can I...borrow a shirt?" she asked.

She scampered barefoot across the grass, Caleb's button-down covering her just adequately. Thank God he was tall. It was hot and midday-feeling, the sun centered overhead through the thick air, which made her brain feel heavier and more muddled. Her right arm was still sore from sleeping on it all night, and she rubbed out its kinks as she weaved through the oaks and elms. The grounds were empty and silent, and she targeted the stage door that Dottie had blocked the night before. Today it was flanked by a pair of techies, smoking. They snapped to attention as she approached, stomped out their cigarettes, and parted so she could pass, which she longed to read as a newfound respect, although she knew it was their latest version of mean-girl mockery. Avoiding their faces, she slipped past them and down the hallway, found her bedroom door.

Phyllis's bed was pristine and tightly made, as it was every morning, its pillow guarded by an open-armed Winnie the Pooh. Her own top bunk was similarly made, courtesy of Phyllis, most likely.

Gwen's bed was stripped, her mattress bare. Betty Rose looked around, at the dresser, the bedside table, under the bed. She pulled out Gwen's assigned drawer. No sign of her.

She opened the closet they shared. Phyllis's Louis Vuitton rolling bag lined up along the bottom; hers and Betty Rose's outfits hung in their assigned places. Gwen's section was empty, her suitcase gone.

The alarm clock read 11:13. She hadn't slept that late in years.

Betty Rose took a pair of dusty rose overalls from its hanger. Unearthed a faded floral top from her drawer, got dressed.

The kitchen and dining room were clean and empty, the tables already set for the next meal. The gristmill sat idle and seemingly injured, a hand-scrawled *Do Not Use!* sign taped across its hopper. Betty Rose wondered if they'd found an artifact repairman after all.

The hallways were deserted, her footsteps the only sound as she passed the communal phone, which, according to its sign, was also out of order, the message chalkboard wiped clean. She tried the receiver, clicked it twice, to confirm it dead. She hung up, hurried on to the lobby.

The box office window said "Closed," and the concessions stand was locked up. She glanced up at the framed divas, back on the wall where they belonged after visiting her in last night's weird, booze-fueled dream. *Hallucination,* she told herself, feeling her hangover anew, even as she redoubled her efforts to shake it.

She peered out the front door window: a ghost town, the grounds empty, the benches and front porch wicker chairs vacant and gently rocking with the breeze. A glint in the distance caught her eye. She looked closer.

Sutton knelt on the Journeyman Bridge, at the edge of the flower bed. She was gardening with a spade that reflected flashes of sunlight. Next to her was the red fire bucket, from which she scooped compost. She mixed it with potting soil from a yellow-striped bag and gently layered it around the base of a brand-new rosebush—a thin, fragile sapling with a single lavender bloom. Clyde the baby goat hovered near, darting hungrily at the mashed-up leftovers in the bucket. Sutton swatted him away with her gloved hand, which perplexed but did not deter him, as he circled around and targeted the bucket from a fresh angle.

Betty Rose was tempted to open the door to say hello, but Sutton seemed so engrossed with her gardening, so peaceful in her solitude, it would be rude to interrupt. Not to mention the dripping compost she kept scooping from the bucket made Betty Rose somewhat queasy on sight. And she wasn't quite ready to face up to her humiliating debacle from last night; she'd thank her, and Phyllis, later.

"You guys missed a spot!" Dottie bellowed from behind, inside the theater. "Do I have to do everything myself around here?"

Betty Rose turned to the closed theater doors, lorded over by Carla the gatekeeper. Her downward smile this morning seemed less impish than taunting. Betty Rose slowly pushed open the silent doors and crept inside.

The house was empty; Dottie, alone, swabbed the bare stage
with a mop, down center. She still wore her dish gloves, her
hair pulled back and wrapped in a red bandana. She plunged
the mop into a blue plastic bucket and sloshed suds onto the
stage. Irritated, she muttered as she scrubbed a stubborn spot,
unaware of Betty Rose moving down the aisle and toward the
stage stairs. They creaked as she stepped on the bottom one.

"Stay off the stage! It's wet!" Dottie ordered and then
looked up with a jolt. "Well, now, *good morning*, Betty Rose!"
She checked her watch and resumed her scrubbing "Just barely, I think," she grumbled.

Betty Rose stood on the bottom step. "Where is everybody?" she asked, her voice still dry and weak.

"Members have off until dinner," said Dottie, focusing on a
small area. "Although the techies clearly didn't finish cleanup.
We can't load in *Brigadoon* on a filthy stage!"

"Do you need help?" said Betty Rose, and Dottie quipped,
"Not *yours*, for chrissakes. You're a walking disaster zone." She
waved her back and laughed. "I'm not sure I could survive your
help!"

"Where's...Gwen?" asked Betty Rose.

"You can thank Phyllis for covering your breakfast shift,"
Dottie went on, now on her knees with sponge, swirling angry circles. "Apparently, you were AWOL." She shot her a look,
raised an eyebrow, and then dropped it.

"Where's Gwen?" Betty Rose asked again.

"What?" Dottie looked back up, perturbed. "Gwen? You
didn't hear? No, I guess not." She brightened abruptly. "Gwen
booked a soap. A three-year contract, allegedly. Isn't that
thrilling?"

"Really? Gwen's...gone?"

Dottie nodded. "First bus of the morning. She has fittings today. Those soaps move like lightning."

"Which soap?" asked Betty Rose, and Dottie stopped scrubbing and looked upward for the answer. "*Safe Passage*, I think," she said. "Way over on Sixty-Sixth. With those great dressing rooms overlooking the Hudson."

Betty Rose thought. "She booked it yesterday? On a... Sunday?" she asked, and Dottie shrugged. "She's been on avail for over a month. She tested before she came here. We thought we might lose her," she said. "Honestly, that's why we brought you in as backup. We only need two interns. Not three."

Dottie squeezed the sponge's murky water into the bucket. "You're full of questions today," she said to Betty Rose's silence. "Do I confuse you? Gwen booked a good gig. You should be happy."

"Oh, I am," said Betty Rose, standing still. "It's wonderful. I just...didn't get to say goodbye." "She hasn't gone to the moon," said Dottie. "You'll see her in the city, I'm sure. Frankly, she didn't belong here. Never seemed happy. A soap suits her better. Fast fame."

"I had the weirdest dream about her," said Betty Rose, sorting through her confusion. "Well, a nightmare, really."

"I'm not surprised," Dottie said, dabbing sweat from her forehead with her arm, scrubbing on. "Gin on an empty stomach. Gin on anything, really..." Then she looked up and said, "You certainly heard the call of the wild last night. For your sake, I hope you don't remember much." She peered closer. "Especially your diva moment. Do you?"

"Oh God," said Betty Rose, more dawning on her. "My stupid speech! In front of everybody." Dottie said, "Yes, that was a showstopper. Perfect casting if we were doing *Next to Normal*."

Betty Rose said, "I'm so embarrassed. I was just...bummed." Dottie seemed perplexed, so Betty Rose added, "About...you know...getting the ax." Dottie still didn't get it, so Betty Rose clarified: "Fired."

"Fired?" Dottie dropped the sponge in the bucket and stood up. "What the hell are you talking about?"

"Aren't you...sending me home?" she asked, having made peace with it.

Dottie scowled in confusion and exasperation. "Why would you think that?" she snapped. "Young actors are such paranoid basket cases. Pins and needles!

"Did you not just hear me?" she went on, punching her words. "Gwen is gone. We need two interns for the season. You're not going anywhere, not even if you wanted to!"

"Oh!" said Betty Rose, surprised at her own gasp of relief. "You did just say that, didn't you?" She nodded. "Yes, yes. Sorry, I'm just a little hazy today."

"Gin on an empty stomach!" Dottie repeated. "Gin on anything, really..."

And then she added, "Although running crew is clearly not your forte, unless we all have a death wish. So Daddy's put you in the chorus for the new show."

Betty Rose lit up. "Onstage?" she said, her voice awakened, and Dottie said, "No, the chorus on the roof. Of course onstage! Am I speaking pig latin this morning?"

"Thank you!" said Betty Rose. "Oh, thank you!"

"Rex made the call. It's just chorus, mind you. Don't get any grand ideas."

"I thought I'd ruined your show," Betty Rose babbled. "I don't know what was wrong with me. I think I was trying too hard, but that's no excuse...." Dottie, feigning a migraine, raised her hand to shut her up. Then she smiled down at her.

"It takes a while to get your sea legs around here," she said. "You're doing better than most, believe it or not."

Betty Rose bounded to the stage, an eager volunteer. "I can finish cleaning up, really," she said, and Dottie came at her with the dripping mop. "Go away!" she yelled with playful rage. "Be back at five sharp. You're on KP. It's surf-and-turf night."

Phyllis intercepted her at the sign-out sheet. "Well, hello there, Drunkie McDrunkster!" she teased. "You'd better have some news from your sleepover."

"None," Betty Rose said, heading out the stage door. "Caleb was a perfect gentleman."

"Bleh." Phyllis stuck out her tongue as she kept pace. "Gentlemen are overrated."

"Did you hear about Gwen?" Betty Rose asked, and Phyllis said, "Isn't that exciting? She's on her way. I'm not surprised. It can happen in an instant, especially when you're Gwen."

Which was true, Betty Rose knew. She remembered the young girl from Michigan she'd trained at the Rum House. Right before her first paycheck, she booked a TV series and was whisked off to Toronto. Granted, it was just a recurring role on Nickelodeon. But still, it was instant. For some. Like Gwen.

"Everyone's meeting at Café Carla," said Phyllis as they approached the Journeyman Bridge, and Betty Rose said, "I'll catch up with you later."

On the bridge, a flock of fat black birds clustered around the baby rose Sutton had planted, pecking the soil. They took flight as the girls neared, disturbing the air.

"What...kind of birds are those?" Betty Rose asked, squinting as they disappeared into the thick elm tree. She struggled to shake off the last remnants of her hangover haze.

"Big ones!" Phyllis laughed, hurrying across the bridge, as if chased. She shouted above the rush of the rapids below. "Freaky ones!"

Scene Two

JULIAN WAS BESIDE HIMSELF.

"I left a million messages!" he unloaded into the phone. "I almost called the police. I've started looking at milk cartons for your photo!"

Betty Rose laughed, apologized, tried to calm him. His overcharged protectiveness was atypical and endearing.

"I haven't had a second, for real," she insisted. "And the phone's always crowded. Or broken. Or something."

She sat at the polished mahogany bar while Mr. Arbor stacked clean highballs onto glass shelves and pretended not to eavesdrop. His cozy Boathouse Tavern resembled more a private study than a pub, with tufted, tattered, rolled-arm leather sofas, tarnished brass lamps with pleated shades, and bookshelves stuffed with well-worn first editions. The floors were strewn with patchwork Oriental rugs, the walls lined with vintage regatta posters, sepia sailing photos, and framed antique maps. Crowning it all was a Princeton crew shell and oars and battered pewter tankards suspended from the ceiling, flanked by drapes of nautical flags. "May the Wind Be Always at Your Back," beseeched the carved wooden beam propping up the ceiling.

It sat at the end of a wide gravel alley across from an arti-sanal florist and nursery and a spare, foodie-looking restau-rant. It peeked out on the Delaware. It was clearly built with love.

"Yes, they're all very nice, and normal," Betty Rose said, struggling to keep pace with Julian's interrogation. "Well, sor-ta normal. They're looney, in their way. Which I expected."

"But it's not a cult," she stressed when Julian kept probing. "Or if it is, it's a harmless one. Adorable even. It's more like grown-ups at summer camp." She glanced over at Mr. Arbor in apology for her odd conversation. He inventoried bottles against the smoky bar mirror, ignoring her. In a corner wing-back chair sat his only other customer: a distinguished gentle-man of post-retirement age, dressed in summer sport coat and khakis, making his way through the *Wall Street Journal* while nursing a Bloody Mary.

She prattled on about her exhausting schedule, the baby goat, the Gristmill's gristmill. She described the eccentricities of Dottie and Alistair and moody Baub and the steely control that Rex, the benign dictator, held over them all. She left out her drunken debacle, her waking up naked in Caleb's bed, as innocent as it was.

"The only kooky thing they do, and it's not all that weird, is they sing this song together," she said. "They link hands and sing. It's like their alma mater."

"Huh," said Julian, and Betty Rose said, "But it's a lovely song. And they harmonize beautifully. I should sing the so-prano line, but they need alto more, so I sing that now."

Her excitement building, she finally fessed up: "Julian, I to-tally ruined their show, all week long. I was a goon. I don't know what got into me. I dropped a spotlight on an old woman. Well, it bounced near her; she was fine, just freaked out. I thought they were going to fire me. I mean, they should have…"

"Huh," Julian repeated, and Betty Rose barreled on: "But they didn't, because one of the interns had to drop out, for a gig. So they need me. And they actually promoted me, to chorus! For the new show."

Mr. Arbor stopped counting bottles and peered at her in the mirror's reflection. She winked at him, and he smiled faintly and kept counting.

"Are you still there?" Betty Rose asked to the silence, and Julian said, "Huh? Yeah, yeah, I'm here. Sorry, in the middle of something. Hey, why is it so hard to reach you there?"

"I told you, there's bad cell reception, and the theater's phone is hopeless," she said, darting a devilish look to Mr. Arbor, who poured goldfish crackers from a carton into bowls. "Luckily, a generous fellow here loaned me his."

"What fellow?" Julian demanded, and Mr. Arbor, anticipating the question, dropped his busywork act and said, "Tell him a very *old* fellow."

"You should come visit!" Betty Rose said. "And see me in the show."

"Well, my show's busy, too," said Julian. "Can we get a room? Make a whole weekend of it?" Betty Rose frowned and said, "That's against the rules, I'm sure. I can't be gone that long. But I get an hour after the matinee. I can show you around town." "An hour…," said Julian. "Huh."

He added, "I'll see what I can do. Let's talk more often, B.R. Deal?" Betty Rose said, "Deal. Yes. Hey, Julian…I miss you." She cupped the phone for privacy and whispered, "And I love you." She hung up. An unsatisfying call. Julian's payback, which perhaps she deserved. It was difficult to explain the Gristmill and its crazed routine to an outsider who'd never experienced it.

Mr. Arbor refilled her glass with club soda from the gun and plopped in a fresh cherry. "You've already lost an intern?" he asked, sliding it to her. "Midseason?"

"Yes, she booked a soap, if you ever watch those..." She nodded up toward the bar television, which ran CNBC, muted. Doubtful. "Or maybe your wife does."

Mr. Arbor wasn't married. Born and raised in New Hope, to an ice delivery father and seamstress mother, he ran his bar alone, closing only on Sundays and his yearly September fishing trip to Montana, after the summer season. "And the occasional personal day," he added, including the New York Auto Show, each April at the Javits Center.

Betty Rose sipped her club soda and luxuriated in her own personal day, her first away from the Gristmill. She felt rehydrated and centered, her fog increasingly dissipated. It was cool and still in the Boathouse, the only sound the white noise from the relentless air conditioner, or the occasional creak from the *Journal* gentleman shifting in his chair and turning pages. She glanced over at the paper's matrix of headlines and turned back, nonplussed. "Phyllis was right," she said with a laugh. "You forget there's a whole world outside...."

From nowhere, she shuddered with a flashback of last night's bizarre dream, which should have seemed comical by now but still lingered potently—the last dying gasp of her retreating hangover with its abrupt mood swings. What had conjured up such a vivid and monstrous, blood-soaked vision in her subconscious? The gin, of course, like Dottie said. Mixed with tequila, she just now remembered, and God knows what else. She knew better, having sworn off hard liquor after the closing-night party of *Once Upon a Mattress* junior year, when, on a dare from Linda Regelman, she performed "Shy" in her underwear in the theater's front courtyard fountain—or so she was told the next day, having similarly blacked out and apparently thrown up. She promised Julian she wouldn't embarrass him like that again, and she hadn't. Last night was a one-off—and entirely excusable, she consoled herself, considering the week she'd had—and Julian need never know the full story. She refused to beat herself up over it.

She tried to relive the hallucinatory parade of titans from the wall, each stooping to talk to her directly, like chummy old friends. That was the thrilling part of her dream, in its own weird way. They all looked so different facing her straight on, as opposed to the carefully staged angles from the movies and photos, and were generous and insistent in their frantic advice. She wished she could have heard their urgent messages, but such was the murky nature of dreams. Her subconscious shortchanged her there.

But Gwen's message—warning, really—had started long before the dream, before Betty Rose took her first drink and eventually passed out onstage, hadn't it? In the dressing room, right after the crashing spotlight disaster. Gwen's panic had escalated at the after-party, by the river, as if danger were imminent. Who knew she was such a drama queen?

Gwen needed to cool it with the pot. It made her paranoid. Betty Rose had tried it only once, before a particularly stressful dress rehearsal in college, having been told it would calm her. It had a disastrously opposite effect and took two days to shake. No wonder Rex forbade it. It was extremely unprofessional.

But Gwen's nonsensical paranoia was contagious and clearly had influenced Betty Rose's dream, although the sequence of events and distinction of real and non-real was still blurry. That's why they called it a "blackout." And why she swore off hard liquor again, starting now. It made her too wiggy, her dreams too fantastical and freakish.

Her mood shifted again, this time brightening and flooding her with fresh relief that she'd passed her crucial first week test and graduated to the chorus. She hadn't been voted off the island, and a solo, unthinkable just yesterday, was plausibly in reach before the end of the summer. It was her new goal and obsession, eclipsing her humiliation over last night's debacle and unseating the nagging alarm of her nightmare, which was, after all, a fleeting figment of her booze-addled imagination.

She just wished the terror in Gwen's eyes weren't so graphic and undreamlike. And haunting.

"Betty Rose?"

"Sorry, what?" She snapped back from the window on the river.

Mr. Arbor slid over a bowl of orange goldfish crackers. "Help yourself," he said, and Betty Rose smiled and shook her head. "Thank you, but they've got me on a diet," she said.

"Diet?" he asked. "How much thinner can you get?"

His gold wedding band caught her eye, and she reached for his hand. He smelled of Clubman talcum, like her grandfather used to. "I thought you weren't married," she said. "I'm not," he replied. She gently turned his palm over, revealing the Gristmill mask logo signet, which faced in.

"You're a member, too?" she asked. "Not officially," he said. He slid off the ring and handed it to her. "I've been going since I was a toddler. They give an honorary membership to the townies.

"I saw my very first show there," he added. "I'll never forget it."

Betty Rose held the ring close, to read the worn initials "M.A." engraved on the underside. It needed a cleaning.

"So you saw all those legends...," she asked, "before they were legends?"

Mr. Arbor perked for the first time, nodded. "The locals eat that up. That sense of discovery: Who's next? And it keeps the tourists flocking." His face tightened a bit. "It's a very... codependent setup."

She gave the ring back, logo facing up. "Well, it's an honor. You should keep it polished. And show it off." He turned it toward his palm again. "I used to," he said. "But it gets in the way."

She looked past him, to the bar mirror, partially shrouded with stacked bottles. She squinted. In faded, antique colors, it was muraled over with the same tableau as the Gristmill's fire curtain: the playhouse, the Delaware, the locomotive, the joyous, worshipful townies. And dead center, towering over them all, the freakishly giant coquette Carla.

"Oh God," she said with mock irritation. "Now, that chick, I've seen about enough of her. She's *everywhere*." She laughed and added, "She's even started showing up in my dreams!"

Mr. Arbor stopped spooning pickled onions into his bar container. He looked over her shoulder toward the *Journal* gentleman. Betty Rose spun her stool to see him peering over his half-glasses at them both, and quickly spun back, so as not to seem rude.

"Now, Richard," Mr. Arbor said with a poker face, checking his watch. "When your wife calls asking for you, which lie should I tell her this time?"

The gentleman chuckled and folded his paper. When he reached for his wallet, Mr. Arbor said, "You know I don't charge you on Mondays. See you tomorrow." The man and Betty Rose politely nodded at each other as he left.

"Yes, the town loves its Carla legend," Mr. Arbor said, putting aside his work. "If it weren't for her, none of us would be here. And, of course, she makes it easier to forget the *Cady* legend..." He twinkled with mischief.

"Ruh-roh," said Betty Rose, rubbing her hands. "Who dat?"

"Her sister. Looked so much alike, people thought they were twins."

He took center stage, behind his bar and leaned in.

"See, until the Great Drought of 1899, New Hope was a thriving farm town," he explained. "When it all dried up, the town faced ruin. But the mill family had a pair of very talented daughters who entertained the locals."

The mural, worn dull from years of cleaning, needed a touch-up, thought Betty Rose. She strained to make out the town features so vibrantly illustrated on the Gristmill's fire curtain.

"Word spread, tourists flocked to see the sisters, a real vaudeville phenomenon," Mr. Arbor went on. "Soon the town was housing, feeding, cashing in. The economy changed and thrived...."

The afternoon light off the river shifted a bit, brightening the town.

"Broadway's top producer came a-calling," said Mr. Arbor, spinning his yarn. "But the night before the girls' big audition, *Cady* disappeared." He paused for effect, and Betty Rose panned the town for the illusive sister, Waldo-style. She glanced back at Mr. Arbor, expectantly.

"Rumor spread that the more ambitious Carla had killed her sister—with a mill pick—piercing the nape of her neck, severing her spinal cord."

Betty Rose recoiled, sitting back on her stool. "Oh God!" she said with titillated horror. "More! More!"

Mr. Arbor pointed at the miniature man and woman flanking the Godzilla Carla. "And that her mother and father, mortified by what she'd done but also afraid of losing her to the local gendarme, had destroyed the evidence—Cady's body, that is—through the gristmill." He held her gaze, still twinkling, and said, "Then the legend gets really twisted...."

"Oh goody," said Betty Rose, giggling. "Because so far it's been oh-so-normal."

"What did they do with Cady's grist?" he asked through a devilish grin, not waiting for an answer. "Some say they tilled it into their garden. Others say it wound up on Carla's dinner plate. As punishment. So she would never forget her horrible crime and sin."

"Eek!" she cried, now laughing through her sour face. "And I thought my family was dysfunctional."

Mr. Arbor stood up straight, releasing the story's tension. "Carla became a big star on the vaudeville circuit, touring the country, but returned each summer to perform for the season, blackmailed by the town, to keep the economy booming. Thus the Gristmill Playhouse was born."

He pointed at the dollhouse-looking barn on the mural. Her own summer home. "When Carla died, dozens of young girls were poised to take her place. A few special ones became the legends we all know. And so the cycle continues to this day." He turned back from the mirror, his hands braced on the bar. "The Gristmill and the town permanently linked—in a dark bond born of blood...."

The sunlight hid behind a cloud, and the mural dulled again. Betty Rose watched it dim, then pivoted to Mr. Arbor and exhaled. "Well," she said with force, "that certainly hit the spot!" She swirled her straw. "I love these quaint old-town tales. Each trying to one-up the others."

"Perhaps it's grown taller over time," said Mr. Arbor with a slight shrug. "Old-town tales usually do."

The Alpine cuckoo clock by the TV whirred and chimed. Betty Rose sprang up.

"I hope I didn't scare you off," he said, and Betty Rose said, "Not at all! But I'm on kitchen patrol, and I can't be late again." She hiked the strap of her overalls higher on her shoulder. "Thank you for the phone, Mr. Arbor. And that yummy bed-time story." She took one last sip and patted her pockets in vain. Mr. Arbor waved her off. "It's on the house," he said.

"When you get older and see things clearly, you want to pass it on," he added, stopping himself. He smiled. "You do me good, Betty Rose. Come back soon. I'll share some more...."

Phyllis loved the tale. "Poor li'l Cady, all ground up in the gristmill!" she said, after squealing her way through the story. "Gives me goose bumps!" Betty Rose had run into her and Caleb coming out of the Blue Penguin with cups of swirled frozen yogurt on her way back.

"A bartender told you this?" Caleb said, licking his pink spoon. "Were you at happy hour or something?"

Betty Rose ignored him. "Such a nice old man," she told Phyllis. "So fascinating and full of stories. Probably lonely, too."

"Full of shit, you mean," Caleb added, and Phyllis punched him. "Show Cady some respect!" she ordered. "She's part of our history, too! As much as Carla."

Clyde the goat, his hooves muddy from digging, greeted them on the Journeyman Bridge, sniffing their hands hungrily.

"Poor Clyde," Betty Rose said, her own stomach churning as she pet him. "I know how you feel, babe.…"

Scene Three

The lobster's scream pierced through the kitchen.

"Good God, no!" Dottie cried, rushing to rescue the flailing creature from the boiling pot. "That's not how we do it!" She grabbed it with tongs and moved it to the chopping board, where it wriggled on, stunned.

Betty Rose jumped away from the counter, horrified by its suffering. "You told me to boil them!" she protested. "I didn't say torture them!" Dottie shot back. "If you must kill a creature, you must make it as painless as possible."

She gave Betty Rose a crumpling stare. "The amount of what you don't know has yet to disappoint me," she said.

Another test failed, but it scarcely fazed Betty Rose. She was preoccupied with *Brigadoon,* humming the alto line on "My Mother's Wedding Day" and going over the steps for "Jeannie's Packin' Up" for her debut the following night. They'd tuck her in the back, a hybrid of chorus and light-duty running crew, but she was determined to shine, or at least not screw up. She focused on the rehearsals she'd caught only glimpses of during her first hell week, running them in a loop through her brain.

So when Dottie had pointed to the plastic crate swimming with lobsters and told her to boil them, Betty Rose had followed orders literally. Now her dazed and terrified victim lashed feebly on the block.

Dottie snipped the ties off its claws. "And you have to give it a fighting chance. Or at least the illusion of one. It's only humane." The lobster reached up and around, clacking at all aggressors. Betty Rose stepped back from it.

Phyllis chirped in from her frying pan, popping with pungent sausage. "On Nantucket we put 'em in cold water, then heat it up a little at a time," she said. "They don't know they're gonna die until it's too late!"

"We don't have time for that," Dottie snapped. "Sutton, can you show them how Daddy taught us? I gotta make the sauce for the lasagna."

Sutton took a break from chopping herbs and fished an ice pick from the drawer.

"A knife can slip off the shell," she instructed. "An ice pick is much safer. And use two hands."

She positioned the slowing lobster, now resigned to its doom, in the center of the chopping board. She lined up the pick just below the head, then raised her arms. The lobster clacked up both claws in a desperate, final defense, and Sutton drove down in a sharp thrust, piercing the shell through to the board. The claws dropped, now still.

"Easy and guilt-free," said Sutton, smiling. She handed the ice pick to Phyllis.

"Whoa, that feels good!" said Phyllis, killing her first. "Who knew?" She pouted at her victim. "Sorry, Mr. Squirmer," she said.

Betty Rose cupped both hands around the pick handle and cracked down through the shell, as easy as killing a bug. She tossed the lobster into the boiling pot and grabbed another from the writhing box. The faster, the better, she thought. Her aim and form improved with each kill.

Dottie stopped her as she went to add the latest to the pot. "Scrawny ones are bitter," she said, nixing it. "Throw it away." She pointed to the mill room off the kitchen. "Into the grist-mill?" asked Betty Rose, hesitating.

"We fixed it," said Dottie, waving her on. "But chop it up before you feed it in. I don't want it jamming again."

Betty Rose whacked off the claws and head, dropped them into the mill hopper. It effortlessly churned and spat the pu-réed debris into the slop bucket like a well-oiled and newly refurbished grinding machine. Its output, however, was as re-pulsive as ever.

The surf-and-turf combo was odd, but popular neverthe-less, as members picked lobster tails or squares of Dottie's aro-matic, rich-looking lasagna, or both. "Enjoy!" said Betty Rose, tonging whole shells onto plates, happy to discover a new grate-ful attitude from the company, owing either to their rejuvenat-ing day off or their growing acceptance of her as potentially one of their own. Even Baub thanked her as she plunked a steaming tail onto his tray, along with extra butter.

Her diet was the same, however, spooned up by Dottie. It had grown on her, and she had started to appreciate the lean, light-headed feeling that signaled progress toward her skin-nier, more actress-appropriate figure. "How much thinner can you get?" Mr. Arbor had asked. *Just watch*, thought Betty Rose, proud of her achievement.

Still, she found herself coveting Phyllis's plate, drawn by its unusually savory aroma. She glanced once again at the thick lasagna slab stuffed with sausage and beef chunks and smothered with melted mozzarella. Phyllis took pity, sliced off a healthy chunk, and with a furtive flick, landed it on Betty Rose's plate, while maintaining her animated conversation with the rest of the table. She snuck in a quick wink, surprisingly smooth.

The first bite overwhelmed her senses with its explosion of flavor and texture. It was a shock she relished, and her tongue held and explored the complexities she'd never take for granted again. Had any lasagna ever tasted this rich and exotic? She reluctantly swallowed and wolfed down a second bite, lest the flying monkeys catch her and take it away.

She bit down on gristle, breaking the spell. It was round and gummy, yet hard, and she rolled it to the front of her mouth and slyly lipped into her napkin. A strand of hair—probably Dottie's—stretched from her teeth, as if floss, and she leaned down to pull and yank it free. She gulped water, swiftly nauseous, and swallowed before she could gag. She ran her tongue, probing for any remnants.

"You okay, B.R.?" asked Phyllis, puzzling at her.

She nodded. "It's weird...eating again," she said, settling. She remembered an experimental three-day cleanse from college, after which a hamburger first thrilled her and then nearly made her ill. Such was the point of her cleanse, to heighten sensitivity to the repulsiveness of modern-day food. Maybe vegans had it right.

Across the mess hall, Alistair riveted his table with tales of working with Elaine Page in an *Encores!* revival at City Center, until Dottie interrupted with, "Five minutes till run-through, gang! *Ándele!*"

Betty Rose tapped her leg and lowered the last bite of her lasagna to the floor for the circling Clyde, who took to it instantly.

● ● ●

Surprisingly, she fit perfectly into Gwen's old petticoat and corset for the *Brigadoon* costume parade. Becky called the run-through from the control booth and moved Betty Rose farther downstage for the group numbers, close enough to interact with the stars.

"Shit, I'm sorry!" Sutton said, flubbing a verse of "Waitin' for My Dearie." She grabbed Betty Rose by the shoulders and shook her playfully. "You spooked me! I thought you were Gwen," she said with a laugh. Betty Rose said, "It's the bonnet!" and Becky yelled, "From the top, pleeeze!"

Phyllis was positioned across the stage, almost a mirror image to Betty Rose, who couldn't help but fret she was being compared to and judged against her fellow intern. *Cool it*, she told herself. Her competitive streak, which often walked the line between healthy and nasty, had already soured her budding friendship with Gwen, for which she felt petty and slightly guilty. She now knew Gwen had only been trying to help—not sabotage—since she already had one foot out the door on her way to soap opera stardom. Betty Rose had simply created a duplicitous rival out of her own bitchy imagination. Someday she'd track Gwen down in the city, fess up, and apologize.

"Let's speed to the wedding scene," called Becky, and a tartan-kilted Alistair said, "I sherr coud use a Balvenie neat right about now!" in his best Scottish brogue.

Rex roamed the rear of the darkened house, his white Santa beard ghosting as he moved back and forth, the metal from his ever-present clipboard winking in the reflected light. Hovering nearby were Dottie and others from the production team, at the ready for new orders and directions, which he gave, fine-tuning the show. The cast kept one eye on him from the stage, gauging his moves and craving his approval.

The choreographer, Baayork—short and feisty, and as an original cast member in *A Chorus Line,* affording a reverence bordering on worship—broke off from Rex and came down the aisle. "Take fifteen, guys!" she ordered the cast and pulled Betty Rose aside to tighten her routine, since she was late to the game and struggling to catch up. She was flattered by the personal attention from the icon, instead of being pawned off to the uppity dance captain Mimi. "That's it! You've got it!" Baayork encouraged. "It's a lilting step, skipping through the clover. Not a care in the world. La-di-da...Step, together. Ankles touch, please! Atta girl!"

"Cooking with gas!" Baayork cheered on as Betty Rose perfected the moves, dipping with her basket to collect imaginary heather. "Off to the races! Now go take five, champion...."

The cast took their breaks outside on the grassy knoll, chatting and sneaking smokes, which was forbidden in costume. Betty Rose wandered through the moon shadows, smiling at her fellow cast while she replayed Baayork's dance routine in her head, determined to nail it in the final run-through. Rex, after all, was watching.

Alistair held court to a small group, explaining how Lerner and Loewe had "more bombs than Joe Allen's flop wall" before hitting it big with *Brigadoon.* "And thank God they did," he added, "or there wouldn't have been *My Fair Lady.* I owe my pension to Colonel Pickering, coast-to-coast. Oh yes, my dear, he vested me."

Rachelle flicked her ashes into the cigarette-speared sand pail on the picnic table. "Gwen wasn't gonna last anyway," she told two girls in their clan sashes gathered by the elm. "But holy fuck what an exit."

"I never liked her attitude," said one girl. "She was dragging everybody down," said the other.

"As Rex says: Everyone is replaceable. *Everyone*," said Rachelle. "Oh, hi, B.R.! Congrats on the promotion. You'll be the bomb." And Betty Rose said, "Thank you," grateful for the change in attitude and relieved to be on Rachelle's good side. "I'm nervous but excited." She was tempted to go to bat for her former roommate but didn't see the point. Gwen had earned her reputation, fairly or not. And in any event, she was now gone.

"I think you're a natural," Rachelle added, and her friends agreed. Betty Rose thanked them again, overwhelmed by their sudden support and generosity, but declined their cigarette offer. She had cleared her first hurdle and felt, if not part of the group, at least no longer its pariah.

"We're back!" Becky called from the playhouse. The cast migrated toward the stage door.

● ● ●

"Should we ask your new boyfriend for a hand?" said Phyllis, and Betty Rose said, "I don't have a new boyfriend. And we can do it ourselves."

They had decided, with Gwen gone, to make extra room in their cramped quarters by leaning her bunk against the wall. "Murphy bed style," said Phyllis.

The mattress, thin and rubbery, was light but awkward. The metal cot frame was heavy and required heft, but they managed.

"Such a palace now," said Phyllis, grandly sweeping through the tiny new space. "And dusty, too," she said, scowling at the floor.

Betty Rose repositioned the bed, so it wouldn't tip over. She stood back to test it.

Right above eye level on the now-vertical bed, near the head where Gwen's pillow once lay, hung her black night mask, tucked into the metal spring coils. Forgotten and of little value to Gwen now, thought Betty Rose, who could use it to block out the erratic exit sign that distracted her at night. She gently pulled it free, untangling its elastic band from the coils until it popped loose. Something small and pink fell from behind it and clattered to the floor.

"Rachelle is such a dressing room hog," Phyllis complained, moving a stack of her underwear to Gwen's old and now vacant drawer. "She's always encroaching on everyone's counter space, and it makes my cleanup duties more complicated, and then I get the blame. It's so low-budge of her. I'm going to put down masking tape to hem her in. Is that too passive-aggressive?"

"Who?" said Betty Rose, reaching with her foot toward the small pink piece of plastic, lodged between the frame and the wall.

"Gertie. Well, now she's Jane. She's always the bitch. That's her line. Spot-on casting. Diva attitude without the looks. She's really just a glorified journeyman. She'll never be a true star like Sutton."

"Oh, yes. Rachelle. Of course." Betty Rose toed the object, carefully pulled it out and away. "I like her." She picked up the tiny pink flamingo.

It was Gwen's computer flash drive. Where she kept her journal of her summer at the Gristmill, as brief as it turned out to be.

"Did you hear they booked Laura Osnes to play our Maria?" Phyllis said, behind her. "They recast her pilot, so she's available."

"Did they?" said Betty Rose, fingering the drive. "Is she?"

"Just for the one show, but still! She gets here Wednesday morning. I saw her in *Into the Woods*. Ahh-maazing. Thank God she's not wasting her talent on network TV. The Kristin Chenoweth curse, you know..."

Unlike Gwen's night mask, her flash drive had value and needed to be returned. Better yet, she could return them together, in the same envelope. With a little note of apology, and of congratulations, ending with the hope that they might continue their friendship, in the city, in the fall.

Fat chance, she knew. Those who'd made it to the next level never looked back at those left behind. It went against natural law.

Still, it was a nice gesture. She'd ask Dottie for the address. Gwen would surely be missing it by now. Especially if she cared enough to hide it under her mattress.

"Did you?" said Phyllis. "Did I what?" said Betty Rose. "Did you see Laura in *Cinderella*?" Phyllis said, adding, "Why are you staring at the bed?"

"Do you have Gwen's number?" Betty Rose asked.

Phyllis shook her head. "I'll Facebook her when I get back to the city. Why?"

Betty Rose slipped the pink flamingo into her overalls pocket and turned.

"I didn't see *Cinderella*. Was it good? Let's sweep up and go to bed."

The night mask blocked out the strobing, but Betty Rose still couldn't sleep. She was too excited about her Gristmill debut.

Scene Four

LAURA OSNES WAS A SWEET DELIGHT AND SINFULLY TALENTED. She arrived late Tuesday and started rehearsals for *West Side Story* on Wednesday. Offstage, she was surprisingly shy, almost shrinking, and usually retired after dinner to her guest cabin. She did stick around her first night to catch the opening performance of *Brigadoon* and toasted the cast backstage afterward. When not in rehearsal, she went off to explore New Hope on her own. She did not wear a Gristmill medallion.

"*Holding!*" Becky called over the intercom, aborting "places" moments before Betty Rose's first performance on Tuesday night. "*We're holding, everybody! Stand by.*" Apparently Strudel the monkey was loose in the aisles, titillating the audience while the Panama Man chased him down. "What a ham," said Phyllis. "What a simian stage hog."

Betty Rose's onstage debut was seamless and smooth. It had been years since she'd performed in the chorus, having graduated to lead roles her sophomore year at Northwestern, but the bar was so much higher here that it felt like a giant step forward. It was her first time on a professional stage, and she got every note and step right. She beamed and bowed at curtain call and shot a wink to Mr. Arbor in the tenth row, where he always sat.

On Wednesday morning at eight thirty, she started a fresh round of rehearsals for the next show.

"Half of you are flat on the high notes, and the other half are sharp," said Myron, the balding musical director, banging notes from the piano. They gathered around him in the mirrored rehearsal room off the kitchen. They held sheet music for "America," although most already knew the words and harmonies. "Come down on top of the note, not at an angle," he told them. "Right on top!"

"Diction!" he stressed, overlapping their singing. "Teeth! 'I want to live in A-mer-i-KAH!' You won't overdo it. Punch it!"

"Relax your jaw, B.R.," he called out as she sang. "Relax everything. Go down to hit the high notes, deeper in your gut. Don't use your jaw. Just let it hang."

"Oy vey," he muttered on her third attempt. "Bernstein is rolling in his grave, like a kayak." Betty Rose was relieved that Laura Osnes wasn't in this number to watch her struggle. She would have tensed up even more.

Rachelle was Anita this time, and she was simultaneously fiery and vulnerable. Impressive from day one. Always perfectly coiffed and made-up, even in the sweatiest rehearsal, she cut an arresting figure in her red leotard and dancer heels. She was a hot-blooded and salty vision of pro. And yet, as Phyllis had noted, she'd never reached the same starry heights that Sutton had. Betty Rose pondered the intangibles between star and journeyman and concluded that luck, or lack of, played a central role.

Baayork choreographed the number in front of the mirrors, the floor dotted with orange tape to mark the set. "Eat nails!" she shouted, flinging precision kicks and twirling with a gusto that would have exhausted a woman half her age. The girls, in character shoes and bias-cut dancer skirts of rayon, struggled to keep up. None of them could pass for 1950s Puerto Rican teens, but makeup, wigs, and a summery suspension of disbelief would fix that.

"Let's take it to the stage," she announced at noon. "Rex wants a peek before lunch."

"Oh God," said Phyllis, dripping sweat. "Don't stress," said Betty Rose. "We've got it down. I think."

They started the number from the top.

"It's a sultry, freestyle intro," coached Baayork from the house, swaying with them. "Just a slow-motion samba. Don't anticipate the cha-cha...."

Betty Rose, staged in the center of the girl pack, swirled her hips and arched her back to the slow rhythm. She ran her hand up her forehead and through her hair.

"It's broiling," said Baayork. "A summer night in Manhattan. You know what that's like. You're up on the roof to escape, to get some air. Feel the heat..."

"Are you getting this, Betty Rose?" Rex called from the back of the theater. The music stopped.

Betty Rose stood straight. "Yes, sir," she said. "I...think so. Am I doing something wrong?"

He emerged into the light, coming down the aisle with his clipboard. He looked concerned but not angry.

"You're doing great in *Brigadoon*," he said. "You've got virtuous and chaste down pat. You're very good at frigid." He smiled, and the cast laughed, and so did Betty Rose.

"Well, thank you," she said.

"But we're off to a different world now. It's steamy. You're restless. Pent-up. You're about to burst. You're *horny*. Do you get me?" The cast laughed again.

"Yes, sir," said Betty Rose. "I understand."

"No, I don't think you do. You see, we"—he indicated the room of empty seats—"we won't go there unless you take us there. Right now you're indicating. You're showing us what you think it's supposed to look like. You're trying to be *interesting.* But I want you to be *interested.* Remember: If you're thinking it, the audience knows it.

"And stop calling me 'sir,'" he added, sticking out his tongue to more laughter. "Some call me 'Daddy,' but I don't encourage that either." He glanced over at Dottie, who shrugged in defiance and mouthed the word in elaborate slow motion.

"See, it's a common fallacy, a trap really, for young actors. Or just bad ones," he continued. "This idea that musicals are fluff. Surface. They pose and mug and saw the air, like you're doing up there. Like a big fake and phony." Betty Rose flinched, as if spit on, and Rex waved it away. "It's not terminal," he said. "And it's not a capital crime. We won't put you to death for it. At least not on your first offense." He narrowed his eyes at her and said, "You can laugh at that, you know." And so she did.

"Musicals aren't the silly court jesters of the theatre or the redheaded stepchild," he went on, opening up his lecture to the whole stage. "A good musical cuts deep and twists the knife, with the euphoric highs and woeful lows of the most searing, gut-wrenching of dramas. The very best musicals bleed as much as any Shakespearian tragedy."

He turned back to Betty Rose. "Are you bleeding?" he asked her, and, she thought, already knowing the answer. She shook her head, and he said, "No, I didn't think so. And neither will your audience. You've got to bleed, Betty Rose." He paced.

"There's something…there's something amiss," he said, sizing her up, tapping his chin, hard in thought. He considered her for a moment and then shooed his hands out. The cast scattered to its semicircle.

"Not you, Betty Rose," Rex said. "Stage center, won't you?" It was a pleasant invitation.

She walked to the middle and faced him. She held a tight smile. Rex walked nearer to the orchestra pit, so she wouldn't have to shield the light to see him clearly.

"How does that feel?" he asked. "Do you belong there? In the spotlight?"

"I...think so," she said, and then off his skeptical look added, "Yes. I do."

"That's better," he said. "That's a good girl." He cocked his head as if hearing a voice, and then saw the lightbulb. He snapped his fingers. "That's it! That's our problem."

"See, I've noticed this in you from the first day," he went on, putting down his clipboard. "You're hiding something. You've wrapped yourself in a protective cocoon. That's fine in life, but it doesn't really work in acting.

"You have to let go of thinking. That's not what acting is all about," he went on. "Acting is raw. It's emotional. And yes, bloody..." He held her eyes for a moment.

"Let's break out of that cocoon, shall we? Right now? It won't take long."

Betty Rose nodded. She knew she was uptight. She'd done similar relaxation exercises before and was eager to try his. Nervous, but ready. They typically involved improvisations that were clownish and embarrassing but ultimately liberating. She was unafraid.

"I call it the 'good girl syndrome,'" he said with warmth. "Your parents meant well, of course. But it's hard for a father to train his own daughter. They don't let surgeons cut up their own children, do they?" Betty Rose laughed once, then stopped because Rex didn't.

"Daddy taught you to avoid sexuality...to stay chaste and virginal. A puritan," he said. "But we do things in our imaginary world that we would never do in real life. You can be a bad girl here. Very, very bad. Daddy will still love you. It's just pretend, you know."

Betty Rose nodded, because Rex was staring at her. Her bottom lip quivered.

Rex squinted at her. "What's this?" he asked. "Are you getting emotional?"

She shook her head and raised her chin. Strong.

"Oh my, there's the rub," Rex said. "*Daddy*. That's the sticking place." He inched closer, to the edge of the pit. "Your whole life, he's been your biggest fan, hasn't he? Your foundation?"

She felt her face contort. Fought it. "Yes...," she said, looking ahead toward the back of the house, avoiding his stare.

Rex inspected her. "But now...he's gone. Isn't he? Your biggest fan is gone. Isn't that right?" Betty Rose didn't respond, so he probed further. "He left you recently, didn't he? A sad, slow goodbye...wasn't it?"

Her eyes dropped to his. She blinked. "Six months ago," she said through a swallow.

Rex nodded in sympathy. "But you were there for him, Betty Rose," he said softly. "You put your dreams aside and stayed with him to the very end. Didn't you?"

"Absolutely. *Yes*."

"That's a good girl. He knows it. And he loves you so very much. Forever."

She heard her own abrupt sob and suppressed it. "I love him, too…," she said, cradled in his eyes, bolstered. No longer aware of the cast encircled behind her.

He cocked his head again, as if listening. "Oh…but Mommy. She's different, isn't she?" He frowned in solidarity with her. "Mommy wants your dreams to die with Daddy. She doesn't want you to win, does she?"

"No…," said Betty Rose.

"Mommy tears you down. Your foundation is crumbling. Isn't that terrible? What a monster. She doesn't mean to be, but she can't help it." He thought a moment and then decreed: "Mommy is a monster."

"Yes…," said Betty Rose, feeling a flash of fever.

"You have to cut her off, don't you? To follow your dreams, you have to cut off Mommy."

She trembled and nodded. "Yes."

"So make it official. Write her a letter. You don't have to send it, but just write it. Cast her out. You'll feel better. Trust me."

"Yes," she said. "I will."

"She's dead to you," Rex said, reddening. "Isn't she?"

"She is. She is…"

"That's right!" he said with growing wrath, his Santa face morphing into Zorba. "She's poison to you. To all of us. 'I can't have *my* dream, so you can't have *yours*!' Oh, she's vicious. What a fucking cunt!"

He widened his tirade toward the rest of the cast. A teachable moment. "We disconnect from those who cage us. Do you understand?" he asked, and Betty Rose and the group said, "Yes, Rex," in unison.

He calmed and focused on her again. "She'll come around again, after we make you into a star."

"Maybe," she said, through competing anger and sorrow.

"They always do. You'll show her, won't you, Betty Rose? You'll win. For you...and for Daddy...."

Her dam burst. "Yes!" she cried out, erupting through heaves. "*Yes!*"

Phyllis broke from the semicircle, rushed to her.

"Don't tamper, you stupid twat!" Rex roared, shaking the room. Phyllis, stung, retreated from his fury.

"I'm killing a bull here!" he raged on. "I've got it cornered in the ring, and I'm sticking the sword through its fucking shoulder blades, and I'm going straight for its fucking heart! Stay the fuck out of my way!" Phyllis cowered.

He settled again. "You're breaking out, Betty Rose. Make it happen. Let it happen...."

"How...do you..."—she struggled through hyperventilating sobs—"know all this?"

He smiled. "Contrary to rumor, I don't have special powers. But I've seen so many of you, for so long. Hundreds. Thousands. I know you better than you do, Betty Rose. Vulnerable inside, a warrior outside. That's what we want. That's what you've got. That's a star."

"Thank you, Rex," she said, submitting, empowered. "Thank you...."

"I didn't do anything. It's all inside you, busting out. You don't need me for anything." He climbed the stairs to the stage. "Now...how does that feel?"

She wiped her eyes and exhaled. She checked herself, wanting the honest answer. "It feels...liberating. Free."

"Isn't it, now?" he said, standing on the apron. "But more than free, isn't it? Reborn?"

"Yes. It's almost like that."

"A newborn. Naked. Like a baby."

"Sort of…," she said. "Yes."

"But you're not naked. Are you?"

Betty Rose laughed. "No. Of course not." She looked back at the cast surrounding her and laughed again.

"Then you're not finished, are you?" said Rex, smiling pleasantly. "You're not really like a baby…."

She stared at him. He stared back.

She forced a slight grin. "You…want me to…?"

"I want you to finish what we started," he said simply. He indicated her blouse.

Her grin dropped.

She'd performed *Fool for Love* in a flimsy, almost transparent slip for full houses over three weekends in college. She'd done countless quick changes right offstage in front of cast and crew alike. Theatre wasn't for the modest.

She unbuttoned her blouse. Untucked it from her skirt, unbuttoned more. She flung it open, sliding it down her body and arms, dropped it to the floor. She stood up straight.

Rex held his expression. Waiting.

"You're getting there," he said. "The others can join you, if you want."

Dottie threw her best Norma Desmond stare his way. "Oh, Rex," she begged. "Please. No."

He stayed locked on Betty Rose.

Betty Rose reached behind, fishing for the zipper to her skirt. Her fingers trembled, but they found it. The zipper stuck, she yanked it back on track and pulled it down to the end. The skirt, of its own weight, fell down her legs, to the stage. With careful balance, she stepped from it and kicked it aside.

Rex didn't budge.

She knew what he wanted. Her leg spasmed, and she lifted it until it calmed. She put her weight on it again.

She looked ahead, into the spotlight from the catwalk.

Betty Rose reached behind, high up her back, and searched for the bra clasp. Remembered it was in the front, in the center. She unhooked it, and it sprang open. She shrugged it off, and it fell to the floor.

Eyes forward, she tucked her thumbs under the elastic of her faded pink panties. Peeled them over her hips, down her thighs and calves. Stepped out of them and flicked them away.

Betty Rose stood tall and straight, in her character heels.

She felt Rex's gaze upon her.

"That's my good girl," he said. "My good, good girl. You want it, don't you? For Daddy…"

"Yes…," she said, still staring ahead. "…Daddy."

"More than anything in the world?"

"Yes, Daddy."

"Whatever it takes."

"Yes," she said. "*Yes.*"

"Say it, Betty Rose!"

"*More than anything!*" she shouted to the back of the theater, filling the room. "*Whatever it takes!*"

Rex exhaled.

"Welcome, Betty Rose," he said, nodding with a smile. "Welcome to the family. Welcome, Betty Rose." He opened his arms.

She heaved again, but with joy. She laughed through her sobs, and Dottie rushed to her with a terry-cloth robe and swaddled and embraced her. The company followed suit, closing in from all sides with hugs and caresses and kisses and more laughter and squeals of delight. Phyllis was beaming and teary, and Betty Rose greeted each dear friend, loving them back, twirling in circles to get them all. "Thank you," she said to Baub and Mimi; "Thank you" to Alistair and Sutton; and "Careful now," to Caleb, who shoulder-clapped her just a bit too roughly.

Rex backed away, retreated up the aisle. Betty Rose spun to him before he disappeared into the darkness.

"Thank you, Rex!" she cried out. Her hand shot up to the sky. "Thank you, Daddy!"

Scene Five

NOW SHE WAS PART OF THIS PLACE, if not as an official member, then at least as an accepted, valued, respected colleague. She belonged.

Her daily schedule was no less grueling than before, but she attacked it with a fresh confidence and familiarity and, most important, the newfound support of her fellow company members. She still woke at six to Dottie's jolting cowbell, but Dottie's crabbiness took on an endearing and quasi-comical quality that she herself seemed to milk. Betty Rose mastered scrambled eggs and bacon and biscuits, and even the groggiest company members couldn't resist her cheery greetings as she filled their plates in the mess hall line.

Although stuck on the lowly intern rung, she'd passed her trial by hazing, as had Phyllis a scant few weeks before. "Nope," said Phyllis when asked if she too had disrobed in front of the others. "But I would have. I'm very comfortable with nudity."

Betty Rose thought her own initiation, which she knew would seem bizarre and abusive to outsiders like Julian, was strangely beautiful and ultimately beneficial to her as an artist. It freed her imagination and bonded her with the cast and crew, to boot. She was still a rookie but, with Rex's new blessing, closer to their equal, and they treated her as such. Even the techies.

Perhaps most important, they let her eat. It took a while to adjust to real food again after so many days of the stinging oatmeal concoction. She started slowly and ate little, proud of her newly svelte figure and determined to maintain it. Her first meal of steak—just a few bites—flooded her with energy and sharpened her mind.

How Rex knew so much about her and her father's death from leukemia several months prior mystified her that first night after the euphoria and elation of her stage-center catharsis had dissipated somewhat and she lay in bed puzzling, too revved up to sleep. She hadn't mentioned his death to anyone at the playhouse—not to Phyllis or Gwen, or even the agent Wes who'd recommended her in the first place. It was such a personal sadness, a private family matter, and still too raw to talk about, especially to strangers. It was also, she knew, a bore and downer to anyone outside her inner circle and inappropriate in a professional setting. It was simply the hand she'd been dealt, and she honored her father's memory by enduring his passing with grace and dignity. Like he had.

But Rex, like a seer, had somehow known it all.

Then again, he hadn't mentioned death or illness at first. He'd only talked in broad terms of a "slow, sad goodbye," which could have meant anything that affected the relationship between parent and child: a divorce that shattered the household, or even just a personal falling-out. She remembered how her high school friend Emily had lost her father to alcohol— still alive, but certainly dead to her family. There were many varieties of slow goodbyes, all sad.

Rex had, by his own admission, seen hundreds—maybe thousands—of actors like Betty Rose over the decades, whose stories were likely similar if not identical. Surgeonlike, he'd gently probed until he uncovered her secret, her "resistance," he called it, and exposed it to sunlight, unblocking her. He'd correctly diagnosed her family dynamic, deciphering her responses to his questions like a highly tuned therapist. That's how he connected the dots and gleaned the secrets of her life that he couldn't possibly have known otherwise:

The loving and supportive father, encouraging his baby girl's most impossible and fairy-tale dreams; the pragmatic mother, demanding her only child chart a realistic life path closer to home. The father's insistence, as he neared the end of his life, that she live hers at full stretch. And then ultimately, the embittered widow, betrayed and abandoned, punishing her for doing just that.

That's why her mother scoffed at her theatre major, ignored her college stage triumphs, boycotted her graduation, and railed viciously against her moving to New York to pursue her acting career, demanding she take up teaching, or even law. And why she tried, at every turn, to sabotage her relationship with Julian—a terrible influence, she claimed, and untrustworthy, based on nothing but motherly prejudice.

Nonsense, thought Betty Rose. Julian's only sins, in her mother's eyes, were chasing his own theatre dream and taking Betty Rose along with him. Her mother's hostility burst open after her father's death a few months ago. It had unleashed a sad ugly that Betty Rose avoided and cut off, long before Rex suggested it. Would she accept her daughter again, like he predicted, after they made her a star? Acting was, Betty Rose realized, the only profession where the losers were pitied and ridiculed for even trying while the winners were worshipped with a near-mystical fervor. Doctors and bankers and truck drivers who fell short of their field's pinnacle were still afforded respect by the world; not so with actors. There was no "A" for effort.

At least she wasn't alone. All her actor friends faced similar family obstacles. Few parents wished for their child a life of instability and rejection; fewer still realized their advice, no matter how shrill, would be heard and ignored simultaneously. No wonder neither Phyllis nor Gwen told their families they were at the Gristmill either.

"B.R., just let them soak! We'll be late for dance call!" Phyllis jolted her at the kitchen sink where she scrubbed hash brown pans after breakfast. Betty Rose snapped to and ran after her.

She rehearsed every day with the ensemble, now that she was one of them. Mornings kicked off with Baayork, who even on the hottest days dressed *Flashdance*-chic with leg warmers and off-the-shoulder sweatshirts, leading the company in stretching and relaxation, followed by choreography of the next routine and production number, honed to precision in chorus lines across the mirrors. For *West Side Story*, she brought in a fight coordinator to teach stage combat to the Sharks and Jets. The boys were quick learners, the results real-looking and violent and impressive. Caleb startled with his intensity and gymnastics skills, the leader of the pack.

After a two-hour dance practice and an "Equity ten" break, the chorus would herd to Myron's piano, divided and grouped by vocal part until they knew their harmonies well enough to intermingle as they would onstage. He stressed accuracy and projection, since the Gristmill, as a point of pride, did not use stage mikes.

Baub, ever multitasking, would recruit the sopranos for preliminary costume fittings while the altos learned their part, working his way through the cast. Roger, the set designer, would steal anyone he could for painting and light carpentry in the scene shop, where Betty Rose found herself with a brush and stencil in between rehearsals. She became expert at sponge-painting walls to give the illusion of texture, earning the nickname "SpongeBob BossyPants" from the playful techies. Their acceptance was a watershed.

But Rex's daily sermons, right before lunch, were what she looked forward to the most. No longer outside the circle, she sat huddled with the others, knees to chest, waiting for him to emerge from the *Panic* and make his way across the knoll to his disciples under the elm. Often they would cheer and applaud his arrival, and, seemingly bemused, he'd shake his head and tamp down their ovation as he held court in the middle of the ring. He would start with specific notes and direction about whatever show they were working on that week. They were sharp and sometimes biting, and pity on those who got the same note twice. After, he would expand to pragmatic advice about the harsh realities of show business they were sure to face throughout their careers, based on his decades of experience.

"An actor must have the hide of a rhinoceros," he would remind them. "And the soul of a baby."

"The reason most actors fail to achieve their dreams is because they flinch," he'd tell them often. "They work hard—*for years*—do all the right things, and when their golden opportunity arrives, they drop the ball. It's intentional, even if they think it's subconscious. It's self-sabotage. You feel lowly, submissive, unworthy. Dear friends, please listen to me: When your big break comes—and it will, for all of you, I promise—do not flinch!"

"In this game, *un*blessed are the meek," he stressed on many occasions. "Sure, there's a little fate involved, a bit of a lottery, but luck is simply when opportunity meets preparation. It's a cliché because it's true."

"And Jiminy Cricket was full of shit!" he bellowed to the group's laughter. "When you wish upon a star, absolutely nothing happens!"

Rex would then toss his clipboard to the grass, and Betty Rose and the others would lean in. He would always end his sessions on a loftier note, spurring them to their best selves and rousing in them a zeal to elevate the audience, and the world, with their dedication and passion.

"Strive to be an artist," Rex urged. "Not just an artisan."

"You're not in Kansas anymore," he told them. "You're not the little boy or girl in Oregon or Nevada or Indiana. You're not your mother or father, your aunts or uncles, with their petty limitations, hang-ups, and rules. Forget about them. Leave them behind. They no longer exist for you. You're out in the world now, on your own. You've got to forge your own way, kids. Whatever it takes."

"Steer clear of *tsuris*!" he admonished, scouring his charges. "You know *tsuris*? Trouble, woe, aggravation. It's a distraction, a subtle and malicious form of self-sabotage. It usually comes from your family, an evil seed they plant to hold you back. You know what the Greeks say about that? 'Fuck it!'" He paused for their laugh and then added, "It's your mind playing tricks, to keep you from your full potential. Hear me out: All drama must be left on the stage!" And they all laughed again, since they knew what he meant and loved him more for saying it.

"Dare to accept there's genius inside you," he demanded. "That you're worthy of the world's adulation. Explore, probe, and maximize the joy of this beautiful journey. Are you guys hearing me? Really getting it?"

"Artists like you built the pyramids, the Taj Mahal, Versailles," he insisted on another day. "They painted the Sistine Chapel, the *Mona Lisa, Guernica.* They wrote *Hamlet* and *La Bohème* and, yes, *The Sound of Music.* They lived short lives, mostly shorter than ours, but they pushed aside their puny fears, blew past the naysayers, and left their mark on the world, forever. They weren't dilettantes. They were warriors!"

"A warrior races into battle," he said at the crescendo of one of his most riveting lessons. "A warrior never flinches. A warrior knows that thinking leads to doubt and fear and losing and death. A warrior perseveres toward something grander, more important than himself."

"A warrior," he punctuated, "kills what must be killed, so that something more noble and vital and enduring can blossom in its place."

The lessons concluded with the inspired students, on cue, springing up to sing the Gristmill's anthem, linked and in harmony, fueled with fodder for their eager chats over lunch. The excitement carried and thrust them through their afternoon stumble-throughs and evening performances to overflowing crowds.

The weeks tore by, as *West Side Story* begat *Gypsy,* which led to *Guys and Dolls,* rehearsals and shows and load-ins and strikes and closing-night parties blurring together in a continuous propulsion through the summer of sold-out houses and standing ovations. After each show, the band would play the exhilarated audience out the door with a spirited rendition of "When the Saints Go Marching In" while the charged-up cast launched their own dance party behind the curtain.

Most rewarding for Betty Rose was, for the first time, feeling like a pro, surrounded by pros. The shows ran like clockwork, with a precision and control that started at Becky's half hour and soldiered on through curtain call and eventual placement of the ghost list at night's end. There was a zeal and commitment, but it was focused and non-giddy. It was a *job*.

Even eccentric oddballs like Dottie and Alistair impressed each time they snapped into character and took the stage with surprising versatility and command. Cocky jackass Caleb had a brighter career ahead than she'd initially thought, so nimble and charismatic he was; the audience couldn't take its eyes off him. Rachelle the tigress practically demanded the crowd's attention and got it, expert at wringing dry her supporting roles and stealing nearly all her scenes. And no one could top Sutton when she unleashed the "eleven o'clock number"—the act two, cathartic showstopper that set up most musicals for the big finale finish. Betty Rose admired her from the wings whenever possible. Sutton, so sweet and vulnerable, was explosive and fearless under the lights. Betty Rose was proud to be among them all, to count them as teammates and friends.

"They booked Andrea McArdle for *Mame!*" said Phyllis, jolting her with a near squeal during KP duties one night. "She was the original Annie, even before Sarah Jessica Parker. I wore that album out!"

Betty Rose thrilled at her photo added to the ensemble in the playbill, at her headshot posted on the marquee sign with the others. She scarcely contained her own squeal when Phyllis showed her the *New Hope Gazette* with both their photos under the headline: "Rising Stars at the Gristmill."

Rex, who was demanding and occasionally brusque during rehearsals, regressed into a child every opening night. Before curtain, he would pop into each dressing room, in his "showtime" uniform of navy double-breasted blazer, striped shirt, and tweed driving cap, and urge the cast to play. "Get in the sandbox! Kick up some sand! Open the gates and let the beagles run!" he'd spur them. "It's all just a game. A game of pretend." He monitored their attitudes and would adjust any moodiness or other bad energy. "Check your worries and squabbles with your outside clothing," he often said. "Never track mud into the theater."

The interns still had extra duties, from postshow cleanup to dresser's assistant for quick changes. Betty Rose marveled how, in spite of established theatre protocol against street jewelry onstage, the Gristmill members wore their round medallions and insignia rings in every performance, like badges of honor. Her college theatre professor would have howled at the inauthenticity of gold jewelry on Oklahoma ranch hands and Scottish shepherds, but their member pride trumped purity, and they flashed and glimmered and sparkled no matter the time and place.

After nightly performances, they mingled with the audience in the lobby and outside under the canopy of rope lights, where they watched the Fourth of July fireworks over the Delaware. On their days off, Betty Rose and Phyllis swept through town like celebrities, greeting locals and accepting praise. They would split sugary goodies from the Pudge Cakes Bakery and flirt with the bohemian deadbeat boys whom Phyllis called "dirty and sexy...

perfect for summer." They rode the Disney-esque Ivyland Railroad on its loop around New Hope and were invited to blast the steam whistle in the conductor's booth. One Sunday, before the *Damn Yankees* matinee, they even joined the fabulous gay pride parade in costume, right behind the Dykes in Bikes motorcycle procession. They perched in the Big Banana Car as it cruised down Carla Avenue surrounded by scantily clad hunks, leather-harnessed "bears," and sequined and busty drag queens. "A girl cannot have enough gays in her life," Phyllis decreed, waving and scattering playhouse flyers at the startled tourists like Evita.

On rare afternoon breaks, the company would skinny-dip in the swimming hole just off the rapids, underneath the Journeyman Bridge. Innocent and shameless, boys and girls would sun naked on the house-sized boulders, and Caleb led the most brazen daredevils, jumping *au natural* from the bridge to cannonball into the water far below. Betty Rose averted her gaze and dipped her feet but stayed dressed, having filled her quota for nudity, she felt, for the time being. "Come on, B.R.!" a bare-ass Phyllis urged, proving she had no hang-ups as she bobbed and splashed about with the others. "They locked the gate to the bridge. Outsiders won't see you!" Betty Rose begged off anyway. "Next time," she promised, kicking back Caleb as he threatened to pull her in.

No, No, Nanette bled into *Annie Get Your Gun,* and local children joined the cast of *The King and I.* They were rowdy in rehearsals and fooled no one as Siamese heirs, but they delighted the audience, the company, and themselves each time they formed their living hoop skirt and swirled around Sutton during "Getting to Know You."

Betty Rose, in between greeting the *King and I* audience and racing to change for Friday's midnight *Rocky Horror Show,* paused in the lobby at the season board. They were more than halfway through, well on their way to the final show. The summer would soon be over, which was depressing on its own. She never wanted to leave her loving Isle of Misfits. But it gnawed at her that neither she nor Phyllis were any closer to their Equity card. She faced the disquieting prospect of returning to New York empty-handed for fall casting season. More experienced and enriched with memories, but unemployable nonetheless. And nothing to write home about, literally.

There were five shows left, her final opportunities to take the stage as her own character, with a name and lines in the script and a song. Her best bet, she knew, was the season's closer, *Godspell*, with its loosely structured parables and myriad minor characters, any one of which would score her a card.

But *Godspell* was now gone from the board, replaced with a hand-painted sign that read, "Special Performance! Invitation Only." It was yellowed and chipped, as if packed away and trotted out for rare occasions.

It stumped Phyllis, too. "Maybe they couldn't find the right John the Baptist," she said, morphing into a freakish, whore-like Transylvanian in their dressing room before *Rocky Horror.* "Anybody can play Jesus, of course; you just have to be serious and odd. But John the Baptist needs to be soulful and relatable. Jonathan Groff is my dream choice, for anything, really. If wishes were kisses…"

Dottie didn't like the question. "How 'bout you mind your own business?" she snapped the next morning in the kitchen. "Must we submit our repertoire for your approval? Good God, these newbies…"

Rex surprised the interns during that week's rehearsals for *The Pajama Game.* He rarely paid much attention to the chorus, except for initial staging and minor adjustments, but he stopped Rachelle in the middle of "Hernando's Hideaway" and suggested a change. A "bit of business," he called it. Betty Rose and Phyllis, both factory girls at the Sleep-Tite Pajama Factory, would be made-up as lookalikes, to the increasing confusion of the other characters throughout the show, culminating with their dancing together in the finale. This didn't strike Betty Rose as particularly funny, just a visual sight gag, and it didn't qualify as a solo, but she and Phyllis attacked it with gusto.

"I think it's genius, Rex," said Dottie. "*Pajama Game* is so quirky anyway. It fits."

Baub costumed them identically in dress, belt, and shoes, with matching wigs and hats. As an afterthought, he gave them beauty marks on opposing cheeks. Baayork tweaked the choreography to keep them far apart in the group numbers.

The opening-night audience loved it. It took them halfway through act one to notice, until Rachelle's first double take before "Her Is," which she milked. From there on, the gag grew and blossomed on a parallel track from the rest of the story. Betty Rose and Phyllis hammed it up, seemingly unaware of the other, until the "Hernando's Hideaway" reprise at the end. They sized each other up—with a protracted triple take—clasped hands, and launched into their own passionate tango, cheek-to-matching-cheek. The audience howled and cheered through the finale, and the stage manager whipped up the frenzy with a surprise double curtain drop timed with clashing cymbals, which brought the crowd to its feet. Strudel the monkey hopped on top of the Panama Man's hat and, mimicking the others, clapped and shrieked out his approval.

Betty Rose and Phyllis bathed in the sustained ovation during curtain call, where they stepped out from the lineup and took a special bow together, the "rising stars of the Gristmill." There were hoots and whistles from the house, and they giggled at each other, overwhelmed by the jubilant response, and Betty Rose beamed and blushed and held the loving room as long as she could, until the curtain slowly, reluctantly, came down for good.

Chapter Six

"*COMPANY MEETING ONSTAGE*," Becky announced through the loud-speaker, and Dottie bellowed, "Company meeting onstage!" not needing one. "La-di-da-di-everybody!"

Betty Rose and Phyllis were in their dressing room on the seventh floor of the silo tower, still giddy from their opening-night triumph. Theirs was the highest and farthest from the stage, but tonight's trek up the stairs was a celebratory gauntlet of hugs and high-fives and bravos.

"I swear I thought it'd fall flat," said Phyllis, swabbing cold cream on her pancake makeup. "But Dottie was right: It works. Rex is sorta brilliant, you know?"

Betty Rose agreed. "And generous," she added, freeing her hair from the wig cap and shaking it out. "To showcase us like that, I mean. So sly. He knows his audience."

He certainly knew the locals, who made up the majority of the opening-night audience. Mrs. Ellsworth's hearing aid alerted the cast to her presence in the quieter moments, and Betty Rose glanced out to see familiar faces, looking up and then down, scribbling on comment cards. She'd never noticed this before, but her role as factory girl afforded her more stage time to survey the audience, subtly, from her fake sewing machine. It was a sea of scribbling, right from the start.

Only Mr. Arbor, in his usual spot, stayed focused on the show. He didn't smile, or laugh, or join the standing ovation at curtain call. She couldn't tell if he applauded or not. Clearly, he wasn't impressed by the production, or by her, or just wasn't in the mood for the show's quirkiness. He seemed to be there out of duty, to make use of his season ticket. He looked bleary.

"And no offense to Sutton or Rachelle, but the show needs our extra kick," said Phyllis, straightening her pink dress with white trim. "I think we nailed the right tone. I mean, it's just *shtick*, as the Yiddish say." She handed Betty Rose a similar-looking dress from the rack.

There was a rap on the door. Caleb poked in.

"Downstairs, ladies!" he said. "Rex wants us all."

"Am-scray!" hollered Phyllis. "We're getting ready."

He waited outside while Betty Rose threw on the dress and Phyllis zipped her up. They did final touch-ups in the mirror, and Phyllis flung the door open with dramatic flair. "I hope this meeting doesn't take long," she announced with a plummy, British accent. "Our *public* awaits!" Caleb bowed and offered his hand. Laughing, Betty Rose followed behind.

"Hey, let's take the slide!" he said, pushing open the fire escape door on the narrow landing. "C'mon! It's the maximum drop from up here." Right inside was a metal corkscrew slide, twisting downward.

"'Tis verboten," trilled Phyllis. "For emergencies only."

"Suit yourself!" he said, jumping through the door.

Betty Rose watched him spiral into darkness. She then peeked down through the landing window as he popped out at the bottom, onto the grass. It looked fun. "Should we?" she asked Phyllis, who replied, "And ruffle our gowns? Puh-lease.

Stars do not take the slide." She descended the stairs slowly, waving at imaginary throngs.

The company applauded their entrance onstage, and the girls curtsied, until Rex arrived and got down to business.

"Apparently there has been some confusion about the change in our lineup," he said from the stage apron, dressed in his opening-night uniform. "While we typically end our season with the spiritually uplifting *Godspell*—one of my favorites—this year is different." Towering behind and over him was the giant Carla on the fire curtain, surrounded by her worshippers scattered through the village. It was, Betty Rose decided, a remarkable work of art, clearly crafted with love, in spite of its oddness. It sparkled in the stage lights and framed Rex theatrically.

"As is our custom whenever one of our legends passes on," he went on, "we're calling our Gristmill family back home."

He looked out over his followers and tipped his head at Sutton.

"You remember, don't you?" he asked with a smile, and Sutton beamed and nodded back, pulling her knees to her chin, little-girl-style. Rachelle leaned forward, at attention, grabbing the seat in front of her. She flashed her own excitement, and Rex acknowledged her with a deliberate, knowing nod.

"Replacing our season ender with an A-list reunion," he continued. "Stars, producers, agents, friends—a Gristmill Homecoming to bid farewell to our dear Marian. And a fresh start to revive and rejuvenate our beloved playhouse. Look how excited Sutton and Rachelle are." He winked, and the company laughed. "For most of you, it'll be a wondrous first you are unlikely to forget." Sutton cackled, and Rachelle joined in, relishing their shared history.

He drank in the company members. "We'll whip up a very special show, just for our extended family," he said. "And who knows? Perhaps it's the perfect opportunity to introduce some new talent?" He glanced down at Betty Rose and Phyllis and then shrugged.

"We shall see," he said, making his way toward the wings. "We shall see."

● ● ●

Betty Rose tried to keep the lid on Phyllis.

"Calm down," she said. "He said 'perhaps.' And only one of us can get our union card anyway."

They stood on the edge of the lobby, by the bathrooms, watching the show's stars greet the opening-night audience, signing playbills, and posing for photographs.

"Who cares about a stupid union card?" said Phyllis. "This is so much bigger, B.R. We're talking New York agents, producers, all the bigwigs together, at once. Right before the fall casting season. You can't buy that kind of opportunity."

Betty Rose knew she was right. She just didn't like to think about it. It seized her stomach. Resistance, like Rex warned about. Self-sabotage. The artist's worst enemy.

There was a yank on her pink dress. She turned to an adorable blond boy in little blazer, shorts, and knee socks, holding a program and a pen.

"Can I have your autograph, Betty Rose?" he asked, grinning up from a wide, freckled face.

"Mine?" she said, charmed and flustered. "I'm just...chorus."

He held up his pen and program. "I'm Phillip," he said, and she gently took it from him and said, "Why, thank you, Phillip. What a sweet little boy." She felt a blush and a thrill. She opened the program to the title page, pristine and full of white space. She thought for a moment and then wrote his name, a simple greeting, and with unpracticed flair, signed her name. Her first autograph.

"My mommy says you're the real deal," said Phillip, and before she could respond, he ran off, newly shy. Betty Rose turned to Phyllis and said, "I never wanted children until just now," and they both laughed.

More autograph seekers gathered, full-grown adults. A mid-forties local woman who ran a custom lamp shop on Mechanic, a freshly retired couple visiting from Alberta, and suntanned honeymooners roughly her age, from Kissimmee. They were eager and twinkly, almost apologetic for bothering her. They were starstruck. She was overwhelmed, hosting her new fans.

"Wow, all the way from San Francisco!" she said to an older dandy, spiffed up in silk summer tweeds with a cornflower in his lapel. He was with a strapping buck young enough to be his son but clearly not.

"We just love New Hope," said the jovial gent in white saddle oxfords and whale-embroidered pastel salmon khakis, while the much younger man looked down and around. "I come every year."

"What's not to love?" Betty Rose said, laughing with him. "So nice to meet you, Clancy. Thanks for coming." She signed his program and handed it back.

"And I can say I knew you when," he added with a final wink. "I feel lucky."

"That kid's not gonna be lucky later tonight," jabbed Caleb after the mismatched couple wandered out. "I wonder what he charges that old queen." Betty Rose punched him in the shoulder and said, "Watch it, buster. Those are my fans." "And you're their fag-hag," he answered, earning another punch.

Over by the box office, Dottie unlocked the wooden comment box, choked and overflowing with cards the opening-night crowd had stuffed into it. She eyeballed a few, agreeing, disagreeing, and then organized them into a thick, tidy stack, which she ferreted away. Young Phillip raced to catch up with her, holding out his own card. She smiled and took it and tousled his hair, waving a special thanks to his mother just outside.

Mr. Arbor waited until the lobby had cleared out to congratulate Betty Rose.

"I see they're grooming you for bigger things," he said, without smiling. She hugged him and said, "I'm so glad you came tonight, Mr. Arbor." She introduced him to Phyllis and Caleb.

He pointed to the board by the box office. "And a special show in a few weeks."

"Yes, it's a Homecoming show," she said, and Mr. Arbor nodded and said, "I've seen many."

He looked around, glanced at Caleb and Phyllis, then back at her. "I was hoping you'd be back to see me," he said. "To use the phone. Or just to chat."

"I'm so sorry," she said. "I've been meaning to; it's just been so busy here." She laughed and said, "They keep me locked up!"

Mr. Arbor nodded again. He seemed more subdued than usual. It was late.

"There's more to that little tale, you know," he said. "I think you'd find it interesting."

"I know I would," said Betty Rose. "Especially if it's anything like the first part!"

"I think you should hear it," he added.

"We'd love to, sir!" Caleb piped in, clapping his arm around Betty Rose's shoulder. "I hear you're quite the yarn weaver."

Mr. Arbor ignored him and said, "Soon, won't you?" He walked toward the exit and turned back and said, "Good night, Betty Rose. Soon, yes?" Betty Rose said, "Tomorrow on my lunch break. I promise." He went out on the porch and into the night.

"What the hell was that all about?" asked Phyllis, and Caleb said, "Yeah, what the fuck? You got a granddaddy complex or something?"

"He's just lonely," Betty Rose said, looking after him. "And sweet. I think it's so cool he's been coming all these years. By himself. In a way, we're the only family he's got."

She turned to Caleb. "'Yarn weaver'? Seriously?" she said. "Were you raised in a barn, too?"

He grinned at her. "If you're a wiseass bitch, I won't tell you what your new fans are saying about you. I heard it all." Phyllis said, "Tell us!" and Betty Rose dismissed it with, "Get outta here." And then she said, "Seriously? What did they say?"

Caleb shook his head. "Nope," he taunted. "You blew it." Betty Rose swatted him, and he said, "I gotta run to get notes from Rex, but if you decide to come correct, meet me on the bridge in ten."

"On the bridge. In ten," Phyllis purred after he left. She jimmied her eyebrows and said, "Methinks it's your turn, B.R."

"Don't be an idiot," Betty Rose said with a huff. "He's an imbecile."

Scene Seven

THEY MET ON THE BRIDGE, but she made him wait.

Caleb's reports of her growing stardom were hard to believe, yet he had no reason to make them up. "Sizzle," he called it. From the streets of New Hope, to the aisles at the pharmacy, even at the counter at Fred's Breakfast Club Diner, he swore the locals were talking about her.

"Tonight sealed the deal," he said. "Everybody was buzzing after the show."

Betty Rose fought her excitement. "Why?" she asked, demure. "I've only done a few shows. In the chorus. In the back."

"Stars stand out," Caleb said, shrugging. "They leap to the front, no matter where they are. Tons of stars got discovered from the chorus. The biggest ones. Shirley MacLaine blew up from *Pajama Game*, too."

"Rex calls it 'the motor,'" he went on. "You have it or you don't. You can't fake it. Or hide it."

"I don't think I have the motor," said Betty Rose, and Caleb said, "It's not up to you. It's up to the audience. Rex talks about it all the time."

She turned to him. "Did Rex say something about me, too?"

"Who? Rex who?" Caleb pivoted back to peer out over the rushing cascades, ignoring her. She pushed his arm. "Hey!" she said.

He smirked. "I don't want you to get a big head or anything. But everybody means *everybody*, B.R. You've already leaped to the front."

She took a breath, joined him at the railing, in between the flower beds. Gazed out over the rapids, the stars, the moving galaxy of fireflies. The air was warm and blanketing and jasmine-edged. She felt dewy, absorbing it all.

"Rex is right," she said, exhaling. "You get beaten down so much, for so long, you think that's where you belong. Like a subspecies. A rodent racing to slip through the door before it slams for good."

Down below and beyond, the crickets and frogs sang in separate rhythms. The amber moon was low but not quite full.

"But that crystal moment—when you're up there, and you've worked so hard to get there, and at first you're terrified, and then the love from the audience lifts you up, and you grab it and zing it back to show them you love them, too, and you're all in it together—it's as close to magic as any moment could be. In that instant, there's no place safer. No place on the planet."

The Rum House seemed a world away. And a different life, not hers.

"It's like the flip of a switch, isn't it?" she said. "It can happen so quickly. Like that."

She turned her head to brush away a tear and decided to let it stay. "It's my favorite summer, Caleb," she said.

"It's not over yet, you know," he said. "It can still get better."

She turned, and he was close, too close. She felt his breath on her chin. He gently caught her tear and perched it on his finger. He leaned in.

"No, I don't think I can take any better," she said with a laugh, backing off. She pivoted to the other side of the bridge and, relieved at the distraction, said, "Clyde! What you got there?"

The goat, doglike, had dug a hole in the flower bed and unearthed a prize with its mouth.

"Hey! Get away from Janet!" Caleb yelled, lunging at the animal. It made a high-pitched bleat, dropped its booty, and scampered back toward the playhouse, protesting in its retreat.

"Janet?" said Betty Rose.

Caleb nodded and pointed at the other rosebushes of different colors, size, and age. "And Lydia and Stacy and…Jessica, I think? I forget all the rest. The journeymen. We plant a flower in memory of each. I mean, the playhouse has, from the beginning. It's a ritual."

Betty Rose looked at the long rows along the bridge; she'd come to take them for granted. Too many roses to count. "Who were they?" she asked.

"The Gristmill actors who never became stars. The workhorses. Without the journeymen propping them up, there wouldn't *be* any stars. Rex says they're our most important members. So we immortalize them here. Forever."

"Does everyone get one?"

Caleb shook his head. "Rex says only those who gave it their all. No half-assed dilettantes on the Journeyman Bridge. It's a big honor. I've never seen them add one in my three summers here."

He refilled the hole from Clyde's excavation and smoothed over the soil. Betty Rose knelt next to him, by a small, weak rose sapling, its color hard to distinguish in the goldish moonlight. It was stooped and wilted. "This looks like a brand-new one," she said, remembering from her mother's rose garden the shocked look of fresh transplants, and Caleb said, "They replace them if they get sick or die. 'Perpetual care,' they call it. Clyde's usually to blame."

"That's really beautiful," she said. She indicated the lavender "Janet" rose he was tending to. "Sutton's always looking after that one." And Caleb nodded and said, "They started here as interns together." He stood up, dusting dirt off his hands.

"Together?" Betty Rose asked. "But that would make her…I mean, how did she die?"

Caleb peeled off his T-shirt in one smooth motion. He was glistening underneath.

"It's fucking hot," he said, "Perfect night for skinny-dipping."

"Ha, no, thank you," she said, avoiding his look. "I'm fine."

"C'mon, they've locked the gate for the night. It's another Gristmill rite of passage!" He kicked off his sneakers and unbuttoned his jeans. "The ol' swimmin' hole!"

Where he'd no doubt "initiated" Gwen. She refused to make the same mistake.

He kicked off his jeans and yanked off his socks, tossing them aside. He stood tall like a gold medalist in his briefs.

Betty Rose turned away. "I have a boyfriend, Caleb."

"So? It's just swimming," he said. "It's not like we haven't seen each other naked before." She heard him lose the briefs. And felt him watching her.

"Suit yourself," he said, and she glanced back to see his naked dive into the dark water below. His form was perfect, slicing through with barely a splash.

She called his bluff, refusing to be the Sandra Dee of the summer. But she walked down to the water's edge and made him face the other way while she undressed and waded in. While not a prude, she was neither a stripper nor an exhibitionist.

The water was cool and clean, like the lake at her childhood church camp. She sank down to her shoulders and treaded with ease, side-stroking toward the rapids as she passed Caleb. He dove under, dolphinlike, and sprang up spouting water, which she swatted away from her hair.

He disappeared again, and Betty Rose spun in her spot, trying to locate him. Just when she started to get antsy, she felt a grasp on her ankle and a gentle yank, submerging her for an instant. She popped back up, now fully soaked, and he resurfaced inches away, grin-first.

She splashed him off and retreated toward the rock outcrop. He followed, pinned her against it, daring her to hop out and expose herself. She laughed, his naked body floating up against hers. It was indecent.

He braced his hands on either side, trapping her, and moved his face closer. She stared into, and then away from, his liquid eyes.

"That's enough, Caleb," she said, pivoting to pry his hand off the rock, so she could swim an escape. His finger glistened with the Gristmill ring. She held it up and scrutinized it, mesmerized. It was such a beautiful piece of artistry.

Caleb dipped in and tenderly locked lips. She kissed back and then pulled away, hypnotized by his mouth, and sadly shook her head. "No," she said.

He relented, bobbing up to grin down at her. "I hope your boyfriend knows how lucky he is," he said.

"We're *both* lucky," she said, her face level with his chest. She tapped her fingertips against it, wishing him away.

"Caleb!" Alistair called from the water's edge. "When you're done molesting that poor girl, Rex would like to see you."

Caleb laughed and said, "Got it!" and Alistair said, "Now, please." "Okay!" Caleb whined. "I'm coming! I'm coming!"

"TMI, Caleb," said Alistair, who dropped folded towels on the ground and then turned and trudged wearily back up the bank toward the playhouse.

"Damn!" said Caleb. "This was supposed to cool me off!" And Betty Rose smiled and glided from his reach and said, "You'd better hurry. Mustn't keep the master waiting."

She swam to shore but shielded her gaze as Caleb scampered to retrieve his clothes on the bridge. He clumped them over his privates and ran up the bank, waiting for her to sneak a peek before flashing her in one quick, cackling motion. Mock horrified, she giggled and shrieked and waved him away.

Once he disappeared inside, she waded out and toed her way up to the towel.

●　●　●

Phyllis upbraided her.

"Are you nuts?" she said when Betty Rose returned to their dorm. "You give me a crack at that bat, and I'd never strike out!"

Freshly showered, Betty Rose positioned her pink dress on a hanger. "We were just swimming!" she said. "God, is there no privacy in this place?"

"Oh, relax. Nothing wrong with a summer fling. As Rex says: What happens at the Gristmill stays at the Gristmill."

Betty Rose opened the closet door. "I've never heard Rex say half the things you claim he has...." She stopped.

Hanging side by side from the bar were two aged red sequined dresses. Faded, tattered, and worn.

Betty Rose took one out. "What are these?" she asked.

"Costumes for the Homecoming show," said Phyllis, sitting Indian-style on her bunk. "Antiques. Dottie wants us to mend them. Aren't they groovy?"

Betty Rose put it back and took out its twin. It was ratty and wrinkled and grand all at once. She twirled it on its hanger.

It was ripped down the back, from just below the neck to halfway to its sashed waist.

"What happened here?" she asked Phyllis, who was tucking in.

"Dottie said it's been in storage for years," said Phyllis with a yawn. "Moths, probably. Or a quick change rip, you know. Easy fix..."

The rip was off the seam, straight through the fabric. Not an easy fix at all. Her mother had taught her mending as a young girl, but she'd lost her skills. She hoped they could hide it from the stage.

Guilt kept her awake, and her night mask was useless. She'd never cheated on Julian before—and hadn't tonight—but he wouldn't see it that way. Nor would she, if the tables were turned. She wondered if he'd hear it in her voice the next time they spoke.

But hear what? There was nothing to confess. And if she couldn't act innocent enough to keep him from suspecting, then she had certainly chosen the wrong career. She settled down.

A clunking noise interrupted her dozing. Someone running the gristmill off the kitchen. It complained and stalled and then crushed and spat. Betty Rose turned and covered her head with the pillow. Did they have to use it at this late hour?

Phyllis was right about her non-dalliance with Caleb. Harmless flirtation, she knew. Summer silliness.

But it couldn't happen again. No more late-night swims, or quick, loaded glances in rehearsal. No hint of a shared secret or special bond between them. And no sighs or gazes. People would suspect things.

People would say they were in love.

Scene Eight

BETTY ROSE TRIED THE KNOB AGAIN, then knocked and waited. She cupped her hands on the window and peered inside.

The Boathouse Tavern was empty. She squinted at the cuckoo clock on the far side of the bar. Mr. Arbor was probably on his lunch break, just as she was, after her first morning of rehearsals for *Me and My Girl*.

If she remembered correctly, this was roughly the same time she'd first bumped into him, outside the pharmacy on Carla Avenue, when he was picking up a prescription. Perhaps he ran errands this time each day. She hoped he'd return soon. She had to be back at one.

And she needed to do a drugstore run herself to get a black Sharpie for autographs. The ballpoint pen she'd used last night was inadequate for glossy playbills. Every pro needed a Sharpie on hand. She still had most of the twenty Dottie had lent her from the box office several weeks ago, since Phyllis usually sprang for the sweets at the Blue Penguin and Pudge Cakes.

She'd likely pass Mr. Arbor on the way, unless he hadn't gone to the pharmacy or Carla Avenue at all. He could be anywhere, even at the foodie restaurant across the alley, although that seemed too tony for his taste.

She peered in again, through a different window above a low hedge. The cash register was covered with its brown plastic protector, the bottles locked away in their cabinets below the bar. Maybe he didn't open until later in the day. But she'd promised to come on her lunch break, and he hadn't objected. In fact, it was his idea. He'd been surprisingly insistent about it.

She sat down on the front steps, out of the sun, and practiced the mouth positions Myron had taught them for the new show's cockney accent. She could do an upper-class British dialect with ease, having studied that in college when performing Shaw and Coward. But this was Eliza Doolittle in reverse.

She'd slept fitfully and woke tired and had iced down her eyes in the kitchen to jolt her awake, not to pop them open bright and clear for Caleb when he passed through the cafeteria line, which she still manned. Even Sutton and Rachelle wore full makeup to rehearsals, out of respect for the process, and they were certainly worthy role models to emulate. She was copying the pros, nothing more.

Fortunately, Baayork had paired her with a different dance partner for "Lambeth Walk." Caleb twirled the ginger from Cleveland, who, while perfectly pleasant and attractive, was hardly competition. If such thing even mattered.

"May I help you?" called a woman's voice.

Betty Rose looked up to a tall, smiling lady in a straw hat and gardening apron. She wore an open-collared white shirt and work gloves and carried a spade. She was tending a row of young roses in black vendor pots across the wide alley, by the side door of the florist and nursery.

"Thank you," said Betty Rose, smiling back. "But I'm just waiting for Mr. Arbor." She thumbed back toward the Boathouse door and shrugged. "He's meeting me here."

The woman tilted her head slightly. "Mr. Arbor passed away," she said.

Betty Rose shook her head. "You must be mistaken."

"I wish I were," said the woman, touching her chest. "I'm so sorry to be the one to tell you."

Betty Rose stood up. "No, I just saw him last night. At the playhouse. At my show."

"Yes, he was quite excited about that. I saw him right before."

Betty Rose went down the steps to the gravel alley. "How?" she asked. "When?"

"Peacefully, thank goodness," the woman said, splaying her fingers across her neck, a sympathetic gesture. "In his sleep. Early this morning, I believe."

"That's really not possible," Betty Rose insisted.

"At that age, anything is possible."

"He was perfectly healthy last night!" Betty Rose said, too loudly. Her voice bounced off the buildings.

"And you entertained him," the woman said, as if an honor. "That's a beautiful gift, Betty Rose."

Betty Rose started. "How...do you know my name?"

The woman fingered the gold medallion around her neck. It glinted in the sunlight.

"We're all so glad you're here," she said, and then turned back to the potted roses for sale outside her shop.

● ● ●

The woman was an oddball and gossip and didn't know what she was talking about. It was vicious, really, to spread such rumors.

Betty Rose waited for Mr. Arbor as long as she could—at the end of the alley, away from the creepy woman—but eventually gave up on him. Her lunch break was almost over, and she still had to get her Sharpie.

She was tempted to ask the pharmacist if he'd heard about Mr. Arbor or seen him that day. He'd surely have answers, if there were answers to be had, but the pharmacy line was long with old, slow customers, and she didn't want to cause unnecessary alarm. She'd ask someone in town and even get Mr. Arbor's address so she could check on him during her dinner break and before the evening's performance. He couldn't live far. Then she remembered she was on pearl-diving duty after that night's dinner. Unless she begged one of the others to sub for her, but even then she wouldn't have time. She had *The Pajama Game* tonight. And she was a hit in *The Pajama Game*.

She'd go first thing in the morning.

She crossed Carla Avenue toward the playhouse parking lot. Past the "Now Playing" marquee billboard with her headshot adorning the frame with the others.

How did the flower woman know Mr. Arbor died peacefully in his sleep? Who could know such a thing? Childless, unmarried, and single, Mr. Arbor almost certainly lived alone. Had he not opened the Boathouse by late afternoon or evening, one of his regulars (even the *Wall Street Journal*–reading retiree with the scold wife) might get concerned and go in search, but who looked in on him first thing in the morning?

It could have been anyone, she realized, nearing the Journeyman Bridge. A close friend, a morning walking partner, a diligent neighbor. Mr. Arbor had been a permanent fixture in town since birth; it wasn't surprising that a fellow local would pop in regularly, especially given his age. It was a kind, responsible, *neighborly* thing to do.

And he hadn't looked so healthy lately, she had to admit. Over the past few weeks, at least in the audience, he'd seem detached, distracted, and, frankly, glum. The shows held no thrill for him, if they ever had. Even his coloring last night was slightly off, compared to his rosy hue when they first met just a few weeks ago. Less pale than ashen, with heavy lids and dark circles, as if he hadn't slept well. He seemed weary.

She hurried through the open gate and across the bridge, past the roses, ignoring Clyde, who sniffed and pawed the flower beds. The young, injured rose had perked up a bit and reminded her of the potted ones lined against the creepy, straw-hatted woman's shop. Undoubtedly, that's where the playhouse bought them.

Maybe that's why Mr. Arbor urged her to come visit him again, one last time. He knew he was ill, in failing health, but didn't want to tell her, to bring her down. He just wanted a final chat over the bar, to tell stories, or pass along wisdom to a young up-and-comer. Especially given that he had no children of his own.

Yes, the nursery woman was eerie but not a gossip nor rumormonger. She was a friend of Mr. Arbor's and shared an alley with his tavern—a longtime local herself, honored with a playhouse medallion—and if she claimed he'd passed away, then that was just the sad truth. Betty Rose didn't handle death well, and this had shocked her, but mostly her denial was root-ed, she knew, in guilt.

After all, he was the first person she'd met in this town. He'd pointed her to the Gristmill when she was lost and offered his phone and a club soda with a cherry and fun, spooky tales about the town and playhouse. She'd promised to return soon and often, but she hadn't bothered to make the ten-minute walk again—even though he made the same walk weekly to see her on opening nights—so consumed she'd been with rehears-als and performances and showing off. She'd ignored him. And now he was gone.

She couldn't remember how long ago she'd been to visit him. Had she become so self-obsessed as to lose track of the days or weeks? Had time itself become a casualty of her ego?

The playhouse lawn was freshly mowed, and the orchestra's flautist, whose name she could never remember, pruned aza-lea bushes along the front porch. Surprisingly handy, border-ing on macho, Alistair sprayed an angry hornets' nest under the eaves with a garden hose, standing his ground, unfazed, as they rebelled and scrambled. He didn't even notice her.

A reordering of her priorities was required, she decided. People first, then her career, lest she turn into a fame monster. They always ended up sad and lonely. She'd go to Mr. Arbor's funeral. She hoped they didn't schedule it on a matinee day.

Rounding the playhouse, she saw company and crew scat-tered about the grassy knoll, making the most of their final lunch-break minutes. A handful of techies laughed and passed a neon Nerf football in the clearing just beyond the loading dock, near the Delaware. She nodded a greeting at one, and as she reached the stage door, she stopped and backed away and then turned toward the river and froze again and squinted.

Betty Rose's face opened.

"*Julian?*" she called out.

● ● ●

"There you are!" he called back, hurrying toward her without making a scene. He looked gorgeous and self-conscious, almost sheepish, which made him even more irresistible. He was a stranger here, out of his element.

"Oh my God!" she cried, flinging her arms around his neck and then palming his face. "Julian!" She kissed him, not caring who saw, but he did, gently breaking it off and blushing.

"Why were you lurking back there?" she asked with a laugh, pointing toward the river. Julian said, "I was looking for you. The funny old man in the front said you'd be here." Betty Rose said, "Yes. Alistair."

Julian looked around at the others staring at them, stage center.

"Oh, who cares? They're harmless," she said, taking his arm and steering him away toward the more private front lawn. "Are you staying for the show?"

"Is this your costume?" he asked, pointing to her pink denim overall dress, and she said, "Of course not. It's just what we...wear."

"You look like a Mormon," he said, and she said, "They're our work clothes. Mine are missing anyway. It's a long story." She kissed him again, which he still resisted, and she said, "When did you get here? Did you take the bus?"

He shook his head. "I rented a car and drove down." Betty Rose said, "Why didn't you tell me you were coming?"

"How?" he said, erupting. "You never call me back! It's been weeks!"

Betty Rose did the math. "That long?" she said. "I'm so sorry, honey. Time totally slips away here." She'd left him messages from the playhouse phone, and he'd left more on the chalkboard, and now she'd lost track of who owed whom.

Softening, Julian dabbed her eye, which felt heavy. "What's wrong?" he asked. "Have you been crying?"

She squeezed his hand. "Just sad news," she said, not wanting to get into it. "A friend of mine here...but I'm okay. I'm just so glad to see you, Julian." He embraced her in a protective hug and said, "I miss you so much, B.R. This has been the longest summer of my life."

"How long can you stay?" she asked. "You'd be so proud of me in my show, Julian. I signed my first autograph!"

"I'm driving back tonight," he said. "With you."

She released the hug. "With me?"

"That's why I've been calling! A girl in my show dropped out. I talked to my director and got you the part, as her replacement. You start rehearsals tomorrow."

"...tomorrow...?" she said.

"It's small, just two short scenes, a walk-on, really," he said. "But you've got lines, four to be exact. And it's a real contract. With an Equity card."

Betty Rose took a step back. "Well...thank you, Julian."

"We can beat traffic if we hurry," he said. "Did you say your clothes are missing? What's up with that?"

"But I can't go back with you," she said.

"Why not? What's up?"

"Because I'm a hit here, Julian. I have fans. People are talking about me, all over town."

Julian fought a smirk. "But it's summer stock. I'm talking about a real show. In a real theater."

"The Gristmill is a real theater," she said. "A very famous one. They make real stars. And they take care of their own."

Now he laughed. "Are you serious?" he asked. She nodded and said, "Yes, of course I'm serious."

Julian's face tightened. He moved a step, drank her in. "It's true, what they say. It's really true."

"What's true?"

"This place is a cult," he said. "A mind-controlling cult. And they've already got you. You're hooked."

She looked closely. He was joking. Except he wasn't.

"Oh God, are you back to that again?" she asked, and when he didn't retract it or back down, she said, "The Gristmill Playhouse is not a cult! What the hell is wrong with you?"

"It's not one to you. You've drunk the Kool-Aid!"

"Stop it, Julian," she said. "Just stop making an ass of yourself."

"You're in so deep, you can't even see it. Do you even know how cults operate?"

"Shh! Keep it down," she ordered, as Baayork and Becky passed by together on their way back from town. "You're embarrassing me."

"They prey on the needy," Julian went on, closer. "Like, say, a girl whose father just died! And on the ambitious. Hmm…a young actress desperate to be a star!"

He'd gone mad. Delusional.

"Nobody is preying on me. They are my friends!" she insisted. "Oh, you wouldn't understand, Julian. We're artists. We're different. Special."

"Special?" he said, with a guffaw. "You're a chorus girl, B.R. You're basically an extra. You're nothing here!"

Betty Rose looked at him.

"I'm nothing?" she said. "Is that what you think?"

He quickly retreated. "I'm sorry, hon. I didn't mean that," he said, course-correcting. "Just...come back with me, Betty Rose. Please. I love you."

The damage was done. She saw him now. The argument was over.

"You don't want me to win, do you?" she said as it dawned on her. "Because I might...eclipse you. So you...you degrade me and suppress me. To keep me down. You've been doing it for years, from the beginning. I just didn't notice." He was the poison Rex warned about. She told him so.

"Fuck Rex!" he pleaded, grabbing her wrists. "This is Julian! Wake up, Betty Rose!"

She struggled to free herself. "I am wide-awake. Let go of me!"

He restrained her. "I'm not leaving you here with these freaks!"

"She said let go," said Caleb, standing at the edge of the playhouse.

Julian, irritated and amused, released her. "Who the fuck are you?" he said.

"One of the freaks," said Caleb, still. "I think you should go now."

"I'm okay, Caleb," said Betty Rose, diffusing the tension. "I can handle this." She turned back to Julian and said, "But he's right. You should go."

Julian looked from her to Caleb and laughed. It was awkward. He seemed confounded.

He nodded at the ground and tucked his thumbs in the belt loops on his jeans. He gave Betty Rose another quick look and sauntered close to Caleb, leaning in to impart advice.

"I think you should go to your dressing room, dancer boy," he said quietly.

Caleb broadened a full-wattage, devilish smile and with a smooth, powerful motion cracked Julian across the jaw, knocking him back and down. He pounced.

"Caleb! No!" Betty Rose cried, rushing to them.

Julian rebounded and got in a pair of licks, but Caleb overpowered him. He was ferocious.

The pummeling migrated toward the back of the playhouse, and Betty Rose inserted herself to shield Julian from the rage of Caleb's blows, barely missing one herself.

"Stop it, Caleb!" she shouted, one hand on his chest, the other stopping his fist. "Go! Go inside!"

Caleb huffed and panted, sweaty and riled up and not inclined to stand down.

She shoved him back. "Now!" she ordered.

He collected himself, and with a final glare of challenge, sauntered to the front porch and into the lobby.

Julian was seething but chagrined. He seemed bewildered. His eye and lip would swell and blacken soon, she knew. Fortunately, there was no blood. Caleb must have pulled some of his punches.

"Are you all right?" she asked, still tender toward him. He'd need ice.

"Is that prick one of your 'friends'?" he asked.

"He's just protecting me," she said, and Julian stepped back from her.

"From *me*?" he said.

She followed his look over her shoulder. Behind, her new family fanned out, watching from a distance. They did look like Mormons.

"They build me up," she explained. "And you tear me down. And yes, they are controlling. Because...they want me to soar. And it breaks my heart that you want me caged."

She refused to cry in front of him.

"We're gonna be late, B.R.!" Phyllis called from behind. "Don't forget to sign in!"

"I have to go," she told Julian, turning.

"Betty Rose!" he called after her. She stopped.

"No one joins a cult," he said. "They just put off the decision to leave. Until it's too late."

She nodded and forced a weak smile. He looked so pitiful. "Take care, Julian," she said, and marched around the playhouse, through the artist's entrance, and signed her name on the sheet. Then she went to the chalkboard by the telephone and erased his.

Scene Nine

"*FIVE MINUTES TO PLACES, EVERYONE!*" Becky called over the intercom. "*Five minutes!*"

Betty Rose rechecked her eyeliner and dabbed powder on her cheeks and forehead. The dressing room was tense and silent, as it always was moments before a show.

She'd thrown herself into afternoon rehearsals, pushing out the day's distractions. She was focused, like a pro. She didn't track mud inside the theater.

No one mentioned the lunch-break clash, even though most had witnessed it and those who hadn't had surely heard about it. Betty Rose got the sense they understood, or had had similar confrontations with their own loved ones at some point along their journey. Caleb, unscathed, attacked the musical numbers with his usual gusto. Only Sutton tipped her hand, with a knowing smile and a gentle squeeze on Betty Rose's shoulder. Not the Tony winner and reigning queen of Broadway, but Sutton, her colleague and friend.

Julian's slings and arrows shocked her. His warnings unnerved her, not for their content, but that he'd made them at all. He was normally even-tempered, bordering on aloof. It was part of his sexy charm that becalmed her most frantic and anxious moods. Today he was irrational and panicked and nonsensical. What had set him off?

The pressures of his new show as it neared the countdown? That had never unhinged him before. Indeed, he usually grew more serene in the run-up to opening night. His humiliation at having nabbed her a role in his show only to have her turn it down? She had to admit that was a huge favor he'd called in, getting the director to cast her in an off-Broadway show sight unseen. It would score her an Equity card, which was the goal of the summer. But it was pity-casting and would haunt her through her career. She could earn her card on her own.

Maybe Julian had lashed out because he was lonely. She should have made a better effort to keep in touch with him over the summer. But he'd been MIA last summer, when her father was so ill and she was the most vulnerable and desperate for a sympathetic ear. Julian was nowhere to be found then, consumed with his own work, which had propelled him to the next level of his career. She hadn't punished or degraded him the way he'd so viciously done to her today. It was unconscionable and revealed an ugly side her mother would use as exhibit A in her ongoing case against him, had she not been guilty of the same thing.

Unless Julian meant his warning about the Gristmill. He'd always been uneasy about the place, but today he'd come down hard, as though he'd done more investigating. There was authentic fear in his eyes. He'd seemed like a different person.

And his attacks on the playhouse seemed less outlandish the more she thought about them.

Phyllis reached across the makeup counter and put her hand on hers, gently toggled it. "When you're a star, he'll come around," she said with care. "They always do."

"Do you think…this place is a cult?" asked Betty Rose.

Phyllis gave her a startled look and then reached over to push the dressing room door closed. It swung shut with a jolt that echoed through the silo.

"Of course it is," she said quietly. "I knew that before I came. Didn't you?"

"I mean, I heard things.…"

"*Holding!*" Becky announced over the speaker. "*We're holding, everybody. Stand by.*"

Phyllis zeroed in. "We all heard things. This place made its reputation the old-fashioned way. It *earned* it."

She went on. "I heard your boyfriend's rant. Drama McDramster. But very cute. Got that Tom Hardy thing. Gentleman-killer. You know he went easy on Caleb."

Betty Rose smiled and said, "Yes, he probably did, thank God."

"And yes, this place checks all those cult boxes," said Phyllis, powdering touch-ups. "But so does my college society. And my roommate's field hockey team. Really, every group tries to control its members. That's why I'd never survive in corporate America. Yuck!"

She gave herself a final once-over and turned back to Betty Rose. "But so what? This place works, doesn't it? And we put up with it because we want to act so bad! Why? I don't know." She puzzled it over and said, "We're probably mentally ill. Or just so starved for love and attention, we'll sacrifice anything to get it." She shrugged.

"Would you…sacrifice anything?" Betty Rose asked.

Phyllis dropped her usual giddy act and spoke like an educated Wellesley scholar breaking down a class assignment. She was real.

"You wanna know the real reason?" she said. "We want to live forever. Even in the memories of strangers out there in the dark. We don't want to be forgotten."

"You're right," said Betty Rose, realizing. "We don't...want to die."

"Look, I'll never be a star," Phyllis said. "My name won't be in lights. My picture won't hang in the lobby. I'm cool with that." She thought and then continued. "But I'll settle for a flower on the bridge, you know? And to be remembered long after I'm gone. That's why I'm here, I guess. If that makes me a cultie, then hand over the tambourine!"

"I think Hare Krishnas play the tambourine," said Betty Rose. Phyllis scrunched her nose and said, "Ew, not them! They're bald!"

Betty Rose laughed and threw her arms around her. "Oh, I love you, Phyllis!"

"Me too, B.R.," said Phyllis with a broad smile. "If nothing else, at least this freak show brought us together." She opened the dressing room door.

"We gotta stay in touch back in New York," said Betty Rose, and Phyllis said, "Bitch, we're gonna be together foreva!"

"*Places!*" Becky called. "*Places, everyone!*"

Phyllis jumped. "God, my heart skips every time." She frowned at her factory-girl reflection in the mirror. "So square. I can't wait to play a hooker in *Sweet Charity*. God, I'd love to get paid for sex."

"Phyllis!" Betty Rose said in mock reproach, as they rushed down the stairs. The drum kettled the overture.

Their *Pajama Game* shtick worked again that night and worked all week. Betty Rose signed autographs after each performance. Closing night came too soon.

● ● ●

Phyllis was right: Cults were everywhere. And most were harmless.

The word "cult" got bandied about a lot, diluting its meaning. Some were truly freaky. There were satanic cults and Wiccan cults. There were more organized and wealthier ones, like the Moonies and Scientologists, although she didn't know what qualified them as cults, other than people insisting that they were. Others were more obviously gruesome. She'd heard of the Branch Davidians and Heaven's Gate on the news as a child and remembered, with a shudder, a terrifying documentary about the Jim Jones cult she'd recently seen on PBS.

She'd discovered it by accident when she thought she had TiVo'd *Live from Lincoln Center* with Audra McDonald in concert. Instead, Channel 13 aired an *American Experience* about Jonestown. It had grabbed her with its horrors, and she'd watched the whole two hours while Julian worked on set sketches at the kitchen counter, scarcely paying attention. Although, based on his overactive imagination today, the documentary must have made a greater impact on him than he'd let on.

The Jim Jones followers were the original "Kool-Aid drinkers," who, under their leader's spell, willingly chugged cyanide-laced punch and even force-fed it to their own trusting children. It was a cult of death: brainwashed lemmings following their leaders over the cliff into mass suicide. The survivors of the Jones cult, interviewed many years later, were mystified by their own submission to such obvious insanity and evil. They still seemed dazed, even frightened by themselves as they choked out appalling tales of those foggy years. Betty Rose felt both empathy and bafflement: How could anyone seemingly sane so fully lose one's mind and sense of self? How could they sink so deeply into the madness?

There were more innocuous organizations that shared cultlike traits: the military, the Catholic Church, her yoga class on St. Mark's Place. Even pyramid schemes like one her mother had joined many years ago, selling berry-flavored diet powders from the kitchen table. Betty Rose remembered the feverish afternoon pep rallies her mother had hosted in the living room, with a visiting rep whipping the neighborhood sales force into chanting idiots. Lonely housewives, Betty Rose now realized, preyed upon by greedy tricksters who leveraged the women's feelings of inadequacy and lost youth in order to swallow whole their thousands in investment. Even now, Betty Rose felt a pang of pity reliving the moment her mother realized she'd been swindled out of their hard-earned money. That was a tense, quiet, bitter evening at the dinner table.

But Julian's claim that the Gristmill preyed upon her was nonsensical. Yes, she was an ambitious actress, but by that logic, any theater that hired her was predatory. And they hadn't targeted her vulnerability after her father's death because they weren't even aware of it until she confessed during her breakthrough a few weeks ago. In Julian's delusional mind, the playhouse sought her out for a weakness they couldn't possibly have known about. How 'round the bend he'd gone, assigning the Gristmill clairvoyant, almost supernatural, powers.

Of course, nobody would admit that their beloved group was, in fact, a cult. Because then they'd have to admit they'd fallen victim to it. A cult was hard to pin down. Betty Rose recalled the common characteristics listed in the Jonestown documentary: They tended to have charismatic leaders and strange rituals, and they flourished in remote, isolated places.

But that would also apply to her church Bible camp, with its magnetic preacher and euphoric baptism rites, which would seem downright peculiar to an outsider. That didn't make it dangerous, or even alarming.

It was preposterous, she had concluded over the week as they readied *Sweet Charity*, to peg the Gristmill Playhouse a cult.

"Five minutes!" Becky called out on the third night of the run. Betty Rose and Phyllis, now Fandango dance hall girls, zipped up each other's short, tight dresses and straightened the seams on their fishnet stockings before racing down the silo stairs.

Yes, Rex was authoritarian—a dictator, really—but hardly messianic like the cult leader A-listers. And there was a decided weirdness to the place, which she considered part of its charm. In any event, the professional theatre had never been a democracy; without an absolute tyrant at the helm, the inmates would quickly overrun the asylum, and what chaotic, scattershot disaster that would bring onto the stage. Successful theatre required strong leadership and *control.* It also required strict obedience.

"Check your line, beeatches!" Rachelle whispered as they fanned across the dance bar, center stage, waiting for the scrim to rise. Betty Rose, near the middle, struck and held her pose—arms draped over the bar, bowlegged, catatonic expression—as Sutton sang her opening solo out front on the apron.

But there were no secret rituals at the Gristmill, notwithstanding her under-the-spotlight strip-down, which was merely an exercise, a tool in unlocking her latent talents, which she had to admit had been successful. She'd blossomed onstage ever since, and both the company and the audience recognized it. She'd grown as an artist and felt empowered, not violated. She needn't explain it to outsiders; it was really nobody's business but her own.

And although the Gristmill Playhouse was certainly isolated, it was part of the larger community of New Hope—a well-known tourist destination and weekend getaway spot for New Yorkers. If it were destructive—*dangerous*—someone in town would know and blow the whistle. But to the contrary, the New Hope locals embraced the Gristmill as its biggest fans and loyal patrons.

Betty Rose adjusted her pose, jutted her hip to the side, one wrist up, one down. A sharp Fosse attitude that Baayork had hammered into them in rehearsal. She gazed at the back of the scrim, waiting.

Another oddity shared by cults, according to the documentary, was a grisly endgame, based on a bizarre mythology unique to them and to which they zealously clung. Ancient pagan cults often performed human sacrifices to please their gods and ensure a bountiful year ahead. For Heaven's Gate, it was a doomsday prophecy that prompted them to poison themselves while wearing black-and-white Nikes in hopes of latching on to a passing UFO. Scientologists prepared for the second coming of an alien named Xenu by confessing their darkest secrets while hooked up to electric soup cans. But for the Gristmill, the endgame was always the next opening night. It was Rodgers and Hammerstein, Adelaide and Nicely-Nicely, or even Sondheim in their ambitious moments. How much carnage could be wrought by people in unitards, dance belts, and tap shoes?

The orchestra teased the opening vamps of "Big Spender," and the knowing audience laughed in anticipation. The light switched, and the scrim rose, revealing another packed house. The Fandango dancers, contorted in impossible positions with blank faces, held frozen as they sang and popped their cork directly to the crowd. Fun-laughs-good-time.

The final cult characteristic she remembered was the most chilling: its violent retaliation against members who turned on it or divulged its secrets. Jim Jones ordered the slaughter of all deserters, and many were gunned down in front of their friends and family. Indeed, rumors had long swirled around ex-Scientologists who went missing or ended up dead. There was a Mafia-like retribution against fugitives who threatened the group, either by abandonment or squealing. Dissent was punishable by death.

The Fandango girls spread out from the bar for their slow-motion dance break. The big tease.

It was absurd to think the Gristmill did such a thing. The worst punishment a balky member could get was extra pearl-diving duty or banishment upstage to the back of the chorus line. And nobody had to stay at the Gristmill against their will. The Trans-Bridge bus came twice daily, and any wannabe defector could hop on and be back in New York in a few hours. Like Gwen had.

Betty Rose crossed her wrists high above her head. She thrust her hips and held; thrust and held.

Gwen clearly thought the Gristmill was a cult, too, even as she avoided that word. And, unlike Julian, Gwen had personal experience with the place, if only for a few weeks. But Gwen didn't understand the place like Betty Rose did. And her daily attitude was so unpleasant, so *un-team-like*. Rachelle was right: Gwen didn't belong here. She was better off on her soap, in her fancy dressing room overlooking the Hudson. Betty Rose preferred her new family on the Delaware this summer.

She felt a soft touch on the small of her back. Fingertips gently rubbed in circles.

Perplexed, Betty Rose glanced back. Phyllis stood behind her, smiling. Had she drifted off her mark? Was Phyllis trying to guide her back?

Another touch from the other side. Rachelle, too close, stroking her bare shoulder. She gave it a tight squeeze.

Baayork hadn't choreographed this. The dance was about the promise, not the follow-through. They were riffing and elaborating. Ruining it. Betty Rose tried to push them away without breaking character. They resisted, closing in.

The Fandango dancers clustered around her, running hands up and down her chest and sides. She felt a massaging touch on her thigh. She turned to Sutton, perched below, smiling up at her. But Sutton wasn't even supposed to be in this number. She should be backstage getting ready for "Charity's Soliloquy."

Was this a prank, another test? She refused to flinch, to break character.

Rachelle unzipped her, pulled down her shoulder straps, peeled off her dress. Phyllis unclasped her bra. Sutton ran her fingers under the elastic of her panties.

Betty Rose looked down to Myron in the orchestra pit. The band played on.

Strong hands enveloped her bare waist from behind. Even without turning, she knew it was Caleb's lips on her neck. She reached back to welcome him and found him naked, pressing against her.

Dottie and Alistair, also naked, eased her down onto the stage, which was carpeted over with the nude and writhing bodies of the company. Betty Rose submitted to their soft warmth, cushioned by their chests and backs and breasts and buttocks. She felt their breath all over her. It both soothed and aroused.

The stage lights shifted to red, more suitable to the mood, and flattering. Betty Rose pivoted her head to the audience, watching intently. She smiled at them, sinking deeper into ecstasy, unashamed. They were family, too.

The mass of interlocking bodies beneath her—twenty, thirty—threshed in all directions, caressing, stroking, moving on to the next. A shared community, radiating heat and exploring one another, but focused on her. She was the nucleus, and she liked it. She peered over a naked shoulder toward the wings.

Rex, fully dressed, stood just offstage. Unsmiling, he nodded at her. Abruptly self-conscious, Betty Rose tried to hide her face, but her hands were tucked under and trapped inside the tangle. She felt a gentle nibbling on her elbow. It tickled. Another mouth latched onto her neck. "Careful," she said, squirming a retreat, lest it leave a visible mark.

The percussion in the orchestra pit overtook the song with a familiar, repeating rhythm. The swarming bodies started to pulse along with it, as if choreographed. Strumming, probing, glistening, and fragrant, more joined in the chant: *Make Things Happen, Let Things Happen.* It grew louder, more insistent. It sounded tribal.

Betty Rose wallowed in the embraces of the young, soft, tanned arms and legs. One led to another in a confusing riot of flesh. Anonymous caresses, love bites, heaving chests. She turned toward a clinking sound and faced a gold Gristmill medallion with the theatre masks dangling from an unknown neck. She nosed the pendant and studied the joy and sorrow in the engraved faces framed by long, flowing, girlish hair. She squinted at the stick in the middle of the medallion, separating the masks. It had a handle at the top and a sharp spear at the bottom. It was, she now saw, a mill pick, like the one they used to stuff the hopper. Carla, Cady, and the pick: the three symbols of the Gristmill. More clinks emanated from the layers underneath her; rings, pendants adorning the naked bodies. She inhaled the jewelry, coveting it.

One slender finger periscoped up from the mass. It looked gray.

The hand emerged, reaching. More ashen and pale than gray, glowing in the stage light. It felt around, seeking.

The arm rose up, translucent and streaked with blue veins. Sickly, but alive. The hand found Betty Rose, grasping, wanting her attention. It squeezed her shoulder, spidered up to read her face. It smelled like rot. Betty Rose recoiled.

The hand clawed at her breasts, urgent, insistent. From below, the head pushed up through the twisted gnarl of bodies, its long dark hair matted, unkempt, and oily. Betty Rose tried to twist away. The trembling head begat the neck, pendant-free, and unearthed the naked torso, skeletal and splotchy, decomposing but alive. It moved with its own desperate rhythm, distinct from the quickening chant.

It lifted its face to Betty Rose. Gwen stared up at her in panic, once-violet eyes now clear and milky, her lips blue, skin cadaver-white and scaling. A black drip of blood trickled from the corner of her mouth. Her dead eyes begged for help.

Betty Rose was alarmed and repulsed. Her instinct to flee overruled her impulse to save. She pushed back and away but was trapped from the waist down by the swallowing mass underneath.

Gwen opened her mouth in a scream, but no sound came. Her neck strained, and her tongue flicked through her teeth, broken and jagged. Betty Rose freed her hands and reached out to drag herself away. Her hands dripped with inky blood, and she smeared them on bodies to wipe them clean. The bodies responded, thrashing with force. The chant rose and intensified.

The more Betty Rose struggled, the deeper she sank into the human quicksand. Soon Gwen was on top, looking down. Her throat contracted in a gag, and she vomited up a thick gush, drenching Betty Rose. It smacked cold on her face.

Betty Rose screamed.

She bolted up, trembling and sweat-soaked. She gasped for breath and stilled herself. Her bedroom was quiet and dark. In the bunk below, Phyllis snored and muttered a slurry complaint.

Betty Rose looked down at herself, naked. She climbed from her top bunk to the floor and steadied herself. Her dusty pink nightgown was wadded on the floor.

She examined her body, unharmed and unmarked. She inspected her neck in the small mirror over the dresser. No hickey, no blemish at all. She toweled off the sweat, donned the nightgown, quietly climbed back to her bunk.

It had been weeks since her last nightmare. She thought they'd passed, along with her anxiety, as her stock rose at the Gristmill and she felt on firmer footing. Her sleepwalking was back, too, if her nightgown wadded on the floor was any indication. She hoped she hadn't wandered naked through the grounds, although that would scarcely cause a ripple at this place, which itself was odd.

The Gwen nightmare was familiar. A rerun from her drunken, pass-out night in her first week. Even now, awake and freed from its spell, it lingered with a haunting and vivid

chill as she lay in her bunk. Such was her hallucinatory vision of Gwen from her last evening at the playhouse: terrified,
pleading, and bloody. Betty Rose's subconscious had conjured up that grotesque image—with the assistance of tequila
and gin—and now boomeranged it back just as she tried to
bury the seeds of doubt and suspicion that Julian had planted about the playhouse. Her mind was playing tricks again.
Damn Julian.

The exit sign flicked its familiar strobe. Its soothing
rhythm had tranced her off to sleep on many nights. Now she
propped up on her elbows, scrutinizing it. Its pattern repeated
in set dashes, like a Morse code. She watched and counted.
Four dashes, a pause, another four dashes. Over and over, an
endless cycle.

Her eye traveled to the molding that ran along the ceiling. The stenciled phrase just below that circled the room in
flowery, nursery script: "Make Things Happen, Let Things
Happen."

She looked back at the exit sign, counted the flickers. To
the repeating script, mouthing the words. She synced them
up and quietly chanted them out. "Make Things Happen, Let
Things Happen." She tried it again, just to make sure. They fit.

The flickering no longer soothed her.

She climbed back down, grabbed her towel and folded it
in half. Hanging off the side of the bunk, she reached out and
flung it to cover the exit sign, smothering its light.

She watched from her pillow. The rhythmic blinking still
bled from the corners of the towel.

Betty Rose turned on her side, covering her head with the pillow. She curled up, knees tight, and breathed deeply into her mattress.

Scene Ten

THE SMOTHERING AUGUST HEAT DROVE EVER-LARGER THRONGS TO THE GRISTMILL, either for the "refrigerated air," or hold-tight-to-summer nostalgia as the season wound down. The sold-out box office kept a wait list, and the most desperate trolled the Journeyman Bridge and grassy knoll for scalpers, in vain. "Sorry, no rush seats today!" the house manager called out to the itchy, clustered mass.

Me and My Girl proved a rowdy crowd pleaser with its jubilant songs and cockney accents. Betty Rose looked forward to each act-one finale—"The Lambeth Walk"—when the singing ensemble would descend into the audience and shake hands as they danced their way up toward the lobby before intermission. Rex called this "confrontation theatre," which he claimed was greatly effective when used sparingly. It reminded Betty Rose of her earliest memories of *Really Rosie* at the Beech Grove Children's Theater, where she'd made sure to sit on the aisle and how frantic she became when Rosie broke the fourth wall to kneel beside her and sing along. Now it was her turn to make others frantic. It didn't feel like confrontation at all; she relished each greeting and was thrilled when starry-eyed audience members would grasp her hand and not let go. She was a rock star, of sorts.

The heat roiled on, through performances and rehearsals. The air-conditioning strained to keep up, and one unit broke down entirely on Wednesday night after curtain call. Dottie called out for emergency repair, and the local serviceman showed up after breakfast with the wrong compressor and promised to get the right one from Lambertville and have the beast working in time for the evening performance.

With all doors open and fans on, the stage was still stifling during afternoon pickup rehearsals, as the thick outside air offered up no breeze. The dog day sat on them hard, and tempers crackled. Even the coiffed and dolled-up Rachelle wilted with running mascara and sweat stains in her tucks, although she soldiered on fiercely. She maintained her stature.

Rex seemed immune to the elements, circulating through the house, checking sight lines and tweaking an act-one production number that had bothered him since opening night.

"Stop! Cut!" he called out, interrupting the ensemble. "Stopfuckingcut!"

He rounded down toward the apron. His exasperation was pure, not heat-aggravated. Betty Rose and the rest of the cast froze.

"Phyllis, are you a moron?" he asked. "Are you another idiot twat actress?"

Phyllis struggled to hold her sunny smile. "No, sir," she said. "I mean, I hope not."

Rex pointed at Sutton, stage center. Then he turned back to Phyllis.

"What am I pointing at?" he asked, simmering.

"That's...that's Sutton?" she said, uncertain. She reddened with humiliation and fear.

"I didn't say *who*. I said *what!*"

"Oh," said Phyllis, flustered, thinking. "That's...the star?"

He nodded and pointed at an imaginary line across the stage, on Sutton's level. Phyllis was standing in front of it, closer to the audience.

"And where are you?" he asked rhetorically. "Where...you told me to be," she answered. The wrong answer.

"You are upstaging the star!" Rex roared. "I never fucking told you to upstage the fucking star!" Betty Rose knew that was false; Phyllis was standing exactly where Rex had blocked her. She fought the urge to correct him.

"But I thought...," Phyllis pleaded, and Rex cut her off. "You're a stupid actor. You're not supposed to think!" Phyllis backed off and said, "Sorry, Daddy." She stepped upstage, past Sutton.

Rex started to turn away but lashed out as an afterthought, expending his fury. "The audience pays to see the swan, not the ugly duckling!" he shouted. Betty Rose gasped at his cruelty, covered it. Stung, Phyllis said, "Yes, Daddy." She shrank back farther, her smile pained and false.

Over Rex's shoulder, in the back of the theater, Betty Rose saw a striking silhouette against the dusty sun pouring in from the lobby. It was a tall, expansive man. He wore a cowboy hat. Turning, Rex saw him, too.

"Good afternoon, Calvin," Rex grumbled, pivoting back to the stage as he forced a lighter mood. "Are you here to audition?" he joked. He seemed slightly chastened and irritated for having been caught bullying a young girl.

"Can I have a word, Rex?" Calvin said. Something on his chest caught the light. Betty Rose focused. It was the reflection from his metal badge. The hat was law enforcement, not cowboy.

"Yes, certainly." Rex simmered down, regaining his parental demeanor to match the officer's. He lifted his eyebrows in Dottie's direction, and she took her cue. "Take ten, gang!" she shouted, waving the cast off the stage. "No break next hour. Don't even ask."

The cast streamed toward the stage door to the fresh air beyond. Betty Rose held back.

She went to the wings, looked around. Kneeled down to adjust the strap on her character shoes. She unbuckled and buckled it, waiting for the stage to clear out. When it was quiet, she stood up and peeked into the house.

Rex moved confidently toward the officer in the back. In his right hand, the officer held a manila folder down to his side. He leaned and said something into Rex's ear; Rex nodded. He gently took the man's elbow and guided him back into the lobby. Then he closed the swinging doors, blocking out the sunlight.

Up in the control booth, Becky and the lighting designer made their escape to the air beyond. They crossed the catwalk over the house and down the spiral stairs to the main floor backstage. Becky was drenched with sweat and fanned herself with a playbill. Betty Rose turned her back and stretched near the fly deck, listening to them pass. When they exited out the stage door, she turned to go.

She walked right into Caleb, shirtless and glistening. He wadded his wife-beater T-shirt in one hand.

"What are you doing back here?" he asked with a smile. "We're on break." And Betty Rose said, "I'm just stretching. I have a leg cramp." He said, "Come outside. It's hell in here."

She said, "It's not so bad," and felt fresh rivers of sweat streaming down her back. She knew it was staining her unitard.

Caleb got closer. "You're not avoiding me, are you?" She touched his chest and pushed him away playfully. "Don't flatter yourself. I'll be right out. Go!" He gave her one last grin and sauntered toward the stage door. He turned back, and she shooed him on. Once he disappeared, she moved toward the spiral staircase in the corner.

She walked carefully so her heels wouldn't clack on the metal stairs. She curled around and up and arrived at the catwalk. She glanced around the theater and the stage, empty and silent. She hurried across toward the lighting booth. The door stood open. She slipped inside.

It was small, dark, and cramped. There were two rolling chairs against the lighting and sound deck, dozens of tiny knobs, levels, and needled gauges. Becky's script, covered in scribbles, sat open in its three-ring binder on the edge. A desk lamp taped over with a blue gel cast a dim glow on the white pages. Two near-empty bottles of water stood on the floor against the back wall, far from the electronic board.

The window overlooking the lobby was open in a futile attempt at fresh air. The booth was torturously suffocating.

"Her *sister* is looking for her?" Rex mumbled from down below. He spoke softly but with an edge that carried in the silence.

Betty Rose perched on the edge of the chair, scooting it up, and carefully peered out the window. Rex and the officer were barely in view at the edge of the concessions stand. Rex stood behind the counter, and the officer faced him, standing erect.

She looked carefully at his badge. Star-shaped. The New Hope sheriff.

She lowered so her eyes were just above the windowsill. She gripped the padded chair seat to steady it. She took shallow breaths and watched and listened.

"The NYPD finally ran a credit card check," said the sheriff. "Her last charge was in mid-May for twenty-six dollars on the bus line. Exact fare from New York to New Hope."

Rex nodded and said, "Huh. And an actress, you say?" His hands were spread and braced against the counter. He drummed his fingers impatiently. His playhouse ring glinted with each cycle.

"Aspiring, yes," said the sheriff. "According to her sister, she came to New York in December. They last spoke in March." Rex said, "I see." The sheriff said, "An aspiring New York actress traveling to New Hope for the summer. So naturally I thought of you first." Rex said, "Yes, naturally. I'm glad you did."

The sheriff slid the manila folder across the counter. Rex took it and backed away a step. Balancing herself on the chair, Betty Rose migrated to the window edge, but Rex's shoulder blocked her view. She heard him open the folder and heard the wobble of the photo paper in his hands. Rex stared down at it for a long moment. He cocked his head, scratched his chin.

"The NYPD thought of you, too," said the sheriff. "They wondered if she might have found her way to your playhouse."

"Yes, that would be an obvious, logical conclusion," muttered Rex, still staring down.

He took a breath and looked up at the sheriff. "No, she's not here," he said. He pushed the headshot back across the counter.

Gwen's headshot.

The sheriff left it on the counter. "Is that all you want me to tell them?" he asked.

Rex shrugged. "I know who's in my company. The NYPD is welcome here anytime if they have more questions."

Betty Rose leaned in farther. Gwen smiled up at her from the counter. She was so beautiful. Her violet eyes popped even from a distance.

The sheriff chuckled and said, "We both know the NYPD wouldn't cross the street to track down a missing actress," and Rex said, "That's one reason why I've never liked the NYPD." Then he added sharply, "You can tell them that, too."

Betty Rose's chair seat creaked.

She dropped down below the window, kneeling on the booth floor. She held her breath. The lobby was silent.

"I wish I could have been more help, Calvin," said Rex finally. "Now, if you'll excuse me, I have a show to rehearse." His steps moved across the lobby and back into the theater.

Betty Rose sprang up, kicking over a water bottle, which rolled across the floor into the darkness under the light board. She groped around and cornered it, set it upright back against the wall. She rushed out the booth door, scampered across the catwalk on her toes, glancing down at Rex, who scribbled new notes on his clipboard, not seeing her right above. She ducked into the spiral staircase and chased it down just as Dottie called out, "We're back early, gang!"

"How's your cramp?" Caleb asked, rolling his wife beater back over his chest as the cast resumed their places. "Much better, thanks!" she chirped back.

The orchestra reassembled in the pit.

Sutton and Rachelle took their last positions. Dottie and Alistair assumed their poses farther upstage.

Baayork called out an adjustment. Phyllis and another girl scrambled to meet it. Myron wanded up the music.

Rex watched it all from the house.

Betty Rose hit every mark.

Scene Eleven

AFTERNOON REHEARSAL WRAPPED AFTER ENSEMBLE RUN-THROUGHS of "Just in Time" and "Drop That Name," two favorites Rex was considering for the Homecoming show and that highlighted Sutton's mastery of both romantic and screwball comedy. Spirits brightened with the abrupt return of the air-conditioning, whose initial blasts promised relief was on the way.

Betty Rose shared a quick, post-song schmooze with the cast as she threaded through the stage and down the hallway. She popped a greeting to Baub in the wardrobe room on her way to her dorm. She slipped inside and closed the door.

She opened her dresser drawer and fished around the undergarments wadded inside. Her fingers caught something plastic, grabbed it.

Betty Rose tucked the pink flamingo flash drive under her skirt waistband and fluffed her T-shirt over it.

Phyllis called after her as she hurried across the Journeyman Bridge. "B.R., you going off campus? You forgot to sign out!" Betty Rose turned and called back, "Can you sign out for me? I won't be long."

"Should I save you dinner?" Phyllis yelled, and Betty Rose shook her head and said, "Nah, I'll peck at something. Thanks, though!" She smiled and waved and said, "Back soon!"

An outdoor art show was in full swing throughout New Hope. Carla Avenue was closed to traffic, and a banner hung across that read "Plein Air Festival—Sponsored by the New Hope Museum of Fine Arts." Betty Rose weaved through a pedestrian mix of tourists and resident artists amid a sea of easels and pastels, watercolors, and oils. There were still lifes and landscapes and the odd caricature, and Betty Rose recognized a smattering of locals in their smocks and fisherman hats. They were consumed in their paintings, and she had no trouble avoiding their eyes as they dipped their brushes and squinted at their canvases.

She passed the skinny Asian mailman on his daily rounds, as intent on his delivery task as always, and spied the pudgy techie grunt from the playhouse on an errand with an oblong, purple velvet tasseled bag, approaching her. She darted behind a streetlamp as he passed and waited until he disappeared into Nifty's Knife Sharpening before moving on.

She targeted the tall white church building with green shutters and a "Public Library" sign above the entry doors.

A book club was meeting just past the circulation desk, in a cluster of pews at the back of what once was the main sanctuary. The benches had been uprooted and positioned around a low table where the mostly female group discussed the latest Harlen Coben, whose cover screamed danger. Elsewhere, tall stacks of bookshelves had replaced the church seating, with a center aisle leading to the pulpit stage. Betty Rose hurried along.

"Excuse me," she stage-whispered to an elderly woman with a volunteer name tag who was restocking shelves from her metal rolling cart. "Can you direct me to the public computers?"

The woman pointed toward the back and said, "Erma can help you."

Betty Rose navigated past the noisy children's section to the periodicals room that was in a newer annex off the auditorium. Two black computers sat empty near the corner window, in adjoining cubicles of blond wood. Across the room, on its own table, sat a hulking laser printer, for common use. She didn't see an Erma or anyone else.

The pink flamingo flash drive woke the computer when she fit it into the USB port. She hadn't used a standard-issue PC since high school and couldn't find the drive's icon on the desktop. She turned around to the room's librarian desk, which was unmanned and Erma-free, and considered going back to the front desk for help, but her time was tight, and she clicked and found and searched through an assortment of folders of Gwen's headshots and résumés and audition songbooks until, through elimination, she zeroed in on the word "freekshow" in the desktop square. Gwen's spelling was off, even if her intention was clear. Betty Rose circled it with the cursor, hesitant.

She didn't know what she was looking for. She'd only saved the flash drive in order to return it to Gwen, and she'd planned on asking Dottie for her address, or at least to call and alert her that it was safe, but the season got so busy, with rehearsals and performances and Betty Rose's own breakthroughs and rising up through the ranks and signing autographs, that it had completely slipped her mind until today. It had sat in her little drawer under Phyllis's, tucked in the back under her socks and underwear and bras, and Betty Rose would have remembered it earlier had Gwen called or sent word that she needed it. It would have triggered her memory, and then she would have mailed it to her pronto.

But Gwen hadn't called or sent word. For weeks.

And now she was missing, according to the New York Police Department.

The drive had several folders, and Betty Rose felt a tinge of unease in accessing Gwen's private files. She was looking, she told herself, for any personal contact information, like an e-mail address or cell number. But a flash drive was unlikely to have any of that, she realized, and even if she did find it hidden away somewhere on a document or saved e-mail, surely Gwen's sister and most certainly the NYPD had already tried it and gotten no response. Hence their investigation, which led them to the New Hope sheriff, Calvin, which led him to the Gristmill. And Rex.

Unless Gwen didn't want them to contact her, for whatever reason, and ignored their messages. She clearly had a strained relationship with her family—she'd said so herself—and it was entirely possible she'd shunned her own sister. Family relations were often tangled and even poisonous, and Betty Rose didn't know Gwen well enough to gauge how plausible or likely it was that she would hide from her sister.

But how did one hide from the NYPD? Especially as an actor on a soap opera with a nice dressing room overlooking the Hudson? It was hard to be anonymous and on daily national television simultaneously. Even the quickest Internet search would turn up her new high-profile acting job—the "fresh face" of daytime drama.

Assuming, of course, that Gwen was both her real name and stage name. Maybe she went by a different name professionally, which was common and which Betty Rose herself had resisted as recently as several weeks ago in Wes the agent's office. A name change would make an Internet search difficult, if not impossible, and if Gwen just started her soap gig a few weeks ago, it was likely that nothing would pop up at all. In fact, it was possible, and likely, that her first soap episode hadn't even aired yet, since they taped them weeks in advance. In that case, it was quite conceivable no one had even seen her on television, which would make it easier for her to hide from her sister or anyone else.

Betty Rose took a breath and checked herself: No, it was completely implausible and impossible that Gwen could evade the NYPD if they were looking for her in New York City. Even if she had changed her name and her first episode hadn't aired, the police most certainly would have reached out to her friends, roommates (every young, struggling actress in New York had them), coworkers—anyone they could find—and at least one of them would have led the cops to her dressing room on the Hudson.

So where was Gwen?

She arched her back to keep the rolling sweat from staining her unitard, which could then darken her T-shirt. It was hot as hell in this library.

Someone sat at the computer in the cubicle next to her. Betty Rose pivoted to shield the view of her screen with her back, which was unnecessary because of the partition, but it provided, she felt, an extra layer of privacy, so itchy she was for probing Gwen's personal files.

She double clicked the "freekshow" file.

The document was written on a diary template, blog-ready. All Gwen would have had to do is upload, hit "publish," and it would have been out there for the world to read. Just like she'd threatened to do.

The first entry was from mid-May, roughly a month before Betty Rose came to the Gristmill. It started with the happy usuals: the town, the charms of the playhouse, Dottie's comical crabbiness. Gwen was amused by her bubbly new roommate Phyllis and cautiously intrigued by a sexy and flirtatious Caleb. She seemed to be enjoying it.

It went south fast.

She railed against the all-controlling rules and rigorous schedule, which were not of themselves all that troubling to Betty Rose. It was simply the way the Gristmill operated, how they churned out a new show week after week and had done so for years. Anyone who couldn't cut it didn't belong.

But Gwen went on to detail her rapidly degenerating state from exhaustion and starvation—conditions unnervingly familiar to Betty Rose from her own first week. It was a cruel and unusual punishment that seemed ancient history now, but reading Gwen's vivid descriptions brought back a flood of horrible memories. Betty Rose's stomach tightened.

Gwen used the word "cult" liberally as her torment wore on.

Betty Rose shivered. She rubbed her arms. The library must have turned on the air-conditioning, full blast. It chilled her sweat, making her feverish.

In the cubicle next to her, the computer user clicked the keyboard and sighed and clicked more.

But this sort of hazing, which Gwen described with unsettling precision and which Betty Rose herself had experienced—almost exactly the same way and on the same timetable—was typical of nearly every organization: clubs, sports teams, even menial jobs. Betty Rose herself had to work doubles and got the worst schedule as a rookie at the Rum House. Why would the Gristmill be any different?

Betty Rose shook her head. It *was* different. She couldn't pinpoint the exact reason, but everything about the Gristmill *felt* different. More controlling and abusive. And, in its own strange way, more nefarious. Because while she put up with a modicum of abuse at the Rum House in order to make money and pay her bills, the Gristmill's dangling carrot was so much more tantalizing: her Equity card and an acting career. Fame. *Love.* To live forever, as Phyllis had so accurately pegged it.

They knew it, of course. Which was why the Gristmill—Rex, specifically—was able to exploit the cast and crew, especially the newbies, and force them into quasi-slave labor and psychological mistreatment.

And if anyone didn't like it, they could always leave. Which Gwen eventually did, albeit in exchange for a contract role on a soap opera and a nice dressing room overlooking the Hudson.

So why was she missing?

Betty Rose checked the clock at the top of the computer screen. She'd be late for pearl-diving duty. She already felt skittish enough for sneaking off before dinner without signing out, although Phyllis had promised to cover for her.

But why should she feel skittish for leaving the Gristmill compound and needing cover in order to go to the public library to use their computer? What strange hold did the playhouse have that such an innocent and normal activity felt jarringly subversive?

There was no strange hold, she told herself, nothing out of the ordinary. Of course the playhouse required sign-ins and -outs; that was standard procedure in any professional theater.

They had to account for everyone at all times, or run the risk of starting a performance with missing cast or crew. It was perfectly logical, a time-tested fail-safe that had existed, certainly, for decades, if not centuries. And it was union regulation.

And if she felt skittish, she had only herself to blame for rooting through Gwen's personal diary instead of turning over the flash drive to Dottie, which would have been the proper thing to do. She wouldn't feel guilty for sneaking if she hadn't been sneaking in the first place.

She reached for the pink flamingo flash drive, paused.

She peered around the partition to the next cubicle. Now empty.

She circled her cursor around the print button on Gwen's diary. She clicked on it.

Across the room, the hulking laser printer whirred to life. Betty Rose closed out the diary file.

"My husband and I loved you in *The Pajama Game*," said a woman over her left shoulder. Betty Rose spun to the librarian-looking person smiling down at her. From her neck dangled a gold Gristmill pendant, peeking under her scalloped blouse.

"Oh, thank you, but I was just a factory girl," said Betty Rose, smiling back, one ear tuned elsewhere as she reached around to eject and pocket the flash drive. Across the room, she heard the printer churning out her pages. She instinctively reached for her purse, as a hiding place to stash her printing pages, and remembered she hadn't had her purse—or her luggage, wallet, ID, phone, money—since the first day she arrived at the playhouse. The first five minutes, to be precise.

"You stand out," the woman said, and Betty Rose nodded another thanks and stood up.

"So very kind of you," she said, as the printer completed its job and idled. "And I've got another one tonight. Can't be late!" She flashed a final smile and made her away across the room to the printer. Her pages were gone.

Betty Rose looked around for another printer.

"Erma, this isn't Playbill Online," Alistair complained from the edge of the librarian's desk, holding Betty Rose's printouts. He shuffled through them, perplexed. "This is more like *Diary of a Madman*. Oh my." His face tightened, reading further.

Betty Rose backed away to the wall, watched him. The printer revved up again. Alistair put her pages down on the librarian's desk and fished the new ones from the printer. He brightened.

"Oh, there it is!" he said, reading the page. "In the back of the queue."

Alistair walked away from the printer and sat back at the computer cubicle next to where Betty Rose had been. She darted to the librarian desk and soundlessly scooped up her stack of pages.

"I *told* my agent they were reviving *Applause*!" Alistair bragged to himself as he read his printouts, to Erma, to the room. He studied his pages and then held it away, exasperated. "A modern-day *reimagining*, they're calling it. Such a stupid word. Really, who came up with such a nonsense word? Although I suppose the story *is* timeless, in its own dark way...."

Betty Rose folded her pages in half, tucked them under her arm, like a clutch. She eyed the exit, past Alistair and his cubicle and Erma. She watched him carefully as he read on.

"They're doing it at the Golden? Egads!" he exclaimed with a scolding gasp. "The proscenium's much too constricting for a full-sized musical. Unless they're scaling it down, as part of their *reimagination*." He spat the word and squinted, engrossed in the article. He swiveled in his chair back to the cubicle desk and drummed his fingers.

Betty Rose, on her tiptoes, dashed across the room and reached the door.

"Miss?" Erma called after her. "You have to pay for those."

Betty Rose froze and turned back.

"The printouts, I mean," Erma added, almost apologetically. She indicated the folded stack that Betty Rose appeared to be hiding. "They're a dime a page."

Alistair swiveled in his chair. "Is that...Betty Rose?" he called from behind Erma, leaning around to get a keener view. He peered over his half-glasses and beamed, and then came up short with his realization. "Was that your diary I was reading? Oh my, a thousand pardons...."

"It's...okay," she forced out.

"Such a violation of your privacy," he added, shaking his head. "My deepest apologies."

Betty Rose looked from him to the librarian, who stood smiling at her, waiting.

"I'm sorry," Betty Rose told her. "I don't have any money."

"Oh my," said the librarian, and Alistair sprang up. He reached for his wallet in the back pocket of his khaki shorts. His legs were white and bony.

"My treat, my dear," he said, plucking out a single. "Least I can do for snooping so. How many pages did you have?"

Betty Rose looked at the folded stack in her hand. The pages trembled.

Alistair plucked out two more dollar bills, held them out to the librarian. "I'm sure that will cover it, Erma. No need to call the jimmies on this dear girl."

Erma smiled at her and said, "Oh, I would never do such a thing."

"Th-thank you," said Betty Rose, forcing her own smile to them both.

Alistair pointed at Betty Rose and said, "That girl's a comer." Erma said, "Yes, I know." Alistair said, "The future of theatre." Erma said, "Oh yes, I know."

"Thank you," Betty Rose repeated and smiled again.

"I'll see you at half hour, dear?" Alistair said.

Scene Twelve

Saturday: Exhausted...Starving...Prisoner...I don't want a damn family. I just want my card...!

Gwen's printed tirade assaulted her as she hurried back across Carla Avenue, worming through the art fair crowds. She sifted the pages, absorbing each sentence, starting with Gwen's first week at the playhouse and quickly moving forward, day by day.

A clanging jolted her, and she looked up to the New Hope trolley bus that had halted for her, blocking its path. The conductor smiled and waved, and Betty Rose nodded an apology and skedaddled out of the way. She tripped on the curb and lurched forward, righting herself to prevent a face-plant. She limped ahead and focused on her steps between pages, lest she twist her ankle and bench herself from the evening's performance.

Wednesday: Some old bitch Marian kicked it last night. Rex lost his shit. Emergency meeting with the flying monkeys on his little boat. Carla? Cady? What show are they fucking casting?

Betty Rose had forgotten how crude and vulgar Gwen could be, especially when agitated. Disrespectful, too. Marian Maples, a true theatre legend, deserved better treatment in her diary. It was shocking, although perhaps not so surprising, that Gwen didn't know who she was. Gwen didn't have much respect for the theatre as a whole. She really didn't belong at the Gristmill.

But why was she missing?

Betty Rose checked the diary entry and oriented herself time-wise. On that Wednesday, she was still a cocktail waitress at the Rum House, desperate for a break. On Thursday, the Broadway theaters dimmed their lights in honor of Marian Maples, who had died onstage on Tuesday, if she remembered correctly. On Friday—which she vividly remembered because it had been easy to get her day shift covered for the incoming weekend tourist crowd—the Siren agency summoned her for a general meeting with Wes, when he first poured cold water on her dreams and then called in a favor to the Gristmill to take her on as a summer apprentice, even though their season had already started. She got the green light late Sunday afternoon—outside, in the rain, while *The Boy Friend* cast was celebrating the end of their work week at her bar—and the following morning boarded the bus for New Hope, where she'd been ever since.

But during that time frame, right before she'd arrived, there had clearly been high drama at the Gristmill, if Gwen's diary was to be believed. Triggered, it seemed, by Marian Maples's death onstage that Tuesday. An upheaval that spurred an emergency meeting between Rex and his top lieutenants, Dottie and Alistair.

I'm not right for the role? Not committed enough? Fine, get rid of me. Can't wait to expose this freekshow from the inside.

So Gwen was eavesdropping—spying really—on Rex and his flying monkeys. Listening in outside his boat, the *Panic*, docked on the Delaware, where Gwen had said he "hatches his plots." Phyllis had scolded her that first night for snooping, which didn't make sense to Betty Rose at the time but seemed clearer now, as she dashed across the Journeyman Bridge, past Clyde digging in the flower beds, and hurried toward the playhouse, already late for pearl diving. Gwen's journal laid it all out.

Rex and his monkeys were right, of course: Gwen wasn't committed enough to cut it at the Gristmill, in spite of her glorious soprano voice and gorgeous, open face that read all the way to the back row. She was the star of the summer and would have most certainly gotten a solo, and her Equity card, were it not for her nasty attitude and sense of entitlement and general cynicism. A waste of great potential. Self-sabotage, as Rex would say. And yet her departure increased Betty Rose's chances of nabbing her own card, since the Gristmill could give out only one.

"Well, look who decided to show up," Dottie snarled, scrubbing a large pot in the kitchen sink, down to her elbow. "I'm so sorry. I lost track of time," said Betty Rose. Dottie hurled the wire pad and then wiped the suds down the front of her apron. She shook her head and stalked from the kitchen, martyrdom in every step.

But was it only chance, a coincidence, that Gwen booked a soap opera (on a weekend), at the same time she'd been threatening to flee and spill secrets about the playhouse, after overhearing that they were going to get rid of her?

And now was missing?

Monday: A new girl arrived. To replace me, I'm sure. Green and clueless. I gotta warn her about this place....

That would be her. She arrived on a Monday, green and clueless. The third intern when the playhouse usually had two.

"Places!" Becky called over the intercom, jolting Betty Rose at her dressing room mirror. She hadn't even started her make-up. "What is wrong with you?" Phyllis demanded, impatient at the door. "We're *on!*" The overture sounded, and Betty Rose raced down the stairs, bare-faced and poorly costumed. She'd finish getting ready after the opening number, "A Weekend at Hareford."

And Gwen *had* warned her about this place, especially on that last night when she cornered Betty Rose—in the down-stairs dressing room and by the Delaware—and urged her to bolt. And then was gone the next morning, without a trace, except for the flash drive she had left behind, hidden in the mattress coils. Gwen had remembered everything else—her clothes, luggage, laptop, bag of pot—but had forgotten her own diary, with her daily account of the abuses of the play-house, which she'd vowed to expose. It had, apparently, slipped her mind.

Betty Rose trudged back up the silo stairs, ignoring glares from Rachelle and others whose names she couldn't remember and wondering what she'd done to earn their evil eye. "You did the wrong number," Phyllis explained in the dressing room, inspecting her. "You did the staging for the finale." Betty Rose said, "I did? Sorry." Phyllis laughed and said, "You're all moon-batty tonight. Wonky McWonkster." Betty Rose apologized again, searching the rack for her next costume.

Had Gwen gone public like she'd threatened to do, it would be, at the very least, a major embarrassment for the Gristmill and would reinforce its notoriety in the theatre world as a strange cult. New York theatre was such an insular, gossipy place—Betty Rose already knew that from Julian and her own brief time around it, even from listening in on actors' chatter at her bar—and a firsthand report from someone who'd been inside the Gristmill, a whistle-blower really, would be enormously damaging to its reputation and could even deter top talent from working there. One blog on Playbill Online could taint it forever, nationwide. It might hurt box office sales. Even more perilous, it could spur Equity to take action and shut the fabled place down.

But now Gwen wouldn't be much of a whistle-blower, because she'd forgotten her diary, which she wrote in every night and took great pains to hide. Even though she packed up absolutely everything else when she left—in the middle of the night—to join the soap opera, which she'd booked on a weekend. And then went missing.

She hadn't just called the Gristmill a freak show. She'd insisted it was dangerous.

And she'd obviously overhead something troubling, perhaps chilling, when she spied on Rex and Dottie and Alistair outside the *Panic.*

"Betty Rose! Betty Rose, you've missed your cue," Becky called over the intercom, and Betty Rose sprinted down the silo stairs, only to be stopped backstage by the assistant stage manager, who shook his head and sent her back. Too late to join "Hold My Hand," fully in progress. Betty Rose grimaced an apology and ran back upstairs to change into her "Lambeth Walk" costume. She couldn't miss the act-one finale and the show's biggest crowd pleaser.

Gwen could tell the world about the starvation, the sleep deprivation, the union-rule-breaking all-nighters, even the public strip-down if Rex had forced her into that, too. It was likely one of his initiation rites for newbies, and if he'd strong-armed Gwen into it, traumatizing her—scarring her, really—then she could blurt it to the world, and out of context it wouldn't seem as harmless and liberating as it had onstage at the time. It would seem downright creepy, if not criminal. It was sexual harassment and the stuff of dirty-old-man fantasy. It was, now that Betty Rose thought about it, outrageous.

Betty Rose steadied herself on the fly deck backstage, dressed and prepped for "Lambeth Walk." She glanced around at Rachelle and Caleb and Phyllis, rocking on their heels, primed for their entrance. She darted a quick look over at Dottie and Alistair, huddled together, also awaiting their cue for the act-one closing number. The flying monkeys always at the ready. Rex's eyes and ears and most loyal henchmen. It was quite the coincidence, she realized, that Alistair had materialized in the library, in the same room, at the same time she had. That he'd intercepted Gwen's diary—by accident, of course— and had skimmed it before handing it back over. Proof positive of Gwen's treachery, from her secret, hidden flash drive, which they'd apparently overlooked when they likely searched her room after her sudden departure.

She looked down at her hands. She'd forgotten her gloves. She'd hide them behind her back during the number, lest Baub unload on her.

Had Gwen been easily excitable or prone to exaggeration—like, say, Phyllis—then it would have been easy to ignore even now her parting shots at the playhouse as sour grapes or a hyperactive imagination or maybe even pot-induced paranoia. But the laid-back, blasé Gwen was, if nothing else, too cool for hysteria and must have heard something especially alarming between Rex and his monkeys the night she warned Betty Rose to escape. It was unlike her to show such urgency, and the fear—terror, actually—in her eyes had been real.

"Breaking you down is their first act," Gwen had schooled her, as that hazy, drunken night when Betty Rose thought she was getting the ax came more sharply into focus. "Molding you is the second." She had spoken with authority and conviction. "I don't even want to know their third...."

Sutton launched into the final chorus of "Once You Lose Your Heart" in front of the scrim, and the cast migrated to their positions in the dark. Betty Rose assumed her spot upstage, in the back. Sutton finished to applause, and the scrim rose.

The flying monkeys anchored each side of the stage, as they typically did in group numbers, per Rex's blocking. Rex positioned them to surround the cast offstage as well. Dottie seemed to pop up whenever anyone mentioned Rex, like a dog whistle. Behind Alistair's affable, fuddy-duddy, fey facade lay a spy and a tattletale. Both stealth drones, reporting back to dear leader whenever someone dared speak up against him or his playhouse.

We've got to get out of here, Gwen had urged her that night by the Delaware. *They're grooming us for something awful,* she'd insisted.

And then vanished the next day, for her soap opera gig and her nice dressing room, according to Dottie, who now crisscrossed the stage as the chorus modulated up a key on the second go-around, shooting a careful glance back at Betty Rose. She was always watching.

But even if Gwen had booked her soap opera gig on a Sunday and left on Monday, the first bus back to the city on weekdays didn't leave until noon, which Betty Rose knew because she'd taken that bus the day she arrived, to get here as early as possible. But Gwen's closet, her luggage, everything was cleared out, without a trace of her, before noon, if Betty Rose had her timing right. That was such a scattered, confused morning when she woke up naked in Caleb's bed and then stumbled back to her (empty, Gwen-free) room to pull herself together.

And then found out about Gwen's abrupt departure from Dottie, frantically mopping the stage. Which was itself, she now realized, odd. The crew mopped the stage before each performance, but it didn't make sense to mop it—frantically— between set strike of one show and set load-in of the next one, when it was bound to get dirty again. Unless, of course, it was unusually dirty or stained from the night before. And in any event, mopping was the stage crew's job, not Dottie's. Unless they'd done a slack-assed job and she wanted it done right, to clean up whatever mess they'd missed. It did seem, Betty Rose now remembered more vividly, particularly important to Dottie to get the stage clean, and to keep her off it. While at the same time insisting that Gwen had not vanished but had simply booked a soap opera gig on a Sunday, and that's why she had disappeared so suddenly. And left "on the first bus of the morning," as Dottie had said. Except there were no buses in the morning. The first bus came, Betty Rose knew, at noon.

On the third repeat of the sing-along chorus, Sutton led the way down the stage stairs to the left aisle. The others followed, and some migrated to the right aisle. They fanned out, dancing their way toward the lobby, shaking hands with the audience. Betty Rose lingered in the back, waiting her turn with the others. She stared outward into the house.

And Gwen wouldn't be in a dressing room overlooking the Hudson, as Dottie had claimed, because there were no more soap operas in New York City. They'd all moved to Connecticut, which every young actor knew, and which Betty Rose had originally thought was a harmless oversight on Dottie's part, since she'd apparently been out of the New York show business scene for a long time, having decamped to New Hope years ago to serve as Rex's number one monkey. But it no longer seemed a harmless oversight. It seemed a clumsy lie to cover a previous lie and likely another before that.

The audience blurred as it had once before, right before Betty Rose passed out that night, when she'd collapsed on the stage, sobbing over what she'd thought was the end of her Gristmill career. Only to be comforted, in her dreams, by a hallucinatory parade of Gristmill legends who'd gone before her. Who morphed, in her dreams, into a terrified and desperate Gwen, begging for help. Who was then rushed by the blurry figures behind her—just like the ones she stared at now—before gasping for breath and vomiting up blood, as if stabbed in the back by some wild mob—with *dull stage knives*—to silence her. A horrific, nightmarish vision that had resurfaced in Betty Rose's subconscious, and her dreams, repeatedly since. As if Gwen—now missing, with her sister and the NYPD and New Hope sheriff looking for her—was reaching out from the grave.

Leaving behind no trace of herself, except her diary, which she'd vowed to publish. With its final entry before she vanished:

I swear there's something deadly brewing here....

You killed her! Betty Rose thought with an explosive charge, looking down at the cast.

They turned and looked back up at her, in silence.

She closed her mouth.

She scanned the audience, also staring at her, alone, stage center. The music had stopped moments ago, or hours. Shock hung in the air, from what she now realized was her own on-stage outburst.

Myron gawked up from the orchestra pit with baffled, pleading eyes. The orchestra held down their instruments.

"*Didn't you?*" she asked the room with sharp accusation. "Didn't you...?" Her voice broke and softened.

She shrank back.

The curtain rang down.

Scene Thirteen

BETTY ROSE CROSSED THE GANGPLANK toward the *Panic*.

She had stayed frozen onstage, prickling with sweat and weighing her bad options, after the curtain came down and the work lights came up for intermission. The stage crew rushed to make sure she was all right, and she nodded and said, "Yes, I'm fine. Thank you," still stunned by her own meltdown and struggling to collect her wits.

There had been neither scolding nor reprimand, and the cast soldiered on past her without glares or snarks, because the calamity was so enormous that to salvage the second act required their focused, steely professionalism. There was, she knew, no excess energy to waste on her.

They parked her in the green room for the second act— even her dressing room was off-limits, lest she pull some fresh stunt and unnerve Phyllis—where she sipped the chamomile tea they brought and breathed deeply and watched "The Sun Has Got His Hat On" and "Song of Hareford" on the monitor hanging from the ceiling. The show did not miss her.

It was during "Leaning On a Lamppost"—her favorite number, toward the end, with its sweet melody and tender longing, not to mention the brilliant special effect of the lead dancing with his airborne cane that the crew had rigged with invisible wire—that Betty Rose finally regained her bearings. The magnitude of her screwup landed hard. It was ridiculous, she now knew, to think that anyone from the cast or crew had a part in Gwen's disappearance. Or that it had been a disappearance at all. It was demonstrably insane to leap to the unhinged conclusion that they had killed her. Dottie and Alistair were nosy busybodies, to be sure, but they were also old and doddering and borderline clownish with their Keds and bony chicken legs and vaudeville banter.

And it was doubly deranged to imagine they had commandeered the cast and crew to do their dirty work for them. Sutton was a Tony-winning Broadway star who would never jeopardize her career being associated with a marauding band of murderers. Plus, it didn't fit her fresh, happy disposition at all. Rachelle was fiercer with a salty mouth, and Betty Rose could envision her potentially killing a cheating boyfriend, but not a young, budding actress with a bad attitude. And yes, they were all slavishly loyal to Rex, but in the same way a sports team was devoted to a charismatic and beloved coach. It was lunatic to think he would have ordered his flying monkeys to order his minions to take out Gwen. Or that they would have obeyed.

Had she really believed that, she would have fled or screamed out for help to the audience members, to rescue her from her deadly cohorts. But she felt no urge to run, no real sense of panic or belief in her fleeting delusions, especially now that she'd had a full second act to sit and ponder how preposterous it all was. It was just the fallout from her emotional overload over the past several weeks, from her sudden arrival and the mood shifts caused by her early failures balanced against the thrill of rising up the ranks and winning accolades and fans, to her nonstop work schedule and lack of sleep, coupled with the dawning reality of what was likely a permanent breakup with Julian, which she hadn't given much thought to lately but had to be taking its toll on her subconsciously. After all, they'd been together for years and were in love, or so she'd thought until she'd unmasked his contempt for her talent. Worse than contempt: his dismissal.

The highs and lows over the summer had destabilized her. No wonder she'd gone wiggy.

After the finale and an especially enthusiastic ovation—fueled, no doubt, by the audience's appreciation of the company's redoubled efforts to save the performance—the cast filed past the green room on their way upstairs, exhaling and reliving their triumph with survivors' relief. Sutton and Rachelle and the others peeked in on her in the green room and smiled with warmth and a tinge of pity. Betty Rose was not well.

Looking back, Betty Rose couldn't even be certain it was Gwen's headshot the New Hope sheriff had shown Rex. She'd seen it from an angle, from high above, and with only one eye when she peered down from the edge of the control booth window. Tons of actresses had million-dollar smiles, glossy, raven hair, and brilliant eyes, especially from fifteen feet away. Any one of them could be missing, for any number of reasons. She'd assumed it was Gwen only because of her recurring nightmares and dazed memory of that night with the desperate pleas and vomiting blood—the same night, she reminded herself, when Barbara Stanwyck and Bette Davis and Katharine Hepburn came to her with both comfort and stern orders to pull herself together and soldier on. Clearly, they had been dreams, so it followed logically that Gwen's grotesque vision had been, as well. That didn't mean Gwen was missing, or dead.

Becky, still on her cordless headset, checked in and told her to sit tight. Then she darted out again.

Betty Rose was heartened that no one seemed angry or even hostile toward her. Indeed, they tread carefully near her. Maybe she seemed fragile. Or perhaps her bizarre spell onstage had been magnified in her own mind and was merely a faux pas, a professional slip no more serious than a missed dance step or dropped line that no one in the audience had even noticed. She'd simply frozen up for an instant, which she'd seen countless actors do in the past without ruinous effect. The cast had covered for her, as she had done for others many times before. After all, they were a team. And it was likely Rex had missed it altogether, since he rarely attended performances once a show opened. He was usually off on his yacht, working on the next one.

Dottie, still in wig, makeup, and costume, stormed into the green room. She seemed frantic on the cusp of panic, which was normal, but composed herself at the door. She approached Betty Rose with delicacy.

"Dottie, I'm so sorry," Betty Rose started, but Dottie zipped her lip and smiled down with almost motherly warmth. She took a breath.

"Rex would like to see you," she announced. "In his room."

● ● ●

The gangplank to the *Panic* was wobbly and rocked with the boat. Betty Rose grasped the rope bannister and inched carefully across from the wooden dock, over a short span of the Delaware.

The *Panic* was forbidden territory that always loomed in the distance. It was Rex's sanctuary, and no one save his monkeys was granted access. The aged artifact houseboat glowed from its curtained windows, as it did every night.

Dottie's orders to report to him had been firm but kind. Betty Rose expected a reprimand, even a dressing-down, but nothing more. She'd proven her mettle over the past two months and had earned a second chance from a minor slipup. The season would be over in a week. Her apology would be passionate and sincere and would get her through.

She paused at the screen door, shrouded by vertical blinds. From inside came a persistent low chatter that echoed off the river, whose crests rhythmically splashed against the sides. The current must have been deceptively turbulent, as the boat rocked with deeper bows than the glassy river would suggest. Betty Rose readjusted her stance to balance out the movement. She lightly knocked on the doorframe and waited.

Moments passed without response. From inside, the chatter continued. Betty Rose sidestepped to the edge to glance down the length of the boat. Two windows were cracked open. She listened. The chatter stopped. She went back to the door, knocked again.

Dottie had told her not to keep Rex waiting. She listened another beat, then gingerly opened the screen door and stepped in through the blinds. She jumped as the door slammed behind her.

Rex's stateroom smacked of adventure. The wooden shelves were lined with leather books and a collection of terrestrial and celestial globes, the walls paneled and covered with framed, vintage nautical maps. A tarnished brass telescope on tripod legs stood by a window facing across the river. His easy chair was indented from years of use and sat by a stack of yellowing *New York Times*. There was no trace of musical theatre. It was a captain's command post.

The room was empty, and the chatter, she now realized, came from a radio floor console under the far window. It crackled with static over an old-time episode of *The Whistler*. The narrator talked her through the killer closing in on his prey, his nasally voice rising with the tension.

She must have found her sea legs, as the boat had stopped rocking.

Betty Rose migrated to the antique, rolltop desk along the wall. It was open and strewn with sharp pencils, papers, and a three-ring notebook labeled "Current Season." Betty Rose hesitated and then, unable to resist, thumbed through the tabbed dividers of each show they'd done throughout the summer. Elaborate handwritten notes and layered directions covered preprinted diagrams of the playhouse stage. Each production number was carefully worked and reworked with specific choreography, light and sound cues, actor positions, et cetera. The shows didn't just happen. Rex sweated out each detail in advance.

She flipped to the final tab, labeled "Homecoming." The stage diagrams were titled "Opening," "Midact," "Ensemble," and, lastly, "FINALE" in all caps. On this diagram were two circles downstage, near the apron, in the middle. Each circle had a "C" inside it. Flanking them across the back of the stage were scattered dozens of numbered circles in various positions.

On the left side of the diagram was a key matching the numbered circles to specific cast members. Dottie was "six";

Alistair was "eight." Each actor, it seemed, was assigned a circle in the final number.

Betty Rose ran her finger down the key list. Her name was not on it.

A woman's scream jolted her. Betty Rose spun, as the room went abruptly silent.

Rex stood by the radio console, having switched it off at the murderous climax. He wore a white terry-cloth robe and leather slippers. His silvery hair was wet and slicked back. He looked up at her and smiled.

"Theatre of the mind," he said, nodding toward the radio. "Back when audiences used, and honed, their imaginations."

Betty Rose fought back dread, less from having been caught snooping than the discovery that her name was missing from the cast list of the season's Homecoming finale.

She stepped away from his desk. Rex padded toward it.

"I apologize for keeping you waiting," he said. "I was in the shower."

"Rex, I'm so sorry about tonight," she blurted, but Rex cut her off.

"Yes, I heard about your…spell," he said with a shrug. "Your call of the wild." And Betty Rose said, "I don't know what got into me.…"

"You have doubts because I planted them there," he said, sitting in his desk chair. "To test you." He swirled around, opened the top drawer, pulled out a white envelope. He placed it on the desk, pushed back on the chair's casters. He smiled at her again and nodded at the envelope.

She opened it. Inside was a ticket for Trans-Bridge Bus Lines. A one-way back to New York City.

"No…," she said, the word catching in her throat.

Rex was already at the coat closet. He wheeled out her rolling bag, set it upright in the middle of the room. From the handle dangled her purse, which she hadn't seen since the day she arrived.

"They returned this weeks ago, from somewhere," he said simply. "I'd forgotten all about it. But you'll need it for your trip home tomorrow."

"Rex," she said. "Please..."

He shrugged again. "You're not one of us. Most aren't. And there's no shame in that. But the show must go on." He tipped his head and wandered toward the galley.

"My mind's been playing tricks on me, Rex...." She followed after him.

He whirled on her, no longer smiling. "I can feel a fly buzzing in my theater. You think I can't sense you snooping around? Doubting me? On a scavenger hunt for clues?"

"I don't doubt you, Rex," she pleaded, collecting her thoughts. "It's just...Gwen's soap opera..."

"...is not even on the air!" he shouted. "I don't know why Dot took it upon herself to lie about that. What goes on between Gwen and this playhouse is none of your goddamned concern." He stormed back to his desk. "But since you refuse to mind your own business..."

He yanked open a side drawer and grabbed a clear plastic sandwich bag, which he tossed on the desk. Inside were dozens of colored pills and a tiny envelope of white powder.

"This is what Gwen was hiding in her room. Her own personal pharmacy." He pointed at the pills, the powder, and little tabs in foil. "Strikes one, two, and three! She's out!"

Betty Rose stared at them. She hadn't known the extent of Gwen's drug use.

"Gwen broke the rules, and now she is gone," Rex declared with a hint of sadness. "Back to wherever she came from. I wish her the very best. But if I got ensnared in the personal, destructive drama of every self-sabotaging wannabe actor who walked in and out my door over the past thirty-odd years, I'd never have a show. I run a business, not a charity!"

He swiveled back to his desk, hunched over the notebook Betty Rose had peeked through.

"I had such great expectations for you," he said. "But alas. A bus unloads a new crop every day, year after year. And so it goes.

"Now, if you'll excuse me," he added, calming, pencil in hand, "I have a show to recast." And with that, he focused on his work, oblivious to her.

Betty Rose stood still, watched him. "I…don't want to go," she said.

"Sorry. Did you say something?" Rex asked, scribbling on his stage plan.

"I don't want to go!"

Rex flew back off his chair, came nose to nose with her.

"What *do* you want?" he demanded. "Why are you *here*? It makes no sense to me. I never asked you to come, you know. You asked to be here!"

"You know what I want," she said.

"What, Betty Rose? *What?*"

"I want to be a star!"

"And how bad do you want it?"

"It's all I've ever wanted!"

"And what will you do to get it?"

"Anything!" she cried out. "*Anything!*" She trembled but stood in place, pleading.

Rex backed a step, softened. He seemed proud of her confession.

"So why all this nonsense, this *tsuris*?" he asked quietly. "Why do you resist? Don't you know I can help get you there? Just let. It. Happen."

"I'm scared, Rex!"

"Of success?" he asked. "Of winning?"

She shook her head. He nodded. She nodded with him.

"It is far better to do what you're scared of than to be scared of what you might do," he said.

He picked up his notebook, showed her the stage plan for the season's Homecoming finale. He pointed at one of the "C" circles downstage and center.

"This," he said, tapping on it. "Is you. The Homecoming. A solo. Your union card. And full membership in our family."

Her hands shot to her mouth. "Oh, Rex," she said, fighting a breakdown. "Thank you. Thank you!" And then, just as abruptly, she added, "What about Phyllis?"

Rex tapped on the second downstage circle. "She'll be there. Right next to you.

"You'll both get your cards," he clarified at her confusion. "Do you really think I let a stupid union tell me how many I can give out?"

"You won't be disappointed, Rex," she said, composing herself. "I won't wig out again. I swear." She stood tall, pro-like.

Rex smiled at her efforts. "This place is strange," he said. "It was strange long before I got here. I warned you the first night, remember?" Betty Rose laughed and said, "You did!" She laughed again and added, "Does it get...any stranger?"

He lifted his eyebrows in mischief, triggering more titters.

"Of course it does," he said, holding his thumb and fore-finger an inch apart. "You're this close to your lifelong dream. Your mind will play all sorts of new tricks on you. Awful tricks. You're about to become your own worst enemy."

Betty Rose shook her head. "I won't let that happen," she insisted. "No, sir."

"I know you better than you do," he reminded her. "And even I'm not sure which way you'll turn."

"I do," she answered. "I'll be just fine."

"Mind over madness," he added, tapping the side of his head. "Will you run from your talent? Escape back to medioc-rity and failure? Will you *flinch*? We shall see...."

"You'll be so proud of me," she said. "I swear."

Rex stepped closer. In the drama and outbursts, his robe had loosened at the belt. She looked down to avert her eyes from the white hairiness of his barrel chest. Then she looked away when she noticed the robe hung open further at his waist.

He lifted her face with both hands, up to his eyes.

"I'm already proud of you," he said. "You only have to do exactly what I say."

Betty Rose stifled a giggle, avoided his gaze. She closed her eyes, nodded within his grip.

"See, you're exactly what we want, Betty Rose," he said, his face closer. "So very much..." His hands tightened and pulled.

Betty Rose broke off, wriggled backward. Stifled another snicker.

"Please don't...," she said softly, with apology.

Rex inspected her, amused. "Now, what's that about?" he asked.

"Sorry, I just don't...do that," she said.

"Do what?" he said, and then it dawned on him. He guffawed. "You think I want to fuck you? Is that it?"

The word stung, making her blush. She recoiled. "I...don't know!" she stammered.

"Do you want me to?" he asked, tickled. "Would you like that, Betty Rose?"

"No!" she said, embarrassed and fevered. She sweated anew. "I mean...no!"

"Whew!" Rex said, fully entertained. "That's a relief. Now, that would be awkward...."

She heard footsteps in a far room. Caleb emerged barefoot down the hallway, a white towel wrapped around his naked waist. His hair was dripping.

"'Sup, B.R.?" he said, flashing his smile. He opened the galley refrigerator, took out a diet Shasta. "That was quite the improv you pulled tonight."

"...thanks...," she said, staring. A bead of water trickled down his chest, soaked into the towel below his navel. He poured a handful of peanuts from a jar. "I'm always so famished this time of night," he said, tossing them back.

Rex stayed focused on Betty Rose. She glanced between the two. Rex in his robe; Caleb in his towel. She stiffened.

"Caleb, I think we're done for tonight," Rex said finally. "Would you escort this young lady back to her dorm? She's had quite an eventful day."

"Sure thing," Caleb said, unknotting the towel. "Just let me grab my stuff."

"I don't need an escort," Betty Rose said quickly, nodding at them as she backed toward the front door. "Really, I can manage. Thank you again, Rex." She beamed and made a slight bow before grabbing the handle of her rolling bag. She slung her purse over her shoulder. "Good night, Caleb," she said, waving as she opened the door, pulling her luggage.

"Good night, everybody!" she repeated as it swung shut behind her.

● ● ●

"I was dying to tell you, but Rex swore me to secrecy," Phyllis explained back in their room. She knelt in her nightgown on her mattress, bouncing like an excited child. "Can you believe it, B.R.? We're going pro. One week from tonight!"

Not soon enough, thought Betty Rose, stitching the red sequined gown they'd assigned her to mend. But she said, "That's great news, isn't it?"

She had told Phyllis about the Rex/Caleb romance, or whatever it was. They didn't hide it; why should she?

"S-s-scandal," Phyllis whistled out with shocked drama, seemingly titillated. "Who knew?"

"To each his own," said Betty Rose, tightening a stitch at the top of the back. "None of my business." She held the dress out and inspected it; the moth hole was nearly closed. The audience would never see it from the back anyway.

"Well...yeah...you know," added Phyllis, daydreaming at the ceiling. "It *is* musical theatre."

Scene Fourteen

THERE WAS NO DAY OFF, NO "SHORE LEAVE" THAT MONDAY. They went straight from set strike of *Me and My Girl* into rehearsals for the Homecoming reunion show on Friday. It was a strictly limited engagement: one night only.

The show would be, Rex announced at the morning company meeting on the grassy knoll, a musical revue. The "best of" numbers culled from shows they'd performed in the past, selected by Rex. And, like all musical revues, subject to change at the last minute and at his discretion.

Betty Rose was showered with hugs and congratulations from all sides. Everyone was thrilled she'd be getting her solo and Equity card. She hugged back and thanked them all, but her mind was already beyond the summer and the Gristmill Playhouse, albeit with one eye trained on Friday night, which could change her career and life.

The thrill of community, of belonging to the place, had abruptly worn off. It wasn't the Rex/Caleb affair, although that had been a shock, like Phyllis said. Not the gay aspect of it, which didn't faze her at all, nor the thirty-year-plus age difference, although that was somewhat off-putting. She didn't feel cheated on, since she and Caleb had shared only a minor flirtation and one quick kiss, which she had stopped as soon as it started. Caleb would flirt with a fire hydrant if it would show him love, which she found rather pitiful and certainly unattractive. His desperate need for attention was sad and commonplace among actors. It would also likely guarantee his future success, up to a point.

Most stars were sociopaths to one degree or another, she'd concluded. Their yearning for the spotlight drove every thought and action, even subconsciously. Rex (and Wes the agent) had called it "the motor"—the internal, spinning mechanism of neediness that set stars apart from other actors. It created an aura that mere mortals mistook for magic.

Betty Rose had a different term for it: mental illness. Perhaps the fallout from childhood neglect, if not abuse. And yet it worked for those who could harness it to their benefit. She'd often feared her own healthy sense of balance and self-esteem would doom her to mediocrity in her chosen profession. Now it was a point of pride that perhaps she was too stable to be a star. She loved acting and the joy of storytelling, but she didn't need adulation or worship. And in spite of her desperate outburst in Rex's stateroom—manufactured for his benefit and to save her hide—stardom for its own sake held diminishing allure as the summer wore on. If it happened for her, she vowed it would come from her talent and persistence, not to fill a void in her soul.

But Caleb's grabby ambition was so naked, his machinations so obvious, that it would likely repel the very audiences he hoped to seduce. His goods were too damaged. It was a trap the true stars—the wily ones—sidestepped. Nobody liked a narcissist, at least not for long. They were dull and exhausting. And self-obsession didn't age well.

"Congrats, B.R.!" called out a freckled dancer whose name escaped her from the rehearsal room as she passed by on her way to a fitting. Her fellow chorus girls looked over from their barre and added sunny good wishes. "Thank you!" Betty Rose chirped back, feigning modesty. "I'm so excited!" She waved and hurried on.

In spite of the unmasking of his pathetic nature, Caleb wasn't a factor in her change of heart about the playhouse. Neither were Rex's advances, which she'd clearly misread and would have seemed funny had she been in a laughing mood. But the episode on the boat just didn't sit right with her, and it took her that first sleepless night to pinpoint why. It symbolized, she now realized, how she felt about the Gristmill in general.

The place made her queasy.

Dear Mr. Arbor had pegged it when he called the playhouse a "jack-in-the-box." She never knew when—or what—it was going to spring on her next.

Betty Rose was tired of being on edge.

Gwen had felt the same way, at least toward the end before she was expelled. It partially explained her perennial bad mood and attitude. Her imagination had filled in the rest, conjuring up outlandish and sinister plots hatched by Rex on his little boat and executed by the Tweedledee -dum team of Dottie and Alistair. God knows what cocktail of drugs she had been on when hallucinating in her paranoid diary. Betty Rose felt sorry for her. But Gwen wasn't her problem.

Her problem was that she had fallen for it herself. So undermined was her self-confidence—so damaged and weakened her ego—by a summer at the Gristmill that her own imagination had run amok. She'd caught Gwen's delusional fever, at least briefly. There had been a time, not so long ago, when she had been top of her class, fearless onstage, immune to the insecurities that plagued most actors. A "tigress," as Julian always called her. Somewhere she had lost that. Now she chased and believed such preposterous fairy tales of doom that left her scurrying around town like a fugitive, afraid of everyone. The "awful tricks" her mind played on her, which Rex warned would only get worse the closer she got to her big break and were symptomatic of the most insidious disease of all for an actor: self-sabotage.

Sutton didn't offer congratulations when she passed her by the loading dock where the crew carried in tall sets wrapped in brown paper. She simply took Betty Rose's face in both hands, kissed her gently on the forehead, and locked eyes for a meaningful moment. Betty Rose blinked back her gratitude before Sutton moved on with a star's grace and confidence.

It was a confidence that she herself lacked, at least these days. And confidence, once eroded, was hard to build back. She realized now the deep-rooted message the Gristmill legends—Davis, Stanwyck, Hepburn—had tried to push on her during her drunken dream. They were her subconscious talking, urging her to be ferocious onstage, and in life. To be indestructible. Such made a true star.

She'd had that before her father took ill and died, before she came to the Gristmill and toiled under Rex's thumb. His boot, really. He was the most responsible for the awful tricks her mind had played. He'd degraded her self-esteem, her sense of power. She feared she'd never get it back.

She'd decided, overnight, on her endgame strategy for her final week at the Gristmill. She would work as hard as ever, deliver a boffo performance in front of the power audience on Friday, securing her Equity card. And then leave Saturday, never to return.

With her card, she would launch into the fall casting season a full-fledged pro. She'd get new headshots and audition daily, with or without an agent. She would book a job, quickly, for regional theatre, a tour, or a Broadway show itself. She would be unstoppable.

"Look at Miss Thang!" Baub gushed, pinning the waist of the red sequined gown she'd mended. She stood in front of the full-length mirror, wearing it for the first time. "You're bringing your diva to this old rag," he added, perched behind her in all his roundness. "You can pin it a little tighter," she instructed, finding it irksome and rather offensive when a grown white man mimicked a black drag queen. It was verbal blackface.

She would not be part of the Gristmill stable, to return year after year, like the other lemmings. It had nothing left to offer her. She was already outgrowing the place.

"Atta girl," Rachelle said, shoulder-clapping her at the sign-in board after lunch. "I had my doubts at first, but you won me over, bitch."

The rehearsal schedule was updated and posted four times a day now, as Rex shifted numbers and casts, honing the show as it drew nearer. It was a wild scramble, with Rex, Baayork, and Myron overseeing different groups: solos, small groups, and full company, in rehearsal spaces throughout the playhouse, even the lobby. Everyone was on call all the time, constantly checking the board for their next assignment. Betty Rose leaned into Rachelle's athletic embrace and said, "You bet your ass, bitch," and Rachelle threw her head back with an exploding cackle before racing off to her next rehearsal.

She'd repair the damage with Julian, an easy fix. It was their first serious falling-out, and they'd bounce back quickly. After all, they still lived together. She would admit he was right about the Gristmill being a cult, albeit a relatively toothless one. And she'd come home with the Equity card she'd won on her own.

She'd keep her skinny-dipping incident to herself. It was an innocuous transgression and not confession-worthy. She wouldn't grill Julian on his either. He'd better not have any.

"*The lips, the tongue, the top of the teeth*," she chanted along with the cast as Myron led them in diction drills before afternoon rehearsal. "*Blow wind, blow! Crack your cheeks! Rage! Blow!*" they repeated over and over, stretching their mouth muscles.

At the ten-minute break, she dashed up the aisle to the lobby water fountain. A fresh stack of the *New Hope Gazette* sat on the concessions stand. Splashed across the front were hers and Phyllis's headshots under the headline "By Popular Demand: The Gristmill's New Members." There was no article, just a reminder of that Friday's Homecoming show, with an invitation to all locals. Although admission was free, advance tickets were required from the box office, with proof of residency.

"We're back!" Dottie called from the stage, breaking Betty Rose's trance as she stared at her face in the paper. "La-di-da-di-everybody!"

The audience, she knew, would include not only locals, but also top-tier producers and agents from New York, all of whom had ties to this funny place. It would be her one shot to wow them and stick in their minds. Armed with her union card and these powerful contacts, the fall casting season would be hers for the taking. The Rum House could go to hell.

Rex watched from the back of the house after staging "Summer Nights," one of her favorite numbers. Sutton was entirely too old for "Sandy," yet she could channel a teenage freshness and was the headliner the audience wanted to see. The cast was segregated in clusters: the boys in tight white T's, the girls in poodle skirts with various colors and motifs. Betty Rose popped her hips to the beat as she'd been told, cheating looks around the theater. Rex checked his clipboard, likely the stage diagrams from the notebook she'd snooped through on the *Panic*.

And to think she'd called him "Daddy." She had only one daddy, and he'd died just a few months ago. It was sick of Rex to demand that.

Except he hadn't demanded it. She'd called him that on her own. But only because everybody else did, and she was particularly vulnerable and exposed—literally naked—in that bizarre moment onstage. It had seemed perfectly normal then. Now it seemed disloyal to her own father, if not blasphemous.

Her eye traveled offstage, where techies unwrapped the painted flats they'd loaded in earlier. They were colorful set pieces: a train station, a barn, a string of quaint shops along a main street, a river, trees. They were familiar; she'd seen them before, but in a different form. The techies leaned them against the backstage wall as she pondered them. On reflex, she looked up to the fly space above the stage where the Carla curtain lived when not in use. The flats were exact replicas of her town, New Hope: the world that surrounded and worshipped her.

"Stop! Cut!" Rex called from the back of the house. Betty Rose snapped back to attention as he stormed down the aisle, waving his clipboard. Myron, not hearing him from the pit, kept the band going.

"*Stopfuckingcut!*" he bellowed, silencing the room.

He leaped up the stage stairs, two at a time.

"Betty Rose, are you with us today?" he demanded. "Yes, Rex," she answered, hand on hip, like he'd told her. "I'm here with you." It came out with more attitude than she'd intended.

Rex grumbled on. "You're upstaging Sutton," he said, indicating the sight lines in the audience. "You should know better by now." Having made his point, he turned to go. He seemed exasperated with her.

Betty Rose stayed in her spot. "I'm standing where you told me to," she heard herself say.

There was a slight gasp from somewhere onstage. The room froze.

Rex turned slowly, puzzled, looking above everyone's heads. "I'm sorry. What did you say?"

"This is where you blocked me," she said, nodding toward his clipboard. "Check your notes." She sensed the cast distancing themselves onstage.

Rex chuckled once and then leveled a look at her, waiting for her to back down. She didn't.

"But I'm happy to move if you've changed your mind," she said.

"I have not changed my mind," he said pleasantly. "I would never have placed you there." Betty Rose shrugged and said, "Then where do you want me?"

"I want you to follow my fucking directions!" he exploded, slamming his clipboard onto the boards. Betty Rose kept cool and said, "I am, Rex. It's okay to admit when you're wrong."

"You stupid twat!" he roared, charging her, stopping inches from her nose. The blood rushed his cheeks, his forehead. "I've been staging this fucking number since before your slut mother was sucking off your dead Polack father!"

Betty Rose slapped him hard across the face. The crack echoed through the theater.

"Don't you ever talk to me that way again," she ordered him.

Rex regrouped. The force of her blow had knocked him back a step. He blotted blood from his nose, inspected his fingers. He smiled.

"Bingo," he said in a normal tone, nodding. "That killer instinct. That's it, Betty Rose. What every star needs." He seemed both proud and a shade fearful. He cowered.

Betty Rose wasn't satisfied. "Shut your fucking mouth, Rex," she commanded, still fuming. "Or you can keep your fucking card. Got it?"

Rex stood tall again, ignored her, which seemed his way of backing down while saving face. "It's just…the number isn't working. There are so many brunettes onstage at one time," he explained, searching for a solution. "It's monotonous. The audience gets confused who is who." He turned to Dottie, still flabbergasted in the wings. "Can we *please* fix that?" he asked her. "Can we get some variety up there?"

Dottie nodded and said, "Yes, Daddy. Of course."

Rex turned and ambled back down the stage stairs to the side aisle, lost in thought. "That would be great, thank you," he called back, still checking his nose. Dottie rushed toward him with a tissue and said, "Take ten, everybody!"

The cast kept an awed distance on the break. Betty Rose strolled past them out the back stage door and wandered around to the side facing the Delaware. She collapsed against the playhouse wall and struggled to catch her breath.

She smiled out at the river, choking back sobs of joy and relief.

She'd gored the bull.

Her kill spirit was back. It must be true. Rex had said so himself.

Scene Fifteen

"Twenty minutes till it sets," Dottie said, turning the dial on the timer. "The longer, the better. Makes the color richer."

Betty Rose sat under an old-school globe hair dryer, her head wrapped in a clear plastic cap.

Dottie had convinced her to change her hair color for the Homecoming show.

She'd cornered her at KP the next morning and made her case. "You'll thank me," Dottie said. "What Rex wants, if I can translate, is to showcase you, to make you stand out. After all, it's your debut, and you really only get one. And we're clearly heavy on brunettes this year."

Betty Rose had dyed her hair for roles before. The last time, her senior year, she'd gone blonde for *Side Show,* and through a sloppy mishap had fried her hair so irreparably that she'd had to wait months for fresh regrowth. Fortunately, the mortar board had saved her graduation photo.

"Can I just wear a wig?" she asked. Dottie considered and said, "Not for your solo. Even the best wigs look fake. You don't want to come across as a female impersonator."

She offered to try blonde again, very carefully this time.

Dottie frowned. "Not blonde," she said. "Tina and Ashley are blondes, and they have bigger breasts. You'll never be able to compete with that. It's your night, Betty Rose. The whole point is to shine."

How many hairs colors were there? Betty Rose wondered and asked. Dottie thought a moment and then led her downstairs to a back area off the laundry room. It was a mini-salon with a hair washing sink and hair appliances. With a stepladder, she reached up to a high shelf and fished out a white plastic jug that was tucked in the back corner. She brought it down, blew off the dust, and poured its dark liquid into a little cup.

"I have dance rehearsal," Betty Rose protested, and Dottie raspberried her lips. "Baayork can take a chill pill," she said. "This won't take long."

She sat Betty Rose at the washing station, tilted her head back into the black sink, and with gloved hands and a special brush, painted the cold, thick ooze onto her hair, starting at the roots. She was meticulous.

"It's semi-permanent," Dottie said, fitting the dryer globe over her head. "We can wash it out after the show. Or who knows? You might like it. Didn't do Lucy any harm."

Dottie brought her a *Bucks County* magazine and a cup of tea while she waited. "If you need anything else, just holler," she said, patting her hand before leaving the room. She'd softened toward Betty Rose. Everyone had. She'd graduated to a new level of respect since she'd made Rex stand down, like the palace guards after Dorothy killed the witch.

Betty Rose ignored the tourist magazine and practiced her solo, concentrating on the high note near the end, where the number ticked up a key. It had sounded thin and shrill in yesterday's rehearsal, when she'd strained for it. *Lazy jaw,* she could hear Myron urge. *Keep the larynx down. Deeper into the diaphragm.* The note had to come from below, she knew. It only passed through the throat, the mouth, on its way to the audience and the world. It was a mental adjustment she was determined to master before Friday.

The high note would have to wait. It was impossible to hit in the sitting position. She practiced the lower tones. They sounded rich and full in the echo chamber of the dryer globe. Effortless, even.

Her eye drifted up to the shelf lined with white plastic jugs. They were labeled in Magic Marker on masking tape. There was a light and dark ash, medium natural, chestnut, mahogany, and on the end, the bottle that Dottie had used on her. Betty Rose squinted. The label read "C/C." It looked older, more yellowed than the others.

When the timer rang, Dottie reappeared quickly. She rinsed and towel-dried her hair. With a roll brush, she blew out its lengths. "No peeking," she said. She conditioned and fluffed it, stood back and admired her handiwork. "Oh, that's nice," she said. She spun the chair.

The mirror shocked Betty Rose. Staring back was a red-head. Not a strawberry blonde or auburn, but a deep, flaming, almost cartoonish explosion cascading down around her shoulders. Betty Rose tensed.

"Oh jeezus," she said.

"It's a bit brassy but will tone down before tomorrow night," Dottie assured her, grinning at the reflection. "It'll pop with your green eyes under the spotlight. So feisty!" She fingered the ends of Betty Rose's tresses. "Now aren't you glad you didn't chop it? The stage demands big hair on its leading ladies." She flounced her own salt-and-pepper bob. "Put off the post-menopausal cut as long as you can."

Baayork shouted, "Aye carumba!" when Betty Rose walked into the rehearsal room. She snapped her fingers like casta-nets and then smiled earnestly and added, "I love it. It's pas-sionate. It's *secksi*."

She led Betty Rose in a solo dance drill in front of the mir-rors, a high-energy, one-on-one jazz class in preparation for a to-be-determined number on Friday night. After an hour, Baayork was drenched in sweat and needed a break. "Oh, to be young again!" she said, clacking from the room. "Take ten, Red!"

The playhouse seemed empty. Betty Rose wandered into the deserted mess hall and kitchen. She scanned the grassy knoll. Finally, she approached the inside door to the back-stage, which was closed. She cracked it and spied in.

"Should we block the back door?" Caleb asked in the distance.

From the stage door, Betty Rose peered past the wing flats to the brightly lit stage beyond. The entire company, it seemed, was in rehearsal. They fanned out across the boards, staggered and carefully placed.

"They usually run for the front." Rex's voice carried from the audience. "Just surround them with love. Makes it a bit eas-ier for them."

The tech crew worked onstage, too, hanging the new flats on fly cables. The church, the shops, the playhouse itself. They tested the train station, flying it up until it disappeared above and then lowering it again just above the floor. At the stage deck, a techie marked the correct measurements and gave a thumbs-up to the crew.

"Phyllis?" Rex called out from the house. "Where's Phyllis?"

Dottie sprang into action from the stage. "I'll find her, Daddy," she said, heading for the wings. Betty Rose quickly backed out the door and turned.

She bumped head-on into Phyllis, who was standing right behind her.

She, too, was a redhead.

"What are you doing skulking around here?" Phyllis said, smiling.

"They...dyed your hair, too?" Betty Rose asked. Phyllis nodded, a bit sheepish, and said, "Rex thinks there are too many blondes onstage." She shrugged and touched her hair, self-conscious. "Yours looks great. Mine looks freaky!"

Betty Rose indicated the stage door. "What number are they doing?" she asked. Phyllis looked at the door and shrugged again. "Something for the Homecoming, I guess," she said. "Rex keeps changing his mind. It's funny to see him so antsy."

"Why aren't we in it?" Betty Rose asked. "It's full company."

Phyllis feigned surprise at the question. "Look who turned diva overnight!" she said with a laugh. "We're getting our solos. I guess we can't be in everything, stage hog."

Dottie opened the door, bumping Betty Rose's shoulder. They both jumped.

"Sorry, B.R.," Dottie said, flustered, and then added, "Why aren't you rehearsing with Baayork?" Betty Rose said, "We're on a break. I was just seeing what—" and Dottie interrupted her, grabbing Phyllis by the arm. "Phyllis, you're on," she said, pulling her past and through the door.

Dottie turned back and looked at Betty Rose. "B.R., the new programs are on the front porch. Can you stuff the inserts? We're so pressed for time. That's a good girl." With that,

Dottie closed the door behind her. Betty Rose heard it lock from the inside.

A chill shot through with the spiking fear that she'd been cut from the show. That Rex, in response to her standing up to him—in retaliation for her disrespect—had shuffled her out of the cast. Taking her solo with him.

But then why the effort to dye her hair or a dance rehearsal with Baayork? Why waste the energy, if they only planned to cut her? The clock was ticking toward the show, and like Dottie said, they were pressed for time.

Relax, she scolded herself. Rex had worked out the running order in his mind, and if Betty Rose wasn't in this particular group number, it was likely because she was in the next act. Maybe even her solo.

Rex was anything but subtle. If he wanted her out, he'd have said so. There'd be no mystery about it.

Then again, Gwen hadn't seen it coming either. He'd gotten rid of her without warning. One minute there, the next morning, gone. Blindsided.

She wandered around the playhouse grounds to the front. Across the porch hung a bright banner with painted balloons that read "The Gristmill Homecoming—Friday Night—Invitation Only." On the porch by the rocking chairs was a large box from the printers. She lifted the cover and found the new programs next to a stack of inserts with hers and Phyllis's headshots and bios. She brightened. Dottie would never have asked her to stuff bogus inserts. The show would go on, with them both.

She sat on the porch floor and got to work. She heard the familiar clanging, and the curious Clyde scampered up to investigate, sniffing at her. She gently brushed him away. "Sorry, Charlie," she told him. "No snacks today." He backed off but kept at the ready, in case she changed her mind.

A large shadow moving across the front lawn grabbed her attention. She looked up.

It was one of the dark birds from the elm tree, swooping over on its way to the Journeyman Bridge. It joined several others already there. A coven.

Betty Rose squinted. The fat, hunched creatures were stooped over, pecking, scratching, unearthing the rose beds. Their long necks bobbed.

She put down her stack and leaned forward. The flock was destroying the flowers.

She took two programs and moved quickly across the front lawn, toward the bridge. She waved her arms. "Scat!" she called at them. "Go! Go away!"

The birds dug in more ravenously. They lifted great chunks from the soil and, tossing back their wrinkled, pink-and-gray heads, wolfed them down. It was a frenzy. Betty Rose yelled louder and waved with increased urgency. She stopped at the bridge's edge.

The birds were vultures.

"Shoo!" she screamed, charging them with the programs. "Scram!"

Seemingly more annoyed than afraid, the beasts spread their wings and lifted into the air as she neared. The most recent arrival was the slowest to evacuate. Earthbound and slow, it buzzed the top of her head with its withered claws as it took flight. She turned to see them lumber through the air and take up residence in the elm, where they settled to watch her.

She turned back to the flower bed, plowed and mangled, its earth spilling over onto the bridge path. The lavender "Janet" rose that Sutton often tended was almost dug up, its roots exposed. Injured, it stooped over, its heavy bloom downcast. Nearby was an empty compost bucket, tossed on its side and raided by the creatures. A buzzing haze of flies swarmed everywhere.

She dropped to her knees to push the moist soil back into the bed with cupped hands. She kneaded soggy clumps, scattering them around the roots. A sharp edge buried deep in the gob lanced her finger. She yanked it back. Her darkened hand stung, but the skin was not broken. She rubbed it and peered down into the clump, blended through with irregular pieces.

She waved off the flies and carefully tilled the soil, picking through grayish shards, jagged and shell-like. She collected several in her palm and studied them. They were bone fragments, splintered pieces from leftover T-bones and drumsticks pushed through the gristmill and dumped into the compost bucket. Once table scraps, now fertilizer. She scattered them back, brushed her hands clean.

She dug deeper, down a few layers, where the soil was wetter and lumpier.

She squinted again.

A wet, bloblike mass glistened in the sun. Spellbound, she flicked away the dirt that encased it and gently poked. It was soft and mushy. It wobbled. She probed the soil around it. More bulbous pieces, jellylike globs, shredded odds and ends that defied classification. They reminded her of dissected baby pigs in biology class. The interior organs she'd had to identify in exams. Lungs, kidneys, glands. Gizzards.

Two of her fingers became entwined with threadlike strands. She pulled them off and held them up to the light, twirling them. They were long, dark pieces of hair. She flicked them away, went back to the soil, picked out more. She was disgusted but fascinated. She held steady.

The soft bell clanging approached as Clyde arrived at her side, nosing in on the action. Without looking at him, she gently pushed his head away. "Back," she said quietly, engrossed.

She grabbed fist after fist of the compost, squeezing out its liquid back into the earth. Brownish-red drops oozed out and cascaded down her hands and forearms, dripping off her elbows. The ground was sodden and cake-batter-like. Red velvet.

"What…," she thought and maybe said, "…is in this?"

She felt a sharp prick on her arm, instinctively slapped it. A large horsefly circled away but returned to the same spot. It turned and stared up at her with fat green eyes. She shook her arm, and it flew up and then back, a dogged pest. She smacked it again, killing it. She tilted her arm, and the carcass fell into the flower bed.

She rested her hands on her knees.

The soil moved at the bottom of the hole she had dug.

It wriggled.

Hypnotized, she took the program she had used to scare away the vultures, dug further into the hole, prodding. An earthworm, a beetle, a buried ant farm struggling to surface, she knew. She flicked away more soil, going deeper, to free it. She jabbed the writhing mass, then poked through. Her hand shot to her mouth, she leaped backward with a sharp scream. A nest of maggots exploded through the guts of the earth.

Thousands swarmed up to the top, twisting around and through one another. The soil burst alive and spread, as the nest pumped more up through the ground.

Betty Rose recoiled, recovered. Drew close again and peered down at the convulsing mess. It stank.

A glint caught her eye. Deeper in the hole, below the squirming maggots, a tiny flash of gold hit the sunlight.

She rolled up the program into a stick shape. Flicked away the covering maggots, raked away the dirt surrounding the gold piece. Saw the round rim of a ring's finger bed. She excavated further, harpooned the ring, lifted it out and up, blew off a clinging pair of maggots with sharp breaths.

It was a crushed signet ring. With the Gristmill's insignia.

She sat back on her haunches. She turned it around, inspected it. Clyde sniffed closer at her dripping elbow.

She held it close and looked inside the finger bed, on the back side of the insignia. Smeared off the wet soil that covered the engraved initials. Clyde licked her elbow, ran his nose up her stain-streaked forearm.

The ring was too mangled. She tipped it toward the sunlight, squinted. Clyde nosed his way to her hand, sniffed her muddied fingers. Licked one.

Betty Rose twirled the ring, zeroed in on the first, marred initial. Clyde bit into her hand with his front teeth.

"No!" she screamed, pushing back. He latched on to the meat of her palm, terrierlike, and bit deeper. Blood poured from the wound, spread quickly across her soiled hand, blended in.

"Clyde! *Stop it!*" she shouted, striking his head with her free hand. The goat released his grip and bleated and scampered back a step. He bleated again and cocked his head.

Betty Rose gripped her gashed hand to stanch the bleeding. She looked from her pulsing wound to the writhing guts of the compost in the flower bed to the befuddled and conflicted goat.

"What…," she said, "…have they been *feeding* you?"

Scene Sixteen

"WHY WERE YOU FEEDING THE DAMN GOAT IN THE FIRST PLACE?" Dottie
scolded, a brown iodine bottle in hand. "This isn't a petting
zoo."

She and Alistair had quarantined Betty Rose on a stool in
the kitchen, having dropped dinner prep when she staggered
in with her gushing palm. After an initial panic and barrage
of questions, they now hovered, attentive and excitable. They
had cleaned and dried her hand; the puncture wound, though
messy, did not warrant stitches or a doctor visit, in their opin-
ion. Alistair gave her a warm towel to press against it until the
bleeding tapered off, and she sat holding it tight while the
company went through the buffet line of pork chops, apple-
sauce, and potatoes *au gratin* and took turns peering through
the door with concern. Dottie barked, "She's fine. Mind your
own beeswax," and they moved along. Seemingly beleaguered,
Dottie mopped her forehead and then, nurselike, inspected
the gash and dabbed more iodine onto her palm.

"I wasn't feeding him," said Betty Rose, wincing as the sting
of the antiseptic sharpened her mind and dispersed the shock
from the incident. "At least, I didn't *think* I was...." She looked
from Dottie to Alistair, reading them.

"Why were you playing in the flower bed anyway?" Dottie quizzed. "You were supposed to be stuffing programs." Betty Rose said, "There were vultures in the flower bed. Eating the soil. I scared them away." She stared at Dottie, who looked up at her and said, "Huh. Weird," and then went back to dabbing.

"That psycho goat," Dottie grumbled, picking through the army-green first-aid kit she'd opened on the counter. "I'll never know why Sutton brought him to us. I wish he'd go play in traffic.

"Do you think he's rabid?" Dottie asked sharply, and Alistair shook his head and said, "Oh, I don't think so. Was he frothing, my dear? Frothing at the mouth?"

"No," said Betty Rose. "He wasn't frothing."

"Thank God," Dottie muttered anew, fishing gauze and medical tape from the kit. "The last thing we need tomorrow night is a cast full of rabies." She snorted a laugh and said, "Wouldn't that be a showstopper?"

"He seemed very casual about it," Betty Rose said. "Like it was normal."

Dottie looked up again, amused. "Oh, did you get inside his little goat mind, B.R.?"

"I mean it wasn't an attack," Betty Rose said. "It was just... food."

"He's a *goat*," Dottie said. "Everything is food." She blotted and positioned a bandage. She pulled a length of tape and tore it with her teeth.

Betty Rose watched Dottie wrap her hand. Dottie, who'd lied to her about Gwen's soap opera gig. She'd lied so effortlessly and convincingly, without an ounce of shame or hesitation, or so Betty Rose had thought at the time. She'd bought the act. Then again, she hadn't been looking for lies, hadn't been suspicious, and she'd been foggy from her hangover that day. Maybe she'd missed some telltale sign of deceit that she'd have caught had she been on high alert. Like she was now.

Or maybe Dottie justified her lie to herself as a means to protect Gwen. It would be an excusable lie, perhaps, to cover for Gwen, so that she wouldn't be tarred prematurely as another drug-addled actress. That could tarnish Gwen's reputation for good, especially in a business as small and gossipy as Broadway. Nobody would hire a loose cannon for the stage. It could have been Dottie's hope that Gwen would straighten herself out before word got around that she was a train wreck. In that case, her lie would have been a benevolent gesture, from a selfless, motherly place. The good kind of lie, and ultimately harmless.

In any event, as Rex had schooled Betty Rose, it was none of her business, even as he'd entrusted her with the real reason Gwen had been kicked out. Although he didn't say she'd been kicked out. He just said she was "gone." And he didn't tell the sheriff Gwen had never been at the playhouse. He merely said she wasn't there now. Rex was clever.

Dottie was a surprisingly good actor, and Rex was a seasoned non-liar who could give a false impression of what he meant without actually being untruthful. Both impressive, in manipulative, shady ways.

In the next room, the kitchen's gristmill whirred to life, as a handful of early diners lined up to scrape their plates. Her "family" in their coordinated *Hee Haw* outfits of dusty pink and blue overalls. The chubby techie grunt had gnawed his pork chop clean and dropped the thick bone into the large, open-mouthed hopper. It churned and clunked, shattering bone with an explosive burst.

"For the love of God, throw bones in the garbage!" Dottie hollered and then turned back when she saw the hapless culprit. "What a troglodyte," she mumbled, taping the bandage. "A rock is easier to train."

Betty Rose stared at the hopper. It was big enough to devour all sorts of things. Not just pork chops, but a whole pig. Practically any animal could fit, if you chopped it into manageable pieces and stuffed it down with the mill pick, through the gnashing gears, and churned it into wet clumps and fragments that spat into the waiting compost bucket.

The same bucket that had collected the pulpy mess that had been tilled into the flower bed on the bridge. A mess that contained bone shards and torn organs that wobbled in the sunlight and bred a writhing nest of maggots. A mess that attracted a ravenous flock of vultures, a scavenger species that feeds on *carrion*.

A mess that included strands of hair. Long, dark hair.

Gwen had long, dark hair.

Stop it, Betty Rose!

Carla's parents had stuffed her sister Cady through the very same gristmill, according to Mr. Arbor, who'd shared the outlandish, ghoulish legend with a glint in his eye and had promised to share more. And who had, on the night the Homecoming show was announced, urged her to come back to visit him, so he could tell the rest of the story. He'd insisted on it. And then, that very night or early the next morning, had passed away, in his sleep, at least according to the shopkeeper across the alley who wore the Gristmill pendant and gave Betty Rose the willies with her glassy stare and eerie adulation.

And whose funeral, if there'd even been one, had completely slipped her mind.

"The Gristmill and the town permanently linked," Mr. Arbor had told her, *"in a dark bond born of blood...."*

The mill clunked and churned and spat.

"Our bewildering superstitions and rituals, traditions that are never written down," Rex had lectured over and over outside under the elm, *"preserve the Gristmill to this day."*

Alistair hovered nearby. Neither had left her for long since she'd stumbled in with her bleeding hand and her discovery of the vulture-and-Clyde feeding frenzy in the maggot-infested compost swamp of the flower bed. They'd stood guard, flustered, almost frantic, watching her.

"Did you hear?" Alistair said to her abruptly, distracting her. "The producer of the *Applause* revival is coming to the Homecoming!" "Oh," said Betty Rose, snapping to. "He is?"

Alistair nodded. "They'll be casting this fall. In just a few weeks. You'd make the perfect Eve I think." "I would?" she asked. "You think so?"

"Oh, yes, my dear," he said, with professorlike encouragement. "You'd best be on top of your game tomorrow night." Her stomach tightened. "I will be," she said.

"Fasten your seat belts!" Alistair quoted with gusto. "It's going to be a bumpy night!"

Dottie shielded her face and said, "For chrissakes, stop spitting!" "I'm a stage actor," Alistair protested with pride. "That's what we do. We spit."

"And that's Margo's number, you old poof," Dottie added. "Eve sings 'One Hallowe'en.'" "Oh yes," Alistair concurred, with reverence. "The eleven o'clock number. Oh, it chills."

Tina and Ashley and Baub and Becky lined up to dump their scraps into the hopper. The gears chewed their leftovers into an unrecognizable puree, liquefied in the bucket. It was almost a magic act before her eyes.

It would be the perfect way to make practically anything disappear.

Poor li'l Cady, all ground up in the gristmill.

"What's so funny?" Dottie demanded. "Sorry?" asked Betty Rose. "You're giggling like a mental patient," Dottie replied. "Oh," said Betty Rose, stifling. "Nothing."

"Before I forget," said Dottie, retrieving a manila folder from a kitchen drawer. "You need to fill these out before tomorrow night." Betty Rose took the folder with her good hand and said, "What is it?"

Dottie grabbed it back and opened it for her. "Well, let's see," she said, shuffling papers and showing them. "W-2, so you can get paid, like a real pro...all the taxy, *guvmint* stuff." She paused for an instant and feigned surprise. "And, my, my, what do we have here?"

From the bottom of the pile, she extracted a stapled stack. Across the top was the unmistakable logo of Actors' Equity. "Could this be the new membership packet?" Dottie asked, taunting. "Does this mean that tomorrow night, after Rex signs this, you'll be eligible for your union card?" Dottie mock inspected the form before handing it to her. "I can't imagine what else it would mean."

Betty Rose took the stack. It was real. There was a jubilant letter on top, welcoming her to the union. There was a long application document with open fields for her personal information. There was a line at the bottom, awaiting her signature. And Rex's.

"Congratulations," Alistair said in earnest. "I remember mine like it was yesterday…1956, *Sticks and Stones*. Alas, we didn't make it past New Haven.…" Dottie cut him off with a pleading "Somebody shoot me!" and warned her, "We have to get through tomorrow night first, you know." Then she smiled and winked. "But I bet we will."

Dottie took back the membership packet, slid it into the folder, and tucked Betty Rose's good hand around it. Then with a grand, presenting gesture, she pressed it to her side.

She paused, puzzled. She pat the elastic band around Betty Rose's waist. With quick efficiency, she popped and released it.

Out fell the crushed Gristmill insignia ring that Betty Rose had hidden. It clattered to the floor. Dottie snatched it up.

"Where…did you get this?" she demanded, rattled. "Was this in your food?"

"In the flower bed," said Betty Rose, eyeing her. "In the compost." Then she asked, "Why would it be in my food?"

"It shouldn't be anywhere!" Dottie said quickly. "How the devil did it wind up in the compost?" She turned for help to Alistair, who was none.

"You old fruit bowl," she said, exasperated. "Did you leave your ring on your plate again!"

Alistair stared at Dottie, at the ring, and then *eureka*'d. "Thank heavens you found it! I thought it was gone forever!" he said. He grabbed it from Dottie and turned back to Betty Rose. "I have a terrible habit, really for decades, of removing my ring when I eat." He shrugged with a nervous laugh. "It's an obsessive thing, I fear. For sanitary reasons."

"And then you scraped your plate into the mill!" Dottie chimed in, accusing. "I guess I must have, and not for the first time," admitted Alistair with a sad clown face.

"Good grief. No wonder it keeps jamming," Dottie grumbled, and Alistair said, "Alas, alack, I'd lose my head if it weren't stitched on!"

"But you're wearing your ring," said Betty Rose, nodding at his hand.

Alistair grabbed his ring finger. He nodded at Betty Rose.

"I'm wearing my *replacement* ring," he clarified. "It's not the same at all."

"Oh," she said.

Dottie ushered her toward the kitchen door. "Go rest your hand," she said. "Phyllis will help you with costume changes."

She strained her neck back toward the dining room.

"Giddyap!" she called out to the company. "Tech/dress in twenty!"

● ● ●

Julian answered on the third ring.

She was calling him, she told herself, to make sure she still had a place to stay when she returned to New York in two days. They hadn't spoken since their clash.

"Hey, B.R.," he said, sounding surprised. "How've you been?"

"I'm great!" she said brightly through a stage whisper. "We're in the middle of dress." She huddled by the message board, her back to the stage. She was costumed and made-up as a zombie-Transylvanian for a *Rocky Horror* crowd pleaser that Rex had decided to include in the Homecoming show.

Betty Rose filled him in on her good news.

"A solo? That's awesome, B.R.! Wow. Good for you!"

"Thanks, Julian. I'm very excited. It's what I've…always wanted."

"Can you speak up? I can't really hear you."

"I wish you'd come to see me," she said, a little louder. "I can sneak you in."

"Aw, babe, I'd love to. But I'm in tech. We start previews next week."

"Oh, right," she said. "I forgot. I hope it…goes well."

"Unless we wrap early tomorrow. We're ahead of schedule. But you never know."

"You never know," she echoed.

"Is…something wrong?" he asked.

Alistair and Caleb and the boys filed offstage past her. From the audience, Rex called out cues for the crew.

Betty Rose hugged closer to the message board and cupped the mouthpiece. "No. Nothing's wrong. It's just…you were right." She forced a carefree laugh. "This place…is a little strange." She relished the strength and sanity of his voice.

"What's going on?" Julian asked, sharpening. "You sound scared."

"No, not scared," she backpedaled. "Just a little nervous. Maybe resisting."

"Resisting what?" he asked.

"Oh, nothing. It's actorspeak. I'm probably excited. That's a good thing, right?"

"I think so," said Julian. "I hope so." And then he said, "I can come if you really want me there. I can come right now if you need me."

"Oh, I don't need you right now," she said, dismissing it with another laugh. She took a breath and added, "But I can't wait to see you when I get back. If…you're cool with that. With me…coming back."

"Yeah, B.R. I'm cool with that."

The orchestra vamped from the pit.

Phyllis raced by, demonically costumed as the others. She pinched Betty Rose.

"Hurry, B.R.!" she said. "'Time Warp' again. Hop to it, missy!"

"I gotta go," Betty Rose said into the phone. "I'm on."

"I'll try for tomorrow," Julian said. "I'll definitely try."

"If not, I mean"—she lingered—"I love you, Julian. You know. Always."

"Well, hey," he answered. "Me too. Always."

She hurried onstage in the blackout and struck her opening pose. An oiled-up Caleb, back from a quick change into his gold leather Rocky briefs and blond shag wig, hit his mark next to her. He didn't belong in this number but had earned special treatment, clearly.

Out of the corner of her eye, she saw him flexing and mugging, trying to catch her attention.

She stared ahead, unplayful.

Scene Seventeen

TECH REHEARSAL WENT SMOOTHLY BUT RAN LATE, as Rex insisted on full performances of the group numbers, instead of the usual cue-to-cue speed-through.

They didn't run hers or Phyllis's solo numbers at all. "Just go over them with Myron," Rex directed them. "Keep it fresh."

Becky ordered everyone to change and report back to the stage for paint call. The tech crew moved in with ladders and big plastic bags to fill the confetti machine up in the fly space.

"I'm having second thoughts about my solo," Phyllis told her in the dressing room, wiping cold cream from her face. "It doesn't have much range. It lacks the 'wow' factor."

"I think it's sweet," said Betty Rose, realizing that this time tomorrow night, it would all be over. "It fits your voice perfectly. You nail it." She glanced up to the video stage monitor on the wall. Techies swept the floor and flew the set pieces up and away, clearing the space.

"Well, what I lack in talent, I make up with sparkle and gumption," said Phyllis, mugging Shirley Temple–style into the mirror before turning. "*Your* number is the showstopper. I'm telling you, the audience is gonna bawl." Betty Rose tilted her head and said, "We'll see.…" She flexed her hand, still sore, but better. She'd change out to a smaller bandage in the morning.

Phyllis abruptly jumped with excitement. "Did you hear Geraldine Roberts is coming?"

"Who?"

"Geraldine Roberts! The Gristmill's oldest living über-legend of all!"

Betty Rose shrugged. Phyllis frowned.

"*Kismet? Silk Stockings?* A gazillion more? Her portrait's in the lobby, next to Sutton's. I thought she was dead, but they're trotting her out for the Homecoming. B.R., she's Broadway royalty."

"Well, then, we'd better sing loudly."

Phyllis held an imaginary cone to her ear and bunched her face. "Speak up, dearie! I can't hear you with one foot in the grave!"

She laughed. Betty Rose forced a smile.

"Don't bother with paint call, girls," Dottie said at the door, having materialized silently, jolting them. "Rex wants you to rest up for tomorrow." Her arms were loaded with costumes to be steamed and mended.

"As if we can!" said Phyllis.

Dottie reached up and switched off the monitor. It went black.

"Put it all out of your mind," she said. "No pressure, no stress. It should be a joy. Remember, the audience isn't a firing squad. They're friends. Family, really." Dottie considered and nodded at herself. "Yes. They're family."

"Family," Phyllis repeated. "Yes."

"B.R.?" Dottie prodded.

"Yes," Betty Rose said. "Family."

Dottie smiled and winked at them. "See you in the morning." And she was gone.

Phyllis stood up. "Easier said than done," she said, then inhaled deeply. "In twenty-four hours...everything changes."

Betty Rose nodded. "You go ahead," she said. "Gotta finish my eyes."

Once Phyllis had gone, Betty Rose quietly closed the dressing room door, easing the latch so it wouldn't spring a noise.

She clicked the video stage monitor back on. After a moment, it brightened.

Rex stood on the apron with his clipboard as a map, positioning actors with precision. Alistair, Caleb, Sutton, Rachelle, all the others strategically fanned out and scattered on specific marks to fill the space, leaving an obvious void stage center.

Betty Rose backed away from the monitor, sized up the stage tableau. It looked familiar.

Rex paced a few steps, heavy in thought. "Sutton, help me out," he said, looking up. "Did we put down plastic last time?" Sutton grinned as if goosed and said, "I was so nervous, Rex. I really don't remember a thing." Rex nodded and said, "Touché."

Dottie hurried onstage and took her position off center, mirroring Alistair. Mother and father.

"Rex, we won't need plastic," Dottie said, brushing it off. "We just mop or paint over if necessary. Not a big deal."

"Done," said Rex, waving a techie to his side. "Glow tape their marks," he ordered, and other crew amassed onstage, fluorescent rolls in hand. They went to work cutting off pieces and affixing them to the stage at the actors' feet.

"Becky, is the thing still on?" he called out, whirling his hand in the air. "The camera thing?"

"Still live, Rex," Becky called back from the control booth.

"Let's kill it for the night," he said, turning back to the stage. "Finish the sets," he told the crew, then pointed at Dottie and Alistair. "Final production meeting in my…"

The monitor went black.

Betty Rose stood in the silence, staring at it.

● ● ●

She crouched outside, by the stage door, watching.

Across the knoll, at the dock, Rex led Dottie and Alistair over the gangplank and retreated into the dark *Panic*. He closed the door behind them. Moments later, the stateroom lights popped on, glowing through the tight sheers.

Betty Rose listened back to the chatter and revelry inside on the stage, where the company painted and joked and sang. She knew the drill.

She scampered across the knoll, past the elm and fireflies, hugging the shadows. She targeted the Delaware.

At the river's edge, she stopped and listened. A breeze tickled the grasses on the bank. The moonlit currents lapped against the shore, sloshed up the sides of the boat in a gentle rock. Through the stateroom window, cracked a few inches for air, came mumbling discussion.

It echoed across the river. She strained.

"We usually have more time to prepare," Rex said, his voice low and concerned. "Do you think they're really ready?"

"Don't worry, Daddy," Dottie assured him. "They'll rise to the occasion. Lord knows they both want that card."

"And you're sure no one knows they're here?"

"Just the one boyfriend," said Alistair, matching Rex's serious tone. "He's known from the beginning."

"Yes, of course," said Rex. "No one else?"

"Phyllis has no one," Alistair said. "Which is, if you think about it, rather sad..."

"The boyfriend won't be a problem," Dottie cut him off. "At all."

"Yes, of course," Rex repeated. After a heavy moment, his tone lightened. "Well, it is live theatre," he said. "Anything can happen!"

Dottie and Alistair laughed in agreement.

"That's part of the thrill!" Dottie said.

The breeze changed directions, scattering the sound. Betty Rose stepped closer to the bank's edge, leaned farther in. She pivoted her head, trying to recapture the conversation. Her foot slid down the side, toward the water. She shifted her weight, causing both feet to slide, drawing her in.

A hand grabbed her arm, halting her skid. Betty Rose spun to a quizzical Caleb, holding her aloft.

"Shouldn't you be in bed?" he asked.

She stared at him.

"I'm too...tense to sleep," she stammered.

He gently pulled her up to solid ground. "That shouldn't be," he said with a predator's grin. "You know there are ways to fix that...." His grip was firm.

She peeled his hand off her arm, backed away.

"I...don't want to fix it," she said, moving quickly back across the lawn, away from him, the river, the *Panic*.

"Come on!" he called after, frustrated. "It's your last night!"

She stopped and turned back to him.

"It is, isn't it?" she said.

She hurried on.

● ● ●

She had to wake Phyllis, who slept peacefully, without a care, snoring softly while Betty Rose paced the dark room.

Rex and his flying monkeys and likely the whole playhouse had a secret plan to be hatched and sprung on them the following night during the Homecoming show. Some sort of initiation rite that had been concocted and brewing to unveil before the invitation-only audience of Gristmill veterans who'd be traveling far just for the special event. A showstopper.

A plan of such importance and potential jeopardy that it was critical that Betty Rose and Phyllis be isolated without the escape hatch of friends or family or boyfriend in attendance.

And a plan that required they both dye their hair red and wear matching sequined gowns. Like twins.

But so what if the Gristmill had a secret initiation rite? Every organization she'd ever joined had one: her college sorority, theatre club, even her summer camp pulled humiliating pranks on newbies as part of their induction into the group. As a pledge in Theta, she was forced to dress up like Little Bo Peep, bonnet and staff included, and roam the campus, like an idiot, calling out for lost sheep. That had caused her embarrassment but hardly the sharp anxiety that plagued her now.

Of course, nobody had accused her sorority or theatre club or summer camp of being cults. No one had even suggested such a thing. It was all harmless play. It was fun.

They didn't knot her stomach like the Gristmill did.

Neither did they offer what the Gristmill did: her union card, membership into an elite troupe of professionals, her first acting paycheck. Each a major, career-moving milestone. And less than twenty-four hours away.

She accidentally kicked the dresser as she paced the room. Phyllis stirred and rolled over and mumbled what sounded like "oyster," although Betty Rose couldn't be sure. She snored anew, worry-free, too young and green to sense the impending threat.

Her mind was playing tricks again, like Rex had warned. Unless he'd warned her to distract from the obvious hazard right before her eyes. There was no end to his cleverness, she'd learned. And his manipulation.

But manipulation of what? She wasn't trapped here; indeed, Rex had expelled her, and she'd begged him, rather shamelessly, to take her back. They'd even bought her a bus ticket to New York, still in her purse, which they'd returned along with her luggage and cell phone, currently charging in the corner. She was free to go at any time. She could call a cab right now.

And then word would get around in the clubby, talky world of the theatre that she was scattered and neurotic and unreliable. An amateur who'd blown her big opportunity, not cut out for the professional trade. A dilettante, as Wes the agent had pegged her. She'd never live down that reputation.

Broadway would welcome Phyllis instead. And forget all about the silly girl from Beech Grove without a single professional credit who was too old to be starting out anyway.

Betty Rose sweated through her chill. She focused on the strobing exit sign to steady her dizziness.

She went to the closet, pulled out her rolling bag, laid it on the floor, and unzipped it. Sorted through the clothes she'd carefully packed and had yet to wear. Unearthed from the bottom edge the small, brown, leather-trimmed lockbox she'd remembered to bring as an afterthought.

Inside, she slid the rubber band off a stack of photos and leafed through the worn and faded snapshots her father always printed up for her. Herself as a toddler and child at the Indiana State Fair, with a dripping ice cream cone on the beach in Panama City, unsure but gamely hugging Eeyore by the Rivers of America at Walt Disney World.

She smiled at her late father, then young and robust and loving. At her mother, whose own smile was once bright and genuine and now nearly forgotten. The only real family she had left, however estranged.

Betty Rose wiped off the tear that had dripped onto the photo, waved it dry.

She found, at the bottom of the box next to a roll of stamps, the stationery she'd had specially made to send as thank-you notes to casting directors and agents. It was still unwrapped. She took out the first note card and fumbled around for a pen.

Betty Rose collected her thoughts, palming more tears from her eyes.

Rex had told her to write a letter. So she did.

Scene Eighteen

BETTY ROSE FINISHED HER MORNING VOICE REHEARSAL with Myron, wrapped up a final dance run-through with Baayork, dashed back to her dorm, and grabbed her purse. She had, according to the posted schedule, a half-hour lunch break, for which she had no appetite and from whose KP duties she and Phyllis were excused on their big day.

She spirited through the theater, up the aisle toward the lobby, while the noisy tech crew amassed onstage with last-minute set tweaks behind the Carla curtain. She clutched the letter she'd spent most of the night writing and rewriting, having gone through six note cards, three of which she'd fit into one stamped envelope. She was, in spite of scant sleep, fresh and highly charged.

She smiled and nodded at Sutton and Rachelle and others milling about in the house, graciously sharing their excitement over the night ahead. "You're all aglow," said a proud Sutton. "You're gonna devour these fuckers," Rachelle chimed in, miming a toothy attack with a rabid growl. Betty Rose laughed with them and shrugged and said, "God, I hope so!"

She hurried up the aisle, through the house doors, into the lobby.

The legends fanned out across the "Wall of Fame" in front of her, each with a challenging stare. Betty Rose paused, noticing something she'd missed before. She stepped closer.

Peeking from under Bette Davis's décolletage was the outer edge of a gold medallion. Betty Rose sidestepped to Katharine Hepburn, an identical pendant hiding under her dress. Ditto Stanwyck and Margaret Sullavan and others. Ditto the recently gone Marian Maples.

She came to Sutton, the newest legend inductee on the end. She wore, in subtle camouflage, the same medallion she proudly wore in real life.

Betty Rose spun to the towering Carla portrait between the lobby doors. The girl who started it all. Her Gristmill pendant, the original, hung openly from her neck. Her hands, as always, tucked shyly behind her back.

"Final stage check!" called a techie from the house. "Fly out fire curtain!"

Betty Rose stared through the lobby doors. The Carla curtain flew up and away, revealing a three-dimensional, mirror image onstage. The town, playhouse, train, trees, and river, all in perfect position. A spotlight hit the empty patch in the center, awaiting the star of the colorful tableau.

She turned to go and smacked into Alistair standing behind her. He cocked his head.

"Shouldn't you be running your number?" he asked.

"I will," she said. "I have been. I will again. I'm on break."

He looked at the letter in her hand. "Would you like me to mail that?"

She moved it down to her side, the front facing her body. "No, thank you. I can do it."

"It's no trouble at all," he said, reaching for it. "Who's it for?"

She snatched it away and took two steps back. "That's very kind, but I hate to be a bother."

She pivoted around him with a broad smile and scurried toward the front door. "But thank you again!" she called out.

● ● ●

She caught the slim Asian mailman in town on his rounds. She followed him down Carla Avenue, from Penny Whistle Toys to the Merry Carver hardware store to the Gypsy Heaven Witch Shop, holding her letter close as she waited for him to finish his deliveries. She moved along with him, head down, pretending to window-shop.

The pudgy techie emerged from Nifty's Knife Sharpening, carrying an oblong, purple velvet tasseled bag with great care, and she turned her back to avoid him. She glanced from the corner of her eye until he'd passed a safe distance.

The mailman marched out of Stuber's Smoke Shop and beelined back toward his Jeep parked in the red zone at the corner, in front of the Mansion Inn at the edge of town. Betty Rose walked briskly to catch up to him.

"Excuse me," she called out, as he put the truck in gear. She waved him down with her letter. "Can I give you this please? To mail for me?"

He nodded and reached out his hand.

"Are you going straight to the post office?" she asked. He nodded, his hand still extended. "Because it's very important this letter get there," she added. He flicked his hand impatiently.

Betty Rose took one last look at the address, double-checking it. She held it out to the mailman, who snatched it and tucked it into a side pocket of his blue messenger bag.

"Outgoing mail, right?" she said, pointing to the pocket. The man pulled away from the curb.

She rounded the corner and watched until the red-white-blue Jeep disappeared down the wooded road out of town. She took a deep breath and turned back to Carla Avenue.

The street, she just realized, was empty.

The sidewalks, shops, the whole town deserted and silent.

The mechanical bear outside Penny Whistle Toys rocked and blew bubbles into abandoned nothingness. With robotic efficiency, it dunked its wand and blew more, the whir of its motor the only sound on the avenue.

She turned back to the Ivyland Railroad in the distance. The steam locomotive sat idle at the station. No one waited to board.

"We're all looking forward to the show tonight," said a woman behind her. Betty Rose spun. The Donna Reed clone swept the front porch of the Mansion Inn. She wore a pink gingham dress under a floral apron. Her bowl hairdo looked newly coiffed. She smiled with genuine friendliness.

"Where is everybody?" asked Betty Rose. "Where are all the tourists?"

The woman surveyed the street. "Just a slow time of year," she said, sweeping.

"It's Labor Day weekend," said Betty Rose.

The woman swept, still smiling. "When the leaves change, we'll be busy again, I'm sure."

Betty Rose stared at the inn's "no vacancy" sign.

"But you're full," she said.

The woman nodded, swept, smiled. "We have special guests arriving soon."

Betty Rose looked up and down the street. "What special guests?"

The woman swept right, then left. "We're all looking forward to the show tonight," she repeated through her frozen smile. From her neck dangled the gold Gristmill pendant.

She looked over Betty Rose's shoulder and perked up. "Oh, here they are. Right on time, too." She leaned her broom against the porch bannister and reached back to untie her apron.

Betty Rose turned to the approaching rumble behind her. The green and white Trans-Bridge bus pulled into town and slowed to a stop across from the railroad. The engine spat and then idled. She stared at the tinted windows, shrouding the passengers.

The innkeeper flounced the back of her hairdo as she approached the bus, prettying herself. The bus door opened outward.

Transfixed, Betty Rose backed away toward the cigar store Indian outside Stuber's Smoke Shop and watched.

Down the bus steps came a happy parade of well-dressed and professional-looking weekenders. They greeted the town with joy.

They wore summer-casual oxfords and seersucker and khakis. A few wore jeans. One woman wore white capri pants. They laughed and looked up and down Carla Avenue and basked. There were dozens of them, milling about the bus, awaiting their luggage.

The innkeeper greeted and hugged them one by one. They squealed and thrilled at the reunion. They babbled.

The mustached driver—the same one who had brought Betty Rose to town—followed the passengers off the emptying bus. He opened and unloaded the undercarriage, lining up overnight bags and rolling cases. The passengers thanked and tipped him. He smiled and thanked them back.

Betty Rose focused. In the bright sunlight gleams of gold flashed around the women's necks, glinted from the men's fingers. Gristmill pendants and rings, all.

One woman in a sleeveless polka-dot blouse caught Betty Rose staring at the group. She poked the youngish man with sandy-blond hair next to her and nodded in Betty Rose's direction. Soon everyone was inspecting her with fresh smiles. She stood holding the arm of the wooden Indian, eyeballing them. They seemed poised to approach.

A middle-aged man in a kelly-green polo shirt and pink sweater tied about the shoulders diverted his attention back past the bus and shouted and waved. The others collected around him, did the same.

Down the main road into town came a shiny black Lincoln Town Car. It pulled alongside the parked bus and stopped. The uniformed chauffeur leaped from the driver's seat and circled back to the trunk, where he unloaded a weathered steamer case papered over with travel stickers. He lifted out a folded wheelchair and shook it open, then rolled it to the side of the car. The wheelchair was upholstered in tapestry fabric and festooned with gold fringe.

The chatty crowd hushed when the chauffeur opened the door to the backseat and extended his arm inside. A withered hand reached out and clutched it.

Out came an elderly woman—slow, shaky, and grand. Her silver hair curled from under a black beret. She wore enormous black sunglasses, a cream blouse with loose black pants, and fiery red lipstick. A black wrap framed her with chic drama. She steadied herself with a rose-painted cane.

The woman muttered something and shuffled with precision into her waiting wheelchair. Her driver hooked the cane over the back of the chair, the cue for the others to come pay their respects. They flocked around her, gushing.

After a few moments of worship, the woman signaled impatience, and her driver wheeled her toward the ramp leading up to the inn's front porch. At the sidewalk, she spied Betty Rose still holding the Indian and ordered a halt. She turned to the hovering innkeeper and asked something. The innkeeper glanced at Betty Rose and nodded the answer. The woman turned back to Betty Rose, took off her sunglasses, and leaned forward in her chair, peering.

Betty Rose recognized the eyes from her portrait in the Gristmill lobby.

The legend got her fill and smiled. She leaned back and waved her driver on. Geraldine Roberts disappeared into the inn lobby, followed by her coven of admirers.

The street was empty and silent again. Betty Rose still clutched the wooden Indian.

The Homecoming reunion had begun. The "special guests" the innkeeper was waiting for had arrived, with surely more to come. Amassing in the deserted town—a tourist-trap village that had been flooded with visitors all summer long and now sat empty on what should have been the busiest weekend of the season—in advance of tonight's big show.

A show that was closed to outsiders, as was the town itself, on a day when it normally would be overflowing, the streets choked with throngs of window-shoppers and weekenders and children pulling parents toward Gerenser's Exotic Ice Cream and Pudge Cakes Bakery and Penny Whistle Toys. With curious passersby poking around the Gypsy Heaven Witch Shop and nosing through the antiques alley and lining up for tickets for boat rides on the Delaware and tours on the Ivyland Railroad.

And now sat empty and desolate. Even Starbucks.

The mechanical bear lifted its robo arm and blew a cloud of bubbles.

The show would start in just a few hours. In the invitation-only audience would be hundreds of loyal Gristmill alumni summoned back by their leader, Rex, and perhaps hundreds more of the local townies whose livelihood depended on a vibrant, resilient playhouse that had recently lost one of its legends in Marian Maples.

A death that had triggered—according to Gwen's journal, before she disappeared to a nonexistent dressing room on the Hudson—a flurry of activity among Rex and his flying monkeys that culminated in the replacement of the traditional season-ender *Godspell* with a private musical revue to bid farewell to one legend and "revive and rejuvenate" their beloved playhouse.

A playhouse that was known as a cult and freak show and had made Betty Rose squeamish and on edge since she'd first arrived. A place from which Erin's actor friend had fled and refused to talk about. Erin who still served drinks at the Rum House and was long past her stardom expiration date, but was still alive and safe on Forty-Seventh Street with Danny and Claudine, although she was likely in the Hamptons with a new boyfriend, because it was Labor Day, and that was the busiest weekend for any summer town. Except for this weekend in New Hope. Where it was deserted and silent.

The bear raised its arm up and down. It was running low on bubbles.

Betty Rose released the Indian and staggered onto the open sidewalk.

She and Phyllis were the showcased talents of the night, the real reason the Gristmill alums had thronged to town on Rex's command, including the icon Geraldine Roberts who was too feeble to get out much but had made the two-hour journey by car on what must have been a traffic-heavy day. Because she wanted to watch, to witness the big event.

An event starring Betty Rose and Phyllis with matching red hair and identical red sequined dresses, like the twins whose ghastly, ghoulish saga had birthed the Gristmill Playhouse and indeed the town of New Hope.

The Gristmill and the town permanently linked in a dark bond born of blood.

The bear's arm whirred up and down. It was empty.

Betty Rose turned around.

The Trans-Bridge bus still idled at the stop.

In her purse was the ticket Rex had given her when he'd thrown her out, before she'd begged to stay. She held her purse close, walked toward the bus.

In two hours or less she'd be back at Port Authority, where she'd stroll past the scurrying crowds and indoor pigeons and Au Bon Pain on her way to the downtown C or E to get off at Spring Street and then on to Julian's apartment.

She'd also stroll past, she knew, giant billboard posters for *The Book of Mormon* and *Kinky Boots* and quite possibly *The Boy*

Friend, whose young cast still celebrated their ongoing hit on Sunday nights at the dark, musty, and touristy bar where she would soon be waiting tables again alongside nosy Erin, who had been awaiting and expecting her return all summer long. "Well, well, well!" she'd call out too loudly, and the fall would turn to winter.

And the young cast of *The Boy Friend* would move on to bigger and better roles as they accelerated their careers. And Betty Rose would wait tables, likely for years, until she tired of the crushing schedule and pushy tourists and sore feet and switched to overnight paralegal, the other survival job where wannabe actors swarmed to pay the rent while their lifelong dreams evaporated in the dark almost without their notice. And then she'd be thirty, past her own expiration date.

And Monica, her half-talent classmate at Northwestern— with neither a high C nor a strong belt and an asymmetrical face—who had already exceeded all expectations, would be the celebrated one at their college reunions while the others looked at Betty Rose and wondered why she—with her drive and talent and fearlessness—had not only fallen short, but had never gotten started in the first place. Why had she gone off the rails?

They wouldn't think about this for long, of course. They'd just register quick pity and get back to celebrating Monica.

Betty Rose stood in front of the idling bus, its door closed.

Once she'd wowed the Gristmill Homecoming crowd—and she would, as she'd nailed her number repeatedly in rehearsals, going deep into her diaphragm to come down on top of the high notes and even mastering the slack jaw that made for a rich resonance up and down the scale—she'd be an official member of the club, just like them, and they'd recommend her for roles and even hire her for some, and she'd leapfrog, not only over Monica, but also over the thousands of aspiring actors who poured into New York each week but lacked her determination and chutzpah and innate gifts that had so far gone unrecognized but would be seen and lauded and remembered, starting this very night.

The bus door opened. The friendly driver smiled at her from his seat.

"Getting on?" he said.

She stood, looking into the open door, the ticket in her grasp.

"Um…back to New York?" she asked.

He nodded. "Last of the day," he said.

Julian would help her there, like he'd promised to do from the beginning, with all the directors and producers who knew and loved him. He'd give her a boost. There was no shame in that.

"Getting on?" the driver repeated, his smile slightly confused.

But Julian couldn't help once word got around she'd walked out on an opening night. There was no greater professional sin. She'd be toxic.

That was a challenge she could plan for, an obstacle, however daunting, that she could anticipate and potentially surmount over time. Whereas she had no idea what to expect that night onstage at the playhouse.

Poor li'l Cady all ground up in the gristmill.

Betty Rose tightened with a chill.

The engine spat again, signaling its departure.

Betty Rose stepped up into the door.

"There you are! You forgot to sign out!"

She spun to Dottie standing behind her in bandana, kha-kis, and white Keds. She looked flustered and sweaty and amused.

"What on earth are you doing?" Dottie asked with a laugh. She reached out and guided Betty Rose down from the bus and back onto the street. "Shouldn't you be warming up?"

"Um...yes," said Betty Rose. "Yes."

Dottie looked quizzical. "Is everything all right?"

"Yes," Betty Rose said, nodding. "Yes."

"Take care, miss," the driver said. The bus door shut.

Betty Rose turned back to it. The driver shifted into gear.

Dottie shepherded her toward the curb, arms entwined.

"Why, you're trembling!" she said, pulling back to inspect her. She felt her forehead and cheeks. "And so flush. My, my. Jitters?" Betty Rose nodded again, and Dottie said, "Now, isn't that silly."

Betty Rose looked back at the retreating roar, as the bus lumbered down the street.

Dottie fingered her hair as she led her across Carla Avenue toward the playhouse. "Curls, I think," she mused. "Yes, defi-nitely curls tonight. Will make you look younger. That's always a good thing."

Betty Rose glanced back a last time to see the bus disap-pear down the wooded lane. Dottie ushered her toward the Journeyman Bridge.

The town sat silent again.

Act Three

Scene One

"FIVE MINUTES!" BECKY CALLED OVER THE INTERCOM.

Betty Rose stared at herself in the dressing room mirror. She wore her red sequined dress and fresh red ringlets.

Dottie had chaperoned her back to the playhouse, arms locked, chatting happily along the way. She was supportive and encouraging, bolstering Betty Rose's mettle and priming her for the night ahead. "The readiness is all," she said. "And Rex wouldn't put you out there if you weren't ready. Just trust him."

The show's running order, which was subject to change, had changed. Gone were the group numbers that included Betty Rose and Phyllis. In fact, the whole second act had been cut.

According to Dottie, Rex had decided that a full-length show, with intermission, would disrupt the festive energy and leave less time for the Homecoming celebration after. "He's mainly thinking about Geraldine," she explained. "She can't stay up too late."

Instead, the show would be a one-act, with a handful of ensemble numbers (minus the newbies) and the requisite Sutton highlight. But the main event, the grand finale, would be the unveiling of Phyllis and Betty Rose with their solos.

"It all leads to that," said Dottie. "Rex will tee it up for a real barn burner."

"That's so terrifying. And thrilling," said Phyllis. "Yes, indeed," said Betty Rose.

During the early dinner, Betty Rose picked at her beef stroganoff with parsley noodles but ate little as she darted looks around the mess hall. Phyllis dug in with more gusto, although she restrained herself with a small portion. The room crackled with a last-day-of-school excitement and anticipation.

Down at the table end, Alistair offered his career diagnosis about a hot young Broadway hunk who'd failed in television. "He's gorgeous, and the ladies loved him onstage, but, you see, he couldn't hide the Nellie," he explained. "And on camera, my dear, you simply must hide the Nellie."

"We've crossed the Rubicon," Dottie called from the kitchen. "Alistair is giving tips on sex appeal!" The room roared.

Betty Rose scraped her uneaten dinner into the gristmill hopper and accepted good wishes from the alto with the pixie cut whose notes were always a bit sharp and headed down the hallway.

Sutton stopped her on her way up the silo stairs. "Where do you think you're going?" she asked, hand on hip.

She led Betty Rose by the elbow to the star's dressing room just offstage and flung open the door. The room was filled with flowers and balloons and cards. Gold metallic streamers stretched from the corners, and two star-capped cupcakes sat on the makeup counter under the electrified mirrors. Phyllis was already there, gawking.

"This is for you two," Sutton said. "You're the stars tonight. And you've earned it." She planted a kiss on Betty Rose's forehead and promised to check back before curtain.

"This is real. This is happening," said Phyllis, drinking in the suite-sized room with striped wallpaper and damask upholstery and marble bathroom with shower. She shuddered with glee. "I mean, this is diva."

Betty Rose stared at her name placard on the mirror—in hand calligraphy—and said, "It is happening."

Baub blustered in with the red sequined dresses they'd mended, freshly steamed and on padded satin hangers. They sparkled as he hung them in the cedar closet. "Wear them gently, please," he cautioned. "They're older than Madge's first face-lift." The crack was neither funny nor sensical, but Betty Rose forced a smile and promised to be careful.

Dottie arrived with a red tackle box to do their hair and makeup. She opened it on the counter to reveal an arsenal of carefully packed supplies. "Full service tonight, girls!" she announced, fishing through them. "Don't get used to it."

Starting with Phyllis, she palmed conditioner down the lengths of her hair and went to work with a curling iron, meticulous and thorough. She moved on to Betty Rose and did the same thing. She tucked towels around their necks and set about their makeup. It was heavy and garish, with thick lashes and bright red cheeks, Raggedy Ann–like.

Out in the orchestra pit, the band tuned up.

"Help me with the dresses," Dottie said, assigning the correct ones from the closet. Betty Rose held a towel around Phyllis's painted face as Dottie carefully lowered the dress over her head and petticoat and knickers and zipped her up. Phyllis returned the favor.

"Nice work on the mending," said Dottie, inspecting the backs. Then she started to unhook Betty Rose's silver pendant.

"No, please," said Betty Rose, her hand shooting to her neck. "I never take it off."

"Well, you will tonight," Dottie replied, removing the chain and wadding it on the counter. "No street jewelry onstage. Very amateurish." The case was closed.

She sized them up side by side in the mirror and could scarcely contain her delight at her handiwork.

"I think my best yet," she told them. "Now, please don't mess it up until"—she paused and considered and then shrugged— "well, until you're onstage. That's what it's for."

She checked her watch and said, "Good grief, I've got to finish my own." She caressed their red ringlets one last time and said, "*Merde!*" and was gone.

Phyllis made a face in the mirror. "Mrs. Lovett as a single girl," she said with a laugh. "No wonder she went batty with the meat pies."

Betty Rose checked the cards on the flowers and balloons that choked the room. They were all addressed to Phyllis. She saw none for her.

"Look, B.R.," said Phyllis at the window, parting the draperies. "High-budge central! Standing room only."

Betty Rose scanned over her shoulder to glimpse the edge of the front courtyard, overflowing with glittering guests. The men wore tuxedoes or dark suits; the women in dresses of various lengths. There were silk scarves and wild hats and the occasional ascot. A mix, she knew, of stars and agents and Broadway big shots, including, according to Alistair, the producer of the *Applause* revival opening next spring. Gold glinted from necks and hands. Several held bouquets of red roses. They chatted and greeted one another over preshow cocktails with grand drama. It was a reunion and a party. High budget indeed.

The front porch bell clanged, summoning the revelers into the theater. They responded with a jolt of fresh energy and urgency, downed their drinks, and migrated toward the door.

"Make room, Phyllis!" called out Sutton, whisking in a vase of long-stem red roses. She was made-up and in costume—a man's white tie and tails with black character shoes—ready for her entrance.

"More flowers?" Phyllis said, blushing. "Here, give them to B.R. This is just embarrassing." She patted the empty space on Betty Rose's counter.

"Girls, savor this night forever," Sutton told them, clasping hands. "It doesn't get better. Broadway, Tonys, whatever. I've done it all. And trust me, nothing compares to this opening night." She gave Phyllis a careful hug to avoid clashing makeup and then leaned in to Betty Rose's ear.

"You should powder up, sweetie," she whispered. "You're sweating something fierce."

Betty Rose checked herself. She was dripping.

"*Five minutes!*" Becky called over the intercom.

"Break a leg!" Sutton said, disappearing out the door, tails flying.

And now Betty Rose stared at herself in the dressing room mirror. Stole a glance over to Phyllis. Both in dress and ringlets.

"You okay?" Phyllis asked as Betty Rose dabbed powder on her forehead, nose, cheeks, and neck.

"I...I think so," she said, steadying her trembling hand.

"Well, you can't be that scared. I mean, you're not giggling."

"No," said Betty Rose. "I'm not."

"That giggling school girl is gone for good," announced Rex from the dressing room door. He looked spiffy and splendid in his opening-night uniform. A bright silk handkerchief spilling from his chest pocket added a new, festive touch. So did his proud smile.

"And so we pay our last respects," he added, whisking a single white rose from behind his back and placing it on the counter in front of her. She stared at it.

"I've compressed the running order," he told them. "This crowd's a bit too charged to sit still for long. I've moved your solos right after the opening. Who says the eleven o'clock number has to wait for eleven?"

Phyllis stiffened. "That's soon!"

Rex shrugged and smiled. "No sense in torturing you two longer than necessary. Let's just get on with it."

He stood tall, drinking them in.

"No pep talk, no hand-holding, no need," he said with parental soothing. "You're both more than ready. Just listen to the song and trust your instincts. Open the gates and let the beagles run. And tonight a new legend is born. You'll see."

He leaned down to Betty Rose at her mirror. "Knock 'em dead," he said with a playful swipe down her nose. And he was gone.

The girls sat in silence.

Betty Rose picked up the white rose from her counter, considered it. "Last respects…," she whispered.

"Did you say something?" asked Phyllis.

From the theater came the Wurlitzer's carousel version of "In the Good Old Summertime" playing the crowd in. Rising above it grew the unmistakable murmur of the gathering audience as they loaded in, talking above the music, finding their seats. There was more laughter, more greetings, the hum of anticipation.

The backstage held a preshow quiet and stillness, waiting.

Betty Rose fought off shallow breaths, struggled to take a deep one, unsuccessfully.

Phyllis reached over and lightly palmed her bandaged hand. "You nervous?" she asked. "A little," said Betty Rose.

"I thought I would be," Phyllis said, staring at her reflection. "I was a basket case a few days ago. But for some reason, right now, I'm just at peace. Maybe the most peaceful I've ever been. Isn't that funny?"

Betty Rose nodded, smiled, tried to breathe.

"*Places!*" Becky called over the intercom. They both jumped.

"Every time!" said Phyllis, laughing. "Every single goddamned time!"

The ensemble, quiet and clustered, filed down the silo stairs and past the open dressing room door on their way to the stage. They all wore white tie and tails and carried top hats, both men and women. They stopped by the props table just outside the door, where the props master and pudgy techie handed out black canes on their way to the stage.

Betty Rose looked up at the video monitor trained on the closed red house curtain. She could see the house lights dim, hear the audience chatter settle down to silence. The theater faded to black.

From the orchestra pit, the kettle drum thundered its opening alert.

The drum unleashed the explosive first chords of an instantly familiar overture. Betty Rose perked and focused to peg it.

It was the overture to *42nd Street.*

"Here we go…," said Phyllis.

The overture coursed through snippets of "We're in the Money," "Lullaby of Broadway," and the monumental title song that demanded attention, just as it had the first time she heard it, as a little girl at the theatre with her father. It sounded new again, like it had then.

She relaxed a bit, took a full breath.

It ended with a clash of cymbals. The audience applauded with vigor and settled again.

After a pause, the orchestra started anew. In the video monitor, the red curtain rose.

The crowd clapped and cheered at the opening tableau: The full company fanned out on two sparkling levels, resplendent in their formal attire, androgynous and glamorous. They launched into the euphoric "Dames." Betty Rose had never seen them rehearse this, but the starting tenor attacked the lead-in with an easy confidence, all pro. It was an elaborate windup and pulse-quickening kickoff to the show.

> *"Who writes the words and music*
> *For all the girly shows?*
> *No one cares, and no one knows."*

"Wow," said Phyllis. "Did you know they were doing this one?"

Betty Rose shook her head. "But he's nailing it."

> *"Who is the handsome hero*
> *Some villain always frames?*
> *But who cares if there's a plot or not,*
> *When they've got a lot of dames!"*

The number started to escalate. It was a delight—hypnotic and strangely soothing—as the full cast joined in the first chorus, notably dame-free.

Betty Rose turned from the video monitor to watch the number live in profile with a backstage view, glimpsing movement through the wing tabs.

From the corner of her eye, she saw the props master poke the techie and point to a separate table along the wall. He reached over to grab the purple velvet bag she'd seen him carrying around town, to and from Nifty's Knife Sharpening shop.

She sat forward in her chair, leaned around for a better view.

He unknotted the gold tassels and opened the bag. With great care, he reached in and lifted out a long, gleaming mill pick. Like a treasured artifact, he carefully laid it on a purple velvet pillow with gold rope trim that matched the bag.

He lifted it from the bottom and carried the pillow and pick from the props table, toward the back of the stage. She watched him disappear behind the backdrop crossover to the other side.

The chorus grew louder.

Betty Rose raced to the dressing room door, shut it, and turned.

"Phyllis, we've got to get out of here. Now!"

Scene Two

PHYLLIS LOOKED AT HER, OVER HER SHOULDER TO THE CLOSED DOOR, BACK TO HER. "Why?" she asked. "What's wrong?"

"They're going to kill us out there!" said Betty Rose.

Phyllis looked past her again, to an imaginary audience beyond. "You think?" She considered the possibility and then waved it away. "Nah. It's a very supportive crowd. They're going to *love* us. You'll see."

"No, I mean they're really going to kill us. Onstage!"

Phyllis scrutinized her with a cautious smile. "What the hell are you talking about?"

"*Look at us!* We're Carla and Cady!"

Phyllis huffed a laugh. "Well, duh. Are you just now figuring that out, McSherlock?"

The full chorus sang.

> "*What do you go for,*
> *Go see a show for?*
> *Tell the truth,*
> *You go to see those beautiful dames.*"

"And the stage is the scene of the murder!" Betty Rose insisted. "Don't you get it?"

Phyllis laughed again and said, "Well, yeah, I guess, if you look at it that way. But it's just pretend. It's fun!"

"No, Phyllis! It's real!"

On the monitor, the ensemble danced with precision.

"Careful now, Betty Rose," said Phyllis with a softening smile. "You're going haywire again. I think you're having another episode."

"It's happening. They're going to kill us both *now*!"

Phyllis patted her hand. "Shh, honey, no," she soothed. "No, B.R. No one's going to kill you, I promise. Why would they do such a thing?"

"It's a ritual. A cult ritual, for the whole town. To re-create the birth of the playhouse. Phyllis, it's a human sacrifice!"

Phyllis snickered and then stopped. She peered at her, reading her closely. Then she pulled back. "Oh, golly," she said. "You're serious, aren't you? Oh my." She pursed her lips with a slight grimace.

She stopped smiling and soothing. "Actually, you just overshot the runway," she said, concerned. "And it's totally bonkers. Please, oh please, don't do this again, B.R. Don't wig out on me right now."

Onstage, the singing and dancing intensified. Caleb and Rachelle did arm tricks with their top hats. Sutton and Alistair stood in place, swaying in rhythm on their canes.

"You spend your dough for
Bouquets that grow for
All those cute and cunning,
Young and beautiful dames."

"You're panicking, B.R.," Phyllis schooled. "This is a panic attack."

The monitor blared. Betty Rose reached up to silence it. She calmed herself and got close to Phyllis.

"Every time a Gristmill legend dies," she said evenly, "they re-enact the Carla/Cady massacre, live onstage, in front of the members and townies. To rejuvenate the playhouse, just like Rex said."

Phyllis grew more serious and Wellesley. "I'm aware of the legend, Betty Rose. But it's truly preposterous, and unhinged, to take it seriously. Or literally."

"Gwen knew it was coming. That's why they killed her. Out there!" She pointed past the door toward the stage.

Phyllis's hand shot to her mouth, to cover a sudden guffaw. "You think they killed her, Betty Rose? This just gets wilder and wilder." She tried humor to neutralize the tension. "Should we drag the Delaware? See if she floats to the top?"

"They *mill* the bodies! They *feed* off them!"

The live singing, growing louder, bled through the dressing room door.

> *"Oh! Dames are temporary flames to you.*
> *Dames, you don't recall their names.*
> *Do you?"*

Phyllis stared at her with alarm. "You're talking cannibalism, B.R. You've gone momentarily deranged. Please come back to earth and simmer down."

"They run the bodies through the gristmill, just like Carla's parents did," Betty Rose unloaded, shocked by her own admission. "They mix it into the food, into the compost. Even Clyde has developed a taste!"

"Clyde?" Phyllis giggled in spite of herself. "And how does Clyde like his humans? Well-done or tartare?"

"Wake up! They're sick!"

"*Who's* sick?"

"But their caresses
And home addresses,
Linger in your mem'ry of those beautiful dames."

Phyllis collected herself. "B.R., listen to me. It's not real. None of this is real." She pointed at their dresses, their hair. "It's acting. It's pretend. It's what we do on the stage." Her wheels turned, searching for a fresh tactic. "It's like, at college, we all dress up for Lizzie Borden Day, but that doesn't mean we're ax murderers."

"This isn't dress-up," Betty Rose said. "This is the real thing."

"Have you been to Disneyland?" Phyllis pressed on. "Do you think that's *really* Mickey Mouse waving to you in Toontown?"

"You've just been blind to it all," Betty Rose insisted. "It's like the lobsters. They've been turning the heat up slowly, and we don't notice until it's too late!"

Phyllis stood up, her patience evaporating.

"Lobsters? Really? Do you hear yourself? This...this...*moon-battery*?" She sharpened with tough love. "This is resistance. Self-sabotage. Just like Rex warns about."

"Fuck Rex!" Betty Rose shouted. "Just think! Nobody even knows we're here!"

"Your *boyfriend* knows!" Phyllis shouted back, and then threw up her hands and turned away. "Oh, forget it. I'm done reasoning with you."

The song tipped up a notch, nearing its climax.

She whirled back, her fury rising. "You know, I thought you were the real deal. But you're just an amateur. A dilettante. Run away, Betty Rose! Run away! Don't rub off on me!"

Phyllis stopped herself and softened, with a pitying look.

"I'm sorry, B.R. I don't mean that. I'm antsy now, too!" she confessed. "But we've worked so hard for this. We're so close. It's why we came here in the first place. I didn't understand it before, but now I do."

> *"Slims and all curvy,*
> *Sweet, shy and nervy,*
> *There is nothin' as refined as beautiful—*
> *No sun can shine as beautiful…"*

"And it's right now, this moment," Phyllis went on, pleading. "Do not ruin the show and blow everything for me, for us. Do not flinch!"

> *"Bring on a line of beautiful*
> *Dames, dames, dames, dames,*
> *Dames, dames, dames, dames—*
> *Dames!"*

She took Betty Rose's icy hands in her own clammy ones. "Let's just go out there and knock their socks off, together!"

The audience thundered.

"Whaddya say, pro?" she said, brightening.

Betty Rose stared at her, listening to the applause swell.

"You're on, girls," said Dottie from the open dressing room door. She smiled.

Scene Three

DOTTIE LED THEM TO THE EDGE OF THE WINGS. She wore a long, ruffled, farmer-wife dress.

The ensemble held their final "Dames" pose onstage, as the ovation wound down. The Carla curtain dropped, the work lights popped on.

The cast scurried offstage, rushing past Betty Rose and Phyllis with a quick-change-urgency on their way to the dressing room silo. They were gleeful and excited but in a hurry as they undid ties and top buttons in their exodus.

"Shh!" Dottie ordered with a stage whisper and frantic gesture. "Quiet!"

Phyllis leaned in to Betty Rose's ear. "If they off me out there, just hightail it out the stage door. But grab my Louis Vuitton first!" She smiled and winked, still clutching hands.

From the far side, Rex strolled onto the apron, in front of the curtain. A spotlight found and followed him. The audience gave him a hero's welcome.

The girls watched from the wings in profile. Rex beamed and basked and almost, it seemed, blushed.

The applause morphed into a stamp-and-clap "We Will Rock You" rhythm.

"Please, please," he projected, tamping down their adoration. "Thank you, now." He abruptly sawed his hands out. "*Stopfuckingcut!*" This triggered a wave of laughter and whistles and then a gradual settling to silence.

He drank them in and took a breath. "My God, you people have gotten old!" More bellows.

"On this very special night," he continued once the house calmed again, "we bid a fond *adieu* to our beloved Marian, no doubt smiling down from a grander stage and cooing, 'Hurry it up, fucker!'" The gladiators responded with fresh howls.

Rex fought emotion. "We'll miss you, dear friend," he went on, looking skyward, his voice earnest and cracking. "But as Carla would say, 'My song plays on.' And while there are young people yearning to make theatre, the Gristmill's song plays on, too."

Betty Rose heard a sigh and turned to Dottie gazing at him with a glassy smile.

He opened his arms. "To our entire family—stars, journeymen, friends—past, present, and future—I humbly and very proudly offer up our newest Gristmill members!" The room erupted.

Dottie snapped to. She poked Phyllis and pointed to the stage.

Phyllis hugged Betty Rose and made a blinking face. "See you on the other side!" she said with nervous cheer and sashayed out onto the boards. She hit her mark in the center.

The curtain rose, bathed her in light.

From her vantage, Betty Rose could see only the orchestra pit and Myron's conducting arms, poised and ready, but she felt the expectation of the full theater. She trained her eyes on Phyllis, who stared out at the audience with a frozen grin. She tipped her head at Myron, whose baton summoned the band.

The intro was simple and pleasant, mostly strings and flute. It weaved its way to the opening line.

Without hesitation, Phyllis hit her cue and sang "Hurry! It's Lovely Up Here" in her clear, lilting, Snow White soprano. She was a delight, pretending to coax flowers from the ground to the sun-filled world above. She was bright and irresistible.

Betty Rose leaned in and around for a glimpse of the crowd; Dottie pulled her back past the masking and wagged her finger, warning of sight lines.

After the second verse, Phyllis broke into an easy, two-step soft shoe for a dance break and twirled once in place before the final chorus, beaming all the while. She showed off her belt in the finale, punctuating the last several notes with sharp knee kicks and a sustained vibrato that was surprisingly strong. Myron and the orchestra capped off the number with an explosive bump.

The audience cheered.

Phyllis, intoxicated, flashed her broad smile and bowed once. As the ovation continued and swelled, she reddened and bowed to each section of the house. From the seats came full-throated "Bravos!" and whistles.

A single red rose landed on the stage apron, followed by more and then a shower. Phyllis, now crimson and teary, kept bowing and roamed the stage, collecting the roses into a bouquet. She stood stage center and dipped into a grand ballerina bow, her forehead almost touching the floor before springing back up and blowing kisses to her admirers. With a beauty queen wave, she reluctantly sauntered offstage right, to a proud Rex waiting under the tree lights.

She looked back to Betty Rose and gave a full, palm-up shrug from across the stage.

The Carla curtain came down to the ongoing applause.

A touch made Betty Rose jump. She spun to Dottie tracing circles on her back, followed by a gentle pat.

"Your turn," she said, planting a kiss on her forehead. "Good luck!"

The audience settled again, waiting.

Betty Rose tried for a deep breath, failed, and walked in a straight line onto the bare stage. She searched for her glow tape mark in the center, picked the wrong one too far left, recalibrated, found the correct one. Her bandaged hand twitched; she made a fist to calm it. It was freezing up here in her flop sweat. Trembling, she faced the back of the curtain and stood steady. She waited.

The curtain bounced and rose, unveiling the audience.

The floodlights blinded her immediately. She fought a squint, staring ahead while her eyes adjusted. The theater was packed: not just the orchestra and balcony, but the aisles and standing room in the back. Overflow folding chairs lined the front just behind the orchestra pit.

The room sat silent, looking at her.

She scanned the rows.

Her vision sharpening, she picked out familiar faces in the crowd: the florist shopkeeper and innkeeper, Calvin the town sheriff, the Panama Man, Erma the librarian, all attentive and expectant. Geraldine Roberts in her wheelchair down front sparkled in a black sequined top and cat-eye sunglasses. She looked chic and grand. And curious.

Throughout the room, gold flickered in the reflected light, from necks and hands.

A shock of flaming hair caught her eye. Wes the agent leaned forward, elbows on the seat in front of him, cupping his face. His festive tie and pocket square stood out in the crowd, along with his Joker-like smile. His finger glinted gold.

The audience waited on her. Myron's arms were poised and ready.

She looked down at him and tried to swallow and nodded her head. His arms moved; the band started.

The music vamped the intro. Betty Rose looked back out at the audience.

Julian was there! Audience left, five seats from the aisle. He was faced backward, nodding a greeting at someone in the row behind him, but he had come. She exhaled.

He turned back. It wasn't Julian. It was a much older person with a hair piece and a goatee. He looked ridiculous. She tensed again.

The music stopped. Myron stared up at her, quizzical. She had missed her cue.

Her gut clenched in the silence. She'd blown it. An amateur and dilettante. She should leave the stage, the playhouse, her delusional pipe dream.

She looked offstage to Rex in the wings. He waved it off, mouthed reassurance, mimed for her to begin anew.

She faced the audience, still rapt and forgiving. Supportive, even. Propping her up with encouragement and understanding. They'd stood where she stood, she knew, at the edge of the diving board.

Betty Rose straightened and focused. She tipped her head at Myron. The music started fresh.

She couldn't remember the first line. The music snaked closer to it. She closed her eyes and took a breath. The moment arrived. She opened her mouth.

There's a secret place I go to brighten up the gloom.
I find a world of peace and love inside this magic room.
A wonderland where I can build a life that brings me cheer.
And sing a song that only I can hear.

She opened her eyes. The verse kept coming.

A note, a chord, a verse, a rhyme, all weave inside my head.
It paints for me a wondrous life far from a world of dread.
And even when the day grows long, and I must pull away.
The magic spell I've cast will stay and stay…

She reached down deeper into her diaphragm to buttress the chorus.

My song plays on,
My song plays on.
When voices fall silent,
The magic lives on.

The audience sat spellbound.

My hymn from the pages
Will sing through the ages.
Long after the music is gone,
My song plays on.

Her breathing came easier in the short interlude before she launched into the second verse of Carla's anthem. From the stage, she embraced the audience, commanding them.

Movement onstage caught her eye and she glanced back to see the painted flats fly in around and behind her. Towering elms, the shops of Carla Avenue, the train station, the playhouse. She smiled at their quaint beauty enveloping her and turned back to sing on.

Her second chorus—even stronger than her first—summoned her fellow cast members, who emerged from the wings, singing backup in unison. They wore overalls and prairie dresses and happy faces as they took slow, deliberate steps in rhythm toward preset positions scattered about. Dottie and Alistair—dressed mother-and-father-like—anchored her on either side. Betty Rose opened her arms, welcoming them into her world.

She felt a wet tickle on her cheek and reached up to find a tear. She let it go, and the others that followed.

Her song took flight during the bridge.

Gone is the spring,
The summer music I sing
And hold so dear...

The backup humming swelled as the bridge rose in intensity.

But my song in the fall
Is winter's proof to us all
That I'm still here!

The cast echoed the line, and together they modulated up a key, unleashing the final chorus.

The stage exploded in golden confetti raining down from above. The floodlights grew hotter. The orchestra crescendoed, and the living tableau onstage fanned into a rich harmony, linking hands behind her as they wrapped her in love.

She stole a look to the wings and saw Rex and Phyllis standing together. Rex was brimming but controlled, while a joyful Phyllis sobbed with relief and pride.

The choir ticked up another key, the bass providing a strong floor while the sopranos lifted the melody to shrill, religious heights.

Betty Rose threw her head back and belted the climactic stanza.

> *My song plays on,*
> *My song plays on.*
> *My final bow taken,*
> *But the love carries on.*

Starting up front and catching on backward, the audience stood at their seats and joined hands down the rows and across the aisles in a singular web of adoration. They raised their arms and swayed in opposing patterns. Even chair-bound Geraldine Roberts lifted one hand and joined in the merry wave as Betty Rose powered on.

> *My hymn from the pages*
> *Will ring through the ages!*
> *Long after the music is gone,*
> *My song plays on!*

Betty Rose hit and held a high C, which the company highlighted by repeating the chorus underneath. It would round back to her one last time, she knew, to knock it home.

She stopped to drink in the room's worship, as the band played on.

She glanced back to the wings for Rex's approval.

He was embracing Phyllis under the light tree. The pudgy techie stood at the ready, holding the purple velvet pillow that cradled the mill pick.

Betty Rose squinted.

Rex carefully picked up the pick and held it out to Phyllis. He laid it across her open palms. The chorus kept singing.

He clasped her by the shoulders and said something of heavy importance and kissed her on the forehead. She nodded and grabbed the pick handle like a dagger.

Rex pivoted her toward the stage and stood behind her, whispering in her ear.

Phyllis held still, soldierlike, facing Betty Rose. The newly sharpened tip glinted in the stage lights.

The musical cue came and went. The chorus kept it alive, waiting for her to pick it up.

Betty Rose's neck spasmed. She shook her head in tiny jolts and locked eyes with Phyllis, who smiled broadly at her. Her mouth was numb, her throat dry.

"No. Not," she thought and might have said, as neither her mind nor voice were in sync or working correctly.

"You're not...*kill*...me," she stammered under the music. She swallowed.

"You're not...going to...kill me," she cried out, full-throated. "*YOU'RE NOT GOING TO KILL ME!*"

Scene Four

BETTY ROSE, SURROUNDED FROM BEHIND AND BLOCKED FROM THE WINGS, ran downstage and leaped off the apron, vaulting over the orchestra pit but falling just short.

She collapsed back onto the drum set and sprang up quickly. She grabbed the edge of the pit and hoisted herself, while the band members scrambled to stop her.

"Gentle! Gentle!" Rex called down from the stage. "Betty Rose, stop!" he commanded her.

She launched into the audience, still linked in a tight mesh. She fought through their web, breaking the chain red-rover-style, as she thrashed up the aisle toward the lobby. Hands from all sides reached out to her.

"Betty Rose!" they pleaded. "Betty Rose!"

Her fellow cast shouted at her as they descended the stage stairs on either side. Rachelle was the bossiest.

"Betty Rose, stop this!" Dottie chimed in, clapping her hands at a naughty child. "Stop it right now!" She sounded crabby again.

Navigating through the snare, shoving people off and away, she made it to the back of the house and raced into the lobby and toward the exit doors. She slammed into one and then the other. She shook them.

They were locked.

The ushers moved toward her, arms out. Others spilled from the house in her direction.

Betty Rose pivoted and ran past the Carla portrait to the door by the box office. She pushed through and scurried down the pitch-black catacombs leading back to the stage. She burst into the wings and set her sights on the stage door.

Caleb stepped in her way. He stifled laughter.

"B.R., please!" he said, composing himself. "Just chill!"

She turned. Techies now blocked the catacombs door. The cast and audience amassed anew in the house, closing in. Betty Rose backed against the stage deck, cornered by the fly cables and power box.

Rex climbed the stairs back onto the apron, silhouetted in the lights. He looked winded and spoke calmly.

"There now," he soothed, diffusing the drama. "Is it out of your system?" He gave a warm smile. "Don't be embarrassed. This happens every time." He stepped gingerly, as if approaching a mad dog.

"*Stay away from me!*" Betty Rose screamed, her mind reeling for any escape hatch.

Rex called back to the audience. "Live theatre, folks!" he explained. "Anything can happen!"

They laughed. He turned back to her.

"Now, settle down," he coaxed. "That's a good girl...."

He got closer.

"You nailed it tonight," he said, nodding with pride. "An eleven o'clock number we'll never forget. But we're not done yet. Not just yet..."

Another step.

"Trust me, Betty Rose. Let me talk you through the finale. You're going to love it.…"

She reached up to the central power box with both hands and cranked the main lever down, drowning the playhouse in blackness.

She darted around Caleb's reach and ran toward the silo stairs. She raced up, two steps at a time. There was noisy confusion and protests behind her.

She stumbled in the dark but recovered and continued her ascent, guided by the railing. She targeted the top.

The building's lights burst back on. She arrived at the seventh floor, looked out the silo window at the grassy knoll far below. Cornered again.

She spun to the clatter of footsteps just behind. Caleb looked up at her from the switchback one floor down, catching his breath.

"Rex!" he shouted back. "Can we just do it up here?"

"Not enough room," Rex called up from the stage level.

"Don't rip the dress, please!" Dottie said.

Caleb turned back to Betty Rose and grinned, no longer hiding his delight in the game as he climbed toward her.

"Sorry. Never done this before," he said, closing in. "It's sorta wild. But, seriously, Rex is losing patience.…"

Betty Rose hoisted herself on both bannisters and kick-punched him in the chest, knocking him down a flight. He landed on his back.

Caleb lost patience, too. He scrambled to his feet and charged her.

She bolted toward the emergency exit door on the landing and pushed through. In the dark cavern, the fire escape slide spiraled downward. She jumped onto it, accelerating in circles as she descended seven floors. Her dress snagged on a screw and tore at the hip, ripping a jagged slit down the leg.

The slide dumped her out at the bottom, through a trapdoor, spilling her onto the grass in a tangle. She sprang up and ran.

She flew around the side of the playhouse, across the front courtyard, toward the Journeyman Bridge, glancing back as Caleb burst through the slide's trapdoor onto the ground. He somersaulted and bounced up and gave chase.

The others poured from the front doors of the playhouse, spotted her, and followed en masse.

She sprinted across the bridge, stumbling and breaking her fall as her hand sank into the flower bed's thick, wet soil. She pulled off the wedge-heeled character shoes that slowed her down and, barefoot, barreled on.

The tall, wooden gate at the end was closed. She grabbed and shook it. Locked. She slammed her shoulder against it. Futile. Caleb sped faster, trapping her.

Betty Rose fought through the dense rose bed and looked over the edge of the bridge. Thorns ensnared her; she beat them back as they ripped at her sequins and arms. She climbed onto the railing, and without hesitation, leaped off the side, plunging into the cascades below.

She surfaced and swam toward the far side in her waterlogged dress, as Caleb splashed down right behind her.

He overtook her, grabbing her legs and working his way up to her waist. She squirreled out of his grasp and paddled toward the shore, kicking harder to leave him behind.

She reached the water's edge and navigated the rocky shoreline, balancing carefully on the shifting rubble as she waded out. Caleb caught up and tackled her from behind, crashing them both onto the muddy embankment. He pulled her back toward the water.

On her stomach, Betty Rose clawed the ground up the bank, straining to wriggle away, but he overpowered her. She reached out to a large, jagged rock at the edge, clutched it with both hands. In one smooth motion, she rolled onto her back, lifted it above her head, and brought it down onto Caleb's face with a crack. It shattered his nose, and she brought it down again to an explosion of blood from the middle of his head. He howled and released her. She scampered onto solid ground and took off.

The mob from the playhouse gushed through the now-open bridge gate and swarmed at her, clamoring for her to halt.

Betty Rose fled across the gravel parking lot and into the dark and deserted town, racing down Carla Avenue toward the far route out of New Hope. A blazing police car sped up from a side street and blocked her escape. She pivoted and ran in the opposite direction, toward the outlet across the railroad tracks.

As if expecting her, the crossing lights flashed and rang, the bars lowered, and the hulking Ivyland locomotive steam-blasted to life and lurched from the station. Betty Rose rushed to beat it but lost out as it churned across the street tracks, cutting her off from the road beyond and stopping in her way. It spewed more steam and idled.

The uniformed conductor leaped from the cab and came at her. Betty Rose scanned her options and dove under the combine car just behind the engine, on hands and knees, to scoot below and beyond. Her hem caught on a valve gear, slowing her. She reached back and ripped herself free as the conductor grabbed at her leg. Thwarted, she rolled back out the way she came, just beyond his reach, and sprang up to run down the length of the train.

The caboose attendant hopped from the last car, waiting for her. She dodged out of his grasp and hurried down the station platform and crossed over to the other side.

The playhouse mob teemed on the street and followed.

Betty Rose ran for her life.

Jumping down from the platform, she moved along a wide canal toward an intersecting side street just ahead. She balanced on the concrete berm at the water's edge as she made her way.

A shiny white car squealed to a stop on the street right in front of her.

Her options were grim. She peered down at the dark canal that led to the Delaware River. Across its wide, strong current lay a different town and more escape routes, if she survived to reach it.

She heard the car door open as her new attacker emerged. She perched at the edge, preparing to jump into the black abyss.

"Betty Rose!"

She turned.

"*Julian!*" she cried out to him. He'd never looked more handsome.

"What the hell are you doing?" he asked, befuddled.

She ran to him, collapsed against him. "Thank God you came!" She clutched his arms. "We gotta go. Now!"

"What is wrong?" He looked her up and down as his confusion shifted to alarm.

She hyperventilated, struggling to speak. "It's worse than you thought. Much worse!" She looked back toward the station, knowing the mob would arrive any second. "We've got to get out of here!" She pushed him back toward the white car.

Julian held and soothed her. "Shh, honey. It's okay. I'm here now. You're okay."

"NO!" she said. "They're coming to kill me! They'll kill us both! Let's go!"

He coiled around her tighter. "Just calm down, B.R."

She tried to wriggle from his clench. "Now!" she screamed. He constricted her more.

She grabbed his hand to pry it off her. "Why are you...?" She felt something hard on his finger. She looked down at the ring, glinting gold.

Betty Rose crumbled.

"Oh my God," she said. "You're one...*of them*!"

Scene Five

Julian gently forced her up the steps to the railroad platform. Everyone was waiting.

She writhed against his grip, knowing it futile.

"Please don't be like this, B.R.," he begged in her ear. "They did me a favor, you know...."

Rex stood in the center of the platform, catching his breath. The others crowded around him. The locomotive, still partially out of the station, billowed smoke and steam clouds from its stovepipe chimney, drifting out and down the platform in a fog.

"Not the way I staged this, Betty Rose," said Rex with good nature. "You're really testing our improv skills." The freak show behind him tittered. Someone in the back laughed out loud.

"And props to you, Julian," Rex added proudly. "Isn't that what the kids say nowadays?"

"I learned from the best, sir," said Julian with a smile. He, too, was winded, breathing down her neck.

Julian, whose career had taken off since the previous summer, those months he was so hard to reach even when she needed him the most. Now she knew why.

"Testing her loyalty, pushing her closer to us," Rex went on, returning the smile. "Impressive stage combat, even. Are you sure you don't want to trot the boards yourself?"

She could feel Julian blush. "I think I'll stick to my day job," he said, demure.

Rex trained his attention on her. "You can let her go," he said, inspecting. "You won't run off again, will you, Betty Rose?"

Julian released her. She found her footing, stood rigid.

Rex nodded. "See? I didn't think so," he said. "I know you better than you do."

She stared back at him.

"You could have left anytime, you know," Rex continued. "No matter how hard we pushed you away, you kept coming back. We even wasted a bus ticket. Deep down, you are exactly where you want to be.…"

"I wrote to my mother," she said. "She knows where to find me." She spoke in defiance. There were no more escapes anyway.

Rex considered and approved. "That's a good girl. Hopefully, she will find you on Broadway."

"Stop it!" Betty Rose screamed. "*Stop lying to me!*"

Rex recoiled, slightly miffed. "I never lied to you. Maybe Dot did.…"

"Oh, please don't pin that on me," Dottie protested from the front row of the crowd. "I was just following the script."

"You killed Mr. Arbor!" Betty Rose said.

He frowned at the name and then nodded in confession. "And someday you'll thank us for that," he said. "That traitor was not your friend, not at all. He didn't want you to win, you see."

"And Gwen!" she added.

Rex looked at her with pity and measured his response. "Don't ruin this moment," he chided. "Just let that one go."

"You did!" she insisted, unloading. "You killed her, too!"

Dottie huffed out her frustration. "Oh, that's rich!" she blurted, and Alistair, next to her, added, "The lady doth protest too much." Rex silenced them both before turning back to Betty Rose.

"That was an accident," he explained gently. "Nothing more."

"I saw her die!" Betty Rose said. "Right in front of me!"

Rex nodded. "Just don't blame yourself."

Betty Rose blinked.

"Myself…?" she said. "For…what?"

"Blame Carla. Her song worked a little too well on you.…"

Betty Rose held his stare, not understanding.

"You trusted your instincts," he continued. "You wanted your union card. And you made it happen. A bit overeager, but nothing to be ashamed of."

She saw Gwen's face, warning her to flee. It morphed into confusion and then shock. She spit blood, then vomited more, heaving.

"She wasn't happy here anyway," said Rex. "She didn't really belong. Not like you do. Clearly."

She looked down at the stage knife in her own hand, clutching the handle, the blade buried deep in Gwen's gut.

"We had to finish what you started, of course," Rex went on. "Out of mercy."

She looked back up to the blurred mass of cast and crew that swarmed toward the wounded Gwen.

"No one will ever know," Rex assured her. "We take care of our own, you see. What happens at the Gristmill stays at the Gristmill."

The nightmare evaporated.

She crumpled on the platform. "No!" she howled. "Nooo!"

"Shh," Rex calmed. "What did I just tell you? It was an accident."

"It *was* an accident!" Betty Rose said, struggling for a breath.

"That's right. And so it doesn't count."

"It doesn't count," she agreed. "It doesn't count!"

He took her hands and, with Julian's help, gingerly guided her up. He cupped her face and softened away her worries.

"There, now," he said, thumbing off a tear. "That's all behind us. Let it go."

"Yes," she said, nodding.

He paused while she composed herself. "That's better, isn't it?"

She nodded again with insistence, avoiding his eyes.

"That's all in the past."

She nodded.

"And so we're not finished," he added. "Are we?"

The mob stirred.

"See, in the theatre, timing is everything," he explained. "And the time...is now."

At the far end of the platform, through the train's steam cloud, emerged Carla in silhouette, strolling toward her, hands tucked behind her back.

She walked into the station's light. It was Phyllis, still in her red sequined dress. She smiled as she drew closer, seemingly in a trance.

Julian restrained Betty Rose again.

From behind her back, Phyllis pulled her hand, holding the gleaming mill pick. She aimed its stiletto tip at Betty Rose and came to a stop.

"Phyllis, no!" she shrieked, still trapped by Julian. "It's me! Betty Rose!"

Phyllis *tsk*ed through her amusement. "I know who you are, silly."

She turned the pick, folded Betty Rose's trembling fingers around the handle, and dropped to her knees in front of her.

"Carla," Rex said to Betty Rose, "meet Cady."

Phyllis gazed up at her with love.

"Isn't it exciting, B.R.?" she said. "I'll be remembered. I'll live forever! On the bridge with the others. With the journeymen…"

Betty Rose stared down at her. "No…," she said. "No…"

Rex got closer.

"And you," he said, casting a spell: "Broadway chorus this fall, a supporting role next spring. Soon a leading lady, toast of the Great White Way and beyond. Creating your own mythology and legend.

"But ever loyal to your family here. Returning in the season, giving back—until your face adorns not just our lobby, but the hearts and minds of millions worldwide. And one day Broadway dims its lights in tribute…like all the legends before you.

"That's far in the future, of course," he added. "Many a new day will dawn before your doom."

Betty Rose raised the pick to stab him. He grabbed and held her arm midair.

"There it is," he said with knowing wisdom. "That final resistance. Here, if it makes you feel better…" He placed the tip of the pick against his throat, right under his chin. He leaned in until it lightly pricked the skin, releasing a single drop of blood that rolled down his neck.

"See, that won't get you what you want," he said. "Only one thing will...."

Betty Rose yanked back the pick. It shivered in her hand.

He touched his wound to stem the bleeding. "It's okay. We all have the jitters tonight. It's been so long for all of us."

Sutton broke from the pack and approached her. "Ten seconds, Betty Rose," she said. "It's over in a flash. You won't even remember it. I barely do." She got closer to her ear. "And it works. I know it works."

"Don't screw this up," piped in Rachelle from the side. "You'll never forgive yourself. I would have killed for the chance you have right now."

Betty Rose looked at the pick. It held steady.

"...I can't...," she said, shaking her head.

"You'll tend to my rose, Betty Rose," said Phyllis below. "I'll bloom for you every year. For you alone."

"Don't let it pass you by, B.R.," Julian urged from behind.

She turned the pick one way and then the other.

Parents herded children to the front row for a better view.

Alistair turned to Dottie. "Technically, we're supposed to do this onstage," he said. Irritated, Dottie shushed and waved him back. "So? We're *on tour*!" she growled. From her hand tick-tocked a new-looking Gristmill pendant in sparkling gold.

Betty Rose looked from the crowd to the kneeling Phyllis.

"Don't worry. It won't hurt," said Phyllis, still glowing. "You know how to do it. I love you, Betty Rose. Do it for *me*."

Rex inched nearer.

"Make it happen," he urged. "Let it happen. You've been dreaming of this moment your whole life."

Betty Rose shuffled a step closer to Phyllis.

"That's my good girl," he coaxed. "Daddy's watching. He's watching right now. Make Daddy proud...."

She stood still, hesitating. Phyllis began to hum Carla's theme.

She added the lyrics, singing softly.

Sutton joined in, then Rachelle and Dottie and Alistair and Baayork and Caleb, still wet and bloodied with a mangled nose that made him manlier and more unique-looking. They sang together in rich harmony.

Others chimed in for the chorus. The sheriff and innkeeper, the florist and baker, the visiting producers and Wes the agent, who belted out the tenor line with surprising power and clarity. He hadn't lost his touch.

The pick rotated in her hand. She gripped it.

Young Phillip stepped to the front row with the other singing children, still holding the program she'd autographed for him weeks earlier. He looked upon her with adoration and sang with an angelic, boy soprano. He tucked the program under his arm and began to clap.

The applause swept through the crowd, and soon everyone was singing and cheering her on.

The Panama Man sang horribly off-key, and a grinning Strudel perched on his shoulder and hammered his paws with spastic, monkey rhythm.

Betty Rose looked out at her audience. She hummed a little with them. After all, it was her song.

She took another step.

It was a brilliant, clear evening with a warm breeze that buffeted and enveloped her. She felt coddled and protected, fully surrounded by love and inspired by the vivid constellations that canopied across the velvet sky.

Geraldine Roberts, sitting ringside in her chair, braced her hands on the armrests and, resisting help, pushed herself up. She struggled her way to a standing position and sang and applauded with gusto. She rose to a legendary stature.

Rex ignored the others, burrowed into Betty Rose. "It's time," he said. "Be a warrior, Betty Rose. Don't flinch."

The choir swelled around her on all sides.

Betty Rose drank in her worshipping fans. All here just for her.

She heard herself chirp and then giggle. It became uncontrollable, and she was laughing and then cackling, with a joy and relief, and she felt tears and let them run. She sobbed with glee.

And she was center stage at the Golden Theatre, under the bright lights in a packed Broadway house, with Myron in the orchestra pit leading everyone in her song. And the opening-night audience, in tuxedos and gowns, with perfect hair and makeup and sparkling jewels, were on their feet, calling her name and yelling "Bravo!" and tossing roses through their cheers and whistles. Not just the rows, but also the aisles and the back of the theater, spilling out the front doors to the street where an even larger crowd clapped and shouted love at her. A standing ovation that went on and on, throughout the city.

She bowed to the center, and then to the left side and right, and swept out her arms for a deep ballerina, not quite touching her forehead to the stage, but she'd get there someday. The audience thundered, showering her in rapture.

And her beloved father was right up front, at the edge of the pit, whistling the loudest (he always had such a strong whistle) and blistering his hands, and he was so handsome and healthy, like he'd always been, and she'd never seen him so vital and glowing and overwhelmed. He was crying, too, with pride in his little girl, so joyous that she'd made it, like he'd told her she would, because he believed in her and always had, even when no one else thought she had what it takes to end up, against all odds, dead center on a Broadway stage with a legendary career ahead of her. She beamed back at him and winked and mouthed "I love you," because her glory was his.

And Phyllis knelt before her on the apron, in her red sequined gown, with her head down and neck exposed, so clear and very easy, and she took a deep breath and nodded, waiting for her cue. Betty Rose reached down and touched the back of her head and stroked her hair and then patted her one last time as the chorus climaxed in the sky.

With both hands, Betty Rose raised the pick high in the air. She threw back her head and screamed up to the stars.

Playoff

May 19

TIMES SQUARE WAS USUALLY JAMMED WITH TOURISTS, but even more so the closer it edged to summer.

Two junior executives in shirtsleeves revolved out the glass door of their office tower and onto bustling Broadway during their lunch break, talking rapid-fire and ignoring the throngs.

"…I swear, all at once, everything went black!" said the first in a Jersey tongue, gesturing with emphasis. "Lights, neon, every damn theater on the block! My girlfriend thought it was an attack or blackout or some shit.…"

"Yeah, I heard about that from Simpson," said the second. He spoke with an outer-borough dialect. "He passed it on his way home. What was it for?"

"Fuck if I know. Some old Broadway chick who kicked it this week. They really gotta warn us about that shit.…"

"Actor freaks." They laughed.

They nearly collided with two oblivious young women barreling out of the Starbucks in post-dance-class gear and sipping iced lattes. They both wore ponytails and strutted down Broadway in boots and leg warmers in spite of the late-spring heat. The junior execs turned back to check them out as they threaded through the swarm, chattering nonstop.

"Nadine booked a gig?" asked one, her voice shrill above the crowd. "When did *that* miracle happen?"

"Few days ago," said the other, pulling her cat-eye sunglasses down from her hair. "It's not a miracle. And it's not really a gig. It's free work. I hear they never go on. Whatever."

They took a sharp turn west on Forty-Fifth Street, weaving through the slow tourist armies that clogged the sidewalks at Wednesday matinee time.

"It's dead here in the summer anyway," whined one of the dancer girls. "When's she back?"

They passed the Music Box and the Imperial with revivals of *A Chorus Line* and *Gypsy.*

"After Labor Day, I guess," said the other, feigning indifference and boredom. "She's been such a buzzkill since Jason dumped her. I've been avoiding her. Everybody has."

"That's cold. I heard they were engaged."

"Didn't stop him from balling half of Hell's Kitchen. La-di-dah."

The biggest crowd amassed around the Golden, spilling off the sidewalk and onto the street between parked cars. Impatient taxis honked and inched their way through the herd.

The crowd was funneling inside for the two p.m. performance of *Applause.*

"Wanna get twofers?" asked one of the girls, stopping to look up at the marquee banner touting its seven Tony nominations, including Best Musical Revival. Peppered alongside were rave reviews from Charles Isherwood, Terry Teachout, and Marilyn Stasio. Along the theater wall were oversized photos of the production mixed in with more fawning notices from *Time Out, Rolling Stone,* and the Huffington Post.

"Fat chance," said the other, sipping her latte. "It's sold out for months. Tara Rubin's casting the first tour in a couple weeks. An assistant at Bruce Leonard is getting me an EPA."

"Really? Can he get me in, too?"

They paused at the full-sized cast photos: Margot, Bill, Bonnie. In costume, posed in action onstage.

In the center, highlighted, was a blown-up photo of a young woman in a simple floral dress and heavy stage makeup, the slim stage mike snaked through her hair to just below her ear, targeting her full, red lips. She stared down her sidewalk admirers with a mix of resolve and challenge, glowing with her fresh hit. The headline at the top announced: "Introducing Betty Rose Miller as Eve."

Across the photo, a newer addition, a bright pink pennant shouted: "Tony Nominee—Best Featured Actress in a Musical."

"Lucky bitch," said one girl. "Out of nowhere."

"Lucky is right," sniffed the other, looking away. "And I hear she's overrated."

On a video monitor, behind glass, the new headliner stood alone onstage in the spotlight, unleashing the eleven o'clock number. Her debut star turn projected in a constant loop for all of Forty-Fifth Street.

"She does have pipes," said one girl, impressed.

"Flavor of the month," said the other, not. "Probably fucking someone. Or everyone."

They watched and listened with the other passersby who had stopped to watch and listen.

"Come on," she added, slinking on past the stage entrance. "I gotta change before work. I'm covering Amanda's shift tonight."

Ticket holders inched farther into the lobby, past the new star's giant photo. From her neckline, under the edge of her costume dress, peeked a glint of gold.

● ● ●

They'd noticed each other in the Port Authority waiting area and on the Trans-Bridge bus, but didn't piece it all together until they both got off in New Hope.

"Gristmill?" asked one young lady, no more than twenty. "So they tell me," joked the other, lively and overeager.

They shook hands. "Great to meet you, Nadine," said one with admiration. "That's a kick-ass name."

They pulled their rolling luggage down Carla Avenue, swapping backgrounds and eyeing the town with an expectant air. They compared their acting classes back in New York and commiserated over survival jobs, the perils of Craigslist roommates, the illusive hunt for an agent and their Equity cards.

They clicked. And shared more.

They marveled at their lucky stars for the chance encounters that had led them here: a cold-reading workshop and a dance class where someone knew someone who heard that the legendary Gristmill was looking for summer interns. That these encounters were months old and the surprise call to New Hope came out of the blue just two days ago reinforced their faith that opportunity could strike anytime for the well prepared.

They brimmed with excitement and a touch of apprehension as they passed antiques stores and ice cream shops and scoured street addresses. A friendly and helpful woman sweeping the front porch at the Mansion Inn pegged them immediately and pointed them in the right direction.

"Thank you," they both said.

By the time they reached the far edge of the gravel parking lot, they'd babbled and bonded over cheating, shifty ex-boyfriends and a series of pleasant nothingness that diffused any potential rivalry. At first glance, they seemed similar types, but their differences came into sharper focus as they let down their guard. One was more statuesque and sat firmly in the classic ingenue camp while the other was just quirky enough for a broad, character appeal. They were both quietly relieved by the distinction.

The ingenue laughed at the other's jokes and barbs and seemed relieved from the slight burden she'd carried off the bus. She brightened with each step.

They stopped and stood, listening to the faint carousel organ music that lured them from a distance. They carried on.

"Oh my God, it's beautiful," they said back and forth over the cascades as they crossed the bridge lined with a rainbow of rose bushes.

"Shoo!" the character actress cried out, scaring off a large, ugly bird that tore at the soil around a fragile young sapling. The bird lumbered through the air and disappeared into an ancient elm that towered just beyond. "Be gone, beast!" She leaned down to inspect the dainty flower's damage. Its pink-and-white-striped bloom wilted downward, but its sturdy, thorny trunk promised a healthy recovery. "Chin up!" she coaxed, gently lifting the resilient bud up to the sun.

A bell-collared adult goat ran up from the shade of the elm and darted in a circle between them.

"Isn't he adorable?" said the ingenue. "That's one fat goat," carped the other, and they both laughed, holding out their hands to him. He sniffed at one and then the other and then bleated a greeting before scampering off to another adventure.

They stepped off the bridge.

"Egads," said the quirky one, looking up. "Bingo."

The Gristmill Playhouse stood square in the grassy knoll, like a giant jack-in-the-box.

The water wheel turned on the side. The carousel music from the front porch speakers beckoned with a soothing yet unfamiliar tune. The chasing-light marquee heralded its exciting summer season.

Together they gazed up and stepped a fraction closer to each other.

"Shall we?" said the ingenue after a pause.

Ahead, the playhouse loomed, welcoming them.

"Hell yeah. Let's do it."

Side by side, the girls moved toward it.

Acknowledgments

Writing a novel is a journey of sorts, and I want to thank those who helped and supported me along the way. First and always, to my parents and sister, Debra. No explanation needed, but much love nonetheless.

To my longtime mentor and friend Harry Mastrogeorge, the renowned acting teacher and director who is Greek-American, from Pittsburgh, and rumored to have the occasional temper, but is in no other way similar to Rex. I promise.

To Michael Starr and Andrew Blau, who are walking encyclopedias of all things musical theatre and were willing to share their thoughts and wisdom while masking their bafflement that I was writing this at all.

To my most loyal readers, whom I now consider friends: Holly Bingham, Marely Cheo-Bove, Christina Evans, Suzanne Fawcus, Devan Hidalgo, Pat O'Meara, and Patty Turrisi. And could a writer hope for a more ferocious cheerleader than Ryan Rayston, herself a beautiful writer?

To my copyeditor, Penina Lopez, whose expertise was crucial to the book you just read. I think I know everything about grammar and usage, and I don't. She does. And to Jacqueline

"Eagle Eye" Mazarella, who manages to find the final few errors that everyone else missed.

To my song collaborator, Kyle Rosen, who can crank out a stellar song per day and spent weeks on the one for this story. He can make magic with his piano. Special thanks to Rick Hip-Flores and Maddy Jarmon for bringing our song to life. You can hear their beautiful rendition at www.DonWinston.com.

To my cover designer and illustrator, Steven Womack, and interior illustrator, Steven Stines, whose talents are a mystery to me and yet seemingly boundless. They both nailed the "Stepford Disney" tone we all wanted.

To the late John Seigenthaler, whose friendship I cherish and whose support I'll always appreciate.

Finally, to my book agent, Helen Breitwieser, not only kind and elegant, but also wise and shrewd. That's a potent and welcome combination in this brave new world.

My Song Plays On

Words and Music by
Kyle Rosen and Don Winston
Piano arr. Rick Hip-Flores

The Gristmill Playhouse: A Nightmare in Three Acts

My Song Plays On

My Song Plays On

5

My Song Plays On

Glossary of Theatre Terms

Against type—Playing a different sort of character than expected. (See *Typecasting.*)

Apron—Section of the stage floor that projects toward or into the auditorium. In proscenium theaters, the part of the stage in front of the house tabs, or in front of the proscenium arch.

Artistic director—Broadly, the role involves being responsible for the overall artistic vision of a production. Normally in charge of the programming of a venue. May also direct shows.

Batten—A tubular metal bar, sometimes known as a pipe, from which overhead lighting can be hung.

Blocking—Stage movements and positions choreographed by the director for dramatic effect. The stage manager makes a careful note of blocking directions for later reference.

Book—1) The non-sung text of a musical. (See *Libretto.*)
2) A musical theatre singer's collection of rehearsed songs for audition purposes.

Booth—An enclosed, windowed area, usually at the back of the auditorium, from which the sound and lights are controlled. Also *Control booth.*

Break a leg—Saying "Good luck" is not allowed backstage. The term "Break a leg" is used.

Call board—The place backstage where the stage manager puts up important information for the cast and crew.

Catwalk—A narrow walkway suspended from the ceiling of a theater from which lights and scenery are hung.

Character shoes—Shoes worn by actors performing, rehearsing, or auditioning for theater productions. Women's resemble a heeled Mary Jane, with a strap over the ankle and pump front, in black or tan. Men's are undecorated, black lace-up oxfords. They are not suitable for outdoor wear.

Curtain call—At the end of a performance, the acknowledgment of applause for the actors—the bows.

Dance break—The part of a musical number devoted mainly to dance, usually separate from singing that precedes and follows.

Dark—A venue that has been closed to the public. Some theaters go dark temporarily during production periods, when the next show is in preparation onstage. Also refers to the production's scheduled days off between performances.

Deck—The stage area.

Downstage—1) The part of the stage nearest to the audience (the lowest part of a raked stage).
2) A movement toward the audience (in a proscenium theater).

Dress—Short for "dress rehearsal." A full rehearsal, with all technical elements brought together. The performance as it will be "on the night."

Equity—also AEA, Actor's Equity Association. American labor union representing the world of live theatrical performance. Strict membership requirements and rules.

Equity ten (or Equity five)—A union-mandated rehearsal break. Either a five-minute break every hour, or a ten-minute break every two hours. Up to members' discretion and vote.

Fire curtain—A fireproof curtain that can be dropped downstage of the tabs to separate the audience from the stage in the event of fire.

Flat—A lightweight timber frame covered with scenic canvas. Most theaters have a range of stock flats made to a standard size and reused many times.

Fly—The action of lifting an item up (out) or down (in) when attached to the flying system.

Fly line—The cables and ropes that form part of the flying system.

Fly space—The empty space above the stage used to attach and house flying scenery.

Fourth wall—An imaginary surface at the edge of the stage through which the audience watches a performance. If a character speaks directly to the audience or walks on/off the stage, this is known as *breaking the fourth wall.*

Front of house (FOH)—Every part of the theater in front of the proscenium arch, including foyer areas open to the general public.

Front of house calls—Announcement made by stage management calling audience into the auditorium, or informing them when the performance will begin. Normally accompanied by bar bells at three, two, and one minute before performance starts.

Ghost light—A light left burning overnight onstage to keep friendly spirits illuminated and unfriendly spirits at bay. Also believed to keep the theatrical muse in a "dark" theater, and to stop people tripping over bits of scenery when they come into the theater in the morning.

Go up—An actor forgetting lines or business.

Grand curtain—Also "House curtain." The main house tabs in a venue. Normally a variation of red or blue in color.

Green room—Area backstage where actors rest before/after a show or have visitors.

Gypsy—Slang. A member of the chorus line in a theater production.

Half hour—The time before a performance by which all actors must be present in the theater—commonly half an hour before curtain up.

Headshot (AKA 8x10)—The actor's official photo for professional use.

Hemp—A type of rope used for flying, made from fibers found within the bark of the cannabis plant. (See *Fly*.)

House—1) The audience (e.g. "How big is the house tonight?").
2) The auditorium (e.g. "The house is now open").

House lights—The auditorium lighting, which is commonly faded out when the performance starts.

House manager—Member of theater staff responsible for front of house staff and organization for a particular performance. Also responsible for audience safety when they are in the theater.

In one—Curtain just upstage of main curtain to divide stage and mask scene changes behind. Simple scenes can be performed "in one" before the reveal of the larger scene and set behind. "In two" curtain performs a similar function, but is farther upstage and offers larger stage space for scenes.

Ingenue—A stock character and a role type in the theater; generally a girl or a young woman who is endearingly innocent and wholesome. Ingenue may also refer to a new young actress or one typecast in such roles.

Juvenile—The most significant role in a play or film that is performed by a young actor.

Leading lady—The actress playing the largest role in the cast performed by a female.

Leading man—The actor playing the largest role in the cast performed by a male.

Legs—Vertical curtains or flats used to hide the wings from view and frame the audience's view of the stage.

Libretto—The sung text of a musical. (See *Book*.)

Line—Summer stock jargon for "type," i.e. the categorization of an actor into roles based on physical appearance. (See *Typecasting*.)

Macbeth—Mentioning *Macbeth* in a theater is said to invoke the curse of the Scottish Play. The only way to break the curse is for the offender to spin on the spot and then spit. The spin turns back time, and the spit expels the corrupting poison. This particular play is always called the Scottish Play.

Marks—Predetermined positions onstage for actors, sets, furniture, or props. Often "marked" by glow tape for easier identification in dark scene changes.

Masking—Drapery or flats used to frame the stage and stop the audience from seeing the backstage areas.

Monologue—A speech within a play delivered by a single actor alone onstage.

Off book—Being able to work without a script. Having memorized one's lines. Opposite of "on book."

Opening night—The opening night of a theater performance often has a largely invited audience of people connected with the show but not directly involved in it. The first official performance with press reviewers.

Orchestra pit—Where the musicians play, usually directly in front of the stage, often sunken below the seating sections.

Paper the house—Marketing technique. Giving away tickets to a performance (e.g. opening night) to make a show seem to be selling better than it actually is, and to start generating word-of-mouth interest.

Parcan—Type of lantern that produces an intense beam of light, ideally suited to "punching" through strong colors, or for special effect.

Pickup—Rehearsal of a show that's already opened, to refine and improve it midrun.

Places—A call by the stage manager that all cast, crew, and orchestra should be in place immediately for the top of the show or to begin again after an intermission.

Position—The placement of feet for dancers standing still. There are five basic positions of various angles and spacings.

Previews—A performance (or series of performances) before the "official" opening night. Previews are used to run the show with an audience before the press are allowed in to review the show. This allows technical problems to be ironed out while ensuring the cast and creative team get audience feedback.

Prompt—To give an actor his/her next line when he/she has forgotten it.

Prop—An object used in a play; does not include scenery or costumes.

Prop master—Member of the creative team who has responsibility for all props used in the production.

Quick change—A change of costume that needs to happen very quickly takes place close to the side of the stage. A quick-change room is often erected to enable changes to take place in privacy.

Rake—An incline, for sight line purposes. Audience seating area on a slope, with the lowest part near the stage. Replaces the raked stage, no longer customary.

Run or **Run-through**—A practice of an entire play or act. "Run" can also mean the length of calendar time that a play is being performed in days, months, or years.

Sight lines—A border onstage indicating the audience's area of vision, to inform the cast and crew where they should stand to remain out of view.

Sixteen bars—The auditioning singer's best sixteen measures of a given song, to highlight his/her strengths and range. Often an audition requirement for time restrictions.

Sock and Buskin—Two ancient theatre symbols of comedy and tragedy.

Speed-through—A fast run-through to practice running order, special cues, and entrances/exits.

Stage door—An entrance to the theater for cast and crew separate from entrances used by the audience.

Stage left/right—Left/ Right as seen from the actor's point of view onstage (i.e., Stage left is the right side of the stage when looking from the auditorium.)

Stage manager—A person who supervises the stage arrangements of a theatrical production. To serve as overall supervisor of the stage and actors (for a theatrical production).

Standby—A member of the cast of a musical or play who understudies one or more of the principal roles but is *not* also in the chorus. A standby often will not even be required to be at the venue at each performance unless he/she is called in to perform in the role for which he/she is an understudy.

Standing room only (SRO)—Admittance to a performance after all of the seats are filled, which requires people to stand to watch.

Strike—To disassemble a stage set ("Strike the set"); to remove props from the stage (e.g., "Strike the armchair after scene 1").

Stumble-through—First rehearsals on the actual stage, to work out blocking, cues, and costume changes.

Summer stock—A type of repertory theater that produces its shows during the summer season.

Swing—A member of the cast of a musical who understudies multiple chorus roles in the production. When a chorus member is not well, has a day off or, in some cases, is performing in a principal role for which he or she is the understudy, a swing performs in this chorus member's place.

Tabs—Curtains separating the stage from the audience.

Tech—Short for "technical rehearsal" or "tech run." Usually the first time the show is rehearsed in the venue, with lighting, scenery, and sound. Costumes are sometimes used where they may cause technical problems (e.g., quick changes). Often a very lengthy process. "Dry Tech" is done without actors. "Wet Tech" includes actors and all technical elements.

Techie—Slang for stage technician. Often used as a nickname (typically by the actors) when referring to anyone involved in lighting, stage crew, and other manual and/or technical jobs in the theater. Pejorative.

Theater—Building where stage acting takes place. An inanimate object.

Theatre—The world of stage acting; the craft, the performing art itself.

Typecasting—When an actor becomes associated with only one type of role or character, often based on physical appearance. Also called a "type."

Understudy—A member of the cast of a musical or play who understudies one (sometimes more) of the principal roles and is also in the chorus. Some understudies have gone on to become stars by outshining the actors they replaced.

Up and Ballad—Slang for "up tempo" and "ballad." Contrasting songs in speed and mood often required for musical theatre auditions.

Upstage—1) The part of the stage farthest from the audience.

      2) When an actor moves upstage of another and causes the victim to turn away from the audience, he is "upstaging." Also, an actor drawing attention to himself away from the main action (by moving around, or overreacting to onstage events) is upstaging.

Vested—Having qualified for a retirement pension based on a minimum amount of union work over a period of years. Currently ten years of vesting service is required to receive a pension.

Wardrobe mistress/master—Person in charge of keeping theatrical costumes cleaned, pressed, and in wearable condition.

Wings—The areas of the stage that are to the sides of the acting area and out of view. Usually masked by curtains.

About the Author

DON WINSTON grew up in Nashville and graduated from
Princeton University.
He currently lives in Los Angeles. His debut novel *S'wanee: A
Paranoid Thriller* hit #3 in Kindle Suspense Fiction. His second
novel *The Union Club* was published in 2014.
The Gristmill Playhouse is his third novel.

www.DonWinston.com

The Union Club

A Subversive Thriller by

DON WINSTON

If These Walls Could Talk, They'd Scream

College sweethearts Claire and Clay Willing are determined to start their married life independent of his rich and powerful West Coast family. But the tragic murder of Clay's older brother, coupled with his own stalled career, suddenly lures them to San Francisco and into the clutches of the Willing political dynasty.

Clay's parents welcome Claire with open arms and ensconce her in their exclusive private club atop Nob Hill, where she mingles with the eccentric Bay Area elite and struggles to maintain her identity in the all-controlling Willing clan.

But her in-laws are the least of Claire's worries as she unravels the freakish mystery of their son's assassination and uncovers the shocking reason they were brought back into the fold. With no way out alive.

The Union Club. Where evil has its privileges.

APPLY FOR MEMBERSHIP

OUR FAMILY TROUBLE

A Domestic Thriller

A child in danger. A family in denial. A mother on the verge.

Dillie Parker has built the perfect life: a fast-track magazine career, a loving and successful husband, a stunning Manhattan home, and, most importantly, a healthy baby boy after a string of failed attempts.

But the birth triggers a flood of weird and disturbing post-partum side effects—mood swings, delusions, paranoia, and ultimately a tragic accident.

Traumatized, Dillie flees with her son back into the protective cocoon of her dysfunctional Tennessee family, where her troubles not only follow, but worsen.

Her strong-willed mother insists her woes are a weakness of character. Her browbeaten father ignores the growing threat. Only her beloved and ailing grandmother prods her toward the awful truth.

As her life and sanity spiral into chaos, Dillie has to confront what is either her darkest delusion or the most horrifying family secret of all: that an unspeakable evil has stalked them for generations. And is back with a vengeance to claim her young son.

Our Family Trouble. You can never go home again.

Prologue

SEPTEMBER

"And how old is Campbell II now?" the ob-gyn asked with a smile, thumbing through her files. "Nine months, is he?"

"He's fine. He's wonderful," replied Dillie Parker with pride, holding her son on her lap. "But no 'II.' Just...plain ol' Campbell." She propped him up straighter, which he didn't protest.

The doctor looked up across her desk and winked at the toddler. Then she scribbled the correction on her file. "Hard to believe just a year ago you were in the home stretch."

"Seems like a lifetime ago," said Dillie, laughing. "I definitely remember sweating through the Indian summer. I love the early nip we're having this year."

"That's an adorable outfit," the doctor said as she wrote, tipping her head toward the boy.

"My mother will be thrilled to hear that," Dillie said. "It's the fourth one she's sent this month."

"Is that sweater Ralph Lauren?"

Dillie shook her head. "It's Khaki." To the doctor's confusion, she clarified: "My grandmother. She's a knitting fiend. If you sit still too long, she'll knit a sweater up around you."

The doctor smiled and said, "It's a gift to have a knitter in the family." And Dillie nodded and said, "Khaki is most certainly a gift."

"And you, Dillie?" the doctor asked.

"Me?"

"How are you doing?"

Dillie glowed. "I've never been happier."

"Yes, I can tell. The first few months are typically the most challenging."

Dillie tipped her head with a knowing stare. "Truer words are rarely spoken."

She and the doctor laughed together. The doctor scanned the file again, made a simple notation.

"You're over the first hump," said the doctor as she scribbled. "It's especially big with the first child. Until you hit your stride, which you seem to have."

"Oh, it's still challenging," said Dillie.

The doctor looked up. "Yes?"

Dillie nodded and shrugged.

"In what way?" the doctor asked.

Campbell squirmed in his mother's lap, and she hoisted him back to a sitting position.

Dillie shook her head, dismissing it. Her fingers fanned across her son's stomach, keeping him on his perch.

The doctor sat still, waiting.

"Oh, you know," Dillie said with a good-natured wave off. "In the normal way. It's nothing. It's just a little different from what I...expected."

"What is?"

Dillie laughed out loud, looking to the ceiling for the answer.

She opened her mouth, collecting her thoughts. "Well...I don't know," she said, searching. "The main challenge, I guess, is that Rupert's been traveling so much. For work. You know Rupert, right?"

"Yes, of course," said the doctor.

"Yes, of course you do. He's been here with me. And everybody knows Rupert, it seems." She paused and glanced up at the doctor and then away. And then: "It's just been such a busy time for him, and there's really nothing he can do about that. I mean, it's not up to him. It's just his job. But the timing's bad, and so that's been a challenge. Which it would be for anyone."

"It is difficult when the husband has to travel a lot for work," agreed the doctor. "I see that often, as you can imagine."

"Right, when the husband and *father* has to travel for work, and I totally get that. It's a high-pressure job, so I try not to let it get to me. And I shouldn't complain, I mean, I have Lola... our baby nurse...but it's just not the same...."

"You still have a baby nurse?" the doctor asked.

Dillie nodded sheepishly. "Extravagant, yes. I'm very lucky that we can...I mean, that we can afford to...well, we had a nanny. Two actually. But they didn't..." She looked past the doctor, inspecting the far wall and its matrix of diplomas. Amherst. Hopkins. "They just didn't work out. So we still have Lola, who is really wonderful, and loves Campbell."

"That's good," the doctor said. "A baby nurse can get pricey."

"Yes, and it's silly, I realize. I'll have to find another nanny soon. If I...can. But Lola is so attached to Campbell, and

Rupert doesn't mind the extra expense. At least he says he doesn't mind. Probably eases his guilt..."

"I see."

"...for traveling so much." Dillie smiled and shrugged. Campbell squirmed, and she pulled him back up to her lap. She glanced out the window, past the tilted blinds, onto the Park Avenue sidewalk. Two older society ladies in light wraps passed side by side and disappeared. Probably on their way to lunch at Swifty's, or shopping on Madison.

"You know, I'm just tired a lot," she finally said. "I think that's my problem. I get punchy. Rupert says I should put Campbell in the nursery, with Lola. I mean, that's why we pay her. So when he cries, it won't wake me up."

"Perhaps you should," said the doctor.

"Yes, but he doesn't cry. He *never* cries. Which Rupert would know if he paid attention to his son. Or to *me*, for that matter. He used to..."

"Campbell doesn't cry?"

"I mean, I *hear* him, but it's not...at least it doesn't seem... It's something else. I don't...and the other noises, you know. I just don't get much sleep. That's the problem, I guess." She stopped, ransacking for her next thought.

The doctor sat still.

"Noises?" she asked.

Campbell started to slide, and Dillie turned him around and held him against her shoulder. She patted his back.

"Oh, you know," she said, rocking him in her seat. "Those old prewar buildings, especially those warehouse ones, no matter how much you renovate and modernize...I mean, the exterminators can't find them; they insist they see no signs of them anywhere, but..."

"What do you hear, Dillie?"

"…and I can't put traps around the crib where they…and Rupert's no help, of course, so I stay up all night looking for them. And I have deadlines, too! I *do* have a career, you know. You think they care if you…? They just don't care."

Dillie stopped herself. She stroked Campbell's back, now fast asleep. She forced a single, quiet laugh.

"Where's that hump I'm supposed to get over?" she asked.

The doctor started to scratch on a pad.

"Are you…happy with your boy?" she asked.

"I…beg your pardon?"

The doctor signed her name at the bottom, tore off the sheet, and slid the prescription across her desk.

"We've talked about postpartum depression…," she said.

"Oh, this is just postpartum bitchiness," said Dillie, sliding the prescription back, pinning Campbell with the other arm. "I don't need happy drugs. Really."

"See me in one month," the doctor said. "Depression is common, of course. But we don't want postpartum psychosis."

Dillie stared at her. Campbell breathed into her neck.

"No," she said, holding an off smile. "We don't."